Carved in Crimson

Heirs of Lirien

Book One

ANNABELLE MCCORMACK

Published by Annabelle McCormack

Edited by Melissa Frain, Marion Archer, Robin Seavill

Proofreading by Caitlin Lengerich, @chronicledbycait

Cover by Maria Spada (ebook, paperback, hardcover)

www.annabellemccormack.com

For anyone who has ever stood in the middle of a crowded room and felt utterly alone. You're a worthy and beautiful soul. Don't ever forget it.

Carved in Crimson

THE CONTINENT OF
LIRIEN
EMBERSTONE
SEREN'S TRIBE
CAIRN HOLD
PENDARA
DREADWOOD
DOBA

EDERYN
VOLKER
SOUMELIN
AMBRA
IBARRA
ZHI

LIRIEN GEOGRAPHY
THE SEVEN REALMS OF LIRIEN

The realms and their traits:

Ederyn

Background: The ruling realm, Norse/Germanic/Scandinavian inspired.

Traits: Authority, politics, royal bloodlines.

Pendara

Background: Realm of warriors, Anglo-Saxon/Gaelic inspired.

Traits: Martial prowess, loyalty, fortress cities.

Volker

Background: Realm of craftsmen and traders, Russian/Slavic inspired.

Traits: Metalwork, trade guilds, industrial cities.

Ambra

Background: Realm of artists and agriculture, Italian/Greek inspired.

Traits: Control over nature's powers, fertile lands.

Zhi

Background: Realm of healers and scientists and seafarers, Persian/Asian inspired.

Traits: Alchemy, medicine, natural science, water.

Ibarra

Background: Realm of magic and priests, Spanish/French inspired.

Traits: Enchantment, spiritual leadership, hidden rites.

Doba

Background: Realm of scribes and scholars, African/Arabian inspired.

Traits: Libraries, script craft, universities.

GLOSSARY

Bloodbinding Rite: A ritual that binds Lirien's children to their realm's magic, restricting cross-realm abilities. Ederyn-born peoples are *Unbound* in their magical skills, but because they do not receive training from Masters, it limits their opportunities to develop.

The Sealing: A ritual in which elite children from each realm are chosen by the King of Lirien—conferring special powers and true mastery of their realm's craft/skill, making them Masters.

The Oath of Bryndis: An ancient soul bond forging a connection by the exchange of blood.

Hrafn Mark: A divine 'fingerprint' marking a mortal as an heir to a dead god's power.

The Sealed Council: Elite council of six Bound individuals chosen every twelve years via blood magic to defend the kingdom.

The Viori: Rebels who oppose the Bloodbinding Rite and Lirien's oppressive laws. They hide in the Dreadwood and fight to end the monarchy's tyranny. They are Unbound by birth.

The Dreadwood: Forbidden forest at Pendara's border, sanctuary for the Viori. Magical creatures lurk within.

PROLOGUE
CALIX

Two years earlier

Waking up in Ederyn's most notorious prison with a splitting headache and an eye so swollen I could barely see was the least of my problems.

The dungeons had gone silent.

I peeled myself from the ground wincing, a putrid piece of straw clinging to the scruff of my jaw. The constant, dissonant moans I'd heard all night had vanished.

He's here.

Fuck.

I combed through my muddled memory, trying to recall a healing spell my childhood nurse had used for scrapes, but the pain in my head clouded my thoughts. Straightening my untucked shirt, I muttered a quick gesture spell to mend a rip in my trousers, then dragged my fingers through my long hair, knotting it at my nape.

The steel door thundered open.

My father entered, dressed in full regalia, his face twisted with displeasure. Only he could command such absolute silence in the dungeons.

A single window provided light, its narrow beam illuminating the swirling dust motes in the early morning sun. He stepped into the glow, the golden hue draping him like a mantle. Love him or hate him, Father was king in every sense of the word, as though the Warrick bloodline had known his destiny from conception.

"Calix."

The low timbre of his voice suggested fury. Father enraged was deadly calm and collected—one of the few traits I admired about him.

"Collecting me in person, Father? I'm flattered."

His steel-blue pupils wreathed with green—identical to my own—narrowed. *Unamused.* Humor wouldn't save me today.

"When my youngest son destroys the most beloved tavern in Suomelin, burns down a city block, and is dragged to prison, a personal call is disappointingly critical."

I crossed my arms, straightening. "The tavern owner was keeping an Ibarran woman as a concubine. In a cage."

"So, you burned the place down?"

"No. I rescued her. The fire was ... accidental." My shirtfront, sticky with dried blood, remained plastered against my skin.

"How so?"

My throat tightened at the memory of her—beautiful and fragile—clinging to me as I carried her from that filthy enclosure. Then the gasp—the bright burst of crimson as a crossbow bolt embedded itself in her throat.

"He killed her," I said hoarsely. "As I took her out. My anger may have ... tipped out of my control."

To be fair, I hadn't meant to cause a conflagration.

On the other hand, I didn't regret it.

The footfalls of Father's fine boots echoed against the stone floor. "And then you killed the man."

"Can I help it that he fell into my sword?"

Father's gaze hardened. "You are a prince and an heir to the throne, Calix. Executing a citizen—no matter how despicable —without trial is forbidden. Even for you. You are not above the law because you are my son. This on the heels of that disaster on the border of the Dreadwood. 'Scourge of the Viori' indeed."

I refused to let him bait me into discussing *that*. And *heir*? I nearly laughed. Convenient, considering six older brothers had claims before me. "You are the law, Father. You could change it. Or grant me clemency."

"And if I don't?"

From the spark in his eyes, I was dangerously close to the edge of his patience. "Then I suppose I'll have to adjust myself to the thought of a shorter funeral pyre."

"You dare jest?" His roar fractured the silence, reverberating off the walls.

I might have pushed him too far this time.

"You're lazy and spoiled," he grated. "The only one of my sons in whom I can find nothing to be proud."

I flinched. "Maybe that's my accomplishment."

His sword came free from its sheath with a ringing clang. *My sword.*

The guards must have handed it to him. He studied the

blade, a family heirloom said to have been forged by fae and carried by the first Ederyn king.

"You don't deserve this gift of the gods. Or my name. You're utterly useless."

"The gods died a long time ago."

His nostrils flared. My blasphemy infuriated him, and some twisted part of me enjoyed it.

"You've relied on my protection for too long. Every realm I've sent you to, you've been more trouble than you were worth." He gestured sharply. "The scribes at Doba wanted me to ban you altogether."

"Because I suggested commoners be educated? Literacy is a right, not a privilege."

"And the swordsmiths in Volker?"

"Their prices are impossible for most Liriens. Our people deserve weapons to defend themselves."

"The soldiers of Pendara protect them. We do not need an armed populace." His voice rose. "There is peace in Lirien."

I scoffed. "The Viori raids leave the borderlands in ruin. The Unbound poison minds against the Bloodbinding. The children of the Bound realms gather in secret, more than ever—"

"Enough." His whisper was more chilling than a shout. "Kneel."

"Why?"

Father sheathed the sword and drew a dagger, its hilt glittering with rubies and emeralds. "You've squandered your powers for too long. It's time you learned discipline ... and fealty."

As though containing my powers was so easy. I *had* tried. And I'd failed, despite my efforts. Maybe not my *best* efforts, but what choice did I have? "There isn't a Sealed Master who would truly train me, even on your orders."

He ignored me. "The tavern keeper's son and the shop owners demand justice. You went too far. I can't save you this time."

Fear slithered through my chest.

He was going to execute me.

I swallowed hard. "And if I demand a trial?"

"There will be no trial. I sentence you to exile for two years to satisfy those who want your blood. But you will not waste this time away from Ederyn, my son. You're going to Pendara. This time, no Sealed Master will refuse you."

I straightened, towering several inches taller than him. *What in Nyxva?*

"Kneel, Calix. You will yield. You will be Sealed as a Pendaran. You must learn fealty to my crown and understand your duty, and why our ways are best, before your rebellious thoughts and ideas of justice take you down a path that excludes you from my protection. Your role requires your head to command your heart, not the other way around."

Sealed? Only Bound children were Sealed. Every ten years, each realm selected three of its most promising. To be chosen was the highest honor in Lirien. The Sealed were masters of their realm's craft. I was a full eleven years older. Twenty-six— and fully aware of the consequences of the Bloodbinding rites and the Sealing.

I retreated a step. "And if I refuse?"

The cell door opened, and the head of my father's royal guard, a beast of a man named Ulf, entered, four more guards at his heels.

The guards' hands clamped around my arms like iron bands. I thrashed, but they shoved me to my knees, my shoulders screaming in protest as rough stone scraped my legs. One man sliced my shirt from my back. My hands fisted as two others pinned my ankles.

My father gripped my jaw. "You do not refuse your king," he gritted out softly. "This is mercy, Calix. Without it, you're already dead."

"And yet, I still refuse."

Pain exploded as his fist connected with my face. Bone splintered. Blood gushed down my lip as his guards held me firmly.

While I considered myself clever and had powers, my inability to wield them effectively, especially against someone like my father, limited me.

This battle was already lost.

"Only the Bound can be Sealed," I gasped. The guards tightened their hold. "You can't seal me—I'm not Bound. It could destroy my powers forever."

Regret flashed in my father's face as his thumb brushed my jaw. The touch felt foreign—almost gentle—but it didn't temper the iron in his eyes. Blood smeared his fingers, and he pulled his hand back, staring at it. His hesitation was palpable.

Seconds ticked by, and my heartbeat was erratic with fleeting hope. He wouldn't really do this to his own son ... would he?

For a moment, I thought he might stop.

"I'm King Magnus Warrick of Lirien. I can seal whomever I want, to whichever realm I want. And if the Sealing binds your other powers forever, so be it." He rounded behind me as Ulf forced my head down in a vise-like grip.

I dug my heels into the stone, thrashing. Futile. Their grips were unyielding. The cool press of the blade against my skin sent a shiver of foreboding down my spine.

My father loomed behind me, whispering incantations in Old Ederyn. The razor-edged blade sliced into my skin, carving symbols between my shoulder blades. Agony radiated through me. The incantation felt alive, heavy with power, each syllable cutting deeper than the blade itself.

Blood spilled in rivulets over my shoulders, its heat trickling down my sides. The metallic scent clawed at my senses, sharp and suffocating. My jaw clenched, a scream trapped in my throat, but I wouldn't give him the satisfaction. I focused on the red drops, desperate to steady my breath.

The Seal burned, alive with magic, etching itself into the flesh between my shoulder blades. I didn't have to see it to know its shape: crimson and black, intricate as ink, a crossed sword and shield—the symbol of Pendara.

When he'd finished, my father faced me, wiping my blood from his blade across my chest in an X. The fire searing my back refused to abate, magic sinking into every nerve, leaving me trembling with rage and pain.

I refused my father's gaze.

"You will leave here today and go to Pendara. Present yourself to the warlord in Cairn Hold. For two years, you'll train alongside their most skilled warriors. Your other powers will be Bound and the name Calix Warrick is forbidden to you. Only when you've proven yourself will I remove the Seal. Do you understand?"

I closed my eyes, my head pounding fiercely. The powerful magic surged through my veins, limiting my speech. The Seal conferred special abilities, honing its recipient's skills. But the process was excruciating.

And in my case, it was destroying every other power I possessed.

The fire that had always simmered at the edge of my veins snuffed out.

Desolation curled through my core as an integral part of my being was ripped away.

The Bloodbinding.

This was what the rite did to every child born outside of Ederyn. On the king's orders, their gods-given gifts were suppressed, unless those gifts aligned with their realm's lawful craft.

Now I knew what it truly meant to be Bound. To have the very essence of who I was smothered, flickering out like a dying flame. This was the fate of every child born beyond Ederyn's borders.

And now, it was mine.

I would never be *myself* again.

Humiliation and anger flooded me. My father's punishment was a stark reminder of why no one—including my brothers—dared disobey him.

"Yes, Father," I rasped.

My father jerked my chin with his fingertips. His gaze softened, the steel in his eyes tempered by something far deeper.

Is that fear?

"This is the only way," he murmured. "You're my son, but you're not invincible. Rebellion isn't strength—it's ruin. You're too much like him. That same fire, that same defiance. It ruined my brother and I won't let it ruin you. Or this kingdom. Fire destroys, Calix."

Then he straightened and set my sword at my feet. "When you return, you'll take your place by my side, in the role I choose for you."

I hated my resemblance to him. Hated those green and blue eyes—the golden hair my brothers and I shared. The sharp, strong cheekbones and firm jaw. The wide, Ederyn forehead.

But he was wrong. I'd never settle for a role chosen for me. Though my other powers were smothered now, I would find a way to reignite them.

Fire consumes everything in its path. Even chains.

My path was mine to forge ... or burn.

PART ONE

THE DREADWOOD

CHAPTER 1

SEREN

Only the strongest survived the Dreadwood—if we didn't kill them first.

As the only humans living in the forbidden forest, our task as soldiers was grim. Liriens were a threat to be eliminated. No questions. No exceptions. That was the *Viori way.*

I unfastened the rope to the watchtower, tension coiling in my gut. No matter how much I'd prepared myself for this moment, the *Viori way* suddenly felt less fair.

Esme watched me with wide, expectant eyes. A leather armor vest hung loosely over her woolen tunic. My sister's skin paled against the silvery moonlight as I placed the soft rope in her hands. The two long brown braids over each shoulder made her look so young. "I'm right behind you."

Esme's knuckles whitened as she tried to lift herself. Her feet swung, seeking a foothold on the evergreen's branches, and I fought the temptation to interfere. Months would pass before she climbed a rope properly. This first, struggled climb to the watchtower was part of the process.

She slipped, her hands skidding against the rope. *That will leave rope burn.* Spots of color stained her cheeks. "I can't do it, Seren!"

"You *can* do it." I kept my tone patient. "There aren't any tasks tonight you can't do."

Esme stomped, then turned back to the rope.

"Tuck your knees higher to your chest," I offered.

"I'd rather climb the branches," she grumbled.

That would be easier. *Faster.* At this rate, we'd spend the first hour of the night shift getting up to the watchtower.

Many minutes later, after crashing through branches and showering pine needles down at me, she was up.

I grabbed the rope, locking my feet as I ascended. Eight practiced pulls and I swung over the watchtower's side.

My bag slid onto the wooden floor, and I squeezed her shoulder. "You did really well."

Her lower lip puckered, and she rubbed sores below her thumbs. "Not as good as you."

"I've had eight years of practice." Not to mention I'd been climbing ropes since I was four—an advantage of being my father's shadow.

"Sit." I knelt beside my pack. My mother's healing potion worked wonders with rope burns. As I dripped some onto her hands, the potent scent of pine stung my nose.

"Rub it in. With any luck, the sores will heal by our next night shift."

Esme sniffled—either from the cold or pain—not meeting my gaze. "I hate this. Why do I even have to be in the stupid Vangar?"

My sister had just turned fifteen, meaning she was ready for initiation—three years of training before pledging compulsory service in the Vangar, our militia.

I'd pledged five years earlier, at eighteen. My twin siblings, Tara and Madoc, had pledged two years before me.

But Esme had never enjoyed traipsing through the forest, preferring instead to follow our mother, snuggle the goats, or tend to the garden. My mother's Ibarran blood ran strong through Esme. The realm of lovers and magic had no propensity for bloodshed.

The twins were thoroughly Pendaran, like our father. Of Lirien's seven realms, Pendara was known for two things: its brutal cold, and deadly soldiers.

While I hadn't been built for the Vangar like Tara and took after my mother's petite frame, I had *wanted* it more. "The Vangar needs our service."

"They don't need mine." She sniffled. "Why can't I just be a cook? I don't want to kill anyone—I can't."

"The cooks that travel with squadrons do all the hunting, fishing, and butchering. *And* they learn how to fight."

Esme groaned and sank on the floor. "What if I fail?"

"They'll still send you on raids—test you. You'll die if you fail. I'm not going to let that happen."

Esme didn't respond. She stared out into the endless dark of the forest, her small form curled up under the blanket I'd spread. The soft sound of her sniffles broke the silence, twisting a knife in my heart. *She shouldn't be here.* She wasn't ready, no matter what the Viori demanded.

Papa had wanted Esme to train with Madoc. I'd trained with Tara, so it should have been my brother's turn. Both Esme and I had protested. We were closer. She still slept beside me when she had nightmares—which was often. Esme feared shadows.

But maybe I should have let Madoc do this as the weight of my responsibility was enormous.

"It won't always be this hard," I whispered. Actually, it

would be harder, but that wasn't the point. "You'll get used to pushing yourself. You're more capable than you think, Es. You're a Ragnall. We're good at this."

"You say that because you've never failed at anything." Esme curled up, resting her cheek against the fur blanket.

If she only knew. I'd never mentioned my many training failures, and thankfully, neither had Tara. I chose not to argue. Spending her birthday evening in a watchtower during a bitter night was miserable enough.

Twirling my fingers, I frosted the tips of the branches above us with icicles that sparkled in the starlight. My ability to manipulate snow and ice mostly felt useless, given that we lived in the cold forest, but Esme had always loved my icy creations.

"Look." I nudged her with a smile. "I decorated for your birthday."

Esme gave the icicles a halfhearted glance, then rolled onto her side, turning her back to me. "I'm not a kid anymore, remember? That's why I have to do this. Unless you also have secret fire powers so I can warm up, ice won't make me feel better."

Ouch.

Would she resent me for training her? It felt possible.

"You know it's not *me* forcing you, right?"

Esme was quiet. After a few minutes, she whispered, "Do you ever wonder what our lives would have been like in Lirien?"

My breath caught. That Esme had voiced such a thought was bad enough ... but what was worse was that I *had* wondered.

What if my siblings hadn't been twins? If my parents had never left?

We would have grown up among the wealthy and elite in

Ederyn, not shivering in the frigid forest, scrounging for food, learning to be soldiers whether we had the inclination or not.

I killed the line of thought before it carried me away. "Father would be in prison or dead—executed for a crime he didn't commit. Tara and Madoc would also be dead. They would have been murdered when their existence was discovered. We wouldn't exist. But if Father wasn't executed, neither you nor I would have the powers we were born with. We would have been Bloodbound to Pendara since Father was from there and only allowed to develop warcraft gifts, if we possessed them—which we don't. And the—"

"I get it."

"Do you though?" I drew my knees up and vanished the icicles with a scowl. "We've all shielded you for too long. Maybe it would have been better to tell you about the atrocities I've seen Liriens commit against Viori. Learning to defend ourselves—preparing for inevitable war—is survival."

Esme curled up tighter. "Or we could all just stop killing each other."

If only it was that simple.

A twig snapped below us.

I peered over the tower.

Something—or someone—moved in the shadows.

The creatures that roamed the forest—and there were many—mostly didn't scare me. Creatures were manageable.

Other humans, on the other hand, were terrifying. Especially Lirien soldiers bent on killing as many Viori as possible. They viewed us as rebels, a threat to their tyrannical king. No matter that we'd set up our territory in the wilds of the Dreadwood, forbidden lands they had no use for.

The musky scent of sweat cut through the forest's earthy aroma, wrong and foreign. The forest held its breath, shadows thickening like predators watching from the trees, the silence too heavy to be harmless.

My gaze locked on the forest floor beneath me.

There. A solid form in the thicket below my post. A Lirien. A Viori would have announced themselves by now.

My heart sped.

I turned to Esme, pressing a finger to my lips. She knew better than to make noise now.

Don't look, I wanted to tell her.

Maybe she needs this lesson, though.

Hurry.

If the Lirien slipped past me and someone farther into the territory had to handle them, I'd be responsible for the failure. Once they moved far enough from the tree for me to lower myself and remain unseen, I'd have to act.

I grabbed the rope. "Stay here," I mouthed.

Esme gripped my forearm, fear on her face. "Don't leave me."

"I'll be right back."

Without waiting for her response, I climbed down. Next year, if I made officer, I wouldn't be assigned posts at the edge of our tribe's borders. Maybe then I'd finally get all the sap out of my hair.

I sank onto the forest floor, damp earth swallowing the sound. Tara had devoted a full year to teaching me how to walk soundlessly.

Crouching low, I searched for the Lirien.

I held my breath, listening carefully. A few pine needles rained down on me and I winced. *Esme.*

How often had Tara seen *me* as a liability?

A soft crunch focused my attention.

The Lirien stood twenty feet away, head cocked. His profile

revealed a strong forehead. Wavy, dark hair, like mine, was tied behind his neck with a strap.

He hadn't seen me.

Pulling a dagger, I rose slowly. The Lirien's reasons for being here didn't matter—one Lirien could wreak havoc. Failing to intercept them meant murder, rapes, executions, or worse, kidnappings back to Lirien, where even grimmer fates awaited. They viewed us as their enemies as much as we did them.

I could do this.

Even with Esme watching.

Still, I hesitated. She'd have to witness death sooner or later—learn to kill—even if she hated me for it.

Esme coughed softly.

The Lirien looked up.

Dammit!

I had to act. *Now.*

The blade spun through the air, a streak of deadly silver—then stopped, caught cleanly in his gloved hand.

His eyes snapped to mine.

What?

Adrenaline surged as I darted behind the closest tree. My cheek scraped bark, pain bursting across my skin.

I'd never seen reflexes like that. Had he been expecting me? *Watching me?* My foolish arrogance stung as I swallowed hard, scrambling for a plan.

I never should have hesitated. My strength was no match against a man his size.

I gripped a branch, sharp needles stinging through my glove as I hauled myself up. Swinging my feet toward my hands, I hoisted myself into the tree as the Lirien's quick footfalls approached me. He lunged from behind the trunk, toward where I'd been moments before.

I dropped from the branch, slamming into his back with all my weight.

He thrashed, his grip faltering as I drew another dagger. This close to him, I had the advantage. My blade slashed his throat, his gurgled choke cutting through the silence.

I let him fall, his body crumpling onto the forest floor in a heap. Blood pooled beneath his twitching body, its sharp tang heavy in the air.

That was too close. My shoulders heaved as I wiped my dagger on the ground below me, my heart still racing.

"Impressive," a deep voice said.

I froze.

Another man stepped from the darkness. A sword tip poked between my shoulder blades.

The chill of the sword at my back seeped into my skin. The muted rustle of leaves broke through a sudden ringing in my ears.

Godsdammit.

I was going to die in front of Esme.

Or worse.

"You might kill me, but my scream will bring dozens of Vangar." I turned slowly, unwilling to admit defeat even while the blade hovered inches from my neck. A flick of his wrist would end me.

This man wasn't as tall as the first. Still, he had a commanding air. A dark, hooded cloak shadowed his face. The earthy scent of pine and decay mingled with his clove-and-rosemary scent, an unsettling blend.

"You won't scream, Seren." His tone was amused, yet it carried a dark weight that twisted my stomach.

He knows my name?

"Then you're underestimating the lengths I'll go to see you dead."

He tilted his head, studying me like a predator weighing effort against reward. "Oh, I've underestimated nothing. The question is: how far will you go to save her?"

He gestured.

Another man stood at the base of the tree below my post.

He held Esme, hand clamped over her mouth. The forest blurred, shadows consuming the pines. All I saw was the blade at her throat, poised to shatter everything I fought to protect.

Her eyes, wide and shimmering with tears, begged me to do something. Trust lingered in her gaze—fragile, undeserved trust. *She thinks I can still save her. Gods, she doesn't see the failure standing before her.*

All my training, all my promises to protect Esme—useless. I was just a scared girl fighting against a man who knew my greatest weakness.

"Fuck you," I gritted, forcing steel into my voice. "She's only fifteen. Let her go, and I might let you live." My heart thundered, every beat a reminder of how close I was to losing her. My dagger felt useless, its weight mocking my lack of choices.

The man tilted his head. "You're just like him, aren't you? Sadly, much smaller, though."

Like *him?*

"Who are you?" I demanded.

He extended a sealed scroll. "Deliver this to your father. Remind him that shadows always follow. That his sins have found him."

I went rigid.

How did he find us?

"My father?"

The shadows of his hood were impenetrable.

"Yes, Seren, daughter of Brogan Ragnall."

I didn't respond. That knowledge meant my entire family

was in imminent danger. "Let my sister go," I managed. "Whatever quarrel you have with my father, she has nothing to do with it."

"True, but as you said, she's just fifteen and much less trouble than you."

The hilt of his sword slammed against the side of my head, a sickening crunch reverberating through my skull.

"Seren!"

Esme's scream ripped through the dark, jagged and raw, as the world tilted violently. My vision blurred, the ground rushing up to meet me. Cold. Unyielding. Pain splintered through my skull, but it was nothing compared to the wildfire of helplessness burning inside me.

I failed her.

I failed them all.

CHAPTER 2
SEREN

"Y ou're not going, Seren." The strain in Father's voice was unusual, and I almost paused while shoving one of my mother's old books into my pack.

I didn't though—didn't slow down.

Wrapping a whetstone in a cloth, I settled on my bedroll. "If you give me that line about this not being a place for women again—"

"It's not." Father sat and set his callused hand on mine. "Trust me. Gods, it's hardly a trip for men. Liriens will kill any Viori man on sight. But a woman, especially one your size ..."

I glared at him. "Which is precisely why I should go. I'm the one who failed Esme. I live with the sound of her screams in my dreams. Me. And you want me to sit idly and let you pay the price for my failure? That's bullshit."

Haunting sadness pooled in my father's eyes. "It's my duty to protect my children."

"Then why are you allowing Madoc to go?"

Across the tent, sitting in front of the small stove, Madoc raised a scarred brow at me. He continued sharpening a knife,

21

his brown-eyed gaze wary. Only Esme had inherited my father's green eyes. The rest of us had Mother's dark ones.

Tara and Mother entered, carrying food stores from the underground cellar. "Is she still at it?" Tara asked, then tossed some longer strands of closely-cropped dark hair from her cheek.

"Hasn't shut up yet," Madoc said flatly. The whetstone rasped against his knife, a grating reminder of the tools he would carry to save Esme—and the tools I wouldn't.

This argument had gone on for nearly a month, since Esme had been taken. I knew the man's name now—Lethos Scalari, an Ederyn spy. He'd captured Esme to force my father into surrender, no doubt aiming for the sizable Lirien bounty on his head.

How he'd found us ... that part terrified me.

For twenty-five years, the Viori had kept us safe. Despite my parents' continued love for Ibarra and Pendara, we'd been protected. But now, someone had betrayed us.

Lethos had found Esme and me with shocking accuracy. The ease with which he and his men had gotten in—and out—of our territory suggested inside help.

"Even if your father relented, Seren, Lord Haldron has not permitted you to go into Lirien. Only Madoc and your father." Mother sat on my other side, sympathy on her face. "We all want to help. I'm as desperate as you are to bring Esme home."

A guttural growl of frustration left my lips. Viori laws had already delayed our ability to rescue Esme. My father, Madoc, and Tara had gone after her the day she was taken, heading toward the Ibarra border where Lethos claimed to be taking her.

The Vangar at the border had turned them back. Going into Lirien was forbidden. When my father had tried to go on without permission, they'd arrested him for rebellion—a crime punishable by execution. Only Tara and Madoc's determination had allowed them to take him back to Emberstone and plead his case before Lord Haldron.

Whatever debt my father owed Haldron, the price would be high. But Father hadn't shared the details of his deal.

"I'm just as angry about it as you are," Tara said from beside Madoc. "But you don't hear me arguing. Like it or not, Madoc is stronger and faster than either of us. Especially you. That's why Father picked him."

I stood and glowered at my father. "Father picked him because he has a cock. He's made that clear enough."

Father reached into my pack and removed the spell book I'd just packed. Standing, he held it out. "If you want to help, stay here and study this. You are more than just one thing, Seren. Being Unbound since infancy means you can cultivate this skill, but you've focused so much on being a Vangar warrior that you've lost sight of your other gifts. Study this, and you'll be what I need the next time I face a dangerous mission."

His words struck like a fist to my chest. My throat tightened, but I refused to let him see how much it stung.

Even Madoc blew out a low whistle.

"I haven't lost sight of anything." I yanked the book from his hands and shoved it back into my pack. The leather strap bit into my shoulder as I slung it over me.

I stormed out of the tent before anyone else spoke, anger churning in my gut. *What does he know?*

Father had always been affectionate. The days when I might have curled into his arms beside the stove on a brutal winter's night were long gone, but he doted on us all. He didn't know how I always took my mother's spell books, studying Ibarran spellcraft. Maybe I wasn't as gifted as my mother was, but I could hold my own. *With simple spells, anyway.*

The cold autumn air stung my cheeks, the scent of damp leaves and earth sharp in my nose. I tugged my woolen scarf higher, my breath misting in the moonlight.

Tara had easily resigned herself to Father's decision. But she commanded her own Vangar squadron now. Maybe she felt needed here.

Tara also had the advantage of not being weighed down by guilt. I'd brought this upon our family.

I hurried down the well-worn path through the woods to the Vangar tents, stationed near the border of the tribe's encampment. My friend Amahle would be in the officers' barracks, which, like most common areas among our tribe, were just larger tents maintained by the community. Amahle knew me better than anyone, and I desperately needed her advice before I did something rash.

Soft footsteps approached.

My heart stumbled at the sight of Seth.

His jet-back hair shone in the moonlight, the pale skin of his arms bearing fresh tattoos on his well-muscled left forearm. Zhi men tattooed dragon outlines on each arm at fifteen. With each man they killed, another section of the dragon was inked in, symbolizing their growing strength and rank.

Seth's dragon was nearly complete.

The sight unsettled me. Seth's ascension had been swift and brutal, his ambitions growing faster than the ink could fill.

Despite looking down on my family's devotion to their realms, he clung to Zhi traditions. The one dictating he could never marry a woman who wasn't Zhi most of all.

Maybe I should have known. But at twenty, it never occurred to me that he'd take my heart in secret while planning to marry my friend, Darya.

I'd learned of his engagement the same day he married her. He'd spent the previous night with me.

I did my best to avoid Seth now. My friendship with Darya had suffered, though I didn't blame her—she'd never known I loved him. Somehow, that made my guilt worse, especially when she noticed the cooling of our friendship. Three years had mostly healed my wounds, but avoiding Seth and Darya was impossible, since he was our Viori tribe's leader—the waldren, our leader.

Seth reached me in a few strides. "Going somewhere at this early hour?"

"I'm free to come and go, aren't I?"

He blocked my path. "You know, you could look me in the eye occasionally."

"No, thank you." I moved to step around him.

He caught my elbow. "Seren, please. I'm worried about you."

His grip was firm, his callused fingers rough against my skin. The faint scent of leather and smoke clung to him, a reminder of the nights I'd once spent in his arms.

I yanked myself free, jutting my chin up as I searched his rugged face. I hated that I still found him attractive—but in a repulsive way, like a food I'd once enjoyed but got sick from. "I'm fine."

His full lips twisted. "Your sister was kidnapped, you were attacked, and now your father and brother are leaving the tribe for gods know how long. You're my responsibility, Seren. You're part of this tribe, and as its waldren, I—"

"You don't care about me, Seth." My voice was ice. "You made that clear enough."

"That's not true." He hesitated, searching my gaze. "I know I hurt you. I've made mistakes, but I've never stopped caring for you. What we had—"

"What we had was a lie," I snapped, my anger bubbling to the surface. "It was always about your ambition. Darya's family had wealth and connections, and that's all you wanted."

He flinched, just barely, and for a moment, I thought I saw regret. Then his expression hardened. "You don't understand the sacrifices I've made for this tribe—for all of us."

"Oh, I understand plenty." My voice turned to steel. "You'll sacrifice anything—anyone—for power. Don't pretend it's for us."

His jaw tightened, but he didn't deny it. "You can hate me all you want but I've done more for this tribe than anyone else."

"Well, maybe it's time for a change. Maybe someone else would do your job better. Someone like my father. Or maybe even me."

"Are you threatening me?"

"Only if you feel threatened."

The low hoot of an owl reminded me of the early hour—how isolated we were out here on the path. Maybe I was a fool for pushing him, but I would be damned if I let him pretend he cared.

Seth's fingers twitched at his side, as if restraining himself. "You have no idea what this job requires."

I laughed bitterly. "You think you're some great savior? You're a coward, Seth. You betrayed me. You betrayed yourself. And you expect me to respect you for it?"

His expression darkened, and his fingers curled into a fist before relaxing again. "You should be careful what you say, Seren. As waldren, I can make life very difficult for you. I could make you untouchable—not out of respect, but fear. No man in this tribe would dare defy me. Not for you."

The threat hung between us. My heart pounded, but I refused to let him see my fear. I stepped closer, lowering my voice. "Do it, then. Show everyone what kind of man you really are."

Something flickered in his eyes—anger, frustration ... and something else. Regret, maybe? Or doubt.

He reached out, as if to touch my cheek, but I slapped his hand away. "Don't. You don't get to pretend anymore."

His hand dropped, and for a moment, he looked almost vulnerable. Then the mask returned, his expression callous.

"You're making a mistake," he said quietly. "You don't want me as an enemy, Seren."

A cold knot formed in my stomach, but my cheeks burned with anger. I met his gaze, unflinching. "You already are."

I hurried away, no longer toward the Vangar barracks, but down a different path—one that would take me as far from him as possible.

When I was certain he couldn't see me, I broke into a sprint, running headlong into the darkness.

My boots pounded against the uneven path, scattering gravel, sending echoes through the forest. The wind stirred the branches overhead, the only sound besides my labored breathing.

The Viori were *supposed* to offer freedom for Lirien's oppressed and desperate. For my parents, it had been the only choice. Lirien law dictated that twins be murdered at birth, thanks to the Rúna that wove all fates. Legends held that the Rúna destined one twin for goodness and the other for evil— but no one knew which was which.

My parents had chosen exile over watching their children be killed. Free, Unbound, and away from Lirien's oppression.

Supposedly.

Seth had shaken my trust in the Viori, and powerlessness pressed down on me. Esme, my family—there was nothing I could do.

I peered through the branches at the moon, its silver light spilling across the forest like a distant promise—a reminder of how far Esme was, and how far I'd have to go to bring her back.

The crisp air sent a shiver through me, but I straightened my shoulders, letting the cold sharpen my resolve.

I can follow Madoc and Father to the border.

I'd need to be careful. One misstep, and Father would send me back, or worse, Seth would find me first. I'd pack light—just enough to keep pace without being noticed. A blade, a spell book, and enough food to reach the border. Once there, I'd be on my own, where even the shadows of the forest couldn't promise safety.

Either way, I wasn't staying behind.

CHAPTER 3

RYKR

"Again." Dalric scowled at me, his sword gleaming under the pale light of the Rookery. Sweat trickled down his brow, catching on the hard line of his jaw.

I swiped my damp face with my forearm, golden hair sticking to my skin. "You're exhausted."

"Am I?" Dalric grinned, shifting his stance. "Or was I just tiring my opponent, waiting for him to grow overconfident?"

"Careful, your wit's sharper than your sword," I shot back, though I couldn't stop my lips from twitching into a smile.

Dalric had a knack for making me second-guess myself. His skill wasn't just in his swordplay—it was in his ability to outthink and manipulate.

"Dalric's right," Thorne called from the sidelines, arms crossed. His voice carried easily over the din of the training hall. "If you're aiming to lead your own unit this year, you'd better prove you've still got some fight left. Getting a bit old, aren't you?"

This line of ribbing wasn't new. Because of my Seal and my age, I'd trained and lived in the Regulation Barracks since my arrival—despite not being a soldier. Unlike my friends, who commanded units, I'd spent every day of the last two years training with younger candidates.

Warlord Ellison hadn't known what to do with me when I'd shown up at his doorstep two years ago with the king's orders in hand.

Magnus ceased to be my father that day.

Ellison was the only one here who knew my identity. Leather bracers concealed my wrists, leading no one to question my lack of a Bloodbinding mark. The Seal visible on my neck convinced them I was Pendaran anyway—as did the speed at which I'd advanced through my training.

"You hard of hearing now, too?" Thorne said.

"Hilarious." I lowered the face shield on my helmet. "Careful, or I'll leave him to spar with you next."

Dalric circled me, his footfalls light on the sparring platform. In the background, the clang of steel and the grunts of soldiers filled the air, mingling with the sharp tang of sweat. I adjusted my grip on my sword, watching for his next move. He was quick—too quick for someone supposedly tired.

He lunged, a sudden strike aimed at my side. I parried, our blades ringing sharply, but his momentum didn't slow. A second blow came, then a third.

"Son of a whore," I muttered, stepping back. "You *have* been holding back."

Dalric's teeth flashed in a grin beneath his helmet. "What can I say? I like making you work for it."

"Allowing me to win won't do me any favors at the commander test."

"You're Sealed." Dalric shrugged. "It's a foregone conclusion they're foaming at the mouth to have you as a commander."

I lunged and narrowly missed the leather of his vest.

Dalric spun, light on his feet, his sword slashing past me as I ducked. "You spent too many days at the harvest feasts." He winked, then called to Thorne, "He's sluggish. I told you not to take him to the dueling pits."

Thorne bit into an apple, watching with mild amusement. "He won me a year's pay. Best investment I've ever made."

"Great." I deflected another blow. My muscles burned, the strain of earlier rounds catching up with me. Dalric pressed his advantage, damn him.

He lunged again, and I ducked, narrowly avoiding his blade. He had me near the edge of the platform—too close for comfort.

Then I saw my opening. With a sharp upward slash, I drove him back a step. Before he could recover, I tossed my sword into the air, flipping over him in a single smooth motion. I caught the hilt as it fell, the movement instinctive.

Dalric laughed, lowering his sword slightly. "Theatrics won't win you a battle."

"No, but they'll win me this match," I said, driving a final strike toward his legs. He stumbled back, conceding the point.

I smirked and bowed. "Victory. Again."

Thorne chuckled, tossing his apple core aside. "Cocky bastard. One good night at the pits, and he thinks he's invincible."

Dalric pulled off his helmet, his golden hair plastered to his forehead. "You're lucky I don't have the energy to throttle you right now." He scowled, though humor glinted in his eyes. "I swear, you're more trouble than you're worth, Rykr."

I removed my own helmet, letting the cool air hit my face. A faint smile tugged at my lips. These moments— however fleeting—made the endless days of training worthwhile.

"You cursed yourself with all that *saving your energy* talk,"

Thorne said, clapping Dalric on the shoulder. "My father always said, 'The silent enemy is the most dangerous one.'"

"That explains your ineffectiveness," Dalric quipped, setting his sword on the platform. "You never shut up."

"Rykr Westhaven!" a deep voice interrupted us. "Warlord Ellison requests you at headquarters."

I turned as one of the warlord's officers approached. Thorne scowled. The Regulation soldiers had about as much patience for the officers as I did—most came from wealthy or noble families whose influence had secured their rank.

In that way, the Bloodbinding kept the realms balanced. Rich or poor, no one could buy a gods-granted gift. Strong lineages increased the chances of being born with a realm's craft, but even that guaranteed nothing. The magic imbued into humans at the start of the Fourth Age, when the gods had abandoned direct intervention, was unruly and unpredictable. I'd seen it here—noblemen longing for the powers they hadn't been born with.

Which was why I could never tell my friends I was Prince Calix. Or Ederyn.

They would see me as an interloper who'd manipulated his way into mastering their realm's craft.

The warlord's officer looked coolly between Dalric and me. "Which one of you is Westhaven?"

"I am." My lips twitched. "Don't tell me you think I look like this sorry hagspawn."

Dalric laughed. The irony was, we *did* resemble each other. He could have passed for my brother, which was unusual for a Pendaran. His mother had been Ederyn, though, which explained the looks.

Thorne, on the other hand, looked every inch a Pendaran warrior—dark hair, intimidatingly broad with massive, well-muscled arms and legs. He also wore a berserker bearskin cloak, regardless of the weather.

Dalric had suggested drunkenly once that Thorne might even be a shapeshifter.

The officer inspected us. "You won't have time to clean yourself up. He's expecting you in ten minutes."

I watched him go, narrowing my eyes.

Something about him was ... *off*.

"What'd you do this time?" Dalric asked with a grin.

I raised a brow. "Who says I did anything?"

"When was the last time Warlord Ellison called you for a private chat?" Thorne asked Dalric, peering over at me.

Dalric shrugged. "Never."

True enough. Most Regulation soldiers, even unit commanders, never met with the warlord. I, on the other hand, had met with him dozens of times. *He probably has news from my father.*

I kept my face neutral. "That's probably because of your stench."

"You sowrutter." Dalric shook his head. "You're confusing me with that bear." He pointed at Thorne.

We left the din of the Rookery and exchanged our training swords for our personal ones at the entrance. I'd blackened my sword's hilt when I'd arrived from Ederyn to make it less obvious. A Pendaran with an excellent blade wouldn't raise suspicion, but a gold-hilted sword would.

Outside, the brisk air hinted at the coming winter. The leaves had begun changing a month earlier, not that it mattered here in Pendara. Once harvest ended, any lingering warmth would vanish. Pendara, the northwesternmost realm, claimed the icy mountains Ederyn hadn't wanted.

After two years here, I understood why Pendaran soldiers made up the bulk of the army. Their realm was devoted to warcraft, and they could outlast nearly all other Liriens in harsh elements. Other realms had soldiers, but only the Askaris of Doba, near the Great Wasteland's deserts, knew such extremes. Unlike Pendarans, though, most Dobans were peaceful scribes and scholars.

"Where are you two going?" I asked as Thorne and Dalric flanked me on the path.

Thorne squinted, amused. "To find out what the hell you did."

I smirked and didn't argue. They wouldn't be admitted to Warlord Ellison's quarters anyway. Would Ellison want to discuss my upcoming departure?

My father had ordered me home in a few weeks. I planned to request command of a Regulation unit. I also expected my father to remove the Seal ... though I wasn't sure I wanted that anymore.

I had no wish to return to being Prince Calix Warrick.

The Seal had honed my warcraft powers—I didn't want to lose them now. Though I missed the other powers I'd possessed before my father gave me the Seal, my training had changed me. No more accidental fires. No more latent simmering at the edge of my veins. No magic I couldn't control.

In truth, no magic at all.

We hurried in silence toward headquarters, following the path that wound near the forest. Regulation soldiers joked that Cairn Hold's training grounds were so close to the Dreadwood to serve as a buffer between Lirien and the monsters rumored to live there.

Jokes aside, they weren't wrong.

The Dreadwood was for the lawless. Monsters—human and beasts alike—dwelled there. No one who entered came out alive. The forest was forbidden. The fortress at Cairn Hold had been built after the fucking Viori began their raids several hundred years ago, meant to safeguard the Pendaran border.

Even the soldiers rarely ventured from the path.

Light filtered through the brilliant gold- and red-leaved trees, dappling onto mosses and twisting vines. Beautiful, really.

Hardly the nightmare legends spoke of, but I restrained a shudder. The only time I had set foot inside the forest, near Doba's border, it hadn't gone well. I didn't want to remember that now.

We were halfway to headquarters when the forest went unnaturally quiet.

The narrow, uneven path skirted the Dreadwood's edge. Dalric walked slightly ahead. Thorne was at my side. He adjusted his bearskin cloak, the faint jingle of his sword hilt breaking the silence.

"This feels wrong," I muttered, scanning the dense undergrowth.

Thorne glanced at me, his eyes narrowing. "Now you're paranoid, too? Gods help us." But his hand drifted to his weapon. He'd sensed it too.

Dalric slowed. "Quiet." His voice, sharp and low, cut through the air.

Ahead, the shadows shifted, wrong and deliberate.

Four figures emerged from the forest like wraiths, their movements unnaturally smooth. Bone-white masks obscured their faces, each one carved with eerie precision.

Thorne stiffened. "Viori."

Dalric didn't hesitate. "Yes?" he called, his tone deceptively casual.

They didn't answer. Behind us, a faint rustling drew my attention. Two more masked figures stepped onto the path, cutting off our escape.

We were surrounded.

The tallest man stepped forward, his voice cold and deliberate. "Calix Warrick?"

My pulse slowed.

They're here for me. I gripped my sword.

"You're far from Ederyn, friends." I kept my gaze down. For anyone really looking for me, my eyes could be a giveaway.

Dalric's lips curved, exchanging a look with me. "The royal prince? At your service," he said with a mock bow.

The man lifted a crossbow and shot.

The bolt struck Dalric in the chest, the sickening thud echoing in the stillness.

"No!" Thorne and I shouted in unison.

Dalric wavered before his knees buckled, his sword slipping from his hand and clattering to the ground. I lunged forward, catching his shoulders just before he collapsed.

"Dalric." His name came out as a whisper. Blood seeped through his shirt, staining the dark leather vest above it. His eyes, wide with shock, locked onto mine as horror seeped through my skin.

"Never ... could keep my mouth shut." He forced a weak smile, blood trickling from the corner of his mouth.

"Stay with me." My voice cracked as I pressed against the wound, desperate to stem the bleeding. "Don't—don't talk. Save your strength."

Behind us, Thorne's sword rang against steel. I barely registered the clash of steel, my focus locked on Dalric.

"I'm sorry," he rasped. "Should've ... been more careful."

"Don't you dare apologize." I choked on the lump rising in my throat. "You're going to be fine. We'll get you to the healers and—"

Rough hands yanked him from my grasp. His body jerked as they dragged him toward the shadows of the forest.

"Get off of him!" Thorne roared, surging forward. His sword sang, a flash of steel cutting through the air.

I drew my own weapon, lunging at the nearest man. Pain blossomed at the back of my neck—a sharp, burning sting. My free hand shot up, ripping out the jagged quill of a common whistler. A Viori weapon, which contained a powerful sedative.

I fought against the disorienting pull as I slashed out with my sword, driving back the nearest attacker.

"Thorne!" My voice was hoarse, desperate.

Thorne turned, his amber eyes wild with rage as he struck down one of the men. But it wasn't enough. More shadows emerged from the forest, closing in.

The world tilted.

Thorne fought on, his blade a blur. He cut down one attacker with a ferocious strike, his roar of fury shaking me to my core.

"They're taking him!" I shouted, my voice slurred. My legs felt leaden.

Thorne didn't answer. He was already moving, strength and fury etched into every arc of his sword. Another masked man fell beneath his blade.

One attacker slashed at Thorne's arm, the blow glancing off his armor. He barely flinched, driving his sword through the man's chest. "Cowards!" he spat, voice raw.

I stumbled forward, every step a battle against the fog clouding my mind. "Thorne ... we can't ..."

He didn't stop. He wouldn't stop. "They're not taking him!"

But they were. The forest engulfed Dalric's captors, his blood leaving a cruel trail.

Thorne faltered, his breathing ragged. A dart struck him in the shoulder. His knees buckled, but he snarled, ripping the quill free and forcing himself upright.

"Thorne ..." I whispered, my vision darkening. The forest around me spun, dark and hazy. I couldn't lose him. Not Dalric. Not Thorne.

He turned, his amber eyes blazing. "Get up, Rykr. You don't get to quit."

My legs gave out, the earth rushing up to meet me. Thorne's defiant roar echoed as I fell, his blade swinging in one last desperate strike.

The remaining men who'd attacked us barreled past, charging behind their companions without another glance at us.

Stumbling, Thorne and I chased them, crashing into the thick brush.

Sluggishness spread like warm wine through my veins.

"How in Nyxva did the Viori get into Cairn Hold?" I managed to ask Thorne. I sounded clumsier than I'd intended, my tongue thick.

I had to keep going. If the Viori believed Dalric was Calix, they'd kill him—or worse, use him as leverage. Because of me. Because I let this happen.

Summoning whatever strength I had, I swung my sword, slicing through the tangled brush.

I had to save Dalric.

Fuck.

I couldn't even see him anymore.

My lungs burned. Sweat dripped down my face, heat searing through me like a fever.

Thorne was gone too.

He must be suffering the same effects. I had no idea how long we'd been separated, or how long I'd been running.

My numb legs gave out as I stumbled into the overgrowth, thorns snagging my clothes and skin. I collapsed, thudding against the hard earth.

Dirt and leaves pressed against my face, but my body refused to move.

The forest swallowed me whole.

Silence.

CHAPTER 4
SEREN

Something hunted me.

Close to the border with Pendara, the forest grew wild and unyielding. The terrain, rugged and tangled with dense undergrowth, formed a natural border between the Viori and Lirien—one we kept that way on purpose.

But the forest didn't just belong to us. Ancient predators had roamed these woods long before the Viori arrived. Most had retreated deeper when we claimed the land, but here, near the border, their territory remained.

Whatever stalked me now was one of them.

The fire I'd built to cook a rabbit crackled faintly, its warmth fleeting against the chilly morning air. I kicked dirt over the embers, extinguishing the glow. The birds had fallen silent, the ever-present hum of crickets gone.

In the forest, silence was a bad omen.

I packed quickly, marking my place in my spell book with a leaf. *Love spells and curses*—useless. My mother had sworn they were important, but I wouldn't waste time reading them twice.

My memory retained anything I'd read, whether I wanted to or not.

The unseen presence crept closer, the seconds stretching taut with dread. My grip tightened on the dagger at my side as I stepped away from the thick pine I'd sheltered under for the night.

I scanned the woods, muscles coiled, ready to run. The colorful leaves sparkled with rime beneath the pale sunlight, fleeting beauty in a world that didn't allow for stillness. Not here. Not now.

I'd been tracking Madoc for a week, his trail growing colder with each step. I hadn't expected him and my father to separate when I'd tried to follow. Madoc had been easier to track, but all signs of him had vanished near the fortress of Cairn Hold in Pendara. Now I was too close to the border, too exposed, and too alone. No sign of him. No sign he'd return this way.

Maybe it was time to stop waiting.

Maybe it's time to give up.

The thought came unbidden, shame curling in its wake. My food stores had dwindled, and though I could hunt, water was harder to find this far out. I needed to move—to get closer to Viori territory, where I'd be safer. Where this hunter might think twice before stalking me.

But if I moved, I might miss Madoc.

The forest went still again, the unnatural hush pressing in. The hunter was close enough that I could almost hear its breath.

The frost crunched softly underfoot, and I winced. No sound escaped this oppressive quiet, not with something lurking so near.

I wasn't easy prey. It would learn that soon enough.

Mid-step, I froze, the hair on the back of my neck prickling.

Crouched ahead in the frost-covered undergrowth—a man.

I gripped my dagger's hilt, instinctively dropping into a defensive stance. His broad shoulders hunched, his attention fixed on something in the distance. The remnants of a tattered shirt clung to his muscular frame, stained dark with blood. Dirt streaked his arms, but the faint gleam of a tattoo beneath a sheathed sword on his back caught the light—crimson and black winding down the back of his neck, the unmistakable symbol of Pendara.

Curpiss.

I couldn't see the full mark, but I knew its shape.

Father bore it too.

A Sealed Pendaran soldier. *What in the gods' name is he doing here?*

The thought barely formed before he moved.

He surged to his feet in a blur of motion, turned, and then barreled toward me. I stumbled back, lifting my dagger, but before I could react, his arms were around me, his momentum slamming us both to the ground.

The impact drove the breath from my lungs. His forearms cushioned the worst of the fall, but his weight crushed me, pinning my dagger uselessly at my side. I thrashed, snarling, but his strength was overwhelming, his grip unyielding.

"Get off of me!" I hissed, twisting against him.

His hand clamped my mouth—large, rough, callused at the ridges where his fingers met his palm, the kind that had seen years of training. The arm around my torso held me taut. A sheen of coarse blond hair, streaked with blood and mud, covered his hardened, well-muscled forearm.

His deep voice was low, urgent.

"Keep still," he said, the command sharp and clipped. "If you want to live."

My pulse thundered in my ears, but his words gave me pause. I stilled, my senses sharpening. That's when I heard it— the low, guttural growl that sent ice down my spine.

He pointed and I followed his gaze.

What in Nyxva?

An enormous wolf-like creature emerged from the shadows, its hulking form blending with the forest as though made of darkness itself.

A vuk.

Silver eyes gleaming, fangs bared, globs of saliva dripping from its maw. A ridge of sharp spines jutted along its back like a dragon, rising with each step, but thick black fur had concealed it against the tree line. The air thickened around it, oppressive and cold.

The man's grip tightened. "Don't move."

As if I didn't know that already. But the predator wasn't looking at him, it was looking at *me*. The silver eyes locked onto mine, a deep growl rumbling from its throat. My muscles tensed, every instinct screaming to fight, to run.

Instead, I breathed, forcing my racing heart to steady. Gripping his forearm with one hand, I planted my boot against the trunk of the tree behind me. Then I *moved*.

With a sharp shove, I kicked off the tree and twisted midair, driving both boots into his head. His grip slackened just enough for me to wrench free, and I rolled clear, my dagger glinting as I rose to face him.

The man staggered upright, blood dripping from a fresh gash on his temple. His expression wavered between frustration and disbelief.

"You're insane," he muttered.

"No," I snapped. "Just not willing to be your shield."

The vuk growled again, prowling closer, its shadow stretching across the frost-covered ground. Its gaze shifted between us, as though deciding which one of us to kill first. My grip tightened on my dagger, but I knew it wouldn't be enough.

The man stepped in front of me, his broad back blocking my view of the beast. "Stay behind me," he ordered.

I bristled and pushed out from behind him. "I don't take orders from Liriens."

"Then try not to get yourself killed," he shot back, drawing the sword strapped to his back. He held it with the ease of someone who knew exactly how to use it.

The vuk lunged.

My pulse spiked, but before I could react, the creature slammed me to the ground. Air fled my lungs as the crushing weight pinned me, claws digging into my shoulders and thighs. The trees above blurred as I struggled for air, a sharp ringing in my ears.

Just as suddenly, I sucked in a ragged breath, the pain of it nearly blacking out my vision.

Saliva dripped onto my neck, searing like acid. Silver eyes bored into mine, pupils black and deep, as if they led to some endless abyss. A faint yellow glowed within them, an unnatural light that sent a chill through my core.

What is that?

I'd never seen eyes like that.

The man's blade sliced through the air, glancing off the beast's scaled side with a dull *thunk*. The creature snarled, unfazed, its fetid breath filling my nose. I thrashed against its hold, but the claws only sank deeper, and I screamed.

Oh gods.

Beneath the black fur, scales armored its body like a dragon's. They were impossible to kill—not that I'd ever been worried before.

Vuks didn't attack Viori. *Ever.*

They were sharply intelligent and respected us as much as we did them.

Maybe it's not me it's after.

With a roar, the man barreled into the beast, locking his arms around its thick neck. The impact knocked the vuk off me. I scrambled backward, gasping, my body trembling as I reached for my dagger.

The vuk snapped at the man, its fangs inches from his face, but he didn't let go. Wedging his knees beneath its belly, he kept it from pinning him outright. Blood soaked his tattered shirt, bright streaks spilling from gashes across his chest and arms. Still, he held on, muscles straining against the creature's immense power.

I couldn't just stand there.

Gripping my dagger, I lunged. The blade struck the vuk's side, searching for a weak spot between its scales, but skidded off harmlessly, the impact jarring my arm. *Useless.*

The Lirien groaned, guttural and raw, as the vuk's claws raked across his torso again. Desperation surged through me. If he died, I'd be next.

A new plan took shape. While he grappled with the vuk, I darted to its flank, searching for an opening. The beast was locked on its prey, giving me a chance. I aimed for the exposed joint near its hind leg and drove my dagger in with all my strength.

The vuk howled, the sound splitting through the forest. Its massive body twisted, nearly throwing the Lirien off. But he used the distraction. With a shout, he drove his sword upward, the blade piercing the vuk's chest in a perfect strike.

The creature shuddered, its silver eyes going wide before dulling. The massive body collapsed, the Lirien trapped beneath it.

I dropped my dagger and braced my back against the vuk's

side. My legs burned as I pushed, straining to roll the beast off him. It shifted slightly, enough for me to drag the Lirien free.

His bloodied body sagged against me, his breaths ragged but steady. Relief washed over me, but it was short-lived. Deep gashes marred his neck and shoulders, and the vuk's black blood coated him from head to toe.

I should leave him here. I should—

No. He saved my life.

Crouching beside him, I pressed a strip of cloth to the gashes on his neck. Blood soaked through immediately, a stark red against my trembling hands. He didn't stir, his chest rising and falling in shallow, uneven breaths. Alive, but barely.

Killing him now would be cleaner. Smarter. Seth wouldn't care that this man had saved me or that I owed him a life debt. All Seth would see was a threat—a Pendaran soldier on Viori land.

But I faltered.

Hesitation was costly—I'd learned that lesson the hard way with Esme.

Yet I hesitated anyway.

Something about him gave me pause. Not just his reckless bravery—charging a vuk—but the way he'd looked at me before the fight began. Like he didn't see me as an enemy. *Knew* me. Or maybe I imagined that.

Mother's voice echoed in my mind, calm and unwavering: *A debt of a life is always paid with a life. Anything less invites ruin.*

It wasn't just the Pendaran belief—it was survival. Refusing a life debt invoked a curse, the kind no Pendaran could outrun. Mother had seen it firsthand, and I'd grown up on her warnings.

Still, it wasn't curses or tradition that twisted my resolve—it was Esme. The memory of her cries as she was taken clawed at my thoughts. I'd failed her because I'd hesitated, because I'd tried to weigh my options when action was needed.

Esme's absence pressed against me like a second shadow. Guilt had been my constant companion these past five weeks, whispering reminders of my failure. If I left this man to die, would I ever shake that guilt? Or would it twist into something even darker, another voice reminding me of my cowardice?

Not this time.

I bit down hard on my lip and sheathed my dagger. If I had to face Seth's wrath, so be it. I wouldn't let another life slip through my fingers.

Even if that life belonged to someone who might kill me when he woke.

The Lirien groaned, his head lolling to the side. Up close, his features were sharper, more defined, though exhaustion and pain had etched lines into his handsome face. A warrior, no doubt, but not one who'd expected to end up here.

His piercing blue-green eyes fluttered open, glassy and unfocused at first. Then they snapped to mine, sharp and assessing despite the blood caking his skin.

"Still alive?" I asked.

"Barely," he rasped, his voice like gravel. His gaze darted past me to the dead vuk, then back, narrowing slightly as if piecing together what had happened. "You ... didn't run."

"I don't run." The words came out sharper than I intended. I didn't like the way his words made me feel. *Like he expected me to abandon him.*

His lips twitched, almost a smirk. "Good. Makes saving you less of a waste."

I bristled, stepping back. "Saving me? You nearly got yourself killed, and now I have to drag you back to camp before something else finds us."

He grimaced, trying to sit up, but his body betrayed him, sagging back to the ground. "Camp? What camp?"

"Mine." The word was curt. Let him think I was leading him somewhere safe—or to his execution. It didn't matter. I crouched and started packing the makeshift bandages more tightly around his wounds. "You're lucky I'm not leaving you for the scavengers."

He winced but didn't complain. Instead, his gaze lingered on me, uncomfortably sharp, as if cataloging every detail—the braid falling over my shoulder, the curve of my dagger's hilt, the tension in my jaw.

"You're not like the others," he said finally.

I froze, hands hovering over the bandage. "What others?"

"The Viori. You don't move like them."

My pulse kicked, but I kept my expression neutral. "And you know how the Viori move?"

His gaze didn't waver. "I've seen enough."

I yanked the bandage tight, earning a sharp inhale of pain. "You talk too much for someone who's bleeding out."

A dry chuckle sent a faint shiver down my spine. "And you're too kind for someone who doesn't run."

I scowled, standing and taking a step back. *He's dangerous.* Not just because of the sword still jutting from the vuk or the tattoo marking him, but because of the way he looked at me— like he saw through me, past the layers I kept so carefully guarded.

"Don't mistake this for kindness," I said coldly. "I'm paying a debt, nothing more."

A faint smile ghosted his lips. "Sure."

I didn't answer. There was no point.

Instead, I laid out my compact bedroll and helped him shift onto it. Then I strapped him to it with a rope. He didn't resist, though his eyes followed every movement. When I was done, I stood, rolling my shoulders and bracing for the long trek ahead.

"If you're smart," I said without looking at him, "you'll stop talking and focus on staying alive."

"Smart," he murmured, voice almost amused. "I'll try to remember that."

I ignored him and hoisted the bedroll's edge. His weight strained my muscles, but I gritted my teeth and started dragging him through the frost-covered forest. This wasn't for him, it was for me—for whatever shred of honor I had left.

Behind me, his voice came again, softer now, almost to himself.

"You don't run," he repeated. "Good."

When I checked on him again, his eyes were closed.

The weight of the Lirien quickly became unbearable, each step a battle against my own exhaustion. Cold seeped into my bones, the strain of pulling his unconscious form made my shoulders ache, but it wasn't the physical effort that made my breath hitch.

It was the thought of Seth.

He would kill this man on sight. No questions. No mercy.

The image flashed in my mind: Seth's face, sharp with anger, his voice cutting like a blade. *Why did you bring a Pendaran soldier into our territory? Why didn't you finish him when you had the chance? Why risk everything?*

The rational part of me couldn't argue with him. I *should* have left the Lirien there, dead or alive. I owed him nothing but the curse that would have followed me if I hadn't paid the life debt. A curse Seth wouldn't believe in. A curse I didn't fully understand.

The forest around me remained silent, save for the soft scrape of the bedroll over leaves and roots. My thoughts filled the emptiness, a churning mix of dread and determination.

What if this man is a threat? I glanced over my shoulder at his bloodied face, slack with unconsciousness. He didn't look dangerous now, but I couldn't forget the way he'd moved in the fight. Fast. Precise. Deadly.

Yet not to me. He could have let the vuk finish me off, saved himself the effort of fighting it. Instead, he'd risked his life—and nearly lost it—for mine.

My lips pressed into a hard line. That didn't mean I trusted him. It just meant I owed him, and that debt had to be paid.

Seth would see my choice as a betrayal. A weakness.

What if he was right? What if I was too weak for this, too soft for the Vangar?

The Lirien groaned, stirring against the ropes on the bedroll. I stiffened momentarily before realizing he wasn't waking—just slipping deeper into unconsciousness. Still, I couldn't let my guard down. Not now. Not ever.

The camp was a far distance. I had time to figure out what to say to Seth, how to convince him not to kill this man before I could repay the debt. Time to figure out if I even believed my own excuses.

But deep down, I already knew the truth: no amount of preparation would change Seth's mind. Bringing this man into Viori territory was as good as handing him a death sentence.

And still, I kept walking.

CHAPTER 5
SEREN

The outline of a watchtower loomed in the fading light, built high into the towering evergreen, signaling how close I was to home.

The Vangar had already seen me—there was no slipping past them. They wouldn't stop me, but they *would* come for me. I'd brought something—someone—they wouldn't ignore.

The path winding through the heart of the encampment stretched ahead. Shadows filtered through the trees as the sun dipped lower, the air growing heavy with the approaching night. I felt the weight of every step, certain I was being watched.

I couldn't risk going to my family's tent. Presenting myself to an officer or council member first would be a show of my good faith.

Speak firmly. Hold your ground. Don't let Seth bait you into anger.

Voices murmured ahead, torchlight flaring against the dark. My pulse quickened, but I kept my expression neutral as the figures emerged.

Seth stood at their head, hand resting on his sword's hilt. Others followed—council members and Vangar warriors— their faces unreadable, though their silence spoke volumes. They'd come to judge me before I'd even spoken.

My body ached from dragging the Lirien, my fingernails torn from gripping for so long. Slowing, I lowered the bedroll to the ground. The Lirien hadn't stirred once during the day-long trek back.

"Seren." Seth broke from the others, closing the distance between us. "Explain?"

"I know this—"

"Who is he? The Vangar reported you had brought a wounded man."

I positioned myself between Seth and the Lirien. "I have."

Olivia Galanis, the council member tasked with checking visitors from other encampments for the Viori rune mark, stepped forward. With a flick of her fingers, a bright green light flared and settled on the man's recumbent form. She lifted her head sharply, eyes wide. "He's not Viori."

Seth's dark eyes glittered. "Liriens have no place here."

"Let me speak."

"There's nothing you can say. You've defied the law—that alone warrants punishment. But bringing him here?" He gestured to the Lirien with a sharp flick of his hand. "You've endangered all of us."

"That's not true." The words felt hollow.

"This is arrogance, plain and simple. You think you're above the laws that protect us." His voice dripped with disdain. "Step aside, and I'll end this now."

Seth's drew his sword.

"No." I'd prepared for this. Pulling out a small crossbow I'd fastened to my back, my muscles trembled. I aimed at him, and he froze. "I won't miss."

Seth's lip curled, but he didn't move. The torches around us crackled, the only sound in the still night.

"What is the meaning of this?" My mother's voice rang out. She ran toward us, Ciaran at her side.

Thank the gods.

Ciaran must have been on duty and warned her. My friend's face was flushed.

"Seren brought a Lirien into the encampment." Seth stared me down.

Stand firm, Seren.

"I have my reasons," I gritted.

"There's never a good reason. Or have you forgotten that Esme remains unaccounted for?" The barb struck deep, and he *knew* it.

Mother reached us, carrying herself with the grace of an Ibarran priestess. "Seth, please." She knelt, prostrate at his feet.

My stomach turned. *Aren't we all supposed to be equals among the Viori?*

Ciaran hovered behind my mother, clearly worried, his presence solid, but that made two people on my side.

"I was attacked by a vuk. This man interfered and risked his life to save mine, killing the vuk, and injuring himself gravely."

Seth barked out a laugh. "A vuk? Even if we were foolish enough to believe one might attack a Viori, it's well-known they're impossible to kill."

Asshole.

"And yet, he did."

Torchlight cast jagged shadows across his face. "And why would a Lirien save a Viori? What reason would he have unless *you* gave him one?"

The insinuation curled between us, unspoken but unmistakable. My cheeks burned. Seth didn't need to say the word *lover*—everyone already understood his meaning.

"Believe whatever you want, but it doesn't change the truth. You'd rather punish him than acknowledge any honor on his part?"

Seth's laugh was bitter, cutting. "Honor? From a Lirien? Or are you the one mistaking his intentions? The last time I saw you, you were sneaking out of the camp. Were you meeting him then? And if he's not a lover, then what? An accomplice?"

The words hit like a physical blow. He wasn't just accusing me of foolishness. He was accusing me of treason.

"Enough, Seth. You know she has Pendaran blood. If what she says is true, she cannot kill him." Mother's long, dark tresses cascaded over her shoulders as she pleaded.

"But *I* can. And she is a Viori first and foremost, Lucia. You Ragnalls may have forgotten that while hanging your Pendaran and Ibarran crests."

The Lirien drew a ragged breath. I knelt beside him to take his pulse, still carefully holding the crossbow.

Slow. Faint.

"He needs healing, Seth. Please," I said. "My mother can heal him and, afterward, he can be held captive. The Harvest Moon is close—he can claim refuge then. If he refuses, at least I've fulfilled my duty."

Soroush, the oldest council member, peered at the Lirien before turning his gaze to my mother, then to Seth. His grey, thin lips parted, tongue moistening dry skin. "It's forbidden. Let nature take its course."

The simple answer. Maybe even the wise one.

But I didn't drag him through the forest to die here at my feet.

"Then I'll heal him. I just need some supplies." My abilities paled compared to Mother's, but I wasn't completely without skill.

I scanned the gathered faces, searching for an ally. Olivia's sharp features hardened with disapproval. Soroush, however, remained calculating, his gaze flickering between Seth and me. He weighed his options. Perhaps he could be swayed.

"Seth, you know I'd never endanger the Viori. No one in this condition is a threat."

Soroush cleared his throat, his thin voice rasping. "Seren, this is reckless. Bringing a Lirien here—did you think we wouldn't notice?"

"I thought you'd listen," I shot back. "I thought you'd trust me enough to hear my reasons before drawing your swords."

Olivia's frown deepened. "Trust is earned, not assumed."

Their words piled on top of each other, a suffocating wall closing in. Ciaran stood at the edge of the group, stoic but alert. Ready to help, if necessary. No one else moved. No one else would step in.

Seth gave me a long, measured look. "If you're so honorable, let the council decide your punishment."

I tilted my head, letting a faint, mocking smile tug at my lips. "Of course, Seth. Just as soon as you explain why you needed to draw a sword on someone carrying an injured man. What are you afraid of? That I might actually have a good reason?"

Behind Seth, the other council members exchanged uncertain glances. *Good.* If I couldn't beat him outright, I could at least make him look like a bully.

"He killed a vuk." I leveled my gaze at Seth. "You're right, it's nearly impossible. Which means this Lirien isn't ordinary. He's *Sealed.* Imagine what we might learn from him if he joins us."

Seth scoffed. "And if he doesn't? What then? He runs back to Lirien with our secrets?"

"Then we execute him," I said bluntly. "But not until we've

learned everything we can. Throwing away a potential advantage is shortsighted, even for you."

A murmur rippled through the crowd, and Soroush nodded faintly. *Perfect. Let them think this is about strategy, too.*

My gaze swept over those gathered, meeting each pair of eyes in turn. "Is this what we've become? We execute those who save our lives without even asking why?"

"Don't twist this," Seth snarled. "You knew what would happen."

"I know what happens to those who break their oaths. If we let honor die in the name of fear, what's left to protect?"

"Admit that he's your lover, Seren. It's the only logical explanation for your behavior. Maybe then the council will have mercy."

Yes, because breaking our laws to rendezvous with and save a Lirien lover made more sense to him than the truth. The bitter irony of it made me want to scream.

But he already believed me to be a liar. *So be it.* "If I admit this man is my lover, you'll allow me to save him?"

Seth's frown deepened. "No. I meant mercy *for you*. You can't claim a lover."

No, but I can claim a spouse.

The desperate plan I'd wrestled with on the journey here might be the only way out. Seth wouldn't back down. Time was running out.

All Viori had the right to claim family or spouses if they fled from Lirien to join us. But born Viori *couldn't* claim spouses—because it was impossible. A Lirien spouse meant you'd lived in Lirien.

But I knew a way around that.

My mother's spell book held an ancient, nearly forgotten incantation. The Oath of Bryndis. A sacred bond, rarely spoken of, but one Ibarrans would be familiar with. The oath would not only tether this man to me—it would heal him. Allow me to claim him as my husband, buying me time to decide what to do next.

And the bond meant the Lirien wouldn't be able to betray me without hurting himself. It was a risk. A gamble. But the only one I had left.

But who knew what the consequences would be?

Bile rose in my throat and I forced it back down. My father's voice echoed through my mind, the lesson ingrained in me since childhood: *Never break your oath. To break it is to break yourself.*

And then Esme's face flickered in my mind as well—small, defiant, and so certain I'd keep her safe. I couldn't fail again.

Not this time. Not this life.

"I claim him as a husband," I declared.

The words sent a ripple through those gathered. My mother's alarmed gaze snapped to me. Ciaran went rigid.

Seth scoffed. "That's impossible."

"No, it's not." I uttered a spell over the Lirien and me and a dome of crystal-clear ice formed around us. Someone with spellcraft might be able to break it, but it would buy me precious seconds.

Doubt gnawed at the edges of my mind. What would this mean for my family? For my mother, who would certainly be scrutinized? For Ciaran, who stood uneasily nearby, looking at me like I'd just thrown myself off a cliff?

I didn't have time for doubt.

Gripping the handle of my dagger, I dragged the blade across my left wrist, carving two adjacent Xs. Blood welled instantly, warm and slick as it trickled to my wrist bone.

Shit, shit. This hurts like hell.

There was no time to do the same to the Lirien, so I yanked

the cloth from his neck wound. Dark and angry blood oozed out as I set my wrist to his neck.

Our pulses beat against each other.

"I take the Blood Oath of Bryndis," I said, projecting my voice through the ice shield.

Mother lunged toward me, her voice muffled. "Seren, no!"

"May my soul be bound to his. I offer him my blade and my protection."

Mother vaporized the ice dome, reaching me, and gripped my elbow, trying to pry it away. "You don't know what you're doing. Do not bind yourself to him."

I met my mother's eyes, which were pleading, *begging* me to stop.

But what choice do I have?

"I bind myself to his fate. I will not raise my hand to strike him, and my blood is his. Let the blood of this oath join our souls forever and let us never be separated, as Bryndis is bound to Varik."

The last syllables left my lips, and for a moment, everything was still.

Then pain struck like a lightning bolt, tearing through my veins. Not just the sharp sting of the wound but something deeper, as though the oath was carving itself into my very being. I gasped, jerking back, but I couldn't break the bond now. Fire licked the edges of the rune I'd carved, radiating outward, spreading through my body like molten iron. *Changing me.*

I clutched my arm to my chest, biting back a scream as I crumpled against my mother, who caught me by the shoulders.

"What have you done?" she whispered, her voice raw with horror.

The rune on my wrist darkened, the edges blackening like

charred wood. The pain wasn't just physical. Something deep within me—my soul, perhaps—had been ripped apart and reshaped. The pressure crushed me, hollowed me out, then filled the void with something unfamiliar and unbearably heavy. A faint, fragile presence brushed the edges of my mind —an echo of pain that wasn't mine, a memory of something I couldn't quite grasp ... *flames engulfing a building.* It vanished as quickly as it came, leaving only a faint hum.

It was as though I felt the Lirien there, a thread connecting us. I wasn't alone in my own skin anymore.

My breath came in short, ragged bursts. Ice poured through my veins now, chasing the fire, and my vision swam with spots of darkness. I gritted my teeth, but my mind raced with panic. What if this oath bound me to more than I'd intended? What if it destroyed me?

The Lirien stirred, a faint movement that pulled my focus back to him. His breathing remained shallow but steady, the wound on his neck no longer bleeding as freely. Relief and dread warred within me.

He lived.

But at what cost?

I sagged into my mother's arms, trembling.

"Seren," my mother whispered, her voice breaking. "You don't understand. This oath is more than a bond. It's a chain."

Her words sent a fresh wave of nausea rolling through me, but I couldn't dwell on them now. Not when Seth's furious gaze bored into me. Mother turned toward Soroush. "You know what that oath means, Soroush. He is Viori now, if she's claimed him. He must be healed." The desperation in her voice unnerved me.

Time beat slowly, each second fracturing my body further.

Soroush blinked slowly, then nodded to Seth. "He is her spouse."

His pronouncement echoed in the air like a gavel striking.

The people gathered spoke, but I barely heard them. My mind latched on to one thought, repeating like a drumbeat.

What in Nyxva did I do?

Seth swiveled toward me. "You'll be given a marital tent, then—strictly under guard. You want a husband?" He sneered. "Fine. You can stay confined with him until the council decides your fate. But you receive no help from your family. You may have one emissary to fetch supplies, food, and water—and to drag that *Lirien* to the tent."

"I will." Ciaran's voice cut from through the crowd. "I'll carry him."

Thank the gods. Ciaran would ensure no one murdered the Lirien along the way. Bending beside me, Ciaran hand rested briefly on my shoulder. "What in the Solric's name did you just do?" he whispered.

"Buy myself some time." *I hope.*

Ciaran hefted the Lirien into his arms with practiced ease, his movements careful but swift. I stayed where I was, slumped against my mother, my limbs shaking. My wrist still burned, but the Oath was done, the bond Sealed. And yet, I couldn't shake the horror that I'd just opened a door I couldn't close.

"What have I done?" I whispered, the words barely audible. They weren't meant for anyone, but my mother heard all the same. She squeezed my shoulders, her grip firm despite the fear etched across her face.

"You've bound yourself to him," she said softly, "but you don't yet understand what that means."

Her words sent a chill through me, colder than the forest air. I didn't need her to explain. I could feel it already. A faint, foreign presence lingered at the edges of my mind, fragile and unfamiliar. The bond. I hadn't expected it to feel so … real.

Ciaran glanced back, his face grim. "We need to move," he said. "Hopefully we can set up a tent quickly, but if Seth's men are on edge—"

"I'm coming." I forced my legs to cooperate, even as they wobbled beneath me. I couldn't show weakness now. Not in front of Seth.

As Ciaran carried the Lirien away, Seth stepped closer, his movements slow and deliberate. The Vangar parted for him like shadows yielding to the flame. I didn't flinch as he loomed over me.

"You think you've won something here," Seth murmured, his voice low enough that only I could hear. "But you've only made things worse—for you and everyone you care about. When the council decides your fate, don't expect me to save you. You chose this, Seren. Remember that."

His words were cutting, but there was something behind them—a flicker of something raw and unguarded. *Hurt.* Seth hid it well, but I caught it before he turned away. He wasn't just angry about the Lirien. This was personal.

But he had no right. He'd done far worse to me. He'd thrown me away—betrayed what I'd thought was love. I owed him nothing. Definitely not remorse for my actions.

He turned on his heel, leaving me standing in the glow of the torches. His words lingered in the cold air, heavier than the bond itself. Whatever trial awaited me next, Seth would see it through—but so would I.

I couldn't falter now.

CHAPTER 6
RYKR

A sharp smell woke me from a deep, unsated slumber. My arms fought against a cool bedsheet, and something warm and damp against my eyelids. A cloth. I flung it away, jerking back, and squinted.

Daylight filtered through the seams of a small, dimly-lit tent, its walls made of patched, weatherworn canvas fluttering in the wind. A wood stove glowed in one corner, filling the air with the scent of smoke. The pillow beside mine on the bedroll had a blanket neatly folded on top, and a low wooden table nearby held an assortment of jars, pitchers, and strange tools. The floor was layered with rough furs smelling of damp earth, and faint voices stirred outside, muffled by the thick tent walls.

A young woman sat beside me, holding a jar close to my nostrils.

Smelling salts?

No, something else. Strong enough to rouse me, but unfamiliar.

The woman I recognized. I'd encountered her in the Dreadwood ...

The wolf-like creature.

I searched for my sword.

She lowered the jar, her gaze intense. "How do you feel?"

Dark, long lashes fringed her large, striking eyes—light brown, pupils rimmed with green and blue ... eerily reminiscent of my family's lineage.

I pushed aside my fascination, keeping my expression neutral. "Where's my sword?"

Amusement sparkled in her eyes. "Really? That's your first—"

"Where am I?" I sat up despite the ache in my limbs, the effort sending a wave of dizziness through me. My body screamed for rest, but something raw and restless simmered under my skin. My hunger was sharp, nearly unbearable.

She leaned back, studying me. "You're in the Viori territory. My tribe's encampment."

Viori. The word stirred my rage. Outlaws. Rebels. Enemies of Lirien. They claimed to stand against the Bloodbinding, but their cause had long since rotted into raids and slaughter, leaving border villages burned, innocents dead.

And now I was their prisoner.

My expression remained impassive, though my pulse quickened.

She set a cool hand on my forehead. "Your fever broke this morning. I didn't want to risk waking you before then."

My lips were raw, my mouth parched. "How long have I been here?"

"Three days. I've been trying to heal you. The vuk poisoned you when it bit you—in addition to the wounds it gave you."

The vuk. The memory rushed back—the beast's massive jaws clamping down, the searing pain as its teeth sank into flesh.

I shouldn't have survived.

I stared at her. "Why?"

Her brows knit together, confusion flashing across her face. "Why what?"

"Why save me? Your kind kills Liriens on sight."

Something flickered in her expression—guilt, maybe. "Because you saved me first."

She tucked her feet beneath her and settled back more comfortably. When I'd first come across her, I'd noticed she was small and lithe, but there hadn't been time to really look at her.

She was striking. My nursemaids had raised me on stories of wretched, hideous forest dwellers, but I'd seen enough Viori women to know those tales were lies. The ones I'd encountered in battle were as rugged as their male companions—short hair, faces painted for war.

She wore a fur-lined leather vest over her shirt, the sleeves cut to expose her shoulders. A complex tattoo of knots and runes wound from her left wrist to her elbow. A tanned complexion spoke of days outside, and her dark brown hair was plaited in a long braid over her shoulder, streaked with golden blond I hadn't noticed during our encounter before. Nor had I taken in the curves of full breasts, or the hint of cleavage above the lacing of her vest.

She'd noticed my appraisal and quirked a brow. "You have a name, Lirien?"

Her composure unnerved me. I wanted to see her as a threat, a captor, but the way her gaze softened when she looked at me made it difficult to hold on to my anger. She was beautiful, yes, but it was more than that. She was steady, utterly unafraid of me.

"Rykr West ... haven." *Idiot.* I shouldn't use that name right now. *Damn breasts, distracting.* "You?"

"Seren." She leaned over to a squat table near the bedroll and poured water from a clay pitcher into a cup. "Drink this."

I hesitated.

She rolled her eyes. "If I was going to kill you, I would have done it by now."

Fair point.

I brought the cup to my lips, the cool relief of water welcome. Downing it in a few gulps, I wiped my mouth with the back of my hand.

What the fuck?

Dark hair covered my forearm. I hurled the cup across the tent, where it landed with a dull *thump* against the canvas.

I shot up, only to realize I was completely naked. Swearing out of fury rather than modesty, I yanked the blanket around my waist, then glanced at my arms and legs.

The hair on my body had turned dark. *All of it.*

Seren watched me cautiously as she stood. If she thought I didn't notice her gripping a dagger in the folds of her cloak, she was a fool.

"What in Nyxva did you do to me?" My voice cracked, betraying the fear I tried to suppress. *This isn't normal. This isn't my body.*

Before she could respond, the tent flapped open. A hulking man stepped inside and grabbed me by the shoulders, shoving me backward. He was young, but taller than me by several inches, which was saying something. And broad. An ox of a man with short, red hair.

"She saved your life," he snapped, grey eyes flashing. "Didn't anyone ever tell you the rules of the Dreadwood?"

Seren stepped between us, cutting him off with a hard look. "That's enough. I don't need your protection, Ciaran." Her tone brooked no argument. "I made the decision to save him, and I'll handle the consequences."

Ciaran's expression made things clearer. He was here to protect her—cared about her. Maybe more than that.

Seren flicked her calm gaze back at me. "I had to use blood magic to save you. Your hair changed because of it. Magic like this always leaves its mark."

Seren moved a few paces away, lifting a small, hazy mirror. She held it up for me to see.

My hair was dark.

I snatched the mirror from her, barely recognizing my reflection. My face was the same, though the scruff of my jaw was as dark as my hair. A long, thin scar with puncture points marred the right side of my neck, healing unusually fast, given what had happened.

A large tattoo had formed over the scar, spreading from the wound on my neck over my right shoulder onto my chest, an intricate design of runes and knots ... *just like the one on her left arm.* Combined with the Seal between my shoulder blades and on the back of my neck, I now had black and crimson tattoos swathing most of my upper right torso.

The dark hair and tattoo disgusted me, not because of how they looked, but because of how I felt—like a stranger in my own skin. Something about me, something deep and irretrievable, was missing. A presence hummed in my mind that I couldn't decipher, pressing into my thoughts.

"I want to know *exactly* what happened. *Right now.*"

"The vuk attacked and somehow you killed it." Seren's voice was surprisingly gentle. "I've never seen a vuk attack. Or heard of anyone killing one successfully. They're immortal. Impossible to kill."

"What happened then?"

Ciaran took a menacing step closer. "Then she should have let you die. Or killed you. The Viori code forbids us from allowing Liriens in the forest to live, except the first day of the Harvest Moon, if they seek refuge."

"But the first day of the Harvest Moon is approaching. Wouldn't I be admitted to your people by your own laws?"

"The first day *only*. Anyone who comes outside that time must be killed."

"So, you're just murderers?" I challenged his glare. "You kill all Liriens, regardless of the threat they pose?"

"I can handle myself, Ciaran," Seren said firmly, then stepped between us, her face darkening at me. "If you're done with your tantrum, I'll answer your questions. Before you throw any more accusations, though, you might want to remember that I chose to save you, even at the risk of breaking the code. You never should have been in the Dreadwood to begin with."

Dalric. Thorne.

What had happened to my friends?

I had no idea if they were dead or alive. Or how to help them.

"The Dreadwood belongs to Lirien. My reasons for being there aren't your concern," I snapped. "Now tell me what the fuck you did to me, and why—if it was your *duty*—you didn't let me die?"

Seren sheathed her dagger. "Because in my family, a debt of a life is always paid with a life."

I studied her. "Your family is from Pendara."

She nodded.

Somehow, that comforted me slightly.

"Am I your prisoner then?"

Seren turned toward Ciaran. "I need a few minutes alone with him."

The ox didn't take his eyes off me. "If he causes trouble—"

"He won't." Her voice held quiet authority. "Stay outside. I'll call for you if I need you."

His jaw tightened, but he obeyed, retreating with a sharp glance my way. "I'll be close."

As the tent flap fell shut, I crossed my arms. "Your lover, I take it?"

"Ciaran is a friend. Nothing more." Seren frowned.

I doubted he saw her that way.

I sat on the only chair, which groaned under my weight. Shifting the blanket over my lap, I felt the weight of her analytical gaze, studying me. She'd been calm and confident up until now, but her demeanor shifted, her eyes darting away from mine.

Seren pinched the bridge of her nose. "You're not my prisoner. But when I brought you back, the leader of our tribe wanted to execute you." She extended her wrist, displaying her tattoo. "I took a blood oath in order to claim you as Viori."

"So ... blood magic?" Even the words made my gut clench. I'd been subject to it before, with the Seal. I arched a wry brow. "Are you a sorceress?"

She shook her head.

"Priestess?"

"I'm Unbound, born with spellcraft gifts. But my mother is an Ibarran priestess."

"What kind of blood oath?" If it had changed my appearance, it had to be powerful. And why had that stopped the Viori from executing me?

"The Oath of Bryndis."

I'd never heard of the oath. While some people, especially Ibarrans, still worshipped the old gods and goddesses, Liriens as a whole had lost devotion to the gods who'd died or distanced themselves from humanity at the end of the Fourth

Age. Most Liriens only worshipped Solric, God of light, and Nyxva, the goddess of the underworld.

Even I, with the finest education Lirien offered, knew little about the old gods. But I knew enough to recognize the name she'd mentioned.

"Bryndis? As in the Eldra goddess of love?" I asked.

"Yes." *She clearly has some education.*

"And ... this *oath* changed my hair?"

"You seem very attached to your previous hair color." A hint of a smile curled at her lips.

"Wouldn't you be?"

"Not if keeping it meant my head being separated from my body."

Her wit was oddly comforting. "Point taken."

She shrugged. "If it makes you feel better, mine changed too. And so did my eyes, though I don't think your eyes did."

I rubbed my jaw, trying to process everything she'd said. "What do you mean by you *claimed* me?"

Seren clasped her hands. "In the strictest sense—"

I got the feeling I wasn't going to like her answer.

"—we're spouses."

Spouses?

She didn't appear to be joking, though. "As in *married*?"

She looked away. "It's more complicated than that, but for the purposes of saving you from being executed, yes. I claimed you as my husband. The bond is both physical and spiritual— it supersedes our laws."

My head spun.

She'd been in a predicament, obviously. Pendaran customs were clear about life debts.

"What if I'm already married?"

Her eyes widened. "Are you? Most of the Sealed aren't."

A few beats passed. Would lying give me any advantage? "No," I finally admitted.

Was that relief on her face?

"The oath was the only way to save you and buy time to figure out what to do next. It's rare, ancient magic—not something I entered into lightly. But it was the best option available, and I'd do it again if it meant keeping you alive," she said. "Ciaran tried to find me more information about the oath, but our repository of books here is limited. Most people don't bring books with them when they escape Lirien."

As though Lirien were a prison.

Her hatred for my kingdom seemed so dissonant with her integrity. Even in front of Ciaran, she'd stood by her choice to save my life, her confidence unwavering.

Don't be an idiot.

Before I'd been Sealed, my idealistic, naive side would have drowned out the voice of caution now ringing through my thoughts. She may have saved me, but she was still Viori. An enemy to my kingdom. I'd witnessed their ruthlessness too many times with the Regulation.

You can't trust her. If she had even the slightest clue who I was, she'd turn me over immediately. Use me for ransom—or worse.

Fortunately, the Seal on my back protected my identity.

"How did you learn about this rare, ancient oath in the first place?"

"I have a ... skill. I memorize anything I read. And my mother brought her spell books with her when she came here. I've studied them."

I gave her a hard stare. "I can't be married to you. Or any other Viori traitor."

"Traitor?" Her voice was hard. Cold. "If I'm a traitor, what does that make you—a Lirien soldier running from your own people?"

She crossed her arms. "Right now, this marriage is the only thing keeping you alive. My tribe is furious. Our laws about Liriens are absolute and they might not admit you. The Viori believe anyone who comes outside of the Harvest Moon is a spy or a threat, and they'll make an example of you."

"If I am admitted, then what?" I demanded. "Will they let me go? Or am I just trading one prison for another?"

Seren's expression darkened. "That depends. If we can prove that I had the right to claim you, you'll earn the right to stay ... and maybe leave, if we can break the bond between us and you find a way to escape from the territory. If we fail, you won't leave at all."

"Sounds like my options are all curpiss." I let the blanket fall away and stood. "I need my clothes. And where's my sword?"

She crossed over to a table where trousers, a clean shirt, and a fur-lined leather vest had been placed. "These are my brother's. I think they'll fit you." She held out the trousers as I approached, her gaze focused on my face.

How respectful.

I smirked. "If we're married, you should be able to handle seeing me naked."

"Don't get too cocky. I wouldn't remain married to a Lirien if you were the last man in the world." Her eyes narrowed. "Your sword is buried inside the vuk. I couldn't carry both it and you, so I chose you."

Anger tore through me, but I forced it down as I tugged on the trousers. They were snug around the thighs and short, but better than being naked. She couldn't have known the sword's value, and I needed to be rational. "Then I have to retrieve it."

She handed me my boots as I finished with the clothing. "You can't leave."

"I need my sword." I couldn't stand being at anyone's mercy—not hers, not theirs. If I couldn't even hold on to my own blade, what did that make me?

"My tribe is convening a council meeting this afternoon to judge us both. If they decide the oath wasn't justified, I'll be punished too—banishment at best, execution at worst. I've staked my life on this, Rykr. On you. You need to understand that."

I had no intention of standing trial. "But I'm not imprisoned, right?" The panels of this tent suffocated me.

"Not precisely."

"Then I'm not staying." My father needed to know about my attack—I'd been here too long already. Surely someone in Lirien could undo this fucking blood oath. The High Magister of Ibarra, at the very least. "If you could point me toward my sword, we'll call it even."

She didn't answer as I pushed aside the tent flap.

True to his word, Ciaran stood only about fifteen feet away, a sword in hand.

Beyond him loomed the Dreadwood, its gnarled trees rising like jagged teeth against the grey sky. Wooden spikes encircled the small tent—more a deterrent than a true barrier—but enough to contain me. The air was heavy, damp with moss and decay, as though the forest itself was watching.

Two large Vangar warriors blocked the exit to the enclosure, their hands resting on their weapons.

"You can't leave."

I should have known.

I spun toward Seren, my temper flaring. "What the fuck is this? I thought you said I wasn't imprisoned."

"Calm down—"

I planted myself between her and the exit, arms crossed, every muscle taut. "No more lies."

Seren didn't flinch, her voice cutting through my rage like a blade. "I haven't lied to you. I told you—you can't leave. Even if you escaped this encampment, what then? Take on hundreds of Vangar scouts unarmed?" She leaned closer, her composure maddening. "You'll get yourself killed, and then my life will be for nothing. Think, Lirien."

Helplessness clawed at me, a loss of control I couldn't stand.

"No." I snatched the dagger from her side, testing its weight in my palm. Seren's lips pursed like I was being *inconvenient*. "You're just going to stand there? Don't think I won't use this if you push me far enough. Tell the men at the gates to stand down."

Ciaran strode toward us. "Get that fucking dagger away from her."

"You stay out of it," I snapped. Ciaran's eyes bulged, as though stunned by my audacity.

Seren rolled her eyes. "Go ahead and leave if you want." The corners of her eyes squinted. "But those guards will kill you. And, like I said, the bond between us is more complicated than marriage. If one of us dies, so will the other. I was counting on all that *honor* you showed when you saved my life."

I froze. No wonder she'd been so calm this whole time.

Clever little bitch.

Something inside me felt different. I'd been Sealed. I knew what blood magic felt like.

I didn't care that I was supposed to be grateful.

If her fucking people weren't savages, she wouldn't have had to "spare me" in the first place.

"Fuck you," I spat, then backed away.

I dropped the dagger, lifting my hands in surrender.

The guards approached with irons.

My gaze stayed locked with Seren's and unrelenting, raging fury spiraled like fire in my veins.

I'd take my chances in escaping. Fight against the best of their warriors. But a fatal life bound to a woman I couldn't trust?

This place isn't my prison.

She is.

CHAPTER 7
SEREN

mahle looked up expectantly as I sank down beside her in the gathering space for the council meeting. I wouldn't have long, as soon I'd have to stand before the platform for judgment. Fortunately, my best friend had been waiting for me in the front row.

I released a slow breath, filling my lungs with the sweet pine-scented air. After days confined to my tent, claustrophobia had set in, and the light filtering through the high tree-tops, the rich aromas of meats roasting over open flames, and the hum of trade at the center of the encampment were a welcome reprieve.

So was Amahle. Ciaran had been my only visitor these past few days, but he'd at least brought messages from her and my family. One of the advantages of being literate in our tribe.

"How was it?" Amahle asked me. "Once you woke him?"

"I'm not sure." At first, Rykr had seemed cautious but willing to listen. But that look he'd given me when he realized how closely we were linked—*that* was pure hatred.

Not that I'd have reacted any better.

"Does he seem decent? For a Lirien?"

"Define decent? That depends on what you value most in a man."

Amahle grinned. "Fair point. Lucky for you, he's decent to *look at*. And if he's indecent in the right ways, you might be very lucky. Could've done worse and happened upon a cave troll instead." She poked me in the ribs. "Though I doubt you'd have taken that blood oath if he had been a troll."

"He's a fucking Lirien." I brushed off the comment about Rykr's good looks. Yes, he *was* handsome. Ridiculously so. I wasn't about to admit those looks had tempted me to stay my hand in killing him before the vuk attacked.

But that's not why I took the oath.

An oath I was quickly starting to regret.

Not only that, but I'd also experienced the monstrous ways of Liriens firsthand. *Why take Esme? Was she even alive or had they already killed her?* The questions haunted me, awake and in my dreams.

Amahle studied me. "But you knew that when you saved him. Do you think we can trust him?"

Him. Rykr. My husband. I shuddered.

"If it weren't for the fact that killing me would kill him, I wouldn't put it past him. I don't know if he's so devoted to Lirien to commit suicide just to rid the world of one Viori, but turning my back to him might be terrifying."

My mother had been right. I'd bound myself to a man I knew nothing about and now that he was awake, the reality was hitting me hard. But I owed him. He'd saved my life.

Still, my limited knowledge of the oath worried me. Hopefully my mother would know more. "Do you know where Tara is? You passed along my message, right?"

Amahle nodded, scanning the gathering crowd. "I haven't

seen her, though. I saw your mother on the way in. But your father and Madoc still haven't returned."

I gritted my teeth. What was taking Father and Madoc so long to find Esme? Each day that passed without their return only fueled my worries. They would have helped me today, too. *Of course, if I had stayed home like Father wanted, I wouldn't be in this mess.* Would he be angry with me when he found out?

All my hopes hinged on Tara. *She should be here by now.*

A deeper fear unfurled inside me. What if she didn't *want* to be here? Facing my family after what I'd done would be difficult—I'd put them all under scrutiny. They'd already been worried about betrayal from someone in our encampment after Esme. My actions made everything worse.

If I'd had doubts about the oath when I took it, they were nothing compared to what I felt now. The changing color of my hair and eyes had been the least of it. The changes I *felt* were more significant. The spell book said nothing about what this bond would do to me.

If Rykr angered the council, he could get us both executed. *Please, please don't be that stubborn.*

Amahle's dark brown eyes reflected understanding. "Tara will be here. And if your Lirien doesn't agree to your marriage, we can always tie him up and make him realize the error of his ways." She set her arm around my shoulders. "If you find any other handsome Liriens in the woods, maybe teach me your oath before you kill them, too. The pool of eligible men around here is becoming damned near incestuous. I don't want to switch tribes just to find a man."

She wouldn't need to. Tall, black-skinned, and beautiful, she was descended from a legendary Doban scribe. She'd rejected all offers that had come her way, though.

I covered my face with my hands. "Much as I agree with

you, I apparently have terrible taste in men. First Seth. Now a Lirien."

As though I'd summoned him, Seth entered the clearing, Darya trailing behind him. The din of the gathered crowd faded into silence. I averted my gaze.

The clearing, nestled at the heart of the encampment, was our version of a town square. Every major decision affecting the tribe was made here, ensuring that nearly everyone would bear witness. I'd never been on this side of the gathering, though—awaiting my own judgment.

The seating—a rough circle of felled logs—ensured I'd be visible to all.

"Are you *sure* Tara is coming?" I asked Amahle, my voice low.

Her lips pursed slightly, then her jaw set. Only my proximity to her made it possible to see the mist that fogged her dark eyes, making them suddenly grey. When she blinked, a hint of fatigue crept into her face. "She's not here yet, but she's close."

I hugged her, my worries ebbing. "Thank you." I wouldn't ask her for more—her spirit gliding ability drained her quickly, and it was wrong to take advantage of her gift. *And Tara is coming.*

I squared my shoulders and took my place before the wooden platform, clasping my hands behind my back to mask the clamminess of my palms. As the other members of the council took their seats, I tried to pretend my life didn't depend on a hot-tempered Lirien who saw me as his captor.

Ciaran had done me a favor by insisting on guarding Rykr himself ensuring he made it here unharmed. *What happens after that ... is up to Rykr and Seth. Two men I can't trust.*

I hated being this vulnerable.

The row of candidates sitting together tugged at my heart

—*Esme should be there.* Ciaran's younger sister, Moira, caught my eye and offered a small wave, her smile quick but warm. She was Esme's friend.

Gods, I miss her.

But I hate the Liriens more for taking her.

I lifted my chin as Soroush began the meeting, his voice so paper-thin that it barely carried over the crowd. He *might* help me, as he obviously knew about the oath. But he hadn't looked at me once.

He gestured to Seth, who stood. "The council calls forth the matter of Seren Ragnall and the Lirien she brought into our encampment three days ago."

Attentive silence followed, and all eyes were focused on me. Everyone already knew what had happened—stories traveled fast here. This would feed the gossip mill for months.

"Allow the Lirien to approach the council." Soroush waved a leathery hand forward.

Ciaran led Rykr down the main aisle, Vangar guards behind them.

Rykr had been striking with his golden hair, but the dark hair he had now suited him even more. Despite the irons binding his wrists and ankles, Rykr carried himself like a man who'd allowed himself to be bound, not one who had been forced. Even in chains, he radiated strength—his broad shoulders set firm, his stance unwavering, as if daring anyone to challenge him.

The crowd noticed him, too. A hum of murmurs arose, particularly among the women, craning their necks for a better view of him.

Ciaran halted when Rykr was beside me, inclining his head toward Seth before retreating to sit beside Amahle. Rykr had been furious with me after being bound, so I wasn't surprised that he wouldn't look at me now.

Seth approached, his eyes sweeping over Rykr with distaste. "What's your name, Lirien?"

Rykr shifted his weight and surveyed the gathering space, a muscle in his forearm flexing.

"Rykr Westhaven."

"And where are you from?"

"Pendara."

"Can you prove that?"

"Really?" Rykr's broad shoulders flexed back, a flicker of annoyance in his face. "I'm Sealed. Unless you don't trust your own eyes, your question is pointless."

Seth's expression darkened further.

I cringed. *Gods, he's arrogant.* I stepped closer to Rykr, lowering my voice so only he could hear. "Don't antagonize him. Keep a level head, or we'll both die today."

Seth studied Rykr, his eyes sharp with unspoken challenge. I knew that look. He'd take advantage of Rykr's temper if he could. "What were you doing in the Dreadwood?"

"Hunting vuks." Rykr didn't bother to look back at Seth as he answered.

Liar. When he'd woken, he'd asked about the "wolf creature"—which meant he didn't even know what a vuk was. Not that I would give him away.

Seth's incredulous scoff made me hold my breath. "Seems like a foolhardy mission, considering they're immortal and impossible to kill."

"Maybe for you." Rykr's eyes flicked back to Seth, lazily.

Dammit, Rykr.

I set my hands on my hips. "Immortal doesn't mean they can't die, Seth. If that were true, the entire foundation of our faith would crumble. Valtheron, Gaelric, and Lysia? They were all immortal gods, and they died at the end of the Third Age, saving us all."

A murmur rippled through the gathering.

"You'll wait until you're addressed, Seren. Unrestricted commentary makes for chaotic council meetings." But he couldn't ignore my point. "For an immortal to die, it usually involves being killed by a god or a weapon of the gods."

"Or decapitation and dark magic," Olivia said from the council's seats. Her tone was clipped, but the fact that she'd spoken up at all made me hopeful. She wasn't on my side—but she wasn't entirely on Seth's either.

Seth cast her a withering glance before turning back to Rykr. "Did you use any of those means to kill this vuk? Because that would be relevant."

"No." Rykr's arrogance dripped, cold and flat.

What in Solric's name was Rykr playing at? He had to know this wouldn't help.

"So, you entered Viori territory for sport?"

"How is this Viori territory? You have no lawful claim to these lands. The Dreadwood belongs to Lirien and is forbidden to all."

I gritted my teeth, wishing I could stop Rykr from saying anything else that might turn the council against him.

Seth smirked, delighted by the resistance. The more Rykr showed loyalty to Lirien, the easier Seth's job would be. "The treaty of King Anders granted these lands to our people."

Shockingly, Rykr laughed in his face. "The treaty makes no such provision. It prohibits Lirien citizens from occupying the Dreadwood. King Anders wanted to protect Liriens from deadly creatures like skinwraiths and wyverns and, after forcing the monsters into the Dreadwood, he warded the border to keep them out. That's all."

Shit. I tensed.

Seth glowered at Rykr. "You dare call me a liar?"

Don't play into his hands. Stop.

Rykr's eyes swept the council with calculated detachment, and he shrugged. "Just ignorant. You clearly haven't read the treaty." A slow smirk tugged at the corner of his lips. "I have."

Seth lunged. As his hand grasped Rykr's throat, my blade pressed into the vulnerable spot at Seth's waist.

A collective gasp rippled through the crowd.

"Get away, Seth," I snapped.

"I'm merely reminding this Lirien of his place. Which, to begin with, *isn't* as a member of our tribe."

Rykr didn't flinch. Didn't back away. He looked Seth coolly in the eye. "I think my wife would say otherwise."

Shivers went down my spine.

The casualness with which Rykr said it—so firm, so certain—sent startling heat through me.

Seth's eyes bored into mine. Maybe I didn't understand Rykr's motivations, but I still felt some small triumph at knowing he'd allied himself with me.

"Your wife." A cruel smile came to Seth's lips, and he lowered his hand. "Then may you have a long and happy marriage. Considering that her appetite led her to our enemies, that might not be possible. She always was hard to keep satisfied."

My fist slammed into Seth's face before I could stop myself. The impact snapped his head back, blood gushing from his nose. Humiliation seared through me. *Fucking asshole.*

And even though my friendship with Darya had completely withered, I still felt bad that he'd said that in her presence, too.

A firm set of hands gripped the waistband of my pants, dragging me back. Rykr's breath was warm on my neck. "I don't like being tied to anyone, least of all someone who dragged me into a fight I didn't ask for," he said in a low voice. "But if I'm stuck here, I'm not going down so easily—and neither are you. One of us needs to prove he's abusing his power, and this won't help."

My left hand throbbed—I'd punched Seth with it thanks to the dagger in my right—and I scowled as I shook it out. Was that what all this arrogance was? *Strategy?*

"If you had a plan, maybe you should have discussed it with me earlier," I hissed.

Seth wiped the blood from his nose, a satisfied gleam in his eyes.

Darya wore deep displeasure on her beautiful face.

"Insult her again," Rykr said to Seth, his voice low and dangerous, "and you'll regret it. Bound or not, I protect what's mine."

Seth addressed the council. "Do you see how Seren mocks everything we stand for? Now her Pendaran lover threatens me, too. He may be her spouse, but he's still a loyal Lirien.

"We've seen this same subversion for years with the Ragnalls," Seth went on. "Their love for their Lirien realms is known to all ... so much so that now Seren has bound her very soul to one, rather than choosing a husband from among us. She should be ejected from our territory and the Ragnalls watched."

What in Nyxva?

I scanned the crowd for my mother, finding her standing at the back, her expression as horrified as I felt.

I'd made the choice to bind myself to Rykr, and I couldn't undo it now, but my family wasn't going to suffer for my decisions—not if I could help it. "If you must punish me, I accept it. But my family has done nothing wrong. I take full responsibility for the oath and my husband, Seth. Leave them out of this."

"Seth, if I may." Macklyn Bryce stood from his seat at the council table.

Ciaran's father was one of my father's closest friends, a man I trusted. Ciaran and I had grown up together like siblings. Macklyn's support meant something.

Soroush nodded toward him.

"The Ragnalls have proved their loyalty for over two decades. To question their honor when half of them aren't here to defend themselves is disgraceful." Macklyn sat with a finality that made it clear he wouldn't allow Seth's attack to continue.

Murmurs of agreement came from others, including council members. But not everyone would agree. And if Madoc or my father had been here, Seth wouldn't have dared to be so bold. *Gods, please let them come home soon with Esme.*

The weight of Rykr's fingers eased from me and I straightened, trying to ignore the heat of his presence.

"I, too, will speak for Seren."

My gaze snapped to Darya as she rose.

"She's in my squadron. As her officer, I've observed both her courage and integrity firsthand."

Shock coursed through me but she didn't look my way.

For Darya to go against Seth … was huge.

Seth dabbed at his bloody nose with a handkerchief. Maybe my provocation hadn't been entirely wasted. He'd miscalculated. Pushed too hard, too soon. He sniffed, then nodded stiffly at his wife. "Does anyone here truly understand what it means to be Sealed?"

The air was tense, thick with suspicion and curiosity.

When no one ventured a response, Seth gestured toward Olivia. "What about you, Olivia?"

Her gaze fixed on Rykr. "It means he's been Bloodbound to the king. Plucked from one of the Bound realms. His powers intensified."

Seth sniffed. "Yes, and no. Explain it, Soroush. You're the

scribe. The people need to understand why *this* Lirien is such a danger."

Soroush rose, gripping his walking stick. Seth handed him a speaking horn, amplifying his frail voice over the assembly.

"When King Ragnor Ederyn founded Lirien," Soroush began, "he faced a troubling reality. The gods, in their wisdom—or folly—bestowed humanity with divine gifts, but unchecked power threatened the balance of the realm."

The crowd leaned in, enraptured. I tightened my grip on my cloak, every breath shallow as Soroush's gaze swept across us.

"And so," he continued, "the Bloodbinding was created. The people were divided—Ederyn, Doba, Pendara, Ambra, Zhi, Ibarra, and Volker—each given a craft. A purpose. A duty." His voice grew heavier. "Thus, only the people of Zhi were permitted powers over the physical body. Only Pendarans were given warcrafts, and so on. But how to enforce it?"

Soroush let the question hang in the air. He was clearly talented at this—which was also why he was so respected in our tribe. I already knew the answer.

"Magic itself. A child is Bound days after its birth, its divine gift stripped away, limiting them to the craft permitted by their realm. For example, if a Volker babe is born with the gift of master stone-carving, it may keep it. But that same Volker babe born with the Zhi gift of healing? They are left with nothing. Weak. Powerless. Bound to a fate outside of the gods' will."

Unease stirred in those gathered. Even among the Viori, we rarely spoke of the Bloodbinding so plainly.

Soroush turned his attention to me. "Do you know which realm escaped this Bloodbinding rite, Seren?"

I forced myself to meet his stare. "Ederyn." My voice wasn't nearly as strong as I wanted it to be.

"Yes. Ederyn. The king's own realm. The only one where a

child could be born with the gifts the gods intended." Soroush's face tilted back toward the council. "Why, Darya? Why free one realm but not the others?"

Darya's lips curved prettily. "The king claimed it was to keep balance. That he didn't want Ederyn to be dependent on the other realms."

Soroush took slow shuffling steps toward Rykr and me. "That's right. Balance. But Ragnor of Ederyn was no fool. He knew the controversy the Bloodbinding would create."

A heavy silence fell over the clearing as Soroush extended a hand toward Rykr. "So, he gave the people the Sealed. Three children, chosen from each realm, every twelve years—the most gifted in each realm. His Seal granted unparalleled mastery to the recipients. The Sealed Masters would teach only their people—ensuring their abilities remained within their realm alone. A Sealed Ibarran would teach spellcraft only to Ibarra's children. A Sealed Pendaran would train Pendarans—but never an Ederyn boy born with warcraft. This allowed the realms to be placated by the king's tyranny."

Seth squeezed Soroush's shoulder in silent thanks, then turned to Rykr with a sharp smile. "And this Lirien is a Sealed Pendaran. His craft is war. He's trained to kill and he's good at it. Lirien, remove your shirt. Show our tribe your Seal."

All eyes were on Rykr, whose jaw was clenched, his head held high. Proudly.

When Rykr didn't move, Olivia stood, her eyes glinting with barely-contained hostility. "Will you defy our chief, Lirien?"

Rykr's gaze locked with mine for a tense beat.

A ripple of unease passed through me. His defiance could determine our punishment.

His lips pressed into a grim line, but there was no hesitation as he untucked his shirt. Even in this moment of humiliation, he stood tall.

With a tense breath, Rykr reached back with his bound hands and grabbed a fistful of his shirt. He pulled his shirt over his head, the cold clink of his irons echoing unnervingly through the space. The muscles of his back flexed, taut with tension, as the scarlet and black mark of the Seal gleamed faintly against the dappled light—an intricate brand carved by blood and magic. A mark of power.

"You see that monstrosity?" Seth's voice cut through the silence like a knife. "Blood magic. Imbued by the cut of a king. That is the Seal of Pendara, binding this Lirien to the throne. He is no mere subject—he's the king's dog."

The gathered tribe leaned in, eyes narrowed, some with suspicion, others with fascination. Rykr's fingers curled, but he said nothing. Instead, he yanked his shirt back down and stood even straighter.

"This Lirien is a grave danger to us. He may have been claimed by a clever trick, but he and Seren should face judgment. If we allow them to go unpunished, we show nothing but weakness," Seth finished.

A slow breath left my lips, my heart thudding. Seth and Soroush had made their case well. Too well. *They're going to kill us both.*

"The Lirien and Seren should be taken to Emberstone," Olivia said suddenly, her voice carrying authority. "They should face the Skorn trial at the Harvest Moon Festival in ten days. We're merely a council—no Viori has been claimed under these circumstances. Their crimes should be decided by the gods, not us."

No, no, no.

The Skorn trial. The harshest punishment outside execution—and it may as well be a death sentence.

"What the fuck is the Skorn trial?" Rykr muttered to me.

Seth overheard and smirked at Rykr, wiping blood from his nose. "A duel to death with the Skorn, our elite Vangar warriors. If you survive, the gods deem you innocent." He cocked his head. "But I'll warn you, Lirien. Very few survive the Skorn trial. It is reserved for only the gravest cases, when guilt is unclear."

I bristled with anger. The Skorn was a trial meant to instill fear and respect of the Viori leadership. They called it justice decided "by the gods," then made it impossible to live through it. My father had always hated the Skorn and believed those condemned to it were simply being made examples of.

Most people didn't agree with my father's opinion, though. Especially not the council members, who were now nodding in agreement with Olivia—including Macklyn and Soroush.

Of course. They would defer judgment to fate, to the gods. They didn't want to be responsible if I died—or if Rykr lived.

So much for justice.

Fear threatened to overtake me but I lifted my chin resolutely, determined not to show my fears in the face of the proposed consequence.

"We shall defer to judgment through the Skorn, then," Soroush said in a low voice. I could only hear because I was close to the platform. "Shall we vote?"

One by one, hands rose in silent agreement.

If the council's decision frustrated Seth, he didn't show it. "As the gods will it. Mark them for the Skorn trial, Olivia. The Lirien will remain in irons until then but may remain in Seren's custody."

Olivia's cat-like eyes gleamed as she flicked her hand, green rune magic curling from her fingertips toward Rykr and me. A glowing "S" settled on the backs of our right hands, then sunk into our skin, leaving no visible mark. The rune ensured that if either of us tried to escape, any Viori tribe that caught us and checked for the Viori rune would recognize our sentence. Only those who survived the Skorn had the rune erased.

Seemingly satisfied, Seth nodded. Then his eyes met mine. "Seren must be punished for striking her chief. I suggest forty lashes. Anything less might encourage rebellion."

I fought to keep myself steady.

Forty? The mammoth-hide flogging whip could split skin in a single stroke, leaving wounds that took weeks to heal.

"No fucking way, Seth." Amahle shot to her feet. "You're out of line."

Ciaran also stood. "You can't do that. You insulted her in front of everyone. She had every right—"

"Enough." Seth glared at them. He turned to one of the Vangar guards. "Vless, escort Seren's friends to the officer barracks. They can expect further censure for speaking out of turn. This is exactly the kind of defiance that breeds disorder."

Even if Vless sympathized, he said nothing. As he reached for Amahle's arm, she yanked free, chin lifting. "Don't fucking touch me. I know the way."

Much as I appreciated their defense, watching them be punished for my sake only twisted the knife deeper. Too many people I loved were suffering because of my choices—my failures.

Seth's gaze swept the crowd. "Anyone else? I don't need the council's approval to discipline Seren for attacking me. I confer with them only as a courtesy, to ensure her punishment is seen as justice, not retribution."

Rykr let out a low, mocking chuckle. "Do your people really drink this curpiss?"

"Careful, Lirien. You're at the edge of my mercy." Seth turned back toward the council.

"Forty lashes might kill her. Render her unable to fight in

the Skorn," Macklyn said. Yet he didn't object to flogging outright. *Dammit.* Ciaran would be furious with his father.

"Lucia Ragnall is a well-known healer," Seth said.

"Ten," Olivia Galanis said, her voice hesitant. Even that would be brutal, but at least it was survivable.

"Thirty," Seth countered.

"Twenty," Macklyn said.

And here I thought he was on my side.

Be strong. Show them I'm not afraid.

But I was terrified.

I dug my fingernails into my palms. Twenty lashes would leave me too injured to prepare for the Skorn for days, at least. It was excessive—meant to cripple me.

I glanced at my mother. She looked ready to speak, but I shook my head slightly. Seth would only punish her for it, as he had done with my friends. Hopefully mother would listen to me. I needed her here.

"Council?" Seth referred the question to them. "Shall we vote? Twenty lashes?"

"Nyxva," Rykr growled quietly.

Indeed, Lirien. This is fucked.

Silence stretched across the clearing. A few council members exchanged uneasy glances, hesitant to raise their hands. Olivia's lips pressed into a tight line, her discomfort evident, but she raised her hand reluctantly. Macklyn followed, though his expression remained neutral.

Slowly, the others complied. Soroush hesitated longer than the rest, a faint cough escaping him as he lifted his hand with a weary sigh.

My heart pounded.

My mother was in tears, and the crowd stirred with unease.

I'd never witnessed anyone—let alone a woman—

sentenced to more than ten lashes. Fifteen was a severe punishment. Twenty was a statement. That, combined with the Skorn, was a cruel message wrapped in the guise of justice.

I shouldn't have expected anything less.

Yet, I bristled with anger. *Not one voice among the crowd crying out at the injustice. All these people so easily cowered in terror to Seth.* I'd already suffered by losing my baby sister, and yet again, I was receiving more punishment. *Where is there mercy?*

Seth lifted his hands, settling the crowd. I hated that they listened to him immediately. Hated that once, I would have been like them—looking to Seth for leadership after his father's death. A handsome, dynamic, and natural choice.

Their devotion to him grew by the day ... alongside *my* hatred.

Blood still dripped from Seth's nose but the satisfaction it had given me had faded.

Even Rykr had remained silent. For a moment, I'd believed we were in this together—that, for now, he'd stand beside me. He'd acknowledged me as his wife, a show of solidarity I hadn't expected.

But I was alone.

Summoning what strength I had left, I strode toward the flogging post, refusing to let the fear show on my face.

"Do your worst, Seth," I said, my voice clear and steady. "If pain is the price for giving you what you deserve, then I'll pay it gladly."

If they wanted to break me, they'd have to try harder than this.

CHAPTER 8
RYKR

The Viori were fucking savages.

As Seren stopped in front of the thick rectangular flogging post, head held high, I gritted my teeth.

The woman might have broken their laws, but she'd tried to be honorable. *Even if it means a cage I don't want.*

Despite my limited mobility, I pulled my shirt back over my head. "I'll take her punishment." My voice was calm as I dragged the shirt to my wrists, leaving my torso bare once more. "Let me take her place."

Seren whirled, her eyes wide. "No, don't—"

Seth, still looming on the platform, scowled. "Tempting, but that would hardly serve justice."

I held his gaze. "I don't claim to know Viori law but in Lirien a man can take a woman's beating. You can flog me yourself if you'd like." Then in a voice only he could hear, I added, "Besides. We both know this isn't about justice. Is it?"

The smug confidence in Seth's face flickered.

I didn't relish the thought of this man beating me, but

Seren *had* saved my life. If Seth accepted my offer, my debt to her would be paid.

His dark eyes filled with temptation.

He wasn't just considering my offer—he was calculating. Weighing something beyond the immediate scene. The cruel smirk that tugged at the corner of his mouth didn't reach his cold eyes. He wanted my blood spilled. This was his chance. A public display of dominance.

At last, he nodded. "I accept your offer." His voice carried through the silent crowd.

With measured, unhurried precision, he unclasped the brooch of his cloak. He wanted me to feel every second before the first lash fell. His every movement was deliberate, designed to keep all eyes on him—on his authority.

He gripped my elbow, tighter than necessary, as he led me to the post, past Seren. Not a word passed between us, but I could sense the satisfaction rolling off him like a storm brewing on the horizon.

Seren's whisper reached me, "You don't have to do this—"

"It's done. Stay out of it."

For a heartbeat, Seren froze. Then she narrowed her eyes at me, her annoyance at my order clear. Her voice was louder as she said, "He had no right to offer himself."

Seth stopped, half-turning toward her. "The law allows it, Seren. Are you questioning the old ways now?"

Her shoulders tensed. "The law doesn't require a spectacle." Her voice was laced with defiance. "He has nothing to do with this. He shouldn't even be standing here."

Seth's smirk faltered, replaced by a flicker of irritation. "You'd prefer we flog you, then?"

Seren's lips pressed together. Her silence was answer enough.

"Exactly." Seth turned back to me, his voice ringing out. "A man steps forward, and the law allows his sacrifice. You should be grateful, Seren. Your precious husband is saving *you* from dishonor."

Her expression hardened at the word *husband,* but she said nothing.

Damn woman.

When I'd seen that vuk stalking us, my only thought had been to warn her. I'd needed to find Dalric and Thorne and get out of the fucking forest. But that had all become secondary when I'd seen her in danger.

Helpless women had caused me trouble too many times.

What type of fucking idiot was I?

The type who ends up exiled and Sealed for two years, apparently.

And now, one who'd be flogged by my enemies.

Seth didn't remove the shirt hanging at my wrists as he lifted my bound hands to the post, tying them with a thick, rough rope that bit into my skin. A chill seeped into my bare back, the air thick with the scent of pine and earth.

My attention focused on the camp beyond me—a ramshackle collection of tents and wooden structures, arranged in a circle, with gathering space at its center. Smoke curled into the air, mingling with the scents of animals and cooking food. The Viori's craftsmanship was evident in the intricate carvings on the wooden beams of the space, including the flogging post, etched with runes and symbols. Despite the camp's makeshift appearance, it was efficient, and easily broken down to be unoccupied and moved. This was no haphazard village—it was the heart of a people who thrived on defiance and survival.

I braced myself as a guard provided Seth with a whip.

Seth uncoiled the whip. His gaze lingered on the Seal between my shoulder blades, resting there for a few beats. Then he stepped back, out of my sight line.

The whip sung through the air with a sharp *snap*.

An intense explosion of pain followed. Deep. Stinging. Nearly unbearable.

I forced my breath to stay even. The sting tore through me, unforgiving, but I made no sound.

Pain was familiar. Manageable.

I could handle it.

But when I heard the sharp gasp from behind me, my focus wavered. I turned my head just enough to catch Seren's expression—wide-eyed, pale, as though the strike had landed on her instead. She swayed on her feet as an older woman rushed to her side and gripped her arm.

The whip cracked again, slicing deeper.

Seren collapsed, barely catching herself. The woman braced her, whispering into Seren's ear.

I hadn't expected feigned grief from her, but I had to admit —she was a damned talented actress. Playing the role of tortured lover was a convincing touch.

My forehead rested against the rough surface of the flogging post, and I willed myself into silence as strike followed strike. With each blow, my ability to stand straight decreased. Warm blood ran down my arms and legs, soaking my trousers, pooling on the pine needles beneath my boots.

I closed my eyes, trying to drown out the sounds of the forest, the sickening, muffled crunch of leather destroying my flesh, the scent of my blood and sweat, and evergreen trees carried in the wind, the sweet smell of bread baking somewhere on a hearth.

Life, carrying on amid my torment.

Seren vomited with the last strike.

Unceremoniously, the guards cut the rope from my wrists, and I collapsed into my own blood, breath ragged. The blinding pain made it nearly impossible to think as I shook uncontrollably.

He can't defeat me. I won't allow him to win.

Maybe it was a sheer act of will—I wasn't sure—but a cool, strange numbness seemed to pass over my wounds, dulling my pain. Enough to make it tolerable. I forced a slow breath, then wiped my mouth with the back of my hand and drew one knee up, bracing my arms against it.

The defiant act drew gasps. By all rights, I shouldn't even attempt to be standing.

Seth towered over me, his face splattered with blood. "You'll go to Emberstone in ten days, Lirien—injured or not. And when you do, you may want to come up with a better excuse for being in *our* forest than hunting vuks. Because we all know you're lying. And you have no proof of your claims."

"He may not, but I do."

A wave of commotion started from the back of the gathering space, where a woman stood.

Dressed like the Viori women I'd fought during raids before, she wore leather from head to toe, her dark hair short and closely cropped, save for a longer section that framed her face. A row of silver hoops looped around her ears.

A foul stench filled the air. An ox and cart was behind her, several paces back. Piled atop the cart lay the carcass of the vuk, my sword still poking from it.

The reek of rot reached the council, sending several members reeling back, covering their noses with their sleeves. Others in the crowd mirrored them, muttering in disgust. The woman strode toward Seren.

"I would have been here sooner," she said with a grim

smile. "But the fucking cart broke down four times, and I had to fix it. Lost a whole day on that. And getting that thing onto the cart? Nearly impossible. But it was right where you said it would be. Are you hurt? What the hell happened?"

Seren struggled to her feet, pale-faced, and then she hugged her. "I'm so glad you're here, Tara."

Seth brushed past me, hurrying toward the vuk. He reached it, then grabbed the hilt of my sword, and yanked it free. The putrid flesh squelched as it sank back. Black blood dripped from the blade.

I staggered to my feet. "That's my sword."

"Not anymore." Seth glared at Seren. "This council meeting is over. Collect your *husband*, Seren. You're free to leave your tent, but we'll be watching. Any attempt to escape will be met with swift justice."

Husband.

What the fuck did that mean for me now?

The crowd began to disperse, but not before I caught several curious glances thrown our way. Seren remained rooted in place for another moment, hands trembling at her sides, then she hurried toward me.

I forced myself to remain upright, biting back a groan. My hands clenched into tight fists, but the numbing on my back continued to spread. Or maybe I was in shock. Either way, the blood loss was making me lightheaded.

"How are you standing?" she asked, a mix of fear and awe in her eyes.

Any attempt at wit died on my tongue. Truth was, I didn't entirely know.

Something about this numbness felt like magic. An unfamiliar sorcery.

"You didn't have to do this." Her voice was a whisper but the tension in her tone was unmistakable.

"I did." My reply was equally quiet, but final.

Any debts between us were paid. We might share a bond, but nothing more—and one way or another, I would escape from this prison.

With my fucking sword.

CHAPTER 9
SEREN

I hadn't expected Rykr to take my place at the flogging—or the blistering pain that had burst across my back with every lash he took.

As though I could feel his pain.

Mother's spell had dulled the worst of it, but it hadn't stopped the sensation entirely. But as I stared at him now, bloodied, raw welts crisscrossing his back, I hardly knew what to say to him.

Why had he taken my punishment?

And how wasn't he curled on the ground, unable to move?

I'd seen my mother cast healing spells before, but none so powerful to lessen the intense pain of a flogging. Men who'd been flogged might spend weeks in recovery, even with Zhi healing practices. *What did Mother do?* I flicked a glance at her. "Have you healed him somehow?" I hissed.

"I've done what I can for now, but no—this is not all my doing." Mother's face was somber. "We should leave. His resilience is attracting attention."

Tara gripped me as the Viori left the gathering. "Let's go, Seren." She flicked a cautious glance at Rykr. "I'm Tara, by the way. Seren's sister."

Rykr didn't respond, either in too much pain to say much or uninterested.

Tara huffed. "Real friendly Lirien you've got here, Ser."

"I figured I'd get the grumpiest one just to make things interesting." Then I gave him a firm look. "Wait here."

"Could I go anywhere if I wanted?" He raised a dark brow, his voice strained.

"You could try, but it wouldn't end well." Even in pain, he had a sharp tongue. *Annoying. And oddly appealing.*

I dashed between people to catch Darya before she left. My back still ached, but the pain was fading. Impermanent. "Darya, wait. I want to thank you for your help."

Seth's wife turned, her eyes dark and troubled. "I'm your friend, Seren. What kind of friend would I be if I didn't speak up when you needed me?"

The words hit me harder than expected. I'd spent so long pushing her away and she hadn't deserved it. Only Amahle and Ciaran had known about my affair with Seth. "Thank you," I repeated, softly.

Darya squeezed my hand. "I can't pretend I really understand what you were thinking, but I'm here if you need me. But I do understand Seth's worry. Liriens don't come into the forest to hunt vuks. They come to hunt *us*. If love exists between you and your Lirien, he should have been willing to respect our laws and waited. He shouldn't have put you at risk. Just ... be careful."

My tongue felt like iron. From the Viori perspective, she wasn't wrong. At last, I managed, "Each Viori has been at risk since the day we fled Lirien. What I did may have added to it, but it didn't create it."

"True, but you deserve more, Seren. And don't worry. I'll keep working on Seth. See if I can lessen his fears. But I'd suggest you not let your Lirien stir up any trouble."

She left me before I could reply.

My mother came up beside me. "We should keep our distance from Seth and Darya. Come. Your husband needs tending to. And we have much to discuss about that oath you took."

I followed my mother without protest.

Tara stayed behind, to dispose of the vuk's carcass and clean our cart. Together with my mother, I led Rykr away. Pain distorted his face with each step.

I should have thanked him, but a part of me still questioned why he had done it at all.

Liriens couldn't be trusted ... could they? I'd be a fool to believe otherwise, no matter how honorable this one seemed.

Much as I hated to admit it, Seth and Darya were right—Rykr, a Pendaran soldier, hadn't been in the forest to hunt vuks ... so what had he been doing there? Whatever his reasons, they couldn't be good for the Viori. I needed to remember that.

We continued in silence. The Viori encampment was laid out like a village, tents arranged with space between them, giving each family a sense of privacy. The closer we got to my family's tent, the fewer neighbors we had. My family preferred living on the edge of the encampment, away from others.

The tent where I'd spent the last few days with Rykr—our tent—was several feet away from my family's. Already, the Vangar were removing the enclosure they'd built around it, and the sight loosened a breath from my tight chest. Maybe it would help Rykr feel less trapped. Trust me more.

"I'm Lucia." Mother gave Rykr a hard look as we stopped at my family's tent. "Before I allow you into our home, you need to swear that you won't lift a hand against my family, Rykr

Westhaven. Allowing you inside is allowing you into our trust. I do not take that lightly."

Dread slithered through me. *If Rykr learns who my father is ...*

Rykr could return to Lirien with details of my family—secrets that could get them killed. I should have thought of that sooner.

Rykr grimaced, then gave one brief nod. "I swear it."

At least he's not being arrogant now. Maybe he's finally realizing this isn't a game—for either of us.

Mother held the tent open.

I removed my boots at the entrance and then helped Rykr with his. The laces were wet and, as I finished, blood stained my fingertips. My hands quivered, my eyes shooting to his piercing blue-green gaze.

Rykr's eyes held an inscrutable expression. Not gratitude, but not complete dislike either.

I shook the thought away, tearing my gaze from his. *Why do I want his approval?*

"Thank you," he said in a low voice as I led him farther inside.

"I'm the one who should thank *you*," I said stiffly.

Mother unfastened her cloak and hurried over to her cabinet of potions and herbs.

"Where I come from, no leader would go unchallenged for giving a woman twenty lashes. Especially for something so trivial. As I've long known, Viori are savages."

I didn't want to agree with him, even though the lack of support I'd received from my tribe had cut through me. "Maybe where you come from, women can't handle a few lashes."

The laughter that lit his eyes was almost as disparaging as his words. "Clearly you've never been to Pendara."

"Stop squabbling and lie face down," Mother said to Rykr, gesturing to the rug in front of the stove. "I'll apply an ointment to your wounds and bandage them, which will help with infection and scarring. Sleep on your stomach until your wounds heal."

Rykr did as instructed and Mother knelt beside him, examining the flayed skin.

I could barely look. As she cleaned his wounds with water and cleaning salts, he winced.

Pain radiated up my back—mirroring his.

Worry creased Mother's brow. "You feel his pain, don't you?"

"Yes."

Rykr twisted his head toward me, his face sharp with disbelief. "What? You felt the lashings too?"

"It's one of the soul-knitting parts of the oath. Souls that are joined cannot be separated," Mother said quietly. "The Oath of Bryndis is ancient—"

"You're saying this bond is permanent?" My throat tightened.

Mother nodded.

Her words settled over me like a shroud. *Permanent?* How had I not known what I was binding myself to?

"From the ages before now, when the Eldra and Skaldra gods roamed the world and had their place among humans ..." Mother's voice was distant, as if recalling something from long ago.

Rykr swore under his breath, shifting as though to sit up, but Mother placed a firm hand on his shoulder. "Stay still if you want to heal."

As Rykr settled onto the rug once again, Mother continued, "The Eldra were gods of order, devoted to love and the land.

Bryndis was among them—the goddess of love. But she fell in love with Varik, a Skaldra god—one of chaos and cunning. Their love was forbidden, an affront to both pantheons. So, Bryndis took an oath to bind their immortal souls as one."

Her finger moved with practiced ease as she applied ointment to Rykr's raw, shredded skin. "The oath is a sacred bond, one that melds souls and bodies."

I gulped a breath, pain rippling through me again as she touched his wounds. "So, I can *actually* feel his pain?"

"Yes. And he'll feel yours. The more you give yourself to the bond, the stronger it becomes. You may hear each other's thoughts. Read each other's minds. Consummating your union would deepen the effects."

I stiffened, my shoulders locking. *Consummating?*

Rykr gave a laugh of disbelief. "You've got to be fucking joking."

"Is it any more unbelievable than an oath that changed your appearance?" Mother flicked a gaze at me. "I warned you, Seren. This is no simple marriage spell. The consequences are far graver. If either of you dies, the other will as well. And worse, anyone who understands Ibarran magic will know how to use this against you. If an enemy seeks to kill one of you, they may come for the other first."

Rykr cleared his throat. "So, you're saying that if I go back to Pendara and someone figures this out ... they could kill Seren in order to kill me?"

"Yes."

"Fantastic." Rykr narrowed his gaze at me.

"Your thoughts should not be on escape, but on how to survive the Skorn trial. You'll both have to live, and if one of you is wounded, the other will feel it. That could cost you your victory."

Dammit. The trial had been deadly enough without the added burden of feeling each other's injuries.

Mother placed a bandage on his back and I gritted out, "Can the bond be broken?"

Mother's normally steady hands faltered. "It's beyond my knowledge."

"Of course," Rykr breathed.

I closed my eyes, trying to process my mother's words. Her books hadn't said anything about this being irreversible. Nearly all magic could be reversed.

What in Nyxva did I do?

"Is there anyone who knows how to break it?" My voice was quiet, uncertainty threading through my words.

"I don't know. I've combed through all my books. The difficulty of the ancient oaths is that the gods and goddesses no longer intervene. Perhaps in another time, a human might have traveled to Eldris, the land of the Eldra gods, or Alvareth, the fae lands where Bryndis ruled, but now ... those paths are closed to us. The Mathema in Doba might have ancient texts, or perhaps the High Magister in Ibarra may know."

Places I couldn't go. People I couldn't speak to.

My arms folded around my stomach, sickness churning in my belly. "I need a few minutes. I'm going to wash."

Fetching a few things from my trunk, I tried not to react to each burst of pain that surfaced as my mother bandaged Rykr.

I left the tent, but my mother followed close on my heels. "Seren, wait. Try not to worry. Given what he did for you at the council meeting, Rykr may not be an evil man."

Easy enough for her to say. I kept my retort to myself. "I didn't know how else to save him, Mother."

"I know." Mother kissed my cheek. "But you must guard yourself around him. Closely. Use only your mind. Let nothing else guide you, including your heart. Your body will yearn for his—that's its nature. And Rykr is an attractive man. Be careful."

I shifted uncomfortably. "I get it."

"I don't think you do." Mother's face darkened. "Don't consummate this marriage. Rykr is powerful. Too powerful to be tied to you through magic alone."

"I can handle myself," I muttered, wishing she'd stop talking.

"Powerful men always believe they're in control. But women can learn the art of wielding control with such men in ways they don't suspect. Be careful, Seren. Bonds can be tricky to manage with someone like him. You'll want to be his lover, but you must resist—"

"Mother, please." I stepped away. "I may not have your skill, but I'm hardly a child without training. Father *and* you taught me well."

Mother's chin ducked with resignation. But I also saw grief. Grief for losing one of her children. Fear for *me*. "Powerful, ancient magic is no trifle. You don't know what you're up against. And the Skorn trial is *meant* to be impossible. If your father were here, he might be able to help you prepare for it. As it is, you'll need to begin training immediately. I can't lose you, too."

I left her, my frustrations mounting.

I can't lose you, too.

Her words echoed in my mind, looping over and over.

I'd been fighting for my life since the moment that vuk attacked. Now all my hope hinged on surviving a trial meant to kill me ... and working with a man who shared my distrust.

He didn't have to like me. Didn't have to trust me. But he needed me to survive as much as I needed him. Convincing him to work *with* me might be as simple as finding leverage.

If I could keep him close, perhaps I could learn more about

what brought him here—*and what he's hiding.* Maybe then, I could find a way to use that to get him to cooperate. If I was going to survive this mess, I'd need to find Rykr's weaknesses before anyone else did.

Because if I didn't, someone else might—and that could be far deadlier.

CHAPTER 10
RYKR

L ucia wiped tears from her cheeks as she placed a bouquet of goldenrods on the single, large bedroll in the tent where I'd woken earlier. Seren's mother had barely spoken to me all evening—like I was the one who had roped her daughter into this situation. This ... *marriage.*

She bowed as she passed me. "May Bryndis grant you—"

"Mother, don't." Seren set her hand on her mother's forearm. "Thank you for all the provisions."

Lucia stiffened. "What sort of mother would I be if I didn't help you set up your own household? I'd hoped it would be a day of celebration. This is not how I imagined any of my children's wedding days—especially not the first one to wed."

Wed was one way of putting it. Being flogged, shackled, and held against my will wasn't how I'd pictured my wedding day, either. Dalric and Thorne would have gotten a hearty laugh from it.

Are they still alive? If I ended up so deep in the Dark Forest, where did Thorne go? Had my father put out a search for me, knowing I hadn't been captured?

Seren hugged her mother. "It's been a long day. Get some rest. If fortune is on our side, Father will return tomorrow."

Paling further, Lucia nodded, then left, closing the panel tightly behind her.

Seren checked the fire in the stove—it was already cold in here—then came toward me. "Hold out your hands."

"Why?"

She sighed impatiently. "Just do it."

I did, and she pulled a sharp metal pick from the braid in her hair. Inserting it into the lock, she gave it a twist, and the irons clicked open. Then she knelt, repeating the process on my ankles. She stood, setting both sets on the chair.

"Impressive." The relief on my skin was immediate—I hadn't realized how much the restraints bothered me until then.

The metal pick twirled between her fingers with ease, then she trailed the tip against the stubble of my jaw. "If you give me even the slightest reason to, I'll carve your eye out with this pick, understood, Lirien?"

So that's how it's going to be.

I leaned down, my voice low and mocking. "You know, there are easier ways to flirt. All this eye-carving talk—it's giving mixed signals."

"Keep talking, and you'll get a clearer signal."

Straightening, I grinned. "See? That's exactly what I mean. Nothing says romance like casual death threats."

Seren's expression didn't change, but her grip on the pick tightened. "It's survival, not romance. Don't get any ideas."

I shrugged. "Trust me, if I ever write a love story, it won't start with 'Once upon a time, I was beaten, bound, and married by force.'"

Clearly despite her best efforts, the scowl on her pretty mouth twitched, the corners of her lips threatening a smile.

I had no doubt she'd try to fight me if necessary, but her threat intrigued me. "If I'm so dangerous, why take my irons off at all? Trying to impress me with your bravery?"

"Because in this tent you're not a prisoner. We have to live here, sleep in the same space. Basic comfort isn't a gift in our camp. It's a necessity. So don't make me regret this."

I studied her, noting the tension in her shoulders. "Or you trust me more than you're willing to admit." I wasn't sure if it was bravado or sheer stupidity. Probably the latter. "You're the one who wanted to kill me. Hell, you would still probably kill me if it didn't mean your own death."

"You want my trust? Earn it. Your kind have hunted my people for centuries. Lirien soldiers killed my friend, just last year. Burned him at the stake to set an example."

"If they burned him, he wasn't innocent. Your people dole out just as much death as they receive."

"You really do want to get stabbed, don't you?"

A smile curved on my lips. "I'd like to see you try."

Liquid anger pooled in the depths of her unusual eyes. "If you think you're the only Sealed Pendaran here, you're mistaken. So is my father. And he taught me well."

Her father was Sealed?

That stopped me cold. No Sealed Lirien in my lifetime had ever left, except for ...

"Wait ..."

Ragnall.

I should have heard it sooner—when that Viori bastard had called out Seren's family. The last name wasn't uncommon but now the pieces clicked.

A slick feeling of disgust coiled through my gut.

Smite me. No. Of all the people to find me in the Dreadwood.

Her skill in fighting me when the vuk had attacked. The

way her sister had brought that carcass back from the forest. Her mother's beauty—a priestess. *It all made too much sense.*

"Your father is Brogan Ragnall."

She stepped back, worry lighting her face. "You've heard of him?"

Fierce, visceral hatred shot through me, tightening my chest like a vise. My pulse pounded in my ears, drowning out everything else. *Heard of him?*

The son of a bitch killed my mother.

And now his daughter was bound to me?

The cruel, laughing twist of fate threatened my temper as cold sweat broke out on my neck. But I'd already shown a lack of restraint earlier that wouldn't help me here.

I had to be careful with what I said and how much passion I displayed. An ordinary man from Pendara wouldn't react the way I desired to. *Revenge could be so easy.*

"The only Sealed child who didn't cry at a Sealing. Commander of the King's Royal Guard and the king's closest adviser in the Sealed Council—until one day, when he murdered the queen and vanished. Yeah. I've heard of him. Every Lirien has."

A flicker of something—uncertainty, perhaps—crossed her face. "He was blamed for murdering the queen, but he was innocent."

"Innocent men don't run."

"And yet, he was innocent. He and my mother both loved Lirien and were prepared to live there forever, despite your kingdom's oppressive laws. Even if my father hadn't been falsely accused, my mother gave birth to twins, and my parents had to flee to save them."

Twins.

The word sent an uneasy ripple down my spine.

I wasn't superstitious. I barely believed in any of the old gods, let alone Solric—the so-called "most important" surviving god after the others had fallen a millennium ago. *Supposedly.* Yet there had to be *something* out there, considering the presence of magic in our world.

But I'd never met twins before. She may as well have said her siblings were unicorns.

The news that Brogan Ragnall had sired twins chilled me. "You do realize that twins are killed for the safety of everyone in Lirien? The prophesies—" I stopped short. Now I sounded like my father.

Wait. Was Tara one of the twins?

And if so, which one was she?

Her eyes flashed with irritation. "Neither my sister nor my brother is evil. They're not going to resurrect one of the dead gods. Infanticide isn't a way to stop ridiculous myths."

"Maybe not the best, but certainly the easiest."

"Callousness is what the Lirien do best, isn't it? Bind innocents out of fear?" She paced, restless in her anger. "I'm starting to prefer the idea of eternal damnation to being tied to you."

"You took the words right out of my mouth."

Fucking Brogan Ragnall.

My skin burned with fury. He wasn't at the camp right now, but when he arrived—then what? Was I supposed to sit at a table with him? Share meals?

"This isn't going to work." Seren stopped pacing. "Like it or not, we're stuck together for now. What will it take for us to call a truce until we find a solution?"

I towered over her. "Nothing. I'm done doing you favors. We owe each other nothing now. And that was before I knew you're Brogan Ragnall's daughter—"

"My father is a good man. A decent one who would do anything for his family. He's never gotten involved in Viori politics because the bloodshed between our people disgusts him. My parents' love for Lirien has practically made us outcasts here. Why do you think Seth said what he said at the council?"

"A man who kills his queen does not love his kingdom."

She scowled. "This isn't about him. This is about you and me. I am not my father, so maybe we can start with that, unless you'd like me to measure you by whoever you happen to be related to. For all I know, they might be the worst sort."

She has a point.

I wouldn't want to be judged by Magnus Warrick's shadow. I'd gotten myself Sealed because of my need to be different from him.

"Fine," I breathed, begrudgingly. "We'll leave your father out of it. For now."

A hint of a smirk showed on her lips, like she'd enjoyed winning that battle.

"But I'd have to be insane to trust a woman who bonded herself by blood oath to someone she'd never met."

Her chin jutted up. "Why did you save me? You could have let me die—run while the vuk had me in its grasp."

I shrugged. "What can I say? I have a soft spot for damsels in distress. Even ones who later threaten to carve my eyes out."

Seren's glare could have cut through steel. "I wasn't a damsel. I was armed."

"Yes. Armed and halfway down a vuk's throat." Slow seconds passed, my pulse throbbing. "I suppose it's impossible to believe that strangers help one another in Lirien." I scanned her face, finding it hard to reconcile someone so beautiful with someone so cold-hearted and deadly. "Do you all really kill anyone that comes into the forest? You only help your own? All Liriens are evil to you?"

"Aren't all the Viori evil to you?"

"No."

A divot appeared between her eyebrows. Shame glossed her eyes. "I know that there may be innocents on both sides. Sorting them from the evil isn't worth the cost, though—not when it's my friends and family who pay if someone who hurts us gets through. Hesitation has cost me dearly."

She looked away. "I've never had a real conversation with a Lirien before you. But you're no better than I am. Lirien soldiers don't always wait for good reason to kill—especially not those in the Pendaran Regulation."

"The Viori often give us a good reason before we can get to them. I watched a village burn to the ground in Ibarra six months ago. Children, murdered. All by your people."

Her stony expression flickered. "Well, it's the same for us. Liriens that aren't killed can expose our whole tribe to danger."

We squared off at an impasse.

Several tense beats passed, then she retreated a step.

"How did you kill the vuk?" She rubbed her arms, clearly self-conscious as she changed the subject.

"Despite my looks, you may be surprised to learn I'm not a god." That elicited an outraged laugh from her. "Didn't use dark magic or decapitate the creature, either."

She raised a brow. "Your sword?"

Exactly. I didn't want to draw too much attention to it, give too much away. I shrugged. "It's an old family heirloom."

Seren narrowed her eyes. "Sounds more like a fancy way of saying 'sharp piece of metal.'"

"That's what people with boring swords say."

"Fine. I'll find a way to get it back from Seth." She loosened her sword holster.

The change in subject offered a tenuous peace, and I didn't want to break that by explaining my sword's significance. But neither could I let her risk her life by going after it. "Let him keep it for now. I'll take it back when the waters settle." I peered at her. "I take it you have a personal history with him?"

Her face shuttered. "We were bedmates. Nothing more."

Oh, there's clearly more to it. Noted.

Had she been in love with the bastard?

He clearly hadn't loved her if he was willing to hand out twenty vicious lashes to her back.

Prying into her past wasn't worth the effort. I sat with effort on the rug near the stove and tugged off my unlaced boots. The damned whip had landed on my ass more than once, making sitting a challenge. But Seren's mother truly was a gifted healer. Considering the beating I'd taken, I should be in much worse pain. The walk to the tent had been agonizing, every step torture, and it had taken enormous effort to keep these people from seeing me falter.

But for now, more pressing matters took priority. I'd managed a quick sponge bath and relieved myself after Lucia finished bandaging my wounds, but I was still thirsty and *starving.*

"This is my first marriage," I said with the vaguest hint of humor. "And I'm not sure what the customs are in—what do you call this place? Viori? Or is that just the name of your people?"

"The people are the Viori. The land is the territory. Each tribe has its own encampment."

"I suppose technically you're all Pendarans since you're in the Dreadwood," I mused, stretching. The movement sent pain flaring through my back. From the widening of Seren's eyes, it was clear she felt it, too. *So fucking strange.* "Either way, do you all *eat* here?"

She smirked and went to the small pack she'd brought into the tent. Kneeling on the rug, she unrolled a bundle of cloth, revealing a hunk of cheese, some bread, and grapes. Then she withdrew dried strips of meat and a corked bottle. "I got a few things to eat from my mother. It's not much. Tomorrow it's market day and I'll get our own provisions."

The food was a far cry from the splendid dining in Ederyn —or even the barracks of Pendara. But gnawing hunger forced me to be humble. "Thank you."

Lifting a strip of meat, I asked, "What is this?"

"Venison."

I sampled it. Not bad—chewy and salted—but edible. The bread was soft, the cheese earthy, but perhaps being famished probably made it taste better. She took a swig from the bottle, then held it out to me.

Wine. It reminded me of drinking with soldiers after training in Pendara, except there we drank mead. I sipped it. Passible, but nothing like the Ambran vintages I preferred.

"So, what happens if I try to escape? Let me guess, your people hunt me down, bind me again, and make me endure another delightful wedding night like this one?"

Seren rolled her eyes. "If you try to escape, they'll kill you on sight. No iron chains, no second chances."

I raised his hands in mock surrender. "Ah, death. The Viori answer to everything. That and impossible trials where, I'm certain, they barely give you a sporting chance before you're murdered in front of a crowd?"

She ignored my barb and popped a grape into her mouth. "The Skorn is meant to be just." With a rueful look, she added, "But you're right ... most people aren't equipped to last in the arena. If we do survive, though, you'll be free to come and go from the territory, which will make it easier for you to find a way to leave for good."

Her brow furrowed in thought. "We'll need a strategy for the Skorn—we'll need to play to our strengths. You're Sealed, so you should be fine with fighting, but they don't always make it a fair fight. In the meantime, if Seth or anyone else suspects you're not really on our side, they won't hesitate to throw you to the wolves—or worse." She paused, glancing at me. "You can't act defiantly like you did today. You'll need to show restraint—act as if you want to belong here. If you can do that long enough, we might have a chance to break the bond quietly and then you're on your own."

I doubted it was that simple. "Unless, of course, we can't break the bond. In which case, I'm not letting you leave my side."

She froze, a grape poised between her fingers. "And why's that?"

"I've spent the last few years training to be the best. The fastest. The strongest. But I'm only as good as my weakest link. And right now, you, Seren, are my weakest link."

Truthfully, I was less worried about surviving her people's fucking test than I was about *her* not surviving it—which would mean my death too, thanks to this bond. This was a nightmare. My eyes narrowed. "And I find it hard to believe you'll *let* me go. I'm dangerous, aren't I? Your logic is flawed."

She rose, a flush creeping down her neck, then flicked a gaze at the food. "Finish whatever you'd like then put it away. There's a clean pair of trousers in my pack for you, since yours are bloodstained. I'm going to bed."

Moving to the bedroll, she removed her boots, then lay on one of the pillows and turned toward the tent panel, not bothering to get under the sheets. She probably had a weapon close at hand.

I wasn't about to eat all the food, so I corked the bottle and wrapped up the rest. She looked so small as I approached her,

her body rigid with tension. Maybe she believed I'd sleep beside her—or try to force myself on her. From the goldenrod her mother had left, I assumed this was supposed to be our wedding night.

Goldenrod. Symbol of good fortune. *How ironic.* Seren had practically tossed them to the side when she'd climbed onto the bed.

"How old are you?" I asked as I sat on the bedroll.

She stiffened. "Twenty-three."

For someone so young, she carried herself with the weight of too much lived experience. And a sadness I didn't understand.

That shouldn't bother me, but it did.

She cleared her throat. "What about you?"

"Twenty-eight." I lifted the second pillow. "I'll sleep on the rug. You have nothing to fear from me. I'm not going to touch you. I promise." Spending the night on the rug wouldn't be comfortable, and I'd be cold, but it was close to the stove. Survival was all that mattered.

She watched me skeptically. "You're such a contradiction. You vacillate between acting with honor and defending Lirien savagery. Which is it? Tell me something true about you."

"If making the woman who saved my life feel safe is a surprising show of honor, I have serious reservations about the way the Viori conduct their affairs."

A dimple flashed in her cheek.

That smile was her best feature—not that the others weren't equally distracting—but I got the feeling that she didn't smile often.

"Something true?"

She nodded.

Strangely, I wanted to see that smile again. "I'm fairly good at juggling."

She rolled her eyes. "Something you'd tell your wife."

"Ah, you want to know about the size of my—"

"No." A blush crept on her face.

Now it was my turn to laugh. I hadn't expected her to be shy. My years in Pendara had desensitized me to sex—not only because soldiers spoke openly about it, but because the lack of privacy in the barracks made modesty impossible.

But I doubted she'd want to know about that. However ... "I'd tell my wife *that*. Show her, too. I believe in good impressions. Though you've already seen me naked, so you know for yourself."

Wariness crossed her features. "This isn't a joke."

"Of course it's not," I said, straightening. "It's my life now. Bound to a woman who hates me, surrounded by people who want me dead, and sleeping on a rug. Truly, I've never been luckier."

A smirk crossed my lips and I set the pillow on the rug. A damned blanket would be helpful, but there didn't appear to be another one. Sinking onto the rug, I sighed, aware of her expectant gaze.

She wanted a reason to trust me tonight.

Maybe even needed it.

As though allowing myself to be beaten wasn't good enough.

"I'd tell her how my father disowned me for protecting a helpless Ibarran woman that a man had imprisoned in a cage. About how she died in my arms when the man came after me. And how I killed him."

She didn't blink, her expression unreadable.

Why was am I telling her this?

It was a moment my father had wanted me to feel ashamed of. Yet I couldn't.

Maybe in that way, Seren and I were alike.

She'd bravely fought to keep me alive. Been belittled and punished for it, too. All because of a sense of duty and honor that went far deeper than anyone around her believed necessary.

"I will never hurt an innocent woman, Seren. I never have. Even a Viori. Good night."

CHAPTER 11
SEREN

I needed a damned *strategy*.

The night had been long, sleepless, punctured by the sounds of Rykr shifting on the rug, his stomach growling occasionally. He was probably ravenous, but that was his own fault—I'd given him food. If he chose to turn his nose up at it, his hunger was his responsibility.

Despite my lack of sleep, I rose with renewed energy and purpose. Maybe I couldn't break the bond while in my encampment, but I only had days to learn as much as I could about the Skorn trial before Seth dragged us to Emberstone. Our repository had books on *that*, some that even elders of our tribe had written.

Unfortunately, today was a market day and my time would be limited.

Every Lysday, each Viori tribe set up a market in the middle of their encampment, selling and bartering goods. Most stocked up on food for the coming week on market day, as I would need to do.

My family also maintained a market stall. Tara and I

prepared pelts and dried venison, while Mother made potions and jars of healing honey infused with Ibarran magic.

Madoc normally sold handcrafted wooden tools and trinkets, and it was incredibly difficult not having him here. He *should* be home. He *should* have found Esme. *Gods, is he okay?*

Has he found where they've taken Esme?

Esme had been gone for over a month now. The longer time passed without her return, the more I worried they'd come up against some obstacle—or, worse, had been captured themselves. If that was the case, how would we even learn what had happened to them?

I'd been tempted more than once to ask Amahle to use her spirit gliding to try to see where they were. She probably would, but the farther away a person was, the more Amahle's gift taxed her.

She'd tried to find Esme the day she was taken, and her heart had nearly stopped. I couldn't risk that again.

Rykr stirred as I strapped on a bandolier for my daggers. Mother had given me an extra set of clothes for him the night before, but he'd need a chance to bathe soon. *I should probably tend to his wounds, too.* Like him or not, he was my responsibility.

"How's your back feeling?" I squatted beside him.

"I'm fine." The timbre of his voice was deep from sleeping.

A rugged, self-assured swagger marked the way Rykr carried himself, and that was unbelievably appealing—in addition to his attractiveness. Ignoring the tug of interest coiling through me, I touched the hem of his shirt. "May I?"

"Go ahead."

"Actually, it might be easier if you just take the whole shirt off."

Rykr said nothing as he complied. I'd seen plenty of men

shirtless before, but with Rykr, I fought the urge to avert my gaze. *Fight temptation.*

Other men didn't make me want to reach out and touch hardened chest muscles, run my fingertips over the flat, ridged plane above their waistbands. I dragged my gaze away, my mouth going dry.

It's just the bond. Isn't it? His razor-sharp wit the night before had made him utterly likable, even as I reminded myself it could all be a ploy to charm and manipulate me.

Shifting so I could see his back better, I peeled back a bandage.

The skin underneath, though slightly pink, had completely healed. Even the redness had faded. Only the barest whispers of scars remained.

I'd seen my mother's salves work quickly, but this was different. His wounds had been severe. This kind of healing wasn't natural.

Then again, he had been able to *walk* away from the flogging, and I'd never seen anyone do that either. And even though I didn't share any marks from the whip, I'd felt the full depth of his excruciating pain until my mother had dulled the connection.

"How in Nyxva did you heal so fast?" Despite my unease, I touched the scar, his skin warm and soft below my fingertips. He didn't flinch.

He attempted to look over his own shoulder, to no avail. "What?" Reaching his hand behind his back, he tugged a bandage away and felt along his skin. His eyes widened. "What did your mother put on me?"

I removed the other bandages, revealing his fully healed back.

What in the world?

I tried to stay calm. This couldn't just be my mother's

medicine. Come to think of it, his wounds from the vuk had healed quickly, too. I'd been proud of my work ... but what if it hadn't been me?

Who was he?

I stood abruptly. "You self-heal, don't you?"

Rykr yanked his shirt back over his head. "No. That's not even possible, is it?"

"Clearly it is." It had to be a rare ability. But Rykr must have known about it before this, mustn't he?

"You sure it's not another one of your 'gifts' from this oath?" He combed his fingers through his dark hair, where the short strands had matted while asleep.

"If I had self-healing, I'd be showing off by now. But you've clearly got something special. So, tell me, how long have you known?"

Rykr sat straight, pulling his shirt down with deliberate calm. "Hate to break it to you, *solwyn*, but you and your mother are the ones with spellcraft. Ask me how I managed to capture a Viori outpost alone and *that* I might have an answer for."

Solwyn. I refused to react to his sarcastic taunt by calling me a term of endearment aimed to belittle me. "Self-healing doesn't have to do with spellcraft. It's inherent to the fabric of a person's essence—like this." A quick flick of my fingers and frost spread over the chair beside the stove. A faint chill prickled the air around us as a fine sheen of ice crackled over the wood, sparkling in the morning light.

Rykr jerked his chin, a wary look crossing his handsome face. "Ice powers?"

I'd always thought of my gift as more nuisance than strength, but the wary way Rykr watched the ice made me feel ... powerful. Just for a moment. Then the self-consciousness returned, creeping in like cold seeping through my boots.

"Remind me to never make you angry in bed."

Tarseholster.

Before I could call him the vulgar word, he quirked a brow. "Are ice powers common around these parts of the forest?"

"Most Unbound have some natural gift like this. Mine is mostly useless—how often do you need ice in the middle of the forest?" I stood, my mouth dry. As I continued to stare down at him, a knot formed in my gut. "But you're right. You wouldn't have self-healing as a natural gift. You're Bloodbound."

He spread his hands out, a smirk crossing his lips that read *told you.*

Barely minutes after waking and we were already on the wrong foot. "Get ready. It's market day and we can get breakfast there. I'll explain on the way."

Rykr scowled and put his boots on. "Unless you mean put my own irons on, I'm ready."

Despite his moodiness, my lips twitched.

He was probably as tired as I was of squabbling. I readied his irons as he used the chamber pot in the corner, doing my best to ignore the forced familiarity of our situation. When he'd finished, he approached. "Where should I empty that?"

"There's a privy with a pit my family uses outside. I'll show you."

"What happens if I don't wear the irons?" he asked after I'd replaced them. He shuffled beside me as we left the tent.

"Seth might transfer you to the dungeon, which is the only permanent structure around here. Impossible to escape."

Rykr's gaze swept over the distant tents. "Why not build houses instead of living in tents?"

"We used to move every year, but as our waldren grew older, we stayed longer in one place. Now it's been several years. He died, but in theory, we try to be prepared to pack and leave the territory at a moment's notice."

"But why?" Rykr almost tripped, then glowered. He was tall and clearly unaccustomed to shortening his stride like this.

"For protection. The elders believed it was safer so Liriens never knew exactly where we were. We also have to negotiate with some forest creatures to allow us to stay sometimes, too. In those cases, we pay for the use of the territory and it's a short-term agreement."

Rykr stopped short. "Creatures?"

I turned to him, quirking a brow. "Why? You're not afraid of the creatures of the Dreadwood, are you?"

"The first one I encountered attacked, so I think that's justified."

"The vuk's attack was unusual. I've never seen one do that." I still hadn't decided whether it attacked because it saw Rykr on top of me first. Would it have left us alone if we'd been by ourselves? "But I meant bigger creatures. Like centaurs. We spent one summer in a dragon's nesting grounds, but I barely remember it. I think I was seven."

"And you regularly interact with these creatures?"

"Rarely. But dragons are hard to miss."

His expression remained skeptical.

But he also probably wouldn't have believed in vuks before, either.

"None of those creatures exist in Lirien?" I continued toward the clearing where the market was held. Much as I hated to admit it, I didn't mind his company. With my friends and Tara and Madoc moving up in rank in the Vangar, conversation was welcome. Our shifts often kept us apart.

"The treaty Seth mentioned yesterday—King Anders's—set aside the Dreadwood for the Lirien's magic creatures. But that was over three hundred years ago. Most of what we know about the forest now is just legend."

"How did you read the treaty?" I plucked a tall blade of

grass as we drew closer to the market stalls. "I thought all those documents were locked in the vaults of Ederyn."

"They are. But I've spent some time in Ederyn." He paused, then added, "For my Sealing."

Ederyn. My parents had recounted so many stories of their life there that I felt connected to it. The realization struck me. Of course the Sealing took place there. Even though I knew more about the Sealing than most Viori, I'd never considered that's where it happened.

"You've seen the Golden City of Suomelin?"

"I have. And walked in the Hall of Kings. The Sealing is usually done in the throne room."

The throne room. The idea of him standing there, where my father had undergone the same ceremony ...

My breath hitched. The thought of my father—of his history with Lirien, of the king who'd put a bounty on his head —settled like a stone in my chest. And now that threat was all too real. For all I knew, the spy who'd captured Esme had dragged Father back to Suomelin now, too.

Instead, I said, "My mother tells me the repositories in Suomelin are so filled with books you can barely see the ceilings."

"That's a slight exaggeration, but yes, the repositories are vast. But I take it you can't go there?"

"None of the Viori are allowed to leave. If we do, we're treated as Liriens if we return. But my family isn't welcome in Lirien anyway. If any of us—" I'd said too much.

Rykr has no intention of staying here.

Not that it mattered now. What my father had always feared had happened. Someone had found him. Tried to manipulate him.

We reached the stall where my mother and Tara were already setting out wares.

Mother's sharp gaze swept over me before flicking to Rykr, her worry barely concealed. *Why do I feel like she's not telling me everything about the oath?*

Or maybe she just hates that I bound myself to a Lirien.

"You're walking upright," Mother said to Rykr, astonishment in her voice.

"Apparently, your salves work better than most. Thank you. The pain is manageable." He offered a polite smile.

"Well, that's lucky for you. How is the happy couple this morning?" Tara teased. "Thanks to you two, I spent most of the night washing our cart—it still smells like death. I can't get the stench out of my hands."

Rykr stiffened beside me. "Thank you for your help yesterday, Tara. And for getting my sword."

"I'm sorry Seth took it before I could return it to you." Tara made a face. "Just so you know, I saw him wearing it today. I'd suggest both of you try to look the other way."

Seth didn't just want Rykr gone, he wanted him humiliated first. He wanted *us* humiliated. Every move he made felt like a calculated insult, daring us to strike back.

The muscles in Rykr's arms went taut. "He's parading around with it? What an—"

"Watch your tongue," Mother clucked softly, nodding toward people near us, setting up their stalls. "We have enough trouble without you stirring up more."

I could practically see the retort forming on the tip of Rykr's tongue. Then he caught my eye and something in his expression softened. "What can I do to help you here?"

Tara nodded toward a crate of jarred honey. "Set those out on that table." She gestured to where she'd started to set out pelts. "The market opens soon."

As Rykr moved over there, irons clinking, my sister's eyes lingered on him.

"I'll help you," Mother said, her voice flat. She probably didn't trust him to do it right.

When Rykr was out of earshot, Tara leaned in. "He doesn't look like a flogged and wounded man ... or a satiated one," she hissed.

"For gods' sake, Tara."

She raised a brow. "People will talk. Besides, I thought you wanted to convince everyone he's your lover?"

"He has healing powers. And he's leaving as soon as we can break the bond, so that's not happening. We don't have a genuine marriage." Seeing her skepticism, I faltered. Tara hated Liriens. Why was she pushing this? "He's a fucking Lirien, Tara."

"I don't care if he's a shapeshifter. If you don't consummate that marriage, it's not valid—even with your oath. You're giving Seth another chance to attack you both. Just get it over with for your own protection. Who knows, you might enjoy it."

"I'm not that desperate, thanks." Not to mention that Mother warned me that sex would only deepen the bond.

Tara's tone was light, but her eyes weren't. I knew that look. Beneath her bravado, she was worried. *Scared.* She hated Liriens, but she hated the thought of losing someone else she loved more.

She has a right to be afraid. Tara rarely talked about her feelings, but Madoc being gone had to be weighing on her. And she was furious about Esme.

"This marriage is keeping him alive. And Mother said if he dies, you'll die too, Seren—and that there will be visible signs you've consummated the thing. That blood oath was reckless. Binding souls is a lot more serious than taking vows. Trust me, if it was only his life on the line, I wouldn't care. But I can't lose another sibling. Not over something as trivial as meaningless sex. And yes, he's a Lirien, but he's also protected you. Twice. A hot and clearly virile man who can't hurt you without hurting himself—and who seems honorable—what's the big deal?"

Visible signs? I didn't show my worry and gave her a hard look. "Even *if* I agreed to it, I'm not the only one involved."

Tara rolled her eyes. "He's a man ... I'm sure he won't object. Give him some wine if it helps. For that matter, drink some yourself. You look like you could use a good roll in the hay."

"It's not that simple," I said. And it wasn't. Not for me.

I hadn't had sex since Seth—a fact I wasn't going to admit to Tara. Even though the opportunity had been there, something had always stopped me. The idea of it made me feel sick to my stomach, a lingering shame that made me shudder when I remembered that last night with Seth. Of being in his arms, whispering my love to him.

What a stupid fool I was.

The distant sound of bells stopped our conversation short. The market was beginning.

I stepped out from the stall, shading my eyes from the glare. We only used this open field for the market, and I was used to the shade of the forest. Once, I'd found the openness refreshing. But after the last month, I felt exposed.

This was one of the prettier encampments our tribe had settled. Beyond the field, the snow-capped mountains hazed in the distance. Streams flourished here, and we never lacked fresh water. We'd even found a hot spring where I occasionally went for a private bath, even in the winter.

A part of me wondered if we hadn't left this place because people were tired of moving. Maybe they wanted to stay settled somewhere beautiful, like this.

The bells from the main square continued to chime. Then came a strange hubbub—people running, cheering, beating drums, and chanting.

Tara and I exchanged a look.

What in Nyxva?

People near our stall had noticed, too. Everyone peered toward the tree line, where a group approached from the forest, hauling a cart. The celebrating throng surrounded them.

A group of Vangar warriors.

Rykr approached me. "Is everyone normally so rowdy this early?"

"No, something's happened."

He frowned. "What do you mean?"

"I-I don't know." The cart rolled out of the woods, revealing a gruesome sight: a dead man, stripped naked and disemboweled, lashed to an X-shaped cross. His head lolled with each jolt of the cart.

Rykr's eyes narrowed, his expression unreadable. Then his body went rigid.

As the Vangar warrior drew closer, Seth emerged from behind them, moving to the forefront. He settled the boisterous group, then shouted, "King Magnus and his sons are dead—the direct royal Lirien bloodline has been *destroyed*."

A deafening whoop rose through the people, shrieks of happiness and drumbeats so loud they rattled through me.

But then something else tore at me.

Pain. *Deep, searing pain.*

I gasped, clutching my chest as though invisible fingers had wrapped around my ribs and squeezed. My balance wavered, and I grasped Rykr's arm, steadying myself against the onslaught of emotions. *What is happening?*

I should have felt joy. This was a victory. And yet, all I could feel was despair.

I turned toward Rykr, my heart pounding as though it might burst.

Rykr's fists clenched at his sides. His face betrayed nothing, but his eyes burned with fury, and the bond between us surged with his seething anger. A flicker of grief pulsed then, so fleeing I almost missed it.

Oh gods. Rykr.

He wanted more than to draw blood. He wanted revenge.

I wanted to believe it was just the bond making me feel his rage. But part of me knew better. His fury wasn't just his, it was ours, shared through the connection tying us together. The bond made it harder to tell where his anger ended and mine began. My body trembled, my hands gripped my sides as I tried to hold on to myself—to something that was just me.

Seth held up his hands again, waiting as the Viori settled. "The king and his sons were all murdered on the same day, at the same hour. Vangar mounted their heads on pikes outside the Golden City for all to witness—all except one, whom our Vangar caught in Pendara. I present to you, *Prince Calix Warrick.*" He gestured to the man in the cart. "Tonight, we celebrate!"

The raucous clamor was even louder than before.

But inside me—inside my soul—agony splintered. *Was this coming from Rykr? Why? What is this feeling?*

My mouth went dry as I stared at the dead prince. His lifeless eyes, his face frozen with shock and pain—as though his death had been torment.

Then I lost the contents of my stomach in the grass.

CHAPTER 12

RYKR

"Come with me. Both of you. Now." Tara grabbed Seren's elbow, dragging her away from the stall.

For someone who claimed to hate Lirien, Seren looked just as shaken as I was.

Worse, actually. She'd thrown up.

But I wanted to kill every person in sight.

Lucia rushed behind us.

I didn't register her words. My mind bubbled with raw, searing thoughts, my heart pounding.

Dead.

My father. *Dead.*

My brothers. *Gone.*

The men who had raised me, who had shaped my world—murdered.

How? And why? *Gods, why?*

The litany repeated, over and over, never inching closer to becoming a reality I could accept.

And—Dalric. Stripped and brutalized, his corpse trussed

up like a trophy. My friend, whose only crime had been his loyalty.

I should be rotting in his place.

The attackers thought they'd killed me.

Fear gripped me.

Seth had only mentioned my brothers and father. *What happened to Malin?* My sister's horror must be unimaginable. My brother's wives and their children—had they been threatened? None of my nephews were of age, but they were still in line for the throne.

I needed to leave immediately and go back to Ederyn, but I was trapped in the Dreadwood with the family of the man who'd killed my mother.

Tara stopped behind the stall, her face dark. "Clean yourself up, Seren." She handed her sister a handkerchief. "And you"—she turned to me—"no one will believe you want to be Viori if you don't wipe that look of hatred off your face."

"For gods' sake, Tara, show some sympathy," Seren snapped, her tear-streaked face hardening. "How would you feel if the Viori leadership was suddenly gone? If Father or Madoc were displayed like his prince?"

Why is she crying?

She hated Lirien. And my family.

Tara gave her a look of horrified shock. "Do you even hear what you're saying?" She pointed back toward the crowd. "That prince out there? You know what his nickname was? 'The Scourge of the Viori.' Know why? Because he torched an entire Viori encampment three years ago after hunting down a group of Viori boys who were playing near the border."

I stiffened, my blood burning with fury. "As I recall, it wasn't quite as innocent as you're claiming. Those boys, as you call them, kidnapped a young Doban child and tortured him for their own amusement."

"So, the response is to start a fire that ruined dozens of lives? That's not justice." Tara narrowed her eyes. "And it has no bearing on you right now anyway. You already have a target on your back. Every ounce of your efforts should be spent showing everyone you hate Lirien, too. That you want to be one of us."

"I don't want to join the fucking Viori," I snapped. "If I could, I'd kill every last one of you barbarians."

Barely able to breathe, I stalked past them into the tall grass until my knees buckled, and I stumbled onto my shins. The irons rattled as I covered my face.

I couldn't think about Malin. That was too close to torment.

How can they all be dead?

How was it possible I'd never hear their voices ever again?

Erik, Gunnar, Bjorn, Evander, Torsten, Hector.

All. Gone.

I'd been cut off from them during my two-year exile.

And now ...

Gods.

And then there was the other grim realization. *I was the true heir.*

I had no desire for a throne. I didn't want to be king. I'd spent a lifetime watching power corrode, politics rot people from the inside out—no one remained unscathed. Even my brothers compromised their ideals in favor of weak stances that "kept the peace."

How could I even be king? Without my father to remove my Seal, was I bound to it forever? What was the law? Or was I free to bend it to my will now, as my father had?

Not that any of it mattered.

Because I don't want to be king.

I was the youngest. Not like Erik, who'd spent his whole

life preparing for the role. By the time I'd been born, no one had given more than a passing thought to the possibility of me being heir.

An icy wind cut through the trees, wrapping me in its desolate, cruel grip. My eyes stung, my jaw clenched so hard that my teeth ached.

Or I could just let them think they'd killed me. Disappear forever. No one would ever know.

No one has to know the truth.

Whatever twist of fate had brought me here, to these savages, to a woman who'd bound herself to me in sacred blood magic to me—the tempting voice in my head threaded doubt and confusion into my resolve.

No. I can't.

If the Viori had murdered my brothers, it had taken precise, strategic planning. They must have had help, too, from within Lirien. Traitors who might kill me the second I returned to Ederyn. Traitors who were likely threatening everything I'd come from. These savages had murdered my family and Dalric.

Like it or not, I had to return. I couldn't abandon Ederyn to chaos—especially not if Malin or any of my other family had survived. They needed a king. And whether I wanted it or not, I was the only one left.

But what was I supposed to do?

A dagger landed in the grass beside me, burying itself into the soft earth.

Tara approached, her expression wary. "Right. So, you're suitably distracted. You didn't even hear it coming toward you." She paused and sat beside me.

Maybe she is the evil twin.

Seren's older sister shared her features, but stood taller, was more muscular. Where Seren's beauty was delicate, inherited from her mother, Tara carried herself differently—sharp, direct, as if she took after someone else entirely.

"Respectfully, Tara, you can fuck off. Unless you can get me back to Lirien, I don't need your advice." I had bigger concerns than anything Tara was worried about.

She grinned. "If you think I'm here to be your friend, then you've got me confused with my sister." She pulled the dagger out of the ground and handed it to me. "The *only* thing I care about is my sister, understood? As it so happens, thanks to that oath she took—which you seem grateful for, by the way—that means keeping you alive. Now get up and start acting like her husband who wants to join our people, instead of sulking over royals who never knew you existed."

I hadn't expected sympathy, but her bluntness was almost refreshing.

She didn't know and couldn't care less that I'd just been served the most devastating news of my life. I wanted to burn the world down and she wanted me to lick my wounds and go play the ridiculous game keeping me alive.

Yet ... what choice do I have?

Without a plan—hell, without someone to trust—I was as good as dead. If anyone learned who I really was, and if I didn't break the bond with Seren, she'd be a constant threat to my life.

For now, I was stuck here.

I scowled, then tucked the dagger into the side of my boot. "Fine. But don't expect me to celebrate." Somehow, I'd retrieve Dalric's body. My friend deserved a proper burial.

"That's fair." She gestured toward the dagger. "I'll get you a sheath later today. Seren didn't arm you?"

I shook my head.

"I'll handle it. She's had a lot on her mind ... Or didn't trust you enough. I'll ask her." She stood, glowering at me. "Oh, and one more thing—"

"What's that?"

"Word travels fast. People are already whispering about whether that bond's real. Seth will use any excuse to call it fake. If he finds out you two haven't consummated the marriage, he'll twist it against you. Either fix it or make sure no one finds out. Personally, I'd pick the first. My mother seems to think there will be signs that ... erm, *your bond* ... is deepening. Others in the tribe familiar with Ibarran magic might expect that, too. And Seth is watching."

Really?

Never once had a protective sister encouraged me to *bed* their sibling. I'd experienced the opposite more than once—Dalric had forbidden me from even *talking* to his sister. The thought of consummating this marriage made me feel like a stud horse.

But if Seth turned the tribe against us, we wouldn't last a day. Not unless I found a way to gain their trust—or at least keep them from stabbing me in my sleep.

"I'll keep that in mind," I lied.

"Good. Since you look better, tomorrow we start training for the Skorn. I gave you the day off today because you were impaired, but you and Seren can join my squadron tomorrow for drills."

I raised my brows. Did she really think she could teach me something? Or did she know Seren was the weakest link but wouldn't disparage her sister? "I look forward to it."

I dragged myself up as she walked back to the stall. Seren and her mother had already returned. Beyond them, the Viori continued celebrating, jeering at the oxcart carrying the body of my friend.

My head pounded, a thousand thoughts assailing me at once.

I needed to block the images swimming in my mind of my family, Malin, my home. Of Dalric. *Does Thorne know?*

This was going to be the longest day of my life.

At least my secrets were buried deep. For now, that would keep me safe.

I gritted my teeth and Seren pivoted her head toward me, then looked away.

"Don't look at him."

Her voice?

No. That was impossible. Just grief playing tricks on my mind. But her reaction ... it had mirrored mine too closely, as if she felt it with me. Not physically, but emotionally. The thought gnawed at me, refusing to let go.

I furrowed my brow.

The bond had me questioning the limits of what was possible. She'd felt my pain yesterday. Now this?

A strange instinct simmered inside me. Her visceral reaction told me we were sharing more than I'd expected. More than I wanted.

The godsdamned bond *was* growing stronger, but how?

No. She was a Ragnall, and I would never trust a Ragnall.

What if she could hear my thoughts, too?

Oh fuck.

If she learned who I really was ... I wouldn't just be trapped. I'd be dead.

Whether or not this bond was broken, I knew one thing— come nightfall, I was leaving.

CHAPTER 13
SEREN

The market had been unusually busy, as though everyone was eager to spend their money ahead of tonight's celebration. But the flurry of activity worked to my advantage—as it wound down, I slipped through the crowd, heading for the repository.

Tara had advised me not to take Rykr. *"You risk emasculating him if you drag him around like a pet."* She was right, and I needed distance. Maybe space would dull the effects of the bond.

Still, as I hurried through the forest toward the center of the encampment, a shadow clung to me, a deep gloom I couldn't shake. I knew its source—Rykr had worn a haunted look. But while sharing his physical pain had been shocking, this was different.

Like an invasion of a private space where I don't belong.

His emotions, so strong that they clouded my own, blurred the lines between us. Rykr had a right to his sadness—he was Lirien—but their intensity gave me an insight into the heart of our enemies, too. What my friends saw as victory, the Liriens would mourn. *Seek revenge.* And there wasn't just sadness in Rykr's heart, but fear, too. Worry. Guilt. Maybe he believed he'd failed to protect his king.

The center of the encampment was unusually quiet as I approached it. This was where the Viori tradesmen had built permanent wooden stalls. Butchers, tailors, bakers, tanners, and others kept actual structures here, unlike the flimsy market stalls dismantled each week. Usually, this area bustled with noise and activity, but today, everyone appeared to be at the market. *Or celebrating the dead prince.*

THE STENCH HIT FIRST—A pungent mix of dung, urine, and animal hides from the tanner's stall. I wrinkled my nose, wishing for the millionth time that they'd built the repository anywhere else. But with so few literate people in our tribe, I was in the minority when it came to frequenting it.

Pushing the tent panel aside, I stepped into the warm, incense-scented space. At least the tent panels masked most of the smell. What lingered, Soroush chased away by burning sandalwood, the rich spice mingling with the old, earthy scent of worn tomes and parchment.

Many tribesmen donated their books to the repository, expanding the shared knowledge available to us all. My mother was one of the few who refused, a choice that had earned Soroush's repeated scoldings.

I heeled to a stop. Darya stood at Soroush's desk, a tall stack of books balanced in her arms.

Both cast their glances at me. I flicked my attention to the nearest shelf, running my fingers over the cool spines. The repository was one of the largest tents in the encampment, with alcoves for study and reading, but despite its size, there was no easy way to avoid her.

I focused on a section about medicinal plants, pretending to search for something. Avoiding Darya had become a habit. She'd arrived three years ago from another tribe, the daughter of a high-ranking Vangar general in Emberstone. She'd been sent to assess our Vangar unit.

I'd liked her, as she'd been reserved but kind. Friendly.

But after she married Seth, I hadn't known how to approach her. She hadn't set out to come between us, yet my heartbreak cast her in an entirely different light. She'd married the man I'd loved, and her position gained her the respect and affection of my tribe.

My senses tracked her as I perused the bookshelf in front of me. Her silky black hair was coiled in a tight roll atop her head, her creamy white skin a stark contrast to her dark clothing. Beautiful, commanding, smart. As my superior officer and Seth's wife, she'd had the ability to make my life miserable in the Vangar if she wanted—but she never had.

Maybe I should have accepted her offer of friendship yesterday, but with Seth's vile behavior, the idea was impossible to stomach. I didn't relax until she moved away from Soroush. Darya paused at the exit, turning just enough to direct her words at me. "Good news today, isn't it?" Genuine excitement lit her eyes.

My unease rose. "The best news for us all." Was she testing me? She seemed sincere enough.

"Your husband seemed unusually recovered today—your mother outdid herself healing him. Will you both be at the celebration tonight?" She dipped her chin, then came closer to me. "This is a good opportunity for you both to cement your loyalty. Seth will be watching."

"I plan on it." The smile I mustered felt brittle.

She paused, as though wanting to say more, but Soroush's watchful gaze seemed to stop her. She bit her lip then said,

"Hope you find what you're looking for. See you at the celebration."

As she left, I cringed. Of course Seth would use the celebration to test Rykr's enthusiasm for his king's death.

A problem for later. Even if Rykr was willing to play along—and he'd made it clear he wasn't—I couldn't bring myself to force him into that charade. Not after I'd felt his grief.

I waited a few minutes to ensure Darya wasn't coming back, then headed toward Soroush's desk. The old man had always been warm toward me, appreciative of my interest in books. But as he peered over his spectacles now, his usual friendliness had cooled, edged with caution.

Sniffing, he set the glasses aside. "I suppose I should have expected you here, now that you're free to roam."

"Don't worry, Soroush, I won't taint you by association." I crossed my arms over the soft leather of my vest.

How quickly things had changed.

Once, Soroush had suggested I appeal to Emberstone to be released from my Vangar duties and train as his apprentice instead—to become a scriptrix, a master of texts. The only way to escape Vangar service was to present a formal letter to Emberstone from a tradesman requesting an apprenticeship.

Exceptions were rare. They passed down mostly from parent to child even if the child hadn't shown an aptitude for the craft.

Soroush would have written that letter for me, though. I had the memory, the aptitude, but I hadn't wanted it. I'd wanted to be a Vangar warrior.

If only he'd made the same offer to Esme. Acid rose in my throat. Esme would have accepted. She would have been safe, tucked away in this tent, learning from Soroush instead of preparing for a militia she'd dreaded joining.

She never would have been in that damned tree the night the Liriens came for me.

Would they have taken me, instead? *Probably.*

Soroush lowered his gaze, meticulously copying a text onto fresh parchment. He'd spent his life ensuring every text in our repository had at least one other copy. "How can I help you, Seren? I'm quite busy."

Annoyance flared through me. If he was dispensing with politeness, so would I. "I need every text you have on the Skorn."

Soroush's grey lips pressed together, and he continued scribbling. "Unfortunately, Seth requested every text we have —on precisely those subjects. Darya just left with them. Perhaps he'd be willing to share while they're on loan."

Heat crawled up my neck. *Solric's balls.* Seth had anticipated me. Ordered Darya to grab those texts before I could. Maybe that was the worst part of being his enemy now. He knew me too well.

"Do you have anything—"

Soroush stood and wiped his red nose with a wrinkled handkerchief. "Forgive me, Seren, but I must find some medicine for my hip. Sitting for long stretches isn't as easy as it once was."

He shuffled away, his grey robes swaying with each limp.

I palmed my face, grinding my teeth. *Dammit.* Time was against me—I had only a narrow window to find anything useful on the Skorn.

I should've seen this coming. I won't make that mistake again.

"Pssst." A soft, feminine voice caught my attention.

In a dim alcove, Giulia Bernardi and Moira Bryce watched me closely from a table.

Giulia was a few years older but small, like me. Frailer, though. Her black curls framed a pixie-like face, blue eyes stark against her pale skin. Her mother had secured her a schoolmaster's apprenticeship, sparing her from Vangar service. But only the wealthier members of our tribe could afford the tutelage the Bernardi women offered.

I scanned the tent for Soroush. He appeared to have left altogether. Biting the inside of my lower lip, I strode toward Giulia, who waved me into the alcove. "What is it?" My voice was harder than I'd intended it to be, my annoyance displaced.

Giulia cringed. Her yellow, floral dress stood out against my Vangar leathers—impractical, too bright for our world. "I heard you talking to Soroush," Giulia whispered, sliding two books toward me. "Darya didn't take everything. She passed these along to me in case I wanted them for Moira's lesson."

My breath hitched, hope surging through my chest.

The Way of Skorn

Mysteries of Emberstone

I met Giulia's wide-eyed gaze. "Are you ... offering these to me?" And had Darya *meant* for her to?

Ciaran's sister watched me closely, reminding me so much of Esme that my chest hurt. How often had I seen them playing together in our tent? She gave me a tentative smile.

"If you need them," Giulia said. "But please don't tell anyone else you got them from me."

Great. Nothing like being treated like a walking plague.

"Why take that risk then? Did Darya tell you to give these to me?"

Giulia shrugged, lowering her timid gaze before glancing at Moira. "Some of us think what you did was really brave." She offered me a small smile. "And if a Lirien who looked like yours wanted me to marry him, I'd probably say yes, too."

I almost laughed, her words oddly comforting. The idea that Darya may have again gone against Seth was even more encouraging. And I wasn't about to argue—I needed all the help I could get. Slipping the books into my satchel, I nodded. "Thank you, Giulia. You have my word. No one will know you helped me."

I turned to go and then hesitated.

Soroush still hadn't returned, and he wouldn't—not until I left. *Fine. I don't need him.* Guilia was a voracious reader, and I suspected she knew more than she let on.

Leaning closer, I lowered my voice. "Do you know anything that could give my husband and me an edge in Emberstone? Something Soroush wouldn't share?"

Giulia moistened her lips. "Most of what might be helpful to you is *in* Emberstone, written in Old Ibarran. Some say the old gods in the Third Age devised the Skorn trial, but that's all just myth as far as I've read."

Curpiss. Old Ibarran. That was something I didn't know how to read. My mother did, but she'd never taught me.

Moira frowned. "There's an Old Ibarran?"

Giulia wrung her hands. "When the world flooded at the end of the Third Age and the people of the Old World came to Lirien by ship, they were a mix of cultures, languages, and races from a much larger continent. Old Ibarran was one of those languages."

Moira's eyes widened. I took for granted that my mother had educated me at home, teaching me the history of Lirien. Moira and Ciaran were lucky—at least their parents could afford tutors. Most Viori never had that luxury. "Was this before Vornfall?" she asked.

Giulia nodded. "Most of the Old World's history was lost after the battle, entire continents and empires erased. Only scraps of the Old World remain, passed down as myths."

"They're not myths." I crossed my arms. Giulia hailed from an Ambran background—she likely didn't believe in the old gods. "Most of the old gods died in the final battle against the Oskir and dark forces of fae and monsters."

I turned to Moira. "The surviving humans united under one common tongue and faith after Vornfall, with Solric, god of light, as the mightiest of the surviving gods. Ragnor Ederyn founded Lirien's kingdom afterward, and was granted divine right."

Giulia's lips thinned, her eyes frosting with annoyance. "Then why don't the gods have anything to do with us? Why abandon us when we fought for them? Really, Seren. You can pretend to be a scriptrix all you want, but you're Vangar. Don't confuse my pupils."

I drew a slow breath. *Because the gods no longer wanted to intervene directly. Because they gave their gifts to humans and the king then stole them from most people with the Bloodbinding.* Moira *should* be taught this. Every Viori ought to know their history—it was what made our cause just.

But proving my knowledge wouldn't win me an ally.

I pressed my lips together. "I'm not sure," I said, my tone conciliatory. "It doesn't make sense, does it? Maybe you could find out and tell me."

After a moment, Giulia dipped her chin. "I'll see what I can find out."

"Thanks again," I said, then offered her a smile before slipping away. My mouth could get me in more trouble. One of these days I'd fill in the blanks Moira's educator refused to—or better yet, tell Ciaran to do it.

The repository encounter rattled me.

Every moment I waited, giving Seth more time to make his own moves. If I didn't learn how to survive the Skorn, we'd be walking into a slaughter.

And if I swallowed my pride, maybe Darya had more information to share.

I wasn't about to walk into Emberstone blind, and I wasn't leaving my fate to chance. If I wanted to protect Rykr and myself, I needed a way to tip the scales in our favor—including learning if there was a way to break the bond that tied our pain, and our deaths, together.

Dusk bled into the sky as I headed back to my tent.

Rykr sat at the entrance, wrists resting on his knees, irons still locked around them. Red marks ringed the skin surrounding them. Underneath would be worse.

He looked exhausted.

"How'd it go?" Rykr asked as I reached him. I'd told him my plans before I left.

Not wanting to get into the obstacles I'd faced, I shrugged. "Fine. Got a few books. Since you can read, we should go through them tonight."

I led him inside. "We don't have to go to the festivities tonight. I can ask Tara to bring us food."

Rykr lifted those piercing blue-green eyes toward me but when he blinked, it was as if he looked through me. Distant. Lost in thought.

"Rykr?" He didn't seem well. Was it still the vuk's bite—or the news about the king?

"Go without me. I have no appetite and want to be alone."

His words shouldn't bother me, but they did. He didn't see us as allies or me as a friend to console him. Darya's warning echoed in my mind—Seth would be watching. But I wouldn't force him.

"You understand you won't be able to wander without me—"

"Understood. I'm a prisoner until the Skorn. Until then, I'll just enjoy the view of your 'free' people crucifying their enemies." Bitterness laced every syllable.

Damn him.

I tried to remind myself that if the roles were reversed, I'd feel the same. But that didn't make his contempt any easier to hear. Especially when I wasn't sure if he was wrong.

When I didn't answer, he stood and held out his wrists. "Any chance you'll free me to be more comfortable while you're gone?"

I pressed my lips tightly, the weight of the decision heavy on me. But trust wasn't a luxury I could afford—not without proof he wouldn't run.

"I can't," I said at last, keeping my voice steady. "Not yet. But I'll find a way to make things easier for you if you give me time."

"Right." He shuffled toward the bedroll. "Your sister gave this to me." Without warning, a dagger flew, burying itself in the post behind me with a soft *thunk*. My heart kicked hard in my chest. I forced myself not to flinch, meeting his gaze steadily, even as tension coiled tight in my shoulders.

"I figured you'd want it where you could see it. Don't worry. I'm not planning to use it." His words were calm, but the tension between us crackled.

Guilt twisted in my gut. I should let him out of the irons. Every time I saw the raw marks on his wrists, shame tightened its grip. But I didn't just distrust him. I distrusted myself, too— my judgment was clouded where Rykr was concerned.

Before I could second-guess myself again, I left. I couldn't afford to make another mistake, not with so many lives at stake. He didn't deserve to be treated like a prisoner—not when he'd saved my life. But if I didn't find a way forward soon, we'd both pay the price in Emberstone.

CHAPTER 14
RYKR

I waited until Seren had been gone for an hour before slipping out of the tent.

The Viori warriors Seth had assigned to follow me were easy enough to spot—my training in Pendara hadn't been in vain—and for some reason my senses seemed heightened here.

I could smell them. Hear them breathing.

Another effect of the oath? Or was my Seal responding to my new environment?

Two men had been shadowing me since morning. Whether Seren had noticed them didn't matter.

The time had come for me to work for my own interests.

I headed toward a stream despite the bracing cold that came with night.

The forest gleamed under the silvery moonlight, a mix of shadows and pale outlines. In the Regulation, I'd learned to appreciate the night for the cover it provided, but I wasn't foolish enough to think the Viori didn't know how to use it just as well.

Even my eyesight seemed sharper as I removed my boots, settling my feet into the cold, slick, leaf-covered stream bank. Then I nearly laughed at myself.

With the fucking irons on, I couldn't remove my shirt or my trousers.

Dammit, Seren.

I didn't have a lot of options. Eventually, I might find a tool to pick the lock like she had. But for now, I needed a quick means to get a head start—one that couldn't be tracked by hounds or humans. Water was the best option.

Fuck it. Lifting my head, I said loudly, "Sorry, boys, show's canceled. I know you were dying to see if I have tattoos in places the irons didn't touch, but you'll have to use your imaginations." I waded into the barely moving water.

When I snuck a glance toward the Vangar warriors trailing me, I almost chuckled. Message received. They'd moved farther away.

The bitterly cold water sluiced past my legs, moving languidly, and my stomach tensed as I prepared to lower myself into the thigh-high current. Holding my breath, I slipped under the surface slowly, trying to behave like a man enjoying the bracing cold, rather than suffering the insane torture that it was.

A thousand sharp needles stabbed into my skin, as I clenched my fists, forcing out slow, deliberate breaths.

Fuuuuuuck.

This better be godsdamned worth it.

I broke through the surface of the water, my chest heaving, and scooted toward a boulder at the edge of the stream, pressing my back against the smooth, frozen stone as my body attempted to adjust.

A soft crunch of leaves nearby made me go rigid.

A lone black bear stood at a distance, barely visible in the dim light.

But the scent ... *familiar*.

A snort, followed by a soft chuckle, came from the other side of the boulder as the bear stepped closer, then drank from the stream. "Hello, Rykr."

Thorne. The hair on the back of my neck bristled.

Maybe Dalric hadn't been exaggerating about his shapeshifting after all.

"Fucking asshole, it *is* you," I muttered under my breath.

"You're being watched." His voice was rough, almost guttural. How he could speak in bear form, I had no idea—but if anyone could defy the rules of nature, it was Thorne.

"I'm aware. Trying to get out as we speak." I drew in another sharp breath and scanned the perimeter for my captors. "You're a shapeshifter."

"And you're the godsdamned heir to the throne." A throaty, bear-like huff followed.

I leaned my head back against the boulder, my legs numb. Cautiously, I glanced over my shoulder as if just noticing the wild animal. My fingers curled around my dagger carefully. "Don't get any closer. Unless you want them to start rumors about me being some kind of bear whisperer. Were you with" —I struggled to say his name—"Dalric? When they killed him?"

An affirmative grunt came.

"I managed to track his scent after I woke from the whistler poison. Saw them kill him. Then I came looking for you once I realized who they'd really been after."

I closed my eyes, fighting the tightness in my chest. Dalric had been my most faithful friend, one of the only ones who'd ever truly seen me—believed I was worth something. And yet, I'd lied to him for years about who I was. He'd given his life for mine, and all I could do now was bury him like a forgotten secret.

Any other question I had about him was too painful to voice. His death hadn't been swift or painless—that much was clear from the way they'd strung him up. That Thorne had been forced to witness it while I'd done *nothing* only deepened my shame.

At last, I managed. "You know about my family, then?"

Another grunt. "Does it mean you're king?"

"Not until I'm crowned by the High Magister from Ibarra. They say the priest calls upon the power of the Everspire to confer the gods' gifts. But who knows."

"But you are the heir, aren't you?" Thorne's amber eyes gleamed in the moonlight, as though he was alert, ready to strike at any moment.

"I believe so. My nephew, Ivar, is only fourteen. He's Eriks's son and would be the heir, but the lineage passes to the closest male heir over fifteen." Just one year older and Ivar would have had a stronger claim than I did.

Thorne exhaled slowly. "So, if you don't return before he turns fifteen, he'll be crowned king."

I rubbed my tired eyes. The distant drumbeats of the savage Viori—reveling in the death of my family—sickened me. I had too much to explain and I had to be almost inaudible.

Hopefully Thorne had a bear's superior senses. My lips barely moved as I whispered, "They think I'm dead and won't wait for Ivar to come of age. But a boy king leaves Lirien exposed—ripe for rebellion, with every rival claiming the right to rule. If they crown him before I return, the gods' gifts—or whatever power my father wielded—might be lost forever. And without a true king, Lirien will tear itself apart."

Thorne growled in a low rumble. "Well, if there are divine

gifts, won't they pass to Ivar when he's crowned? Will your claim be diminished?"

"I don't know," I admitted through clenched teeth, exasperated by his questions and my own ignorance. "I was supposed to grow old, get drunk, and make terrible decisions, not inherit a throne everyone wants to kill me for. I never asked about the coronation secrets because I was never supposed to need them."

Thorne bowed his head. "I apologize, Your Highness."

"No, don't. We're just Thorne and Rykr. I'd like that to remain the same."

"But—"

"For fuck's sake, if you truly view me as your king, take that as a command." I raked my fingers through my hair. "I'm not irritated with your questions. I just don't have the answers. And thousands of highly skilled Unbound Viori warriors who would love to see me dead sit between me and the borders of Lirien where I can get those answers. If my father hadn't locked away my powers, maybe I could've done something clever—like fly out of here. But no, here I am, freezing my ass off and talking to a bear."

I took a breath. "I believe the moment the High Magister utters the words of consecration, any divine powers are transferred to the heir. My father had a large rune of the Everspire on his chest. I think he received it when he was crowned."

I had to get out of this water, unless I wanted my legs to fall off and join the stream, which would really ruin my chances of walking out of this mess alive.

The Viori watching me kept their distance, convinced by my apparent need for a bath.

"I have to get moving before I'm too frozen to run properly. I thought traveling by water would throw off my scent."

"This is your plan? Freeze yourself then travel wet and cold in a forest you don't know?"

"Do you have a better plan?" I grunted.

"No, but I *can* come up with something better than this. Sometimes I forget how green you are. Doesn't do you any good to be able to kill someone with your thumbs if you don't know how to survive the forest. You started training too late."

"No Sealed Master would accept me until my father Sealed me. I'm sorry for lying to you."

Another low growl. "You're my king—it's forgiven. Don't worry, I won't leave the forest without you."

His loyalty didn't surprise me. Thorne was always too noble for his own good. If I told him to march into Nyxva's Domain armed with a spoon, he'd probably ask if I wanted the wooden or metal kind. "Thank you," I said softly.

"Stay here for now. I'll find you in a few days with a plan for escape. Also, you stink of vuk—wash that off while you're in the water."

I winced, swallowing a chuckle. "There's been a complication I can't explain. In the meantime, I need a few favors."

"Anything."

"Steal Dalric's body. Drag him to the forest and bury him. *Please.*"

Thorne let out another grunt. "And?"

"Find out what you can about the massacre of my family."

"Yes, Your—" He caught himself. "I will."

I slipped away from the boulder without a goodbye, moving quietly, like a man who might want to put some distance between himself and a wild beast—and one who needed to get out of the godsdamned water.

I can't leave tonight, damn the gods.

But at least I had one ally. One I *could* trust.

Thorne might be my only hope to get out of this mess. But hope, in a forest of bloodthirsty enemies, was a fragile thing—and one wrong move could shatter it.

CHAPTER 15
SEREN

The heady flush of wine settled my queasy stomach and quieted the noise in my head, and I leaned back on the blanket, resting against Ciaran as I took in the sparkle of the stars. The air was crisp, filled with the scent of woodsmoke and the promise of frost.

"I used to love feasts so much," I murmured, catching Amahle's watchful glance across from me.

Ciaran set a steadying hand at my waist. "You'll love them again someday. The last month has been a lot for your family."

Yeah, that's putting it mildly. Another day had passed with no word from Madoc or my father—one of the reasons I'd gratefully accepted wine tonight.

"You two are looking awfully cozy," Amahle noted, sipping her wine. "Considering one of you is a newlywed ... to someone else." She arched a brow.

I rolled my eyes and scooted a smidge away from Ciaran, taking another swig from the bottle we'd been sharing. "So now I can't have friends, either?"

"Calm down. You're not offending me. I'm just saying you might want to tone it down."

The redness in Ciaran's face was visible in the yellow glow from the oil lamps set in the center of our blankets. "You don't really consider that Lirien your husband, do you?" He rubbed the back of his neck stiffly.

"He has a name, you know." Then I lowered my voice. "But no, I don't. I didn't know how else to save him, that's all."

Some of the tension in Ciaran's shoulders eased.

I chewed on my lower lip. Rykr had mentioned that Ciaran had feelings for me. If I was honest, I'd noticed it over the years, but always brushed those thoughts away. Ciaran was a good friend, but I'd never seen him as anything more, even if I enjoyed the closeness of our friendship. He filled *most* of the need I had for male companionship—though maybe not the one that made me the crankiest.

"You Pendarans have some interesting beliefs," Amahle said. "Like that whole life debt thing."

I sighed, taking another sip of wine. "It's not just a belief, it's a curse—a real one. A life debt is always paid with a life. That's why I didn't have a choice with Rykr."

At Ciaran and Amahle's questioning gazes, I continued, "It's based on an old legend. A man prayed to the goddess of war, Morrga, to save him when he was about to be killed. She granted his wish by sending a soldier to slay his enemy. But when the soldier asked for the man's most beloved daughter as a reward, the man, furious, killed the soldier. So Morrga cursed humankind, saying, *the debt of a life is always paid with a life*. She struck the man dead and condemned his soul to be damned in Nyxva's deepest pit for eternity."

Amahle squinted. "And what does that mean for you?"

"That means that Pendarans believe that if someone saves your life, you owe them a life debt. I couldn't kill Rykr the way the Viori law dictates because he saved me from the vuk. And letting him die when I could save him could also damn my soul. So, I saved him."

"Or maybe you spent too much time reading myths that made you superstitious." Amahle ran her fingers through her curls. "Though clearly something happened when you made that blood oath."

"Yes, but that was Ibarran spellcraft. They mix magic from all the realms." Ciaran's voice carried bitterness. "I still think you should have let him die. It wasn't your fault he was dying—the vuk did that, not you. Rykr stalks around here with an attitude of superiority that makes me want to stab him myself."

"Is *that* why you want to stab him?" Amahle shot back with a smirk.

I didn't want to go down that path. Sighing, I reached for an apple tart and took a bite. "Whether I should or shouldn't have is irrelevant. I didn't have time to ask for opinions and made the best choice I could. And now I need to find a way to undo it. Otherwise, I'm stuck with this bond to him."

"Well, for what it's worth, I like him. He pissed Seth off and held his own at the council meeting and that's not nothing." Amahle leaned back on her hands. "If it wasn't for the damned Skorn trial, I'd say this is one of the cleverest tricks you've pulled."

"Don't encourage her," Ciaran muttered, staring gloomily into his mead. "Seth has blood in his eyes. If it wasn't for Darya, I think he would have done more to push the Ragnalls out of the tribe."

"I don't trust that bitch." Amahle frowned. "She's the one who stole Seth away from Seren in the first place."

I hid a smile. Amahle's loyalty, as always, was unwavering. "Much as I wanted to blame her for that, I can't. And really, she did me a favor. I don't have a lot of regrets, but Seth is one of them."

"She did you a favor at the council meeting, too," Ciaran said. "My father was talking about it last night. The council wasn't going to interfere with Seth due to the seriousness of the law you broke, Seren. Darya probably knew that, and she still spoke up on your behalf. She may be more of an ally than you think."

"She's Seth's wife. She can get away—" Amahle trailed off as Alessia Bernardi approached our blanket.

"Have any of you seen Giulia? I've been looking for her all evening, but I haven't found her."

I exchanged a glance with Ciaran. I *had* seen Giulia but saying so risked the trust she'd placed in me when she'd lent me those books. Fortunately, Ciaran shook his head and said, "No. I saw her earlier, at the market, but not since then."

Alessia frowned. "If you see her, let her know I retired for the evening." She set her eyes on me. "Where's that husband of yours tonight, Seren?"

"He was in too much pain to come," I said, rolling my shoulders back. "Still recovering from the flogging." Hopefully that would be an acceptable excuse—the whole tribe had seen him lashed.

She frowned, then glanced at Ciaran. "Maybe we'll see him tomorrow. Goodnight, then."

She wandered off to the next closest blanket. We'd set up farther out in the field for privacy, choosing the outskirts of the feast.

"Poor Giulia. Her mother watches her like a hawk," Amahle said with a laugh. "She's probably off in the woods some-where, rutting around with Timor Ladette."

"Do you blame her? Giulia is all she has," Ciaran remarked dryly.

He was right. Giulia was her only daughter. Alessia's husband had been killed over a decade ago, during a raid in Lirien. She had no other family.

"Maybe so, but she holds the reins so tightly that Guilia's always sneaking off just to get a good lay," Amahle said, then stretched. "Speaking of which, it's a feast tonight and I'm not spending it with my newly wedded best friend and the one man in the Vangar who might still be a virgin."

Ciaran shoved her, and I laughed. He didn't even have to reach—his arms were that long.

Wow, it feels good to actually laugh with my friends.

Even though I'd been morose at the start of the evening, they'd calmed me enough to even enjoy myself. Forget the troubles awaiting in my tent—and elsewhere. I'd been doing a fair job of ignoring the fact that I needed to prepare for the Skorn.

But the thought of Rykr made my stomach twist. He must be hungry. He hadn't eaten much during the market. Despite our rocky interactions, the least I could do was bring him food.

I hated him for making things so complicated. And yet, as I thought about him alone in that tent, or the way he'd taken lashes meant for me, my confusion toward him only grew.

The extra food on the blanket went into my pack. After helping Ciaran and me pick up, Amahle left in search of company for the night and I regretted seeing her go.

Ciaran watched as she disappeared into the merry crowd. "I'm not a virgin, you know," he said in a low voice.

He still wasn't looking at me. I bit down on the fleshy part inside my lower lip. "I never said you were."

"I just didn't want you to think—"

"It's fine, Ciaran." Truthfully, I didn't spend much time thinking about Ciaran's sex life, but I wasn't about to point that out. My relationship with Seth had always bothered him, and he'd been relieved when Seth had married Darya. Not that he'd said as much. He'd comforted me, but we rarely talked about relationships or sex and even then, only vaguely.

"I just wanted you to know," he said flatly.

I cleared my throat and took his hand. "You know I love you, Ciaran. I would never think less of you for something so trivial, even if it were true."

He squeezed my hand, his eyes warming. "I'll walk you back."

I settled my pack on my shoulder. Much as I wanted to stroll with Ciaran and pretend I didn't have to return to the thorn in my side, Amahle's warning about watching eyes came back to me.

"It's okay. A walk alone will help me clear my head."

Ciaran's expression was guarded. "Just be careful. Seth was threatening you yesterday, and if he felt that emboldened, it's because he has the allies to back him."

Seth's threats were the least of my concerns right now.

"About Rykr ..."

I nearly groaned, then quirked a brow.

Ciaran shifted, uncomfortably. "When I was putting the irons on him, I noticed he doesn't have a Bloodbinding mark."

My brow furrowed. "What ... what do you mean?"

"On his left wrist. It's not there. I've seen the ones your parents and any other Bound Liriens have. Just thought you should know."

I crossed my arms, feeling strangely defensive. "What are you saying?"

"I don't know, Seren. But something about Rykr doesn't add up. A Sealed, Bound Pendaran *should* have a Bloodbinding mark. It's strange. I don't know what it means, but you of all people should be aware of it."

I hated that he was right.

No Bloodbinding mark. How had I missed something so obvious? Every Pendaran bore the mark. Rykr kept his secrets close ... but this? How was it even possible? The thought unsettled me more than I wanted to admit.

Nodding, I stepped toward Ciaran. "Thank you for telling me. Please don't say anything to anyone else. I can't afford any more eyes on me right now."

Ciaran cut his eyes at me. "You know you can trust me with anything, Seren."

That was true. I would trust Ciaran with my life.

"I'm not saying this because of how I feel," Ciaran muttered, his eyes meeting mine with an intensity that left no room for jest. "I just don't trust him, Seren. He's not one of us, and you're tied to him in a way none of us understand."

A faint, shivering whisper seemed to carry in the dark shadows of the forest behind us and I tensed, looking over my shoulder, suddenly uneasy.

Great. Now I was letting Ciaran's doubts control my fears. As if it weren't bad enough having Rykr's emotions confusing mine through the bond.

I pushed my fears aside and found my friend's earnest face.

"Thank you. I'll see you tomorrow. Don't forget—meet me at the stables just after dawn. Tara said she wanted to go to the training fields." I left him in the field, heading toward the forest. The festivities would likely go on until morning. I'd never seen everyone so excited before.

The air cooled farther away from the warm drifts of the bonfires. As the music of the festival turned into a distant din, the tall grasses met the tree line of the deeper forest. The surrounding woods appeared empty and still, but I drew my sword anyway, Ciaran's warning about Seth ringing in my head.

I didn't think Seth would hurt me—he knew better than to attack me outright—but scare me?

Yes, I could see him doing that.

After his fury in flogging Rykr, Seth's threats had become corporeal, hanging over me, ready to strike.

The last few days had been a tangled mess, leaving me unsettled in ways I hadn't fully processed. A royal massacre was disturbing enough, but the changes happening to me because of the bond with Rykr? That scared me even more. The blood oath I'd taken hadn't seemed dangerous at the time, but it was dark magic all the same. Unpredictable and unwieldy.

My parents' tent loomed up ahead, and mine was just yards away from it. I paused, bracing myself for another inevitable confrontation with Rykr. The messiness of our arrangement bothered me—and yet we had to rely on each other to stay alive, as my mother had said. Would anyone try to hurt one of us to get to the other, like he'd suggested? It didn't seem beyond the realm of possibility.

"Rykr? I'm back," I said, pushing my way into the tent.

Empty.

The dagger he'd tossed earlier was gone.

As the ground seemed to tilt beneath me, my heart slammed into my ribs.

Godsdammit, I never should have left him alone.

Turning on my heel, I fled back into the cold night, fear closing in. If he'd tried to escape, he'd be caught and killed immediately. No trial, no sentence. Just instant execution.

Panic rose as I knelt, searching for any tracks or sign of his movement. A faint line of disturbed leaves trailed through the forest—the drag of irons marking his path.

Solric, help me. He'd had hours alone. Who knew how far he'd gotten?

I reached into my satchel, dusted my fingers with spell

powder, then whispered a light spell. A small, golden globe flared above my palm, casting a glow on the ground. Rykr's trail was clearer now, but the light risked drawing attention.

A rustle through the leaves sent my pulse to a sprint. Someone else was out here.

Turning my head toward the sound, I listened.

Nothing.

But my heart sped regardless. Something moved deeper into the woods—as though fleeing at the sight of me.

Rykr?

Lengthening my stride, I followed.

Maybe I should have let Ciaran walk with me.

The rancid stench of death hit me.

My senses quickened, more alert. A wisp of a breeze tickled my cheek and the hairs on my forearms, and the forest was alive with the sounds of frogs and the birds of prey that stalked the treetops.

Something was dead near here.

I followed the scent. Hopefully just an animal. Scouts usually removed any dead carcasses from our territory, to keep the stench at bay. Considering that this one was on the route between the encampment and the market field, it should have been dealt with by now.

Water gurgled from a nearby brook, splashing over stones. Beyond it stood a stump of a tree.

The smell is coming from the tree.

The thought was mad, but my gaze fixed on a dark lump in the center of the stump.

Cold water filled my boot as I stepped into the brook and crossed, drawn by the putrid stench.

In the pale, silvery moonlight, the dark shape on the stump took form.

A human heart.

A scream ripped from me and I staggered back, clutching the hilt of my sword.

A rustle came from behind a tree.

Giulia Bernardi stepped from the shadows, the distinctive yellow dress she'd worn earlier still draped around her frame.

Relief surged through me and I gasped out a breath. "Oh gods, it's just you, Giulia—"

She turned toward me and I stepped back. A gaping hole yawned in the center of her chest. Her skin was blueish, and the reek of decay came from ... *her.*

Run.

My feet stayed rooted in place, as though lead had wrapped around my ankles. A rush of nerves pierced my skin, but my mind didn't seem to fully comprehend what I was seeing— Giulia had been turned into a skinwraith, a hideous monster of the living undead.

I'd never seen one before. Barely believed in them, despite the stories.

The sight of her—of what was left of her—made every inch of my skin pebble in gooseflesh. The Giulia I'd seen laughing just hours ago was gone, replaced by this twisted, decaying thing with lifeless eyes.

This can't be real.

But she stepped toward me, and some primal instinct in me snapped. I grabbed a dagger and hurtled it toward her.

The blade sunk into the cavern of her chest, then thudded to the ground.

"Run, dammit!"

The deep voice in my head wasn't my own, but it shattered my paralysis. I tumbled backward, my hand slamming into a thorn-covered bush. Pain pricked my palm, warm blood blooming over my skin. I spun and lunged for the stream.

Tales said fire could destroy them, but there was none close enough. My grip tightened on my sword. If brute force wouldn't work, I needed another way.

My boots plunged into the water, slipping on algae-covered stones. Once on the other side, my knee slammed into the soft earth. Before I could stand again, a hand grasped my vest, yanking me.

I slashed my sword at Giulia, carving deep gashes into her thighs, but she barely reacted. An unearthly growl rumbled from her throat as her icy hands clamped around my forearm, pulling me into the water.

Fluid filled my nostrils. Gagging and choking, I thrashed. *Kick.* A coughing fit was coming on. *Slash.* The sword felt loose in my hand, my grip unsteady.

She's going to kill me.

Cold air smacked my skin as Giulia lifted me as though I was weightless, then hurled me toward a tree.

The impact sent bright spots of light across my vision. A sickening crack splintered in my ribs, pain following a beat later, slow and searing, as I hit the ground.

Somehow I'd kept my sword, but with my side screaming in pain, it was useless in my hands.

Giulia stalked toward me, her face a mask of pure evil, her lifeless eyes glowing with an eerie yellow light, deep inside the pupils.

After an excruciating breath, I staggered to my feet, working through the searing pain that threatened to rip my senses apart. If I didn't do something, she'd kill me. With every ounce of strength, I drove my sword deep into her gut.

She didn't stop. Didn't flinch.

A chill seeped through my skin where her decaying hand gripped me, the touch of death itself. My breath caught as her rotting flesh pressed into my arm, and nausea coiled within me. No matter how deep I cut, she kept coming, relentless, unstoppable.

A fragment of memory surfaced—a passage from a book.

The damn creature had to be decapitated.

"Seren!"

Rykr. He ran toward me as best he could with his irons still on.

Where in Nyxva did he come from?

And why is he soaking wet?

Giulia turned at the sound of his voice.

As she did, Rykr swung—the heavy irons on his wrists slamming into the side of her skull.

She snarled, rabid and furious, teeth bared as she lunged at him. The shift in her focus gave me an opening. I couldn't retrieve my sword from her body, and my daggers were useless.

I spread my fingers, summoning jagged ice. A sharp, crystalline blade formed in my grasp and with a swift stroke, I cleaved through her neck.

Giulia's head hit the ground.

I stared at it in horror, half-expecting it to keep moving. Then the body disintegrated into black, hissing vapor, stretching out and enveloping us in a cloud of shadow.

Then it vanished.

CHAPTER 16
RYKR

The gruesome head of a woman stared at me with lifeless eyes, but the body had disappeared.

For a moment, I didn't see a woman's head there, but Dalric's.

My empty stomach lurched, then I blinked, and cleared my vision. Not Dalric. Just a girl. Just a corpse, face twisted, eyes vacant. Tearing my gaze away, I bent and grabbed Seren's fallen sword.

She gasped in pain.

"Are you all right?" I didn't dare let the sword go, in case there were more of those *things* out there. If I hadn't seen it with my own eyes, I wouldn't have believed it.

"I'm not sure." Seren's hands trembled as she backed away from the gruesome head. "How in Nyxva did you get here? How did you know where I was? Where did you go?"

She leaned against me as we crossed the stream, moving as quickly as possible. But between her injuries and my irons, we were too slow.

169

Explaining what I'd seen felt absurd, but Seren—maybe her mother, too—might be the only ones who'd understand it.

"I heard you." I surveyed behind me. We were alone. For now.

"You heard me scream?"

"Yes, but also ..."

"But also, what?" She eyed me suspiciously. "How is it you just so happened to be here, Rykr? You were trying to escape, weren't you? And that-that ... *thing's* eyes glowed. Just like the vuk's. It wasn't Giulia it was a—"

"A skinwraith?"

"The living undead. That's why I had to chop its head off."

My skin prickled. Skinwraiths were myths—stories whispered to keep young children in line. I'd heard rumors of a Regulation unit encountering one in the mountains of Pendara, but I'd always assumed it was a cautionary tale.

"And you say ice powers aren't useful."

"I've never made a weapon like that before—it was instinct." Terror shone in her eyes. "How did you know where to find me?"

"I was ..." How to explain this? "I was washing myself. And then ... I was in your head. I saw the forest ahead of me, the stream, the stump ..."

She stared at me, open-mouthed.

"The bond, Seren. Somehow, I can see and hear things in your mind."

Her grip tightened on my forearm. "What?"

"I-I don't know. I can't explain it. You felt my pain yesterday, didn't you?"

She froze.

"So, you *saw* I was in trouble and came to help me?" A mixture of astonishment and horror played across her face. "You can *hear* my thoughts?"

"Only sometimes. I caught glimpses earlier today. But this ... I saw it. Like I was *you*."

She trembled. Not that I blamed her, given the skinwraith and my revelation. "How is this even possible?"

"I was hoping you might be able to answer that."

"You can *see* into my head?" The violation on her face was unmistakable.

"I didn't cause it. I don't even know how it works." My defensiveness was irrational. "If you'll recall, I'm not the one who bonded us."

"Don't remind me. I regret enough already."

Her retort, uttered as deadpan and dryly as I might, nearly made me choke with laughter, despite the circumstances.

"We need to tell Seth about the skinwraith," she said, not looking me in the eye. "If something turned Giulia, there could be more out there."

"That thing was a friend of yours?" The creature had worn a dress.

"I knew her." Seren's voice faltered, and she averted her gaze. "Her mother was just looking for her. My friends thought she was off enjoying herself during the festivities ..." Her lips tightened, before she drew in a sharp breath. "She helped me, Rykr—at the repository. She was ... scared to help. And now she's dead."

What was she implying? That someone had murdered and turned her into a skinwraith because she'd helped? That seemed extreme, even for the Viori. "You think someone in your tribe did this to her?"

Fire lit her eyes. "I hope not, but we can't let this happen again. If something is turning people into skinwraiths, we need to find out what—and stop it. I'll have to tell Seth of the encounter."

I didn't relish the idea of going to see her tribe's waldren again, but she was right. We had to warn them.

The combination of my wet clothing and her words sent an involuntary shiver through me, and I peered more closely at our dark surroundings. What if whatever had turned that girl into a skinwraith watched us now? I'd outrun the men who followed me to get here. And despite them being my enemies, a strange pang of guilt laced the thought that they, too, could be exposed out here.

As we neared the cluster of tents, including her tent, Seren stumbled, and a deep ache flared from my side—a phantom pain, since I had no injury there. I steadied her before she could fall. "I think you have a few broken ribs."

"You *feel* that, too?" she asked, gasping.

"Yes. Why don't we go to your mother first? Your sister might alert others. She's an officer in your Vangar, right?" The connection between us was all-consuming. Her pain bled into me, real and raw, as if the bond had made us one being split into two bodies. And if it was this strong now, what would it be like in a month? A year?

She locked eyes with me. "Tell me the truth, Rykr. Why were you out here? I went back to the tent and you were gone. Were you trying to escape?"

My jaw set. "I was, but I changed my mind. We can talk about it later. We're almost there," I murmured, guiding her forward, though the wariness in my chest didn't fade.

Seren grimaced, a flash of pain in her eyes. Whatever she thought of my admission, she didn't say.

She limped the entire way into her mother's tent.

The tent was much larger than Seren's, with furnishings that made it feel more like a humble but well-equipped cottage. The glow of orange firelight from the stove and several oil lamps lit the warm space. Lucia and Tara sprang from their bedrolls as we entered.

"What's wrong?" Tara asked, reaching us before Lucia did.

"A skinwraith." Seren winced, sitting on a plush cushion on the floor near the stove. "I stumbled across it on the way back from the festival. Giulia Bernardi was murdered—turned into one—and attacked me. Threw me against a tree. Rykr heard and came to my aid."

Lucia went ashen. "I've never heard of skinwraiths near here."

"Can people be turned into them by other humans? Or do they have to be turned by other skinwraiths?" I asked.

Lucia lifted a few bottles from a table calmly, as though mending her children was nothing new. "Anyone can be turned into a skinwraith by a sorcerer, but it's ancient—very dark magic. Forbidden magic. The price for magic like that would be costly, and I know of no one with that skill here."

Tara knelt beside Seren and helped her out of her vest. "Where are you hurt?" Tara surveyed Seren's face.

"I broke some ribs. Not sure what else." Seren drew a shaky breath and Tara unbuttoned her blouse, then pushed it off her shoulders. Her side was dark with an angry bruise, and I turned away, giving her privacy, though Tara seemed unconcerned.

"I'll take care of her," Lucia said, waving Tara to the side.

"Where's Madoc when I need him?" Tara muttered. Lucia met her gaze, a forlorn look passing between them, some unspoken pain there that neither voiced.

Who is Madoc?

Tara straightened and moved toward the sleeping area. She slipped behind a dressing screen, and minutes later, she emerged fully dressed. Grabbing a sword from beside her bedroll, she asked, "Is the skinwraith still out there?"

"Seren killed it," I said, from the corner of the tent. "It vanished. The head was still there, though."

Tara and Lucia looked at me, as though they had forgotten I was there. Tara frowned.

Was that blame in her expression?

"Tell me where, exactly."

I followed Tara outside. If she'd noticed I was still carrying Seren's sword, she said nothing. She didn't disarm me either.

"That way." I gestured toward the direction we'd been in, using both hands. "There's a stream. On the other side of the stream is a stump, and there's a human heart on it—probably that woman's. The head is near there."

If Tara was afraid, she didn't show it, and I respected that. She'd dragged a vuk back for Seren, so she was clearly a capable woman. But the rigid set of her shoulders made it clear she was on her guard around me, as though I'd somehow brought the skinwraith upon her sister.

"Thank you for helping Seren. Again." Her tone was sharp, more accusation than gratitude, as she turned to leave.

"I don't know how to summon murderous vuks or skin-wraiths if that's what you're thinking," I said dryly.

Tara paused, glancing over her shoulder with narrowed eyes. "Maybe not. But you're still a Lirien, and Liriens don't just show up in the middle of the forest at the perfect moment unless there's something we don't know. This will do nothing to inspire confidence in you, Rykr. Don't even think of breathing a word of this to anyone—especially not Seth."

"Damn," I muttered under my breath. "And here I was planning to summon my closest Viori friends for story time."

To my surprise, Tara smirked, but the distrust in her expression didn't waver.

A muffled cry came from inside the tent, and the pain in my side flared, then dissipated just as quickly. And when I looked back, Tara was already gone. Once I returned to the tent, Lucia was smoothing honey over Seren's bruise, but Seren appeared to be asleep.

"Did you mend her?" I knelt beside them.

Lucia didn't look at me as she continued rubbing the honey in. "I gave her a tonic to let her sleep. I can fix some bones, and bruises are easy enough, but I don't have the same power to heal that the Zhi do. My magic works differently. It leaves a mark."

"She told me your connection has deepened." Lucia pulled a strip of cloth from a spool beside her and wound it around Seren's torso. She gave me a sidelong glance. "I can teach you both how to block each other from invading the other's minds, but the closer you become, the deeper the bond will go. Eventually, if you don't learn to control it, you may not be able to separate your thoughts from hers—or hers from yours. It will start slowly. A memory here, a feeling there. But without training, it could consume you both."

She paused, eyes meeting mine. "Some say that bonds like this aren't meant to be controlled, as they're meant to bind two souls into one. But if that happens, you'll lose what makes you Rykr, and she'll lose what makes her Seren. And I doubt either of you want that."

Losing what made us ourselves? That was what terrified me about the bond—how much of this connection was mine, and how much was Seren's? Where did one end and the other begin? And if we couldn't control it, how long before it absorbed us completely?

"She seems to think there still may be hope of breaking the bond." I hadn't really processed anything Lucia had said yesterday as realistic, but that was before I could feel Seren's pain and see into her mind.

"The chance of that is slim at best. I tried to warn Seren

that this oath had deep consequences." Her eyes bored into mine. "I'd like to believe you are worthy of the risk she took. But the bond could also destroy you both if you're reckless. You've been given a second chance here among the Viori, a life that you, perhaps, did not want. But the alternative was death. Don't take that chance for granted."

Her words sank through me. If she only knew how much deeper those truths went.

Had I been in Ederyn, or if Dalric hadn't been mistaken for me, I would be dead.

Even the fact that my father had Sealed me, changed my name, and that Seren's oath had altered my appearance offered me a chance of hiding in plain sight—as someone else.

"I know," I said.

But even as I spoke another, darker thought took shape. If breaking the bond was impossible, then Seren would have to remain by my side or continue to be a threat to me. Forever. Because my place wasn't here.

Lucia finished binding the cloth and buttoned Seren's shirt. "I'll help you carry her back to your tent. Get some sleep. I fear trouble tomorrow."

CHAPTER 17

SEREN

Throughout the night, my dreams had been dark, twisted images of death. The glazed, soulless eyes of Giulia as a skinwraith. A yellow glow, deep within. A crack and shattering of bone as I crashed into a tree, over and over.

My damp shirt clung to me as I yanked myself from sleep, nausea roiling my stomach.

I'd been moved to my tent, back on my bedroll. The last thing I remembered was my mother giving me a tonic. Judging by the depth of the darkness outside, though, it was still well before dawn.

Rykr slept on the rug near the stove, bound in irons.

I'd told him he wasn't a prisoner here, but I'd gone back on my word when it was inconvenient.

And he'd tried to escape.

Except ... he'd come back.

We were no closer to trusting each other. No closer to breaking the bond. No better prepared for the Skorn. But dwelling on it wouldn't change anything, I just had to do better.

Pain shot through me as I rose.

My torso was bound in cloth, but the pain had dulled. Mother's healing skills were unusual, blending Zhi techniques with Ibarran magic, and she'd learned more since moving to the Dreadwood.

Grabbing a jar of healing honey from my bedside, I tiptoed to Rykr.

The bond might be clouding my judgment but, dammit, so was he. He'd upended everything I thought I knew of Liriens.

The Viori had told me they were vicious. Zealots who cared more about enforcing the Bloodbinding than truth.

But I hadn't seen that in Rykr. He'd disarmed my claims with thought and logic, but it was more than that. There was something about him—steady, deliberate, infuriatingly calm —that made it impossible to see him as a mindless soldier. And three times now, he'd gone out of his way to protect me.

The bond pulled me toward him, but it couldn't explain why I was starting to *want* to trust him, and that terrified me more than anything.

Kneeling beside his feet, I studied him in the warm glow of the stove.

Dammit, I like him.

We hardly knew each other and yet I'd spent enough time to come to that conclusion on my own. He'd also kept his promise not to hurt me. Even last night, he'd slept far from my side, never making me feel unsafe.

Liking him—especially when I still didn't know who he was or why he was in the forest—was dangerous, but it didn't make it any less true.

I pulled the pin from my hair. As I unlocked the irons on his ankles, he jerked awake.

He rolled over, blinking at me. "What are you doing?"

"Taking the irons off." I repeated the process with his wrists, my heart clenching at the welts on his skin.

The sweet scent of honey filled the space as I dipped my fingertips into the jar. "May I?" I gestured toward his ankles.

He gave a gruff nod.

I spread the honey over his wounds, using the barest pressure to avoid causing him pain.

"Thank you."

"You have to swear not to run again, Rykr, even though you came back and helped me. At this rate, I'm never going to repay you."

"Believe it or not, I'm not keeping score. But by my count, you saved me from execution *and* killed the skinwraith. If my friends in the Regulation ever hear about this, they'll never let me live it down."

I capped the jar, offering him a wry look. "Don't get used to it. If you don't start pulling your weight around here, I'll have to return you back to where I found you."

"Promise?" The corners of his mouth tipped up with amusement. He drew a slow breath through his nose, then sat as I finished putting honey on his wrists. "That feels surprisingly good."

"It's my mother's secret recipe. Secret because it's magic and she doesn't share all the spells she knows. Which, given my record with you, is probably for the best. How are you feeling this morning?"

He raked his fingers through his hair, then examined his wrists, clearly relieved to be free of the irons. "Exhausted. And cold. My bath outside last night didn't help."

I glanced back at the bedroll, which had the only bedding in the tent. Before I could talk myself out of it, I reached for Rykr's hand, lifted his pillow, then tugged him back toward the bedroll. A few sleeping hours remained, and I couldn't live with myself if I let him shiver in front of the stove.

Rykr hesitated. "What are you doing?"

I threw him a smile. "Don't worry, Lirien, I have no intention of deflowering you. But you might be warmer on the bedroll beside me, where there's warmth from my body, sheets, and a pelt. Plus, it's more comfortable."

In the dim light of the stove, his lips twitched. "Thank goodness. If there's one thing I've tried to do in life, it's guard my innocence."

I laughed softly. "I'm sure you're a paragon of chastity."

"Obviously." He stretched out beside me, his voice turning lower. "Though if you change your mind about deflowering me, just let me know."

The casual banter shouldn't have made my stomach twist with heat, but it did. He made a joke feel like a dare.

Despite my intentions, a familiar feeling of anticipation crept through me at his nearness as I crawled into bed. Facing away, as though he could see the hint of desire igniting within me, I covered us both with the bedsheets, then the blanket. I backed up closer to him.

His clothes were wet and ice cold.

"You're never going to warm up like that." I groped in the darkness for my trunk. I'd washed his bloodstained clothes earlier, leaving them to dry.

I handed the clean ones to him. "Change. And take the shirt off—leave it by the stove. It'll dry better there."

A soft chuckle left him. "How did you know I love it when a woman tells me what to do in bed?"

"Lucky guess." I crossed my arms, biting back a smile. "Hurry up before you freeze. I don't want a half-dead man sharing my bedroll."

"Don't worry. I'll be alive enough to be annoying."

"I noticed." I turned away, giving him privacy. "Maybe I should leave the irons on next time, just to keep things quieter." *Asshole.* I smiled to myself as he stood. "Why'd you take a bath with your clothes on?"

He cleared his throat, the sound of his trousers falling. I tried not to picture him, mostly failing. "At first, it was to use the stream to throw them off my scent."

Right. Because his plan had been to escape. "And after you decided not to run?"

He chuckled. "Hard to strip when you're chained up like a criminal."

His voice was light, teasing, but the reminder stung.

Oh no.

"I didn't think of that," I admitted, voice quieter. "I shouldn't have—"

"You didn't know I was going to try to betray you, or bathe. Next time, you'll think before chaining up a perfectly innocent man." He flashed me a grin as he reclined beside me, one that was impossible to be angry at, even if I wanted to be.

"Why did you come back?"

One arm stretched then bent, his hand settling behind his head. "Because I realized it wasn't worth risking both our lives without a halfway decent plan. Even if your people murdered my ... king."

His answer wasn't wrapped in any romantic trappings. He'd weighed the odds and wanted to live another day. Simple as that. Maybe he'd been slightly motivated not to risk my death, but I doubted I'd been much of a factor in his decision.

I swallowed hard. The depth of his grief simmered through the bond, raw and unfiltered. I wanted to be angry with him. To condemn his actions tonight and scream at the risk he *had* taken. Neither of us would have been in the woods when Giulia had attacked if not for him.

And yet ... I understood his desperation to do *something*, even when he was powerless. That was what had led me to the border when I'd met him. My failure with Esme and my inability to help rescue her had driven me to act foolishly—and my problems had only been compounded since then.

"If you had escaped," I said softly, "they would have hunted you down. And it wouldn't matter if they caught you, Rykr, because they'd also hold me responsible for your escape. They'd hang me for it and then you'd be dead anyway."

He faced me. "I'm not used to thinking about living for two people's survival. I didn't ask for this bond, Seren."

"You think I wanted this?" I raised a brow. "I've gone over what I did to save you a hundred times in my head—both *before* and after I did it. Each way ended with one or both of us dead. I considered dragging you to someplace secret, attempting to heal you there. But the chance of us being found —either by a creature or a Vangar scout—was huge. You were bleeding everywhere and needed healing."

He cleared his throat, tearing his gaze away. "You sure there aren't any more skinwraiths waiting out there for us?"

I shivered then told him what had been plaguing my nightmares. "She wasn't just *any* skinwraith. Giulia ..." I shook my head, the guilt rising like acid. "She gave me the books I brought back. Darya—Seth's wife—had borrowed every other book I needed before I got there, on Seth's orders. I can't help feeling like someone found out and punished her."

"Seth? Or his wife?"

I drew a slow breath. "Much as I want to blame Seth, I don't think forbidden, dark magic is something he knows. I may have broken Viori code, but that didn't suddenly turn him into a dark sorcerer. And Darya was the one who encouraged Giulia to give me the books in secret, I think. It's more likely

Giulia encountered a skinwraith, but the coincidence bothers me."

"Are skinwraiths common around here?"

"I haven't ever heard of one or seen another." My fingertips drifted over my ribs and I gritted my teeth at the pain. I was lucky Giulia hadn't broken my spine. Healing from that might not have been possible. "I'm worried that the vuk might have been a skinwraith too," I breathed. "Its eyes were glowing, deep yellow, inside the pupil."

"I saw that, too," Rykr admitted quietly. "What do you think is turning them?"

"I don't know what to make of it. I don't know how you were able to kill the vuk if it was a skinwraith, either—didn't you say you have to decapitate them?"

He averted his gaze. "I told you ... my sword might have had something to do with that."

Something *else* he clearly didn't want to talk about. *Fine.*

I turned my back to him, abruptly ending the conversation. "Go back to sleep, Rykr. Tomorrow we need to start training for the Skorn, and hopefully, break this bond before it."

He said nothing, tension hanging between us as he released a slow breath, then rolled to his side, facing me.

Even though I couldn't see him, I felt his nearness—the warmth of him against me. I took a strained breath, closing my eyes and trying to relax. At least I wasn't thinking of the awfulness of the skinwraith's clammy touch now.

Instead, all I could think of was Rykr's touch. What would it be like, feel like, to have him run his hands over me?

Dammit. I shifted, pretending to adjust the blanket, trying to will the thoughts away. Beside me, Rykr's breathing was steady, oblivious—or so I hoped.

It had been almost three years since I'd had sex, but this

wasn't just about that. It was him. His presence, his strength. The bond didn't help, either.

Way too long since I'd had a man this close, especially one half naked and with a body like Rykr's. If I was honest, I'd never been with a man as attractive as Rykr, and that was increasingly problematic. My core turned to liquid at the thought. He was all rigid muscle, skin tanned golden from days of training in the sun, tattooed and callused hands. *He's probably good with those hands.*

With Seth, sex had often been slow and languid, a respite from days out in the field. Silent, too, because I hadn't wanted to get caught sneaking into a senior Vangar officer's tent.

But I couldn't imagine anything like that with Rykr.

I *could* picture him shoving me up against a tree and taking me there. Hard. Fast. Unyielding.

My breath went shallow.

Dammit, I'm wet.

Allowing him into my bed had been a colossal mistake—not that he was even doing anything to indicate he was interested. But my body was on fire, my need growing.

If this was the bond, it was winning. But was it only the bond?

Mother had warned me my body would yearn, that the magic binding us would twist desire into something nearly unbearable. But this ... this felt different. More real. Which made it even more dangerous.

Gods, this was much, much worse than yearning, as I was damn near burning alive. My heartbeat quickened and I shifted one knee back.

The thought of his naked back when Seth had demanded he remove his shirt was enough to nearly undo me now.

"Seren?" Rykr's voice was a low rumble behind me. "Are you holding your breath?"

I startled. "Um—"

He doesn't know. There's no way he possibly knows what I was thinking.

... except he was the one person who could hear my thoughts and feel my emotions.

Fuck.

He was silent, then shifted, just slightly. "I—"

"Don't. Don't say a word," I snapped, mortification flooding through me.

Rykr rolled onto his back.

A full minute passed, then in the most insufferably smug tone, he said, "I'm much warmer now, thank you."

Damn him, damn him, damn him.

Furious with myself, I gritted my teeth. I didn't need daylight to see the self-satisfied smirk on his handsome face. I could sense it, practically feel it vibrating in the soft chuckle that came from deep in his throat.

He didn't need a sword to disarm me.

Worse, he didn't even know he'd done it.

I'm in so much trouble.

CHAPTER 18
RYKR

Seren barely looked at me in the morning.

The temptation to allow her to act on her thoughts in the middle of the night had been *strong*. So strong that I'd had to put a stop to it, before I let myself get carried away by the lust I'd felt consuming her.

In the Regulation, sex had been a pastime, just like any other. Find a warm body for the night, forget the day's troubles, and wake up to brutal training. I'd kept to myself more than my friends had, but that only made them curious. They'd started sending young men to my room, new recruits, thinking that my preference had held me back.

After that, I made my interest in *women* much clearer.

But care about one?

That wasn't something I'd allowed myself. Who I married wasn't up to me. I was one of my father's many political bargaining tools.

My father. Even if I'd left him on bitter terms, the loss of him—of my brothers—burned me alive. *Why had they been slaughtered so mercilessly?*

And now ... I had no tether to any place.

If I wanted a beautiful Viori wife, it'd be so easy—especially when the lust between us seemed to be growing.

I'd better stop thinking about it. I could only blame the bulge in my trousers on the early morning for so long. We dressed in silence until Seren crossed her arms by the tent flap. "Ready to go?"

I glanced at my chains, still on the rug where she'd left them. "What about the irons?"

"Throw them in my pack for now. Considering we don't know what's out there, I'd rather take my chances angering Seth than run into another skinwraith while you're unable to run."

Fair enough.

She grabbed a leather knife bandolier and tossed it to me. "Take anything you like from there. I'll see about getting you a sword later."

"Your sister said she'd help with that."

She slipped a sword holster over her shoulders with a grimace. Her ribs still hurt.

"Ready?"

"Yeah." The thought of Seth's men watching me wander without iron nagged me, but Seren was right. And the walk to her mother's tent was short.

Lucia was nowhere in sight as we entered, but Tara waited inside, drinking a cup of mulled morning wine. The scent of cloves hit me as it simmered on the stove, making my mouth water. I was hungrier than I realized. Seren poured us each a cup before settling beside her sister on the floor. The hint of purple under Tara's eyes hinted at a long night of little sleep.

"Well?" Seren asked her.

"I found Giulia's head and turned it over to the Vangar so that her mother would know she's dead. Then I went hunting for skinwraiths." Tara sipped her wine. "I didn't find any or any sign that our encampment had been breached."

"Did you tell the Vangar about the skinwraith?" I asked.

Tara rolled her shoulders back, her expression darkening. "No. Silence might be wiser. For both of your sakes."

I swallowed a gulp of wine. "I had that same thought."

Seren shook her head. "But I don't understand. I killed the skinwraith."

"One of our own is dead, Seren. You're the only one who saw the skinwraith. The tribe won't believe it unless there's proof, and if they don't believe it, they'll need someone to blame for Giulia's death. We can't risk them thinking it was a certain mysterious Lirien."

"But her body ..."

Her body had vanished. All that remained was a severed head—just as dead as it would have been if she hadn't been turned. Seren must have come to the same conclusion, her face paling.

"Thank you," I said quietly. I drained my cup and placed it beside the stove.

Tara stood, her stance protective, wary. "I didn't do it for you. Frankly, I don't know who the fuck you are, Rykr. You show up, and suddenly a vuk attacks, my sister makes a blood oath, *and* a skinwraith wanders into our territory? Who's to say that it's *not* you? For all I know, you bewitched Seren."

Seren's eyes widened.

"How have I never considered that?"

Her thoughts traveled down our bond, loud in my head.

I scowled at her. "You don't believe that, do you?"

"You just thanked me for saving your life." I sent the thought the same way it had come to me.

The doubt in her face only increased.

A bitter chuckle left my lips. "Fantastic. Not even you

believe in me. Ironic, considering you're the daughter of a murderer and traitor."

Tara's expression grew frosty. "Don't you dare speak badly of my father in his own home."

"Unlike your *people*, who take no issue with liars and criminals in their midst, I hold myself to a different standard, Tara. I won't shy away from the truth just to make you feel better about your origins."

Tara set her cup down. She took a menacing step toward me. "Say that again, you hagspawn."

I had to admire her. She wasn't afraid to threaten a man nearly a foot taller than her, someone she had to know was far better trained than she'd ever be.

I crossed my arms, managing a look of boredom. "I'm terrified."

Tara's face darkened and she took another step forward. Then her eyes focused on my wrists. "Where are his irons, Seren?"

Curpiss.

"I took them off. Just for a little bit," she added hastily.

"Fucking hell." Tara looked from me, back to Seren, her face dark, then she stormed out of the tent.

Tense silence descended between us. Tara had dredged up a host of fear inside Seren.

I scrubbed my face with my palms, trying to think clearly. "I'm not the source of all this evil, Seren. You can feel it, can't you? That's part of this bond, isn't it? If I meant you harm, wouldn't you know by now?"

"Will you tell me why you came into the territory?" Her voice sounded empty. *"He can't be what Tara claims. I feel it in my core."*

At least that thought had come through loud and clear, providing a shred of consolation.

I held her gaze, unblinking. "I was lost."

Her voice intruded again. *"He's lying."*

So much for consolation.

"You know I swore to protect you, right? It's part of the oath. And even if I wanted to break that, I can't. So you better start believing you can trust me, Rykr. I'd prefer to defend you against falsehoods, including from my family, but you make it hard when you won't defend yourself by telling me the most basic information."

"You *have* the most basic information." My unyielding stance continued, the muscles in my arms flexing. "Including that I've despised Brogan Ragnall my whole life. You can't expect that to change just because you ask."

She tore her gaze from mine. "Why do you hate my father so much? What difference does it make to you that he's viewed as a traitor?"

I hesitated, searching for a reasonable answer. "I met the princes and the princess when I went to Ederyn to be Sealed. I know"—my voice cracked—"*knew* them well. They were friends. The death of their mother crushed them. King Magnus could be cruel at times, but the queen ... she was beloved. Known for her kindness. She didn't deserve what your father did to her."

Before Seren could respond, Tara strode back inside, brushing past me on her way to a bookcase. She yanked one from the weathered wooden top, then marched back and thrust it into my face. "This book is sacred. Swear on it you didn't bewitch Seren."

I flinched, a slow frown tugging my lips. "And then you'll believe me?"

"I may not be able to kill you without risking Seren, Rykr, but that doesn't mean I won't break every bone in your body if you hurt her. Swear you're an honest man."

My eyes narrowed. "I don't think I can go that far." Still, I set my hand on the book. "But I swear on all the deities—real or fake—of Eldris and Skaldra, I did not bewitch Seren." Leaning toward her, I added, "Also, if you break every bone, she'll feel it, so you'll still be hurting her."

Tara scowled and lowered the book. "You're not taking this seriously."

"I am." I took the book and kissed it. "I seal my solemn oath with a kiss. That's a bigger pledge than I was able to give this delightful marriage of mine."

Seren groaned and Tara knocked the book back against my jaw. "You're a real *swiver*," she seethed.

But she also appeared satisfied, for the moment.

As she put the book back, I scrutinized her. "What, exactly, would you expect to happen to me if I lied? Burst into flames? Drop dead?"

"We could only be so lucky. Honestly, it's your lack of reverence that's more convincing. Someone evil would fear making an oath on a sacred book. You're just a skeptic who doesn't even think about the consequences in the first place." Tara's glare didn't lessen.

"Just so we're clear, do you still want me to consummate my marriage to your sister or not? I'm having a hard time keeping straight the requests you make in the name of being a protective sibling."

Seren's face flamed red, her eyes flying to her sister. "Tara!"

Tara shrugged. "Now that I reluctantly believe you, feel free."

"Glad to know I have your blessing once again." Sarcasm dripped from my voice.

"Will you two stop? My gods, you argue like siblings." Seren crossed her arms, stepping between us. "Since we're starting training today, and I'm still in pain from the skinwraith's attack, I was thinking it might be better for you"—she gestured at Tara—"to work with Rykr, while I do some reading on the Skorn. And I need to learn how to better control this bond with Rykr. It might be to our benefit to go to Emberstone a day or two early. The most powerful sorcerers and priests in our territory are there, so we may as well take advantage of it."

"What exactly is Emberstone?" I asked. My lack of knowledge about the Viori territory frustrated me. That they'd managed to keep their secrets so well was a serious flaw in Lirien military intelligence.

"The seat of our government in the Viori territory, where our leader lives. A city, but it's built into a mountain and warded." Seren didn't bother looking at me as she spoke.

Tara huffed. "You can't go poking around Emberstone asking about how to break the bond that's keeping you both alive at this point. Rykr could be killed, and then where would we be?"

"All I'll ask about is how to control it."

Tara crossed her arms, disbelief on her face. "Your best bet to surviving is staying *here* and training as much as you can. Most people have much longer to prepare, and they still die. The Skorn will test you to your limits, Seren. You'll need to play to your strengths, including any the bond has given you. Instead of seeing it as a weakness, you need to start figuring out how to use it."

Seren scowled. "Right now, it's a liability, Tara."

Tara smirked, shaking her head. "Of course you see it that way. You've always been shortsighted, little sister. Mother says you can use it for mind speak, is that true?"

Seren's face reddened. "Well, yes, but—"

"That's a huge advantage right there. Two people able to communicate like that? That's an enormous gift while fighting elite warriors."

I didn't want to say it aloud, but Tara had a point. She clearly had a sharp mind for strategy.

Though a hint of sympathy softened her hardened features, Tara's lips pursed. A few seconds of tense silence passed between the sisters. "We train today, Seren. Physical skills *and* with your books, even if you're in pain. The Skorn won't take it easy on you and neither will I. My squadron will help." She smiled. "Mostly because they don't get a choice. And I can probably get Madoc's squadron to help too, since they've been running drills with me while he's gone."

There was that name again.

"Madoc?" I raised a brow.

"Madoc is our brother," Tara said flatly.

"The twin?" I met Tara's eyes over the top of Seren's head. "Would that be the evil one or the good one? Right now, my money is on you for the former."

Tara's brown eyes grew frosty. "Thanks for telling him, Ser."

"It's not like it's not common knowledge." Worry flashed in her face. "Has Mother heard *anything*? I don't understand what's taking Madoc and Father so long. Something might have happened."

"She hasn't heard anything, but she's worried, too—hasn't been sleeping. She left a few hours ago, probably to see what magic she can use to track them." Tara glanced at me. From the change in her demeanor, she didn't want to talk about this in front of me.

The conversation raised questions, though. *Just where is Brogan Ragnall and his son?* And why hadn't Seren mentioned them much? Now that I thought about it, it was as though she was avoiding the topic.

Tara's expression closed off. "I'm going to order my squadron to ride to the training field. Grab some extra supplies and bedrolls—we might camp out there the next few nights, rather than coming back here. And your husband needs some clothes that fit him. Get him outfitted in Vangar leathers for training. That's an order."

Seren's shoulders slumped. She might be formidable on her own, but in her family, she was lowest in the pecking order. "Can Ciaran and Amahle come with us? I asked them last night if they'd help, and they were going to meet me at the stables."

"If they're not on duty, they're welcome to join us."

"And what about the skinwraith and Giulia's murder? We're just not going to tell anyone what happened?"

Tara bent to gather her pack. "In the absence of another attack and any other evidence, the Vangar will investigate it as a murder. I'll do my best to make sure no one is falsely accused. Is there anything else that's helpful that I should tell them?"

"Should I mention the glowing eyes of the skinwraith and the vuk?" Seren's voice came through my head.

"Do that and she'll think I'm to blame for certain," I answered.

Seren shook her head. "Not that I can think of."

"Hopefully, it's just a horrific accident. Giulia liked to wander in places she ought not to have. If there's another incident, we'll have to reassess." Tara threw her pack over her shoulder, then jerked her chin at me. "Put your damn irons back on. We don't know if they'll let you out of them for the Skorn, so you'll need to learn to fight with them. And don't let her allow you out of them again."

I scowled at Tara. "Do you know how to successfully control what she does?"

"No, but—"

"Then how in the fuck do you expect me to?"

Tara shook her head. "You two fucking deserve each other."

For the first time that morning, I smiled.

CHAPTER 19
SEREN

ods, Rykr was handsome.

Amazing what a pair of well-fitting leather trousers could do for shapely male legs. I'd outfitted him in black leather armor from chest to foot, with shoulder pads, a kilt that came to mid-thigh, and leather bracers covered his wrists and forearms. High boots came to his knees. Of course, I'd had to do it without the irons and now I faced a new dilemma as we approached the stables—explaining to Seth and Darya, who waited there, how I'd been able to dress Rykr while he was supposed to be chained.

Seth didn't wait for us to reach him, striding forward with purpose, his face a hardened mask. An ugly bruise darkened the skin beneath his eye, thanks to the punch I'd landed a couple days ago.

"Why is he dressed in Vangar clothes?" Seth snapped.

"Tara's orders." I shrugged. "She's sending us to the training field with her squadron today. Speaking of which, our progress to the field will be slower than we'd like because of the irons. I wanted to request they be removed while we ride. I had to take them off in order to dress him." I didn't bother tiptoeing around it. Seth knew I kept a pick in my braid—he'd taught me that trick *and* how to pick locks.

Seth's lips pursed, but his voice was surprisingly gentle. "The irons are for the safety of our people, Seren. You may be proud of flouting the law, but many in the tribe aren't impressed. You'd do yourself a favor by not challenging me in front of others."

Seth turned toward Rykr. "Speaking of the laws of our territory, Prince Calix's body was stolen last night. We found bear tracks. You wouldn't happen to know anything about that, would you?"

Maybe the suspicion wasn't unduly justified, but *bear tracks?*

Rykr met his stare coolly. "It so happens I spotted a bear stalking me as I bathed in a stream last night. I stayed still for a while and moved away without it spotting me, but it must have been hungry. Probably smelled the body."

The unspoken interrogation taking place between Seth and Rykr made my curiosity burn.

How much had Rykr done while I'd been at the feast?

A few beats passed. "We were supposed to turn the body over to Emberstone, but now we'll have to beg for forgiveness while our scouts scour the forest looking for whatever's left of it." He stood straighter. "You won't be training with Tara, Seren. Effective immediately, I'm calling all the Vangar squadrons to the training fields. There's been a murder in our camp. And you're in Darya's squadron, aren't you?"

"Yes." My gaze flicked toward Darya, who'd stayed a few paces back. "A murder?" I asked as innocently as I could.

"Giulia Bernardi's head was found in the forest. Her body is still missing," Darya said.

My mouth went dry. "Maybe it was that bear Rykr mentioned—"

"I found this in the forest," Darya said, unwrapping a cloth in her hands. The remains of the ice blade I'd made. The cold must have preserved it. Unnaturally dark blood marked the surface of the blade—Giulia's.

I restrained a shiver, feeling Rykr's eyes on me. I hadn't even thought about leaving the blade behind in the chaos of the attack ... but how had Tara missed it? *Damn.*

"You know how to wield ice, don't you, Seren? Any idea on how something like this could have been made?" Darya asked. Despite the neutrality of her tone, the implication was clear. Why come to me otherwise?

But she's not wrong.

I raised my chin. "My skills have mostly been limited to frost and small icicles. That looks complex."

"Hmm." The corners of her mouth turned downward, and she covered the blade again. "Her mother is convinced she was murdered, but I'll pass along the bear suggestion to the scouts. In the meantime, our squadron will be reinforcing the Vangar watchtowers today. Seth and I can escort you and your husband to the training field."

Reinforcing the watchtowers? If I was going to prepare for the Skorn, that was a colossal waste of my time—we weren't even allowed to read in the watchtowers, considering we had to stay alert.

"Will we be running drills on the field too?" I asked. "I just want to make sure I packed what I need."

"Perhaps. There's obviously been a breach of security, and we all need to be vigilant. We leave in five minutes." Darya turned abruptly and strode toward the corral, where her horse awaited.

Seth, who had remained silent, watched his wife go before

turning his focus back to us. "I'll allow for Westhaven's leg irons to be removed so he can ride on your horse, Seren. But he rides with you, not alone."

"Riding on a horse together will make for a slower journey." I crossed my arms.

"We can't risk putting him on a horse alone. He'll ride best with you since you're small. I believe your friends are inside the stable preparing horses, so they can help accommodate you."

Unwilling to goad him any further, I didn't argue. At least riding with Rykr might allow me to read along the journey—gods knew when I'd get another chance. "Fine. I'll go get the horse if you'll remove his leg irons." I headed into the stables to where Ciaran and Amahle waited with the horses they'd saddled.

Amahle's dark brown eyes reflected unease as I greeted her. "Did he tell you about Giulia and the new orders?"

"Yeah." I didn't elaborate—better to say nothing than lie. Tying my pack to the horse Ciaran had saddled for me, I glanced at the mare my family owned. She was too old and small to carry both Rykr and me.

Ciaran's horse, a young gelding, would be stronger for the journey.

"Think Rykr and I can use your gelding? Seth says we have to ride together."

Ciaran frowned, his gaze lingering on Rykr as he entered the stable, free of his leg irons. "It'll slow us down, but sure." He hesitated, adding, "Cozy ride, though."

Rykr joined us a moment later and Amahle smiled at him. "I'm Amahle. We didn't meet properly at the council meeting."

"I wouldn't have remembered, with the whole blinding pain thing." Rykr turned to Ciaran. "Callen, right?"

"Ciaran," he muttered, reddening.

Swiver. He knew Ciaran's name.

Rykr caught my glare, his voice slipping into my mind. *"He should worry less about our saddle space and more about himself."*

"Or maybe he's just being considerate," I shot back.

Amahle glanced between us, her brow furrowing slightly. "Everything okay?"

"Just fine." I moved past Rykr to help Ciaran unsaddle the horse. The tension in Ciaran's posture was obvious as he worked, and he didn't look at me.

"Sorry," I muttered.

Ciaran shook his head, placing a sturdy bareback blanket on the gelding. "He's arrogant, and he wants me to know you're his."

I set my hand on Ciaran's arm. "I don't belong to anyone. If Rykr needs to be humbled, so be it. You're my friend, and I won't let him humiliate you."

Ciaran's neck reddened, and he pulled away. "If he dies, you die, right?"

I nodded, regretting that I'd told them about the oath's consequences. But I trusted them. They needed to understand why Rykr's life mattered.

"Then, like it or not, your loyalty belongs to him." Ciaran's voice was low, but there was no mistaking the edge to it. "I'm not so foolish that I can't see it."

His words cut deeper than I wanted to admit. If Ciaran, who knew me better than anyone, already doubted me, how could I hope to convince Seth and Darya? Worse still, how could I convince myself that I hadn't crossed some invisible line, one where duty and loyalty blurred in ways I wasn't ready to face?

He's wrong, I told myself. But doubt gnawed at me as we started the trek toward the training field. What if they refused to see it that way? The bond with Rykr wasn't something I'd wanted—it had been forced upon us. But would that matter to Seth, to the council, or even to my closest friends?

I was proud to be Viori. Unlike Lirien, where power was bound and controlled from birth, we were free to grow into our gifts. No Bloodbinding to sever us from what the gods had bestowed. Amahle had been born with spirit gliding—a Zhi craft. Ciaran could bend metal as easily as a Volker craftsman shaped iron. And Esme, sweet Esme, could speak to animals as though their souls were one, as well as any Ambran. All of them would have been snuffed out in Lirien—the Bloodbinding removed gifts like that from every infant, only leaving them powers if they'd been fortunate enough to be born with a gift that was allowed in the realm of their birth.

"You're riding as stiffly as a corpse," Rykr commented in a low voice behind me.

While it made more sense for me to ride behind Rykr, Seth wanted me in charge of the reins, which meant that Rykr's iron-bound wrists were around my waist, his chest against my back.

"Maybe because it makes no sense for us to be riding on this damned horse together all because Seth is afraid you'll ride off on your own. Not to mention how lovely it is to have you breathing down my neck."

"I wouldn't trust me either, if I were him," Rykr said, more reasonable than I'd expected him to be. "Not that I'd get far. He's had me followed most of the time I've been here. And you didn't seem to mind me breathing down your neck last night, *thistling*." He set his jaw against my shoulder, as though to prove he could.

"Thistling?"

"Yes, little thistle ... beautiful to look at, prickly to touch."

Swiver. Tensing, I moved my face toward his. My breath caught more than I wanted it to, a shiver of pleasure going through me as my cheek rubbed against the dark scruff of his strong jaw. His full lips were only inches from mine and the impulse to close my eyes and sink my mouth against his tantalized.

But if he could restrain himself against any pull this oath was causing, then so could I.

Regardless of how insanely good-looking he is.

Dammit. I hoped he hadn't heard me.

The feline smirk curving that mouth told me otherwise.

"There's nothing wrong with admitting that I find you attractive," I snapped. "It's the fucking oath's fault. And stay out of my head."

Rykr's lips threatened a chuckle, but this time, something softer lit his eyes. Amusement, yes, but also understanding— like he knew exactly how the oath was twisting our emotions and didn't resent me for it. That made it worse somehow, made him harder to hate.

Seth rode up beside us. "What are you whispering about?"

Rykr, asshole that he was, tightened his arms around my waist. "Just how much I'm enjoying having her bouncing on my balls. That a problem, Seth? Or do you need a written account of everything that happens in our tent, too?"

My face flamed as Seth's eyelids practically twitched. Even from here, I saw Amahle's shoulders shake with laughter as she rode in front of us. I bit my lip, trying to keep a smile from my mouth.

"Dammit, Rykr."

"Imagine how much he'll hate it if he finds out we can have private conversations without saying a word."

The exchange was so easy, so fluid, that I *did* smile, despite my best effort. "There's nothing to worry about, Seth," I said, keeping my tone steady. "We aren't planning an overthrow at the training camp, and we certainly aren't foolish enough to try anything with a host of Vangar watching our every move."

Seth didn't seem convinced. "Just remember, Seren. The Vangar oath represents more than any individual loyalty to an encampment. If anything happens there, it won't just be your life on the line." His warning hung in the air like a sword over our heads.

Seth flicked his reins, simmering frustration evident in the rigid set of his shoulders, leaving only Darya trailing behind us —a silent reminder that we were far from trusted.

"Your taste in men is questionable." Rykr pulled away from me. "If that's who you were involved with before. Or has Seren had a long string of suitors?"

I sighed. Maybe this conversation needed to be had, given what Seth had implied about me at the council meeting, but I didn't relish it. "The ten years we're required to be in the Vangar, most Viori don't get married. Everyone turns a blind eye to the amount of bedmates most people have."

Lowering my voice a bit more, I said, "But Seth was my first —and only—lover." I'd considered sleeping with others, just to forget him, but no one had ever appealed enough, and I'd spent my free time training instead. "Being petite put me at a natural disadvantage in the Vangar and I had to work harder to keep up."

And Seth had broken my heart.

Whether Rykr heard that thought or sensed it, he stiffened slightly. "Did you love him?" Rykr's voice was surprisingly gentle, none of the judgment I'd expected.

"I thought I did. But I was naive. And clearly, he didn't love me."

Rykr gazed out at the forest, squinting as we went through a beam of sunlight. "Love and attraction are confusing, no matter what age. It doesn't mean you were naïve, just human.

I'm sure a few years from now, someone else will make you much happier than he ever would have."

I released a light, sardonic laugh. "How very reasonable of you, Rykr. But I don't know about that."

"You're beautiful, obviously, and a force to be reckoned with. A little tornado of fury when you're angry." His lips teased a smile. "I'm willing to bet there are more than a few men in your tribe who'd happily sell their souls to be with you."

He thinks I'm beautiful?

I pressed my tongue to the roof of my mouth, trying to swallow back the strange flutter of warmth that went through me at his words. "I doubt it," I said at last, with a taut smile. He couldn't know that my family had always had a tenuous position here, thanks to the twins and my parents' love for their homelands. Or the lasting effects this *marriage* would have on my prospects. "What about you? Is there a woman in Pendara that's caught your attention?"

I'd wondered about his past several times, mostly because I'd been an interruption to it. While he'd assured me he wasn't married, that didn't mean he didn't care about anyone, either.

He laughed lightly. "Are you asking how many lovers I've had?"

The thought of Rykr with other women made my stomach turn, but I'd be a fool to think he lacked experience. I gave him a flippant shrug. "You asked me."

"What do *you* think?"

The evasive answer was good enough. I bit my lip. Rykr was handsome enough to have any woman he wanted. "Fine. Keep your secrets," I said, nudging the horse forward. "But if you're going to keep dodging my questions, don't expect me to answer yours either."

Rykr tilted his head, a half-smile forming. "Fair enough, thistling."

I ignored the teasing. "If we're supposed to trust each other enough to survive this, maybe it's time you stop hiding things from me."

"My family doesn't do love matches," he said abruptly, in a dry tone. "Marriage is strictly for breeding, according to my father. And pedigree."

He'd dodged my question again.

His bound wrists caught my attention, reminding me of what Ciaran had said about his lack of a Bloodbinding mark. For Rykr to be without it meant something dangerous—either he'd escaped the rite, or he was hiding something far worse.

Even though Darya rode several feet behind us, and we whispered, who knew if she might overhear something if I asked him about it now?

Darya possessed spellcraft powers. Given that could cover many things, I didn't want to risk discussing anything truly suspicious with her nearby, no matter how friendly she'd been over the last few days.

Then again, she couldn't overhear mind speak.

"I've been meaning to ask you something."

Rykr's thumb tapped against his iron cuff. *"Now who's the one in the other's head?"*

"If you're allowed, then so am I." I smirked over my shoulder. *"Why don't you have a Bloodbinding mark?"*

The fingers on his right hand curled slightly. *"Who says I don't?"*

A beat of silence passed before he added, *"Maybe you're looking for something you're not supposed to find, Seren."*

His words, simple and calm, sent a chill through me.

"I noticed this morning when I put on your irons. You don't have one. I may not have noticed before because plenty of Unbound

Viori don't have one. But you should—you're from Pendara." Transferring the reins to one hand, I tapped my fingers on the iron above his wrist. *"Right here, no?"*

His hand slipped down, then grabbed my wrist. His touch sent a delicious sizzle of heat down my veins, and my fingers flexed. *"Sometimes we can't see what's right in front of us, Seren."*

"What's that supposed to mean?" My breath caught, my body increasingly aware of the effect of his thumb brushing lightly over the sensitive skin of my wrist. His palm slid up the back of my hand, then his fingers interlaced with mine, curling down. My fingers curled reflexively, my pulse speeding. I leaned back against him without thinking, heady with mounting desire.

"Sometimes marks don't mean what people think they do," he murmured, glancing at Darya as if to check whether she was listening. His voice was too quiet, too careful.

My fingers tightened around the reins. What kind of secret was he keeping, and why was it important enough to hide even now?

The tension in his answer settled uneasily in my chest. Whatever it was, I couldn't shake the feeling that knowing might change everything.

Rykr's lips skimmed my earlobe. "Don't ask questions you don't want the answers to."

I drew a sharp breath, then scowled, yanking my hand away. "Why don't you make yourself useful and hold the reins? I'm going to read so I can prepare a defense at Emberstone to save your ass. Again." I needed all the information I could get if I wanted any chance of living.

"Yes, because your last plot to save my ass worked so well. If I recall correctly, the death threats haven't let up since then. Not to mention the deadly trial we're facing. Maybe I should take over the plotting for a while."

His teasing tone cut through my irritation. "I don't need to plot. I could outsmart you in my sleep."

His blue eyes sparkled with mischief as he took the reins from me. "You think of me while you sleep?"

I shook my head, struggling to keep the smile off my lips while I tugged a book from my satchel. "It's more like a recurring nightmare, actually."

He laughed and my heart squeezed, a strange mixture of pleasure and worry. I snuck a look toward my friends—my faithful allies—who might view every shared laugh and whisper as further evidence of my shifting loyalty.

But, dammit, even though we bickered, and he was deliberately giving me non-answers, using his tongue to alienate potential allies like my sister and friends, I liked his company. I wasn't sure we'd ever be friends like Ciaran and Amahle, but I was sensing that I didn't only *need* him to live so I didn't die. Somehow, I *wanted* him to live.

Every hoofbeat on the forest trail echoed with unspoken questions, as if the trees themselves were listening. Shadows stretched long beneath the canopy, and with each passing mile, the weight of what awaited us pressed heavier on my chest. Something was coming. Something I couldn't yet name, but it was there, lurking just beyond the edge of sight. Waiting.

CHAPTER 20
RYKR

Fighting in irons had its advantages, it turned out.

"You have to stop doing that." Tara glowered down at me as I sat at the base of a tree, sipping from a waterskin.

I cocked my eyebrow at her. "And why's that?"

"You've put five members of my squadron in the infirmary. We're having to call up extra healers to the training field. You nearly crushed two of their windpipes, Rykr." Her eyes narrowed. "Keep it up and no one will want to fight you and then where will we be?"

I stood slowly, not even slightly exerted. "You want me to train for this damned trial, where I may or may not have irons on while I fight the best warriors your people have to offer? Then this is part of what I plan to do. I can barely move my feet the way I want them to. Disarming them with my chains and strangling them is a good next move."

"You're an arrogant show-off," she growled, crossing her arms. "And the Skorn aren't going to fight like my squadron. They won't let you get that close. I'm *trying* to help you."

"I don't need your help with fighting techniques," I snapped. "You of all people should know what I can do—you're Brogan Ragnall's daughter. What I need help with is blocking the bond between your sister and me, for both our sakes. Sure, maybe talking to her with mind speak can be helpful, but feeling each other's pain is not. *You* can't help me with that."

Tara scowled. "I know that," she said, at last. "Which is why I sent for my mother." Worry flashed across her face. "Seren isn't a strong fighter, though. She did—does—need all the training she can get. She won't last two minutes in the arena with the Skorn, Rykr. She's smart and she's fast, but she's not skilled or strong enough to take on the best Vangar warriors in our territory. And she's young. Darya is screwing her over by making her sit in the watchtowers all day."

Her honesty was refreshing. In that way, Tara and Seren were similar. But her words also confirmed what I already suspected: Seren needed to learn more.

"I'll train her myself at night if I can. It'd be good to have a proper duel with her so I can assess her weakness for myself. One where I'm not wearing chains."

Tara's lips pursed, her gaze distant as she stared past me. "Agreed. That would be helpful for Seren." She paused, thinking. "There might be a way I can get Seth to agree to training *you* untethered, but it'll be exhausting for you."

"What's that?"

"I could challenge the other squadrons to a sparring championship. It'll pit the squadrons against each other in the ring, where the champion of each round keeps fighting until none remain."

She flicked her eyes at me and caught the hint of a smile on my lips. "Wipe that grin off, Rykr. I already know you're capable of winning. That's not the point. The point is that

Darya's squadron will be challenged and Seren will have a chance to fight you. By now, Seth's probably heard about your tendency to crush throats with chains. He won't let you do that in a sparring championship, since we're not supposed to kill each other."

"Just tell me when and where and I'll fight."

"Was Father this annoying when he was young?" Tara asked, looking past me and deeper into the woods.

I swiveled my head to see Lucia approaching, a light blue hooded cloak drawn over her head.

Lucia gave a gentle smile, holding out a jar of healing honey toward her daughter. "Most of the Sealed are arrogant. They've earned their arrogance, though. Your father was uniquely humble among them, which was why I fell in love with him."

I nearly rolled my eyes. If I had to hear anyone else extolling that hagspawn, I might actually hurt someone. "Yes, he very meekly slit the queen's throat, right?"

Lucia averted her gaze, and Tara cleared her throat. "Good luck, Mother. He's a real joy to work with." She turned and strode off toward her squadron.

Gesturing deeper into the forest, Lucia glanced back toward me. Her voice was a low murmur, "Your mother was the kindest, loveliest woman in all Suomelin. And she loved you dearly."

My heart slammed against my ribs. The pounding was all I could hear, deafening.

She knows ...

"Yes, I know who you really are."

Fuck.

My hand shifted to the hilt of the dagger Tara had given me. I didn't want to kill Seren's mother. Seren would never forgive me.

But my secrets were unraveling, slipping free like a loose thread. Seren had figured out I didn't have a Bloodbinding mark. And now her mother ...

"How long have you known?" I rasped.

"Since the moment I saw that scar you carry on your back, just above your left hip. When I was treating your lashes." Her eyes gave nothing away. She started forward again and I followed, helpless to do anything else, her answer only provoking more questions.

"How do you know about that scar?"

"I put it there, when you were an infant. Your mother came to me in a moment of panic and desperation, and I masked a birthmark with a rune, so that it would never be discovered."

What in Solric's name?

"Why?" I demanded. "What birthmark?"

"There's a great deal we must discuss. The farther we are from others, the safer you will be."

I clamped my mouth shut, despite my burning curiosity, following her into denser woods.

She didn't take a path and I stepped through brush, thorns snagging my clothes while she simply parted them with effortless gesture spells. I missed those days—when magic had been at my fingertips.

Adjusting to life without the powers I'd been born with had been hell.

I'd spent the first few months in Pendara hating my father. Imagining the day I'd return, not to win his approval, but to prove I no longer wanted it. That his exile had cured me of any desire to be what he expected.

But had I been fooling myself?

Now that he was gone, robbed from me forever, something raw and hollow gaped inside my chest.

"The only one of my sons in whom I can find nothing to be proud."

Some of his last words to me.

He had died still believing the worst of me.

Lucia and I reached an enormous fallen tree, its hollowed, moss-covered trunk large enough for us to both stand inside. What had seemed like aimless wandering now revealed itself as deliberate—the small altar and tools within the hollow told me differently.

This was her altar. A natural, woodland sanctuary for a priestess without a temple.

Lucia slowed as she approached the altar and pushed back her hood. "No one has followed us, right?"

I furrowed my brow. "Am I supposed to—"

"You can smell them. Hear them." With a quick turn, a knife flew from her grasp, straight toward my chest.

I knocked it away with ease, the clang of steel on wood echoing around us, then stared at her, wide-eyed. "What the *fuck*?"

She didn't smile as she retrieved the knife. "You have new skills. Powers granted by the oath. But they aren't from Seren. She's more powerful as a sorceress than a fighter, but she always wanted to be like her father."

I didn't move, still staring at her, unblinking.

She unpinned her hair, letting it fall over her shoulders. She looked every inch the legendary Ibarran priestess I'd heard about. "You owe some powers to the blood of another present when Seren took that oath."

What the fuck is she saying?

"I'm not following."

Lucia produced a leather pouch and withdrew a gleaming amulet with a long chain, then came closer to me. Too close. I flinched as she raised her arms, slipping the chain over my head, before fastening the remainder of the chain around her own, facing me.

Her finger lifted to my temples.

The world around me shattered.

I lay on the ground, dying. A faint, ice-blue light shimmered around me.

Seren hovered over me, cutting a rune into her wrist.

Dark blood oozed as she pulled a cloth away from my neck and pressed her bleeding wrist to the open wound there—a wound slick with the vuk's black blood.

"I take the Blood Oath of Bryndis," she said. "May my soul be bound to his. I offer him my blade and my protection. I bind myself to his fate. I will not raise my hand to strike him, and my blood is his. Let the blood of this oath join our souls forever and let us never be separated, as Bryndis is bound to Varik."

The vision faded as Lucia pulled away, the hollow strangely, eerily quiet.

"How the fuck did you do that?" I gaped at her, astonished by her power.

"This amulet allowed it. You saw my memory. And you allowed me in. You don't know how to block me yet."

Her memory? That explained why I'd seen it from the outside, watching my own body, covered in black blood—

Oh fuck.

I gave Lucia a hard look, understanding dawning. The healing. The insatiable hunger. The restless energy.

"The vuk," I said at last.

"Seren was careless." Lucia's mouth drew to a thin line.

"Let the blood of this oath join our souls forever."

The blood of the oath. Mine. Seren's.

... and the vuk's. All over me.

A staggered step back was all I managed, my mind reeling. I

yanked the chain from my head. The vuk's blood had bound itself to my soul?

"What about her?" I scanned Lucia's face.

"No. The blood of the slain vuk was inside you, not her. She's not bound to it." She left the amulet on and returned to the altar.

I tried to breathe, but my chest had drawn tight. All this time, I'd though my hair had darkened because of Seren ... but had it been the vuk? "What does it mean? What did the vuk's blood do?"

She studied me. "You have been gifted with its extraordinary powers, on top of the ones you already possessed. I do not know the full extent, but there is no doubt you will discover new abilities for some time."

She lit a candle with another gesture spell. "Why were you in the forest?"

I hesitated. Something in her powers unsettled me—a chilling, formidable presence. Seren *had* inherited her power— enough to perform that oath—but in Ederyn, Lucia had been infamous.

But before I could answer, she set her palm on my forehead.

A dark shadow crept into my mind, intruding without mercy. A sea of memories filtered through ... *my father Sealing me ... sparring with Dalric in the Rookery ... taking comfort in a woman's arms in the Regulation barracks ... laughing with Thorne during training ... the prick of a whistler quill as Dalric was dragged into the forest ...*

No. I wrenched myself free and shoved her away. She stumbled, hitting the altar, but a satisfied gleam shone in her eyes. "Good. You sensed me that time, didn't you?"

The thought of every memory and emotion laid bare for

her perusal made my stomach churn, a sick feeling ripping through me.

"Outraged?" She jutted her chin. "You should be. The ability to read minds is dangerous. The Bloodbinding was meant to control such things—limit them to a select few. It's also why the Oath of Bryndis should never be made without complete trust. If you don't learn to control the bond, you'll have unlimited access to each other's minds. Even for those deeply in love, that's a terrifying prospect. Imagine never being able to hide jealousy, criticism, frustrations—or momentary, misplaced lust."

My voice came out raw. "You saw—"

"I saw what I wanted to see." Lucia drew a sharp breath. "It appears you've been on quite a journey—"

"Don't. You don't get to talk about what you saw. Those were my thoughts. *My memories.*"

Sorrow crossed her features. "Yes, they are. And it is a violation to have them viewed by another. That's why you must learn to block it. We don't have much time. It will be important for the trial, but we both know what you hide in your mind is a greater threat than that. There may be others in Emberstone who can read minds. And your identity is dangerous to Seren. She can never know the truth while you remain in the territory."

"Then I can learn to block you?" I narrowed my eyes at her.

"You can learn to make your mind a steel trap, impenetrable to anyone."

"Why would you help me?" I stepped toward her, using the significant height difference between us to my advantage. "Why do you care if I'm caught or not? Your people are my enemy. Your husband is my enemy. You know who I am."

She blinked slowly, expression solemn. "Your mother was my friend. In exchange for her help in fleeing Lirien, I swore an oath to safeguard your life. And even if that didn't matter to me, your life is tied to my daughter's. There is nothing I won't do for my children, Your Grace. That alone should be reason enough for me to want your survival."

Everything I'd ever heard of Brogan Ragnall told me differently. He'd murdered my mother in cold blood *then* fled—or so I'd been told.

But like every situation I'd found myself in since stepping into this godsdamned forest, I didn't have a choice. Lucia knowing my identity was a threat. Trusting her might be foolish but not trusting her could mean my death. *Or worse.*

"What about Seren?" I asked. "Doesn't she need to know these things too?"

"Yes, but Seth has made it impossible for me to work with her by calling the squadrons to training. For now, I need to work with you, before he makes that impossible too."

I considered her words.

Lucia might be the most dangerous person here.

But right now, she was offering me an olive branch. More than that. *Help.* Outside of Thorne and Seren, my allies here were thin.

I grunted, still unsettled by the option. "Fine. But this doesn't mean I trust you."

She gave me an enigmatic smile, stepping closer to me. "If you're wise, you won't trust anyone in the forest. Including Seren." Then her palm pressed to my forehead and a sea of black flooded my vision again.

CHAPTER 21
SEREN

The scent of woodsmoke drifted through the air as I slid onto the fur-covered floor of the watchtower, stretching my aching feet. The Vangar officers pretended watchtower duty was a noble responsibility—*the first line of defense for our tribe*—but I knew better. Even Amahle and Ciaran had admitted it when they'd become officers: no one wanted this job. It was pawned off on candidates and pledges.

I only had a few months left as a pledge.

If I make it that long.

I nudged my pack with the toe of my boot, anxiety coiling at the thought of the unread books in there. By now it was too dark to read and all I wanted to do was sleep, even though I was sure my racing mind would prevent that, too.

"Pledge Ragnall." Darya's voice cut through the dark quiet.

I shot to my feet, heat creeping onto my face. Being caught sitting wouldn't do me any favors. Looking over the watchtower's edge, I spotted her below, standing beside another pledge from our squadron. And Ciaran.

"Break time." Darya smiled. "Lieutenant Macklyn brought you food."

Thank the gods for Ciaran. I could hug him.

Grabbing my pack, I swung my leg over the edge and descended the rope quickly. "How long do I have?" I asked as I landed beside them.

"You're off shift," she answered. "But stay with the squadron tonight—no conjugal visits. We're being cautious because of Giulia Bernardi's death. We still haven't found her body and there may be a bear stalking the tribe. Don't wander."

Calling the squadrons to the training fields, ordering us to sleep in our squadrons ... seemed excessive. *Unless they suspected something worse than a bear.*

I kept my thoughts to myself and followed Ciaran away from the watchtower, eager to sit, take my boots off, and eat.

"How are you? Did you train today?" he asked.

Concern edged his words. My friends didn't have to say what they were thinking—none of them believed I'd survive the Skorn. "No. Watchtower duty all day. Maybe I'll get a chance to read by a fire before sleeping. Hopefully Rykr fared better."

We reached the edge of a brook, where the grass thinned, a tangle of brush and matted leaves scenting the mud with sweet, earthen decay. Dropping down, I pressed my hands over my face, willing the tension away. "Thanks for coming. I'm starving."

Ciaran sat beside me and pulled a bundle from his satchel—smoked fish wrapped in paper and a small loaf of bread. "My mother packed it for you." He handed me a waterskin.

I took a grateful sip as he snapped a blade of grass between his fingers. "I don't understand why Darya didn't give you time to train. Why put you in a godsdamned watchtower before you have to fight the Skorn?"

It was a good question, one I had pondered too. *Seth's decree?*

"And you should know. People are talking about Rykr."

I frowned. "What about him?"

"They're questioning how he's walking around without a single scratch after that flogging. Whispering about dark magic."

"He has a self-healing ability." I peeled the skin back from one side of the fish. "Rare, yes, but not dark magic."

"Healing is Zhi magic. Pendarans don't have it."

My fingertips faltered.

Dammit, he's right. I set the fish down, trying to think. I'd always considered myself clever, but lately, I was missing things. Sluggish. Too close to the situation to see what was obvious.

"Are you worried about dark magic, too? Or is this just because you don't trust him?"

"I'm worried because he's *Lirien*, Seren." Ciaran tossed a stone into the brook with a splash. "He won't change because of your oath, or what you've done for him. He's just biding his time, waiting for the right opportunity to strike or to flee. You'd make a huge mistake to trust him."

I curled my arms around my knees, resting my chin against them. How many times had Ciaran and I sat like this? As children, we'd spent hours playing in streams, diverting them with rocks to float boats we'd created from reeds.

Then, when we were older, we'd take turns keeping watch while the other bathed after brutal days of training for the Vangar. Binding each other's blistered hands and feet.

Ciaran knew me better than anyone—besides Amahle. I trusted his opinion implicitly.

But his prejudice blinded him. *Jealousy, too.*

As though to confirm my thoughts—which thankfully he couldn't hear—Ciaran lifted a hand, settling it at the base of my neck. He rubbed gently, kneading the tension from my shoulders.

Touch was natural for us. I'd never worried about cuddling with him or enjoying his massages. He was like another brother to me. Although, given Madoc spent more time with Tara than me, he was closer than a brother.

But I wasn't sure if Ciaran saw me the same way anymore. And now Rykr had driven a wedge between us.

"This is all my fault." Breath snagged in my throat. "I never should have brought him back. I should have tried to heal him alone, in the forest, then we could have gone our separate ways. Maybe I would have broken the law, but I wouldn't be under all this scrutiny. My honesty counted for nothing."

The weight of his gaze was on my face, but I couldn't meet his eyes. "Seren, you ... you take too much responsibility for things on your shoulders. Things that aren't your fault. You deserve to be happy. With someone who loves you and treats you well."

I bit my lip. Ciaran wanted that someone to be him, though. *And he loves me.* We told each other everything—our fears our dreams. The deepest things in our hearts.

But despite his hopes, I would never be happy with him. Not the way he wanted. I loved Ciaran, but something about him—his hesitation, his need for certainty, the way his bravery came with a safety net—kept him from ever being the man I'd choose. I wanted someone reckless. Someone *fearless.*

A man who'd dive off a cliff after me without hesitation, even if he had to figure out how to fly on the way down.

His fingers pressed deeper into tight muscles of my neck, and goosebumps rose on my forearms.

I pasted a smile to my lips, turning toward him so that he was forced to drop his hand. I reached for the food once again. "I'm fine, Ciaran. You don't have to worry about me."

His brows drew together. "That's not true, and you know it. You're not fine. And even if you were, I'd still worry about you."

A heavy feeling pressed in on my chest. I didn't want him to say things that couldn't be unsaid. Cross lines we couldn't come back from. "Ci—"

"No. Listen to me." Ciaran's warm hand rested on my shoulder. "I don't care what anyone else in our tribe thinks—I know your marriage to Westhaven is just a sham. A sham because you're a good person and you didn't want him to be killed. And it worries me because you're in danger because of him."

My pulse beat in my throat, heat pooling in my cheeks. Despite my better judgment, I met Ciaran's gaze. "You don't have to protect me from Rykr. He'd never hurt me. If only because he'd end up hurt in return."

"There are plenty of ways he could hurt you without killing you and you know it." Ciaran lifted his hands to my face, cupping my jaw, his thumbs brushing lightly along my cheekbones. "I love you, Ser. I think you know that. And the only thing keeping that tarse alive is that I don't want something to happen to you."

I searched his gaze, my stomach tightening. Ciaran had never been quite this bold. But maybe Rykr's presence had pushed him to say what he hadn't dared to before.

Before he could take it any further, I leaned in and pressed a gentle, platonic kiss to his cheek. "I know you do." I tried to move gracefully out of his grasp, not wanting to yank away like a startled deer, but he caught my hand.

A forlorn expression fogged his eyes. "I don't think you understand—"

"Don't." My fingers tightened against his. "Don't say things you can't take back. Rykr may be a Lirien, but I ..." *I care about him.*

There.

I'd admitted it. To myself, at least, even if I couldn't say it aloud yet. Especially not to Ciaran.

His face flushed. "I don't think Westhaven is doing you any good. You seem ... *different* since you took that oath. He's not a good influence on you."

I rolled my eyes and tore my hands away. Covering the food he'd brought, I stored it in my pack, my appetite vanishing. "I've known him for a handful of days and now he's changing me? Maybe you're just blinded by your prejudice. I appreciate you wanting me to be happy, but you have every reason not to like him. Admit it."

His throat bobbed. "I'll admit it. I don't like him. But who is he, anyway? I understand why you made that oath, but that doesn't have to mean I like what happened. Or that he's here. I'll stand by you, Seren, but Seth wasn't wrong to question what you did. It was dangerous, and it broke our laws."

His words hit me hard. Ugly, untamed anger flared through me. "So now Seth is the good guy? I deserved twenty lashes, then?"

"No, no. You know I hate what he did. But Seth being a hagspawn doesn't mean he doesn't have the best interest of the Viori at heart—especially where Liriens are concerned."

I stood, brushing off the leaves from my backside. "I'm done discussing this, Ciaran. Maybe my decision was extreme, *fine.* But now Seth is right about Rykr and I'm not? That's not loyalty and you fucking know it." I whirled on my heels to go.

"Seren, that's not what I mea—"

I threw him a withering glare. "It doesn't matter. It's what you said. And I'm pretty damn sick of men telling me they know better about everything where I'm concerned."

Ciaran scowled, scrambling to his feet awkwardly. "I never really thought I had a chance with you, Seren. Not really. And I know that you're ... *his*, now. But all I'm asking is that if that's how things are going to be, you be careful."

I covered my face with my palm. "First, I'm not his. I don't belong to anyone, let alone Rykr."

I can't be at war with my friends. Not right now. Not with everything else I have going on.

Lowering my hand, I stepped back toward him, leaves crunching under my soaked feet. He was so much bigger than me—always had that quiet strength—and the sadness in his face broke my heart. Even in the moonlight, the pain in his eyes was plain. "But I want you to tell me anything. Especially if you think I'm being foolish. I care about what you think, Ciaran. More than anyone."

A faint glimmer of hope lit his expression, and I bit the inside of my lip. *Curpiss.* I shouldn't have said it like that. But the damage was done, and I didn't have the heart to take it back.

"If he hurts you—"

"He won't. He saved me from the vuk. Not because he knew me, but because he has integrity. And then again last night, when I was—"

I paused, searching his eyes. We'd agreed with Tara that telling anyone about the skinwraith attack could be dangerous. *But I can trust Ciaran.*

Ciaran raised a brow. "Last night?"

At last, I whispered, "Giulia Bernardi ... she wasn't just murdered."

His red-gold brows furrowed. "What do you mean?"

"After the festival, on the way home, I heard something, so I went searching and found a human heart. On a tree stump. Then I saw Giulia." My body gave an involuntary shudder. "She'd been turned into a skinwraith and attacked me. Rykr heard me scream and came to my aid. We destroyed the skinwraith."

"What?" Ciaran's body went rigid. He ducked his chin at me in disbelief. "A skinwraith? What did Seth say? Why haven't the scouts been informed? There are teams searching for her body."

All valid questions. I bounced with discomfort. "The thing is, only Rykr and I saw the skinwraith. And considering how much controversy we've brought to—"

"No." Ciaran retreated a step. "You're telling me that one of our own was killed and turned into a *skinwraith* and you told no one?" His eyes flashed with anger. "Giulia's mother deserves to know what happened to her daughter."

I didn't blame him for his anger. He was right. "I told Tara. My mother, too."

"Then they're just as guilty as you are." Ciaran's fingers hooked into claws as he paced. "Don't you realize how serious this is? A skinwraith on our territory means everyone we know and love is at risk. We have to tell Seth and the council—alert the Vangar. It's our duty."

My energy seemed to drain. "Please, Ciaran." I stepped closer to him, settling my hand on his arm. "I can't take any more scrutiny. Neither can Rykr. I *know* it's bad, but what else can I do? Everyone would question Rykr, you know it. If I say anything, if they know I was involved ... gods, I'm already heading toward the Skorn. For now, we have to wait—"

"Until what? More people die?"

"I don't know what else to do, Ciaran! Tara thought—"

"I don't give a damn what Tara thought. You're better than

she is. You used to be better than this." His eyes glared with betrayal. "You're just protecting Rykr. Why do you care so much about that swiver?"

I flinched.

"You're making him a priority over everyone you claim you love ... above the honor that used to matter to you before him."

His words gutted me.

Gods, he's right.

I shouldn't have told him about the skinwraith.

"No. You shouldn't have." Rykr's voice cut through my mind, crisp and knowing. I whirled around to find him several feet away, leaning against a tree trunk. He lanced me with his blue-green eyes.

Fuck.

I drew a deep breath, then lifted my gaze to Ciaran. He'd already spotted Rykr and his entire body tensed, his anger barely restrained.

Rykr pushed off the tree, sauntering toward us, despite the irons. "Thank you for being here, Ciaran," he said with deliberate, infuriating calm. "I was worried she might not have someone to wait on her out here, but clearly I had nothing to worry about." He leaned down and grazed a kiss against my cheek. "Hello, wife."

My heart stumbled.

Ciaran's fists clenched, but he forced himself to step back. "Goodnight, Seren," he ground out, then stalked away.

Rykr hooked his thumb into the waistband of my dagger sheath at my hip, tugging me closer. I stiffened, but didn't pull away. "How long were you there?" I asked, fully aware of the war going on inside me.

My loyalty was to Ciaran. He was right. I shouldn't conceal the truth about the skinwraith. He was my friend.

And yet ...

Rykr felt like a piece of me.

Mine.

"Long enough to hear him confess his love for you," Rykr murmured, his gaze never leaving mine. "And watch him put his hands all over you."

Heat flared over my skin, but I met his stare head-on. "What's it to you, Rykr? Or are you suddenly pretending this thing between us gives you the right to give a fuck who touches me and where?" I tilted my chin.

For a moment, his eyes flicked to my lips. The corners of his mouth curved. "Such a dirty mouth on a pretty face." He leaned in closer, his breath warm against the skin of my jawline, and my pulse hammered in my throat. "Makes me want to see what else that tongue of yours can do."

Fire surged through me, liquid heat pooling in my core. My thighs clenched before I jerked away, glaring. "What are you doing here anyway? You had your fun on the horse ride this morning. Leave me alone."

He barked a short, humorless laugh. "What am I doing here? I'm here, thistling, because you dragged me here, remember? And now we're facing a trial in a few days, so I thought I'd come by, see if you were done wasting time sitting in watchtowers, and actually wanted to train for it. But clearly you had the company you really wanted, so I apologize for intruding."

I raised a skeptical brow. "You came to train me?"

"Hard to believe I might want to keep you alive? Yeah, I know. I'm not sure what I was thinking." He smirked.

The last thing I wanted to do was train.

I wanted a bedroll. Food. A bath. A sleeping draft to help me forget the hideous, monstrous face of a skinwraith and to numb the ache still radiating from my ribs. A way to warn the tribe about the attack without condemning myself—or putting more lives at risk.

But I had none of that right now.

What I had was a Sealed Pendaran—irritated or not—standing in front of me, offering to train me for a deadly trial. *Dammit.*

I deepened my glare. "Fine." I started back toward the brook. "Come with me."

"Your gratefulness is oozing from your skin."

"What can I say? I'm learning lots from you already, Rykr."

CHAPTER 22

SEREN

Every inch of my body hurt from the last three nights of training with Rykr. I shifted in my bedroll, my eyes closed, trying to remember what had torn me from sleep just now.

Sleep beckoned. Then the squadron member who'd been sleeping closest to me shook me. "Roll call."

I groaned, blinking, and sat slowly. Sleeping in a sack had done nothing for my healing ribs, but I was cold, too. Exhausted and sore. Rykr's training had been brutal.

The swiver.

Since we'd arrived at the training field, each day had been the same—watchtower duty with my squadron all day, stealing whatever snatches of time I could to read about the Skorn, then sneaking as far as I dared at night to train with Rykr until I begged for sleep.

Strictly speaking, I wasn't breaking any rules—Darya had said no conjugal visits and these sessions with Rykr had been anything *but.*

The close proximity had been a challenge, though.

His hands had been all over me—not the gentle touch of a lover—but the fierce and practiced ease of a warrior who knew every way possible to dismantle his enemy. Unfortunately for me, that hadn't done a damn thing to quell my attraction to him. If anything, it had only sharpened it.

On the other hand, I'd never had anyone like him instruct me before—not even my father. *Had he been holding back?* Maybe he hadn't wanted to see his daughter become lethal. Or maybe Rykr was just better. More skilled. More ruthless.

I'd learned more in these last few nights with Rykr—while he was still in irons—than I had in months of training with my squadron.

"Seren?" Darya interrupted my thoughts. I jerked my chin up, realizing too late I'd missed her taking roll.

"Present," I muttered, raising a weary hand.

A thin layer of snow had blanketed the forest floor overnight and the side of my face that had been exposed to the air felt like ice. With a dry mouth, I started getting ready for the day as Darya continued addressing our group of twenty-five Vangar.

Hopefully Rykr had fared better than I had in the cold.

I missed him.

The thought unsettled me, but it was true. His voice felt quieter in my mind. He'd told me my mother was training him —helping him control the bond, how to block me out. I was jealous, but stuck here, there wasn't much I could do. And if I knew my mother, helping Rykr was as much for her benefit as his. With still no news from Father, Madoc, or Esme, she needed something to occupy her mind.

We all did.

"Today we'll be joining the other squadrons for a sparring championship," Darya announced. "I expect all of you to participate in challenging the current champions in the sparring rings, who have been fighting since early morning." She directed a look at me. "No exceptions."

Apprehension wove through the squadron. We'd been on watchtower duty for three days—most of us weren't warmed up, let alone prepared to fight.

I shouldered my heavy pack, eyes burning from exhaustion.

The scent of chestnuts roasting over firepits drifted through the training field, mingling with the crisp bite of morning air. I rolled my shoulders, trying to unwind some of the tension. *This training exercise doesn't make sense.* Seth had blamed it on Giulia's death, but other than hearing whispers and speculation from my squadron mates, the officers had said nothing else about how the training was connected to that.

I bought a cup of morning wine from an enterprising member of our tribe who'd come up to the training field and headed toward the sparring rings. Better to get Darya's orders over with sooner rather than later.

The areas around the sparring rings were packed. Unusually so. A dense crowd had gathered around one in particular, energy thrumming with excitement. I frowned, leaving my squadron and moving through the crowd to reach the ring master and sign my name.

A roar of cheers erupted just as I broke through the crowd. A half-naked man had pinned some poor fool to the center of the mat.

Not just any half-naked man.

Rykr.

I froze.

He stood in the center of the ring, the champion of the match and free of his irons. Sweat gleamed over his bare chest. A cut marked his temple, there was another on his forearm—seemed that someone had gotten close enough to nick him, but not enough to slow him down. He looked ... relaxed.

The ring master, Jabari Bankole, lifted Rykr's hand in triumph. Another wave of cheers. Rykr's gaze found mine.

As though he sensed me.

The moment our eyes met, the corner of his split lip curled in a smile. My heart lurched and I tore my gaze away.

What the fuck is he doing here?

As another man from our tribe climbed into the ring for the next match, I spotted Tara, who sat with Amahle at the ringside, laughing.

Tara saw me and waved me over. I swallowed back a gulp of wine and pushed through the crowd, nearly spilling my drink as I walked.

"Are you off watchtower duty at last?" Tara asked when I reached her. She scooted over to make room.

I nodded, still thrown by what I'd just seen, then gestured toward Rykr. "What is he doing here?"

"We've been here since three in the morning. I brought my squadron over to get an early start on the sparring. Five hours later and ... here we are." Tara rolled her eyes.

That she had tolerated him this long boded well. Maybe he wasn't as obnoxious with her as he was with me.

"He's won matches for five straight hours?" I gawked at Rykr. He was barely breathing hard.

That also meant that he hadn't slept. *At all.* He'd left me well after midnight.

"He had a couple of breaks, but yes, basically." Amahle leaned forward with an amused shake of her head. "I'd say a few people have gotten their money's worth already this morning. The bets started early."

My gods, why does he have to be so good at everything? I

knew he was skilled after the nights of training—but this? Five hours straight?

What else can he do for five hours?

The heated thought curled through me unbidden, and I prayed he was too busy fighting to have heard it.

"You know how to pick them," Amahle said as the next match began. Her brown eyes glittered in the early morning sunlight. "He's ... impressive. I've heard more than one woman cursing your name this morning."

Just what I need. "They can have him." I avoided looking into the ring. "They won't be able to fit in a tent with him and his ego."

"You should be careful," Tara said in a low voice. "The way some people have been watching him makes *me* want to claw their eyes out."

The idea bothered me more than I cared to admit.

"Madoc is going to be so mad when he realizes he missed this." Amahle smirked. "Not just the sparring championship, but the chance to kick the ass of the man who's sharing a bed with his little sister."

I held my breath, waiting for Tara's reaction. For a second, her gaze clouded, then she blinked brightly at Amahle. "Yeah, he'll be pissed." She threw back a mouthful of mead, her smile tense.

Maybe *that's* how Tara was burying her pain over Madoc's continued absence.

Tara reached toward me, lifting a golden strand of hair in my ponytail. "Your hair looks so pretty with all that new gold in it."

I clenched my jaw. The outward sign of the bond between Rykr and me was so ... profound. Like we belonged to each other.

Except we didn't. And never would.

"I don't like it," I rasped, shifting my legs in front of me. I sipped my wine, thinking about the way he'd acted around Ciaran—who had been avoiding me ever since. "And it's just one more reason for him to act like he owns me when he doesn't."

"Personally, I'd love to trounce his pride, but you're married to him. You're allowed to touch him. Even sleep with him," Tara said. "You should get in there and fight him. It'd be good for you."

"Darya ordered my squadron into the sparring rings this morning, so it seems like I have no choice."

"You're going to fight Rykr?" Amahle's expression turned dubious.

"I may as well. He won't let me forget it if I don't." *And hopefully I've gained some skills from the past few nights. Right?*

Who was I kidding? He knew all my weaknesses. He anticipated my every move. And now, anything I tried would be things he'd taught me. I could only hope he'd show some compassion.

I eyed the ring master as the man sparring with Rykr went flying against the ropes, then fell to the ground with a slump, unconscious.

Wonderful. I'd bonded myself to a weapon.

A Lirien weapon. I cut my eyes at Rykr as he wiped his forehead with the back of his wrist.

A Lirien weapon who didn't have a Bloodbinding mark.

What had Rykr said?

"Sometimes we can't see what's right in front of us, Seren."

The only Liriens who didn't have Bloodbinding marks were Ederyn.

His hair had once been golden, and the Ederyn were known for it.

Of all the realms, the Ederyns were the ones most universally hated and admired. Their exemption from the Blood-binding made every other realm resent them. But they were also free.

Rykr being Ederyn made every single bit of sense—down to his arrogant swagger.

But why was he Sealed with the Pendaran symbol?

Clapping interrupted my thoughts and Jabari lifted Rykr's hand in victory again. I sighed and stood as Tara watched me closely. "May as well get it over with."

I was growing impatient at the thought of having to watch several more fights if Rykr was going to keep winning like this.

I handed Tara my wine then slipped into the ring and took out my sword.

Jabari gave me a steely-eyed look. "You're not on the list, Seren."

"You going to stop me from challenging my husband?" I quirked a brow at him.

Jabari grinned, then stepped back, gesturing toward Rykr. "As you wish. I'm assuming you'd like to challenge the champion with weapons?" He looked back at Rykr.

The challenger of every round could decide what type of fight they wanted. Most challengers played to their strengths.

Rykr's face was expressionless as he took me in. *"You sure you're ready for this?"*

I gritted my teeth. The sound of him filled my body with heat. *"Get out of my mind, Rykr."*

"No swords," I snapped. He'd be more likely to overpower me that way. "But he can use anything else he wants. Or we can start without them."

Leaving the sword at the edge of the ring, I checked the weapons at the mouth of the ring, just outside the ropes. At any point in the match, I could grab one—if I could make it over there in time.

Jabari offered him a dagger and Rykr shook his head. "I don't need it."

Jabari crowed, smirking at me.

"You son of a bitch."

Rykr smirked at me as we squared off. "Now who's the noisy one? I thought you were *working*."

"We were ordered to the sparring rings today."

"And you came to visit me? I'm touched." His eyes glinted. "You could have chosen another champion."

The crowd around the ring had grown more silent, leaning forward with interest. Men and women were treated as equals in battle here, but Rykr had won so many matches that I doubted anyone would hedge their bets on me.

I ignored his tease. "You're doing a good job displaying your skills to the tribe." My gaze fixed on the pulse of the vein near his throat and the jagged rune there. "They're going to see you as even more dangerous and watch you more closely."

He shrugged. "I'm not particularly worried." He gave me a sharp look. "I'm not planning on taking it easy on you. I don't enjoy losing."

"I'm shocked," I said dryly. My exhaustion wouldn't help anything, but I didn't tell him that. He'd just think I was making preemptive excuses.

But he had to be tired, too.

I assumed the starting position, waiting for him to take his place.

The starting bell rang. Considering how easily he'd handled his last opponent, I'd have to be quick on my feet. To win, I'd have to be the first to make three strikes that counted as fatal moves to my opponent—I'd be lucky if I could get one before Rykr did. My best bet were daggers and spears, but I might do well without any weapons at all, too.

We circled each other, our eyes locked. "Did you miss me?" A cocky grin hooked up on one side of his lips.

Gods, he had a way of making me want to punch *and* kiss him at the same time.

My head tilted to the side as I considered a response, a spark of rebelliousness rising through me. "About as much as a hen misses a fox."

"I'm assuming I'm the fox in this scenario?" His eyes glinted.

I launched forward, moving with speed as I jabbed him on his wounded forearm. He blocked my next jab—to his solar plexus—then attempted to catch my wrist as I spun a swift kick to his side.

Surprise lit his eyes and he lunged back, out of my reach.

"No, you're the bastard who's standing between me and breakfast. Stop talking and just fight me. I'm here to spar, not to talk."

"Sounds like you're not planning on winning." One dark brow rose slightly. "My favorite part of sparring with a beautiful woman is when she's *not* quiet. Don't forget, Seren, this time we're playing without chains."

Son of a bitch.

I didn't dignify the taunt with a response, leaping at him with a flurry of precise strikes. He blocked about half of them, but each time my fist or the ball of my foot connected with him, served as a reminder of what I was up against: no softness here—punching Rykr was like taking my fists to a tree.

The pain fueled me, sharpening my focus.

"Why aren't you feeling my pain anymore?" I asked as we circled each other.

"It was the first thing your mother taught me to block."

"But we can still mind speak."

"Different parts of the bond." He tilted his head. *"Is this your attempt to distract me?"*

I gave him a pretty smile. *"If I was trying to distract you, I'd do this."* I sent the raciest, sexual image I could muster down the bond. Then I delivered a hard, fast roundhouse kick to his shoulder, using the momentum to seize his wrist as he stepped back.

My fists wouldn't win against him—I knew that much—so I shifted my approach. Twisting his wrist, I wrenched his arm backward, forcing his body forward, between his legs. I knocked his knee forward with my own and grabbed his ankle with my other hand, dragging his calf up and forcing him onto one knee.

As he caught himself, I used one fluid movement to pull a dagger from the sheath at my side and tip it to the back of his neck.

His shoulders heaved with quick breaths, and I leaned over him, my lips at his ear. "Guess I win this first round."

Rykr turned his profile to me. "Not bad, solwyn. The image was a nice touch." His hand slid up my wrist, grasping my forearm close to the elbow. "But not good enough."

Before I could stop it, he'd flipped me over him onto the mat and I landed hard on my back. Dots spun in my vision and I rolled out of his reach, gasping for breath. As I stumbled to my feet, I rolled my shoulders, the sounds of the crowd sounding oddly distant. My eyes connected with Amahle's by the ringside. Worry lined her forehead.

I needed another win, and fast.

"Where's Ciaran? Too afraid to get his ass handed to him after the other night?"

I struggled for another breath. "I don't know how things work where you're from, Rykr, but hurting my friends will never gain you my respect or trust. If you were wise, you'd stop bringing it up. He's kept our secret, hasn't he?"

He laughed, an easy, careless sound. "Sadly, I can't say anyone has ever accused me of being wise."

"That's obvious." I twirled one of my daggers. I couldn't throw one and risk doing actual damage to him. Who knew how it might go for me if I actually hurt him?

I hesitated too long—Rykr lunged. I dodged, but not before he landed a blow to my side that sent me reeling. Pain exploded up my ribs and I spun, jabbing an elbow into his kidney as I whirled to face him again. He grunted, a flash of pain in his eyes telling me that he'd felt the blow he'd given me through the bond.

Taking advantage of that, I used my left hand to land a savage hook to his jaw, then slashed my dagger up, landing the blade right under his sternum.

A deep ache swelled from my own jaw. *Dammit.*

"I thought you were blocking the pain," I ground out.

"You changed the rules on how we use the bond." His eyes glimmered.

I'd won that round, though. A messy win, but a win, none-theless. If it'd been a real match, he would have been dead. Jabari called the second strike in my favor.

One more, and I'd end the match. "I thought you planned on trying to win." Sunlight glinted off the blade of my dagger.

"Maybe I was taking it easy on you to give myself a momentary break."

I gawked at him. That was impossible. I'd won fairly.

But had I?

We squared off again.

"You're overthinking your moves now, aren't you?"

I scowled and flicked my wrist, my dagger flying straight for his thigh. "Stop that."

He caught it by the flat side of the blade, flipping it smoothly into his grasp before sliding it into his belt. The casual display of skill sent a hot rush of frustration through me.

"And now you've lost a dagger." The cockiness in his voice was just as loud in my head. *"But if that impresses you, you should see how good I am at sheathing ... my favorite sword."*

My cheeks burned. "You're cheating."

"By distracting you?" His face darkened. "Didn't anyone ever teach you that in a life-and-death situation, there's no such thing as cheating?"

Blood rushed my face. *"Obnoxious bastard."*

He smiled, then closed the gap between us in two steps. I twisted, bending backward out of his reach, but he swept my legs out from under me. As I started to fall, one powerful arm shot under the small of my back, catching me before I could land.

"My lady." He'd said it loud enough that the crowd heard and roared with laughter.

I punched his jaw, getting a quick, cheap shot in while his hands were occupied. Some in the audience hooted in response, then I reached for the dagger he'd stolen.

Rykr swung me flat against the mat, knocking my breath away as he pinned me with the weight of his body. Grabbing my wrists, he held them above my head, his face inches above mine.

"I don't know whether to kiss you or disarm you thoroughly in front of your friends and make a statement," he gritted out, voice low and raw as his eyes burned into mine. "Then again ... one is much more enjoyable."

His mouth dropped close to mine. But instead of claiming my mouth, his breath warmed my cheek, his lips skimming my jaw, and he pressed a slow, deliberate kiss into the curve of my neck.

My body jolted in response, the yearning crashing through me with shocking force. The same longing that had gripped me in our tent flared back to life, stronger now. Relentless. His skin was damp with sweat, the raw, earthy scent of him invading my senses. Maybe it wasn't a kiss in the way I'd imagined—but that only made it worse. Somehow, this was more intimate, and I felt completely exposed to him.

His tongue flicked against my throat, and my pulse pounding went wild.

The audience was laughing now, and my heart was rioting with both outrage and need.

Outrage won. I head-butted him, ripping away from the caress and attempting to roll out from under him as he careened back.

He slammed his hips and legs down over mine, immobilizing me further with his massive strength. The sudden weight sent a wicked jolt through me, my body betraying me as I fought against him and the unwanted heat curled between my legs.

"You're not playing to your strengths." His grip on my wrists stayed firm, while his free hand slid over my torso, down to my thigh.

I barely had time to realize his intent before he yanked my second dagger from its sheath.

"You never should have let me get this close to begin with."

The blade pressed lightly against my throat, freezing me in place.

As if to drive his point home, he caught my earlobe between his lips, the same way I'd taunted him before. "Guess I'm catching up."

My indignation boiled.

"Get off me, you fucking bastard." The crowd around us was eating it up—leering, whispering. Enjoying the show a little too much.

He wasn't just trying to beat me—he was humiliating me.

"Block them out. They're not in the ring with you," his voice hissed in my mind.

He released me and then offered a hand to help me stand.

I ignored it. "Stop doing that, Rykr, I mean it." Then I wiped his kiss away from my neck with the palm of my hand. I could still feel him there, and my lips heated, desperate for more.

"Doing what? Talking to you or giving the audience a show? I thought you wanted a kiss." He gave a wicked grin. "Though maybe I missed where you had in mind. Should I have aimed lower?"

Nyxva.

I glared, then skirted around him, making a break for the cache of weapons on the side of the ring. My hands closed around a spear, and I whirled back toward him, keeping him several feet away.

"Good choice."

"Don't you dare, you condescending prick."

I had training. I'd won matches.

But never with someone who could rattle me this easily. Who got in my head, turned me inside out, and set fire to my thoughts.

I didn't need to block the crowd.

I needed to block *him.*

Circling him slowly, I calculated my move. Daggers had been a mistake. He was faster, stronger. Spears were better.

Lunging, I extended the spear, stepping into the strike. He dodged out of it. *"Don't make the mistake of assuming I won't grab that spear right out of your hands."*

I ignored his taunting, certain he was doing it to fluster me. I spun, leaping toward him with a finesse and speed that had served me well before in the past. The tip of my spear grazed his shoulder as he dodged out of the way again.

Then I flipped toward him. He retreated a step, and I swiped his legs, forcing him to jump over the spear.

His teasing vanished, his eyes never leaving me.

But he was still flawless.

I lunged again and he side-stepped, then charged. Swinging out, I drove the shaft of the spear into the side of his head. He caught the spear by the shaft, stopping it cold.

Shit.

Using my momentum, I flipped out of reach and let go. I landed on one knee, behind him.

"And now I have your spear." He turned toward me, slowly.

I rose, breath steadying.

Rykr gripped the shaft, eyes glinting. "Word to the wise. Don't hit your opponent in the side of the head with it. Stab them through the eyes with the pointy end and make it count." With an effortless motion, he snapped the spear clean over his knee. "But you did a better job blocking out the crowd."

He was right. I hadn't heard anything they'd been saying or their responses to my movements—until then.

The noise all crashed back in an instant, a cacophony to my ears.

He flew in the air toward me, stopping the tip of the broken spear just above my heart. *"Strike two."*

My eyes narrowed at him. "Godsdamn you, Rykr."

"Who says they haven't already?" His voice was dry and unamused.

I was ready to be done. He'd embarrassed me enough.

My defeat must have shown in my face, or he'd heard it.

"Don't give up now." His order was flat, without goading. *"It's going to be much worse than this in the trial."*

"It's already over." Exhaustion weighed down my throbbing limbs. I needed sleep.

Rykr came closer. "Fight me. You're one strike away from winning."

"What's the point, Rykr?"

"The point is that you don't stop fighting until it's over. You go down swinging." He tossed the spear away. *"Or we both die."*

I sighed. *"There's no winning with you."*

He frowned. Then he swung at me.

Instinct took over. I blocked him.

A sharp kick followed, which I dodged, followed by another punch.

The more he pressed, the less I thought. My body moved on its own, muscles responding in fluid, automatic precision. I fought him back like he knew I would. But I still wasn't on the offensive.

His hand caught my shirt and he hauled my back against his chest, his bleeding forearm snugly pushing back against my breasts. "Fight me," he growled in my ear.

"And what? Have you keep playing mind games?" I twisted slightly, glaring up at him.

"Don't you get it? Mind games *are* a strategy. A strong mind is your most valuable weapon."

A flash of silver hurtled in the air toward him.

A dagger. The sharp blade flying with precise aim right at his head. He had me too firmly in his grip to do anything, and I watched as time slowed as it drew closer.

Then Rykr's other free hand shot out, at lightning speed, and he caught the blade inches before it reached him.

My heart slammed into my ribs.

How had he caught that?

And who had thrown a dagger at him?

Rykr dropped the dagger, only the faintest of scratches on his fingertips, and a hush fell over the crowd.

Seth stepped into the ring. "This match is over. I challenge the champion."

CHAPTER 23
RYKR

My head still reeled at the fact that I'd only seen that dagger flying at me because of Seren. The blade had been seconds away from impaling itself on my face, but I'd seen it through her mind.

I shouldn't have been able to catch it. But somehow, I had.

And I knew who had thrown it.

Seren tensed in my arms, her back rigid as Seth stalked toward us, his black trousers without blemish, unlike my thoroughly stained and torn ones.

"Swords," Seth said, pulling my blade from his side.

I doubted Seth had used it before now and I didn't know if it would work for him—but I wasn't fool enough to find out the hard way. The sword had an ancient curse on it and using it always resulted in a lethal blow. *Always.*

If Seth used it against me, I was dead.

"No." I released Seren, shifting to put myself between them. "I'm not fighting you."

Seth appeared unimpressed at my words, then gestured to Jabari. "You don't get to decide."

The fuck I don't.

I set my lips to a line. He'd been waiting for this opportunity and I wasn't about to play into his hands. "No."

An ugly shadow came over Seth's expression. "You're in our territory, Lirien. You don't get to rewrite the rules of our games." He peeled off his shirt, revealing a body hardened by years of training—and Zhi tattoos that proved his deadliness.

A shiver of hatred rolled through me. The thought of his hands ever being on Seren ignited rage in my blood.

If I gave into that, I'd kill him where he stood.

Jabari came to my side and raised my hand, declaring my fight with Seren over. I barely registered the crowd's reaction.

She was already gone.

I'd been at it for hours, yet I wasn't tired. My body had moved with speed and power I'd never known before, and I'd barely tested its limits. I'd been holding back—especially with Seren.

The stark truth was that I barely felt as though I'd unleashed my power. Everything that Lucia had told me about the vuk's blood made sense now ... and it had given me a freedom and level of skill that even the Seal hadn't done.

But a match with that sword meant someone would die.

"I'm not fighting you," I told Seth once again.

Jabari approached me, worry lining his dark brown face. "A champion can't decline a fight," he announced to the crowd.

Boisterous cheers erupted but Jabari stepped to my side. "Before a fight, anyway," he added in a low voice only I could hear.

His meaning was clear. *I can forfeit* after *the fight had begun.* Unusual—at least in Pendara. Forfeiting at the beginning of a match was unheard of in the Regulation. Dishonorable.

I didn't give a shit about honor here, though. Not if my death was all but assured.

I made my way toward the center of the ring, circling Seth. Zhi maneuvers and fighting techniques were nothing like Pendaran. They were physical fighters, their ancient war making blazingly fast. My father had always said that if Pendara's army ever failed him, he'd turn to Zhi. Had Seth trained in those arts, alongside his Vangar skills?

Seth's mouth formed a straight, hard line. "It's not enough that you don't deserve her—is it? You feel the need to humiliate her in front of everyone she knows."

What?

He was trying to defend Seren?

As though he had the right.

It would be so easy to give in to the swell of malice clawing through me.

Which is what he wants.

The bell rang and I knelt immediately. "I forfeit," I declared.

Silence descended upon the crowd.

Jabari rushed to Seth's hand and lifted it. "The champion!"

The Vangar audience booed, hissing at me as I turned away.

Seth stalked toward me, cutting me off. "Fight me."

Godsdamn, you have no fucking idea how much I want to. I didn't want to lose to this fucking swiver. I certainly didn't want to be called a coward for forfeiting.

But had I learned anything in the last two years? Patience was a formidable skill as any weapon.

I shoved him back. "No."

"Coward." The tips of his teeth bared.

"Perhaps. But I don't trust you for a clean fight. That dagger stunt proves I'm right." I made sure the crowd heard me, then moved past him, hopping out of the sparring ring and shoving past the ropes.

Amahle grabbed me by the elbow. "Come with me. You won't have any friends around the ring right now."

She dragged me through the crowd as jeers and vulgar gestures followed in our wake. As though I hadn't been here for hours, growing their purses with bets. *Fucking Viori.*

We didn't slow until we were far from the sparring rings. Amahle plucked an apple core from her collar, where someone must have thrown it. "That was quite a stunt." She scanned my face. "Why didn't you fight him?"

I couldn't tell her about the sword. "I don't trust him. He had hours to study my fighting techniques and I'm unmistakably his enemy." *He's an unworthy opponent.*

"You should know that forfeiting a fight is considered a great insult among the Viori."

I smirked. "It's considered a great insult among the Pendarans, too."

"You're playing with fire, Rykr. Seth wants you dead. He'll punish you any chance he gets."

"Well, in this case he wanted to punish me for fighting Seren. Or at least that's what he implied."

Amahle gave me a curious look, tilting her head for me to walk with her. "I'm not in the habit of talking about my friends to anyone, but you should know ... Seren and Seth had an intense love affair. Secret. I was shocked when he ended it. One day, he was just ... different. And then Darya was his wife. But I've always suspected, deep down, he still has feelings for Seren."

Seth? "Are we talking about the same man who ordered her flogged with twenty lashes?"

"I know it sounds crazy. But I also think the flogging was more about you than her. I'm worried about her. We all are." She studied my profile. "Given how closely your life is tied to hers now, I think it would be in your interest to help her, rather than push her away."

"What do you think I was doing in that sparring ring? If I can't see where she's weak, I can't help her."

Amahle hesitated, her intelligent gaze alert as we headed into the darkness of the woods from the clearing. "The Skorn trial isn't a game. I know there's tension between the two of you, and that was painfully obvious in the ring. You want to help her, but you can't tear her down in the process. All I'm asking is that you be worthy of the sacrifice she made for you. She saw good in you worth saving. Help her—without an agenda. She's one of the best and bravest women I know, and since the moment she decided to honor her debt to you, she's done nothing but fight for you."

Shame trickled through me. I *had* been trying to help. But maybe that required a little less arrogance.

"Thank you for your honesty." The way the spark had gone out of Seren's eyes while we'd been fighting had worried me. She'd seemed so defeated—so flat. Ever since I'd interrupted her conversation with Ciaran, she carried the weight of more guilt on her chest. Guilt I'd made worse by straining her friendships.

What was worse, I didn't know how to handle what I felt each time I thought of Seren Ragnall. Raw, fiery lust was easy —that's why the taunting on the sparring ring floor hadn't bothered me, despite my better judgment.

But when I let myself feel? I saw the strength and bravery Amahle spoke of.

I was starting to care about this woman.

Someone I had every reason to hate. To distrust.

That was new, unchartered territory.

And it scared the curpiss out of me.

The blaring of horns cut through my thoughts. Amahle and

I both lifted our heads, sharply. I might not know much about the Viori, but even from where I came from, horns weren't a good sign. "What is it?"

"An attack in the encampment." Amahle's eyes glittered. "Come with me. Hurry."

We tore through the forest. I'd managed to slip out of the sparring ring free of irons. What I needed, though, was a fucking sword.

Chaos had overtaken the field where the sparring had been, as Vangar warriors rushed to extinguish fires, grab horses, and run.

"Rykr, where are you?" Seren's voice in my head cut through the noise.

"Near the sparring ring. You?" I scanned the field, but she was nowhere in sight.

"With Ciaran. Getting the horse. Stay there and I'll find you."

Tara spotted us and strode forward, her face set in grim determination. "You two, come with me," she ordered.

"What the fuck is going on?" Amahle asked her we fell into step with her.

"I'm going with your sister. I'll meet you at the encampment." Better to stay with people I knew wouldn't take the opportunity to stab me from behind for now.

Tara didn't answer but led us to a group of Vangar with horses, including Seth. "Get on a horse," she said, then paused beside me. Her eyes darted to mine and she lowered her voice. "That horn is only used for the severest level of attack, Rykr. Regulation soldiers. Stay with me. If it is Liriens, this won't go well for you."

A tangle of hope and worry gripped me as I swung into the saddle. What if this was Thorne's escape plan? He could have gone back to Cairn Hold, gathered reinforcements, and brought them here.

But if Seren encountered them before I could? Even Thorne didn't know the risk she posed to my life.

The group launched into a gallop, tearing toward the encampment. Tara kept to my side, Amahle behind me. Seth, too, stayed close—either escorting me or ensuring I wouldn't take advantage of the attack to flee.

The wind bit my skin as we rode, and the tension on my companions' faces was unmistakable. The sky darkened the closer we got, thick clouds billowing overhead, heralding an oncoming storm.

A sharp, rancid scent curled in my nostrils. I inhaled again and turned to Tara. "What's that smell?"

"What smell?" Tara frowned.

A prickle of warning swept down my spine. Our horses suddenly balked, whinnying and rearing—trying to turn back.

I leaped from the saddle as my horse bucked, narrowly missing a kick from Tara's mount.

Shouts rang through the group as the remaining riders fought to regain control. Those still in the saddle wheeled their horses around, bolting back the way we'd come. The rest of us—Amahle, Tara, Seth, and a Vangar man and woman I didn't know—had all been thrown or forced to jump.

Each of us scrambled from the forest floor, covered in leaves and dirt as we took stock of who remained.

Not a single bird chirped above us.

A different sort of fear slithered through me. A dark premonition brought about by an eerie, unnatural silence.

"Something's not right," I said, squinting toward the encampment, still too distant to see clearly.

No movement.

Amahle met my gaze. "I smell something rotten."

Fuck. What in Nyxva had happened here?

To his credit, rather than hesitating in the trees, Seth kept moving. He motioned to Tara. "Follow me."

"I need a sword, Seth." I followed him.

Seth gave me a wary look, then continued forward without offering one of the extra swords strapped to his back.

We followed Tara and Seth closer to the encampment, but no one emerged. A low rumble of thunder sounded, and the wind stirred, carrying with it the unmistakable stench of decay.

My stomach soured. Behind me, the Vangar man gagged. "What is that?" he asked.

"Death," Seth answered flatly. He exchanged yet another glance with me.

Did he somehow think *I* had something to do with this?

Movement up ahead drew us to a halt.

A herd of bulls blocked the path to the encampment, their heads low to the ground, as though grazing. But not a single blade of grass grew in the forest there, the ground was rock and dust and leaves.

"What the fuck?" Tara asked. Her eyes narrowed as she peered closer at the bulls.

They weren't chewing on grass, but bone.

"Those aren't bulls." The foul scent was stronger now. More familiar. I'd smelled it the other night, when Seren and I had been attacked.

One of them lifted its head.

Cold, dead eyes—human ones—stared at us. Flesh, rotting, hung from the skulls visible below their faces.

"Skinwraiths," I said in a low voice.

The rest of the herd lifted their heads in unison.

"Skinwraiths?" Amahle asked, incredulous.

"They've shapeshifted," Seth said, readying his sword.

"What the fuck?" The color drained from Tara's face. She

exchanged a look with me. "My gods. All our best soldiers are still back at the training field ..."

Oh gods. She probably thinks I did this, too.

The bulls stood on their hind legs, shifting back into human form. Then, with bloodcurdling shrieks, they hurtled through the forest, sprinting straight toward us.

My horror grew as some of them veered toward the trees, scrambling up the trunks like spiders, moving unnaturally fast.

"We can't stay here," I yelled. "There are too many of them."

We'd be overrun within seconds.

Fuck. One skinwraith had been enough of a challenge. But fifty or more?

We were dead.

I grabbed Tara by the back of her vest, then hurled her back. Seren would never forgive me if I let anything happen to her sister, no matter how brave she was. "Run," I roared. "Get me a fucking sword, Seth!"

This time Seth didn't hesitate. He yanked one free of its sheath, then tossed it toward me.

The Vangar man was the first to fall, the skinwraith dealing a savage bite to the back of his neck, then lifting the man's body and crushing it against a tree. A swarm of others crowded the body.

"They're going to kill every last one of us," Tara growled, then stormed headfirst toward them.

Amahle released a battle cry and followed her, sword in hand.

Seth and I remained behind them, but the skinwraiths had already reached Seth, who plunged his sword into one of their chests.

The man might be my enemy, but right now we had to be allies. One more living soldier against the dead.

"Decapitate them," I shouted, slicing the head clean off a skinwraith. The body exploded into that black mist I'd seen before. "It's the only way to stop them."

Seth didn't question me, his sword cleaving off the head of the skinwraith he'd stabbed. No black mist followed, but the skinwraith's body fell and stayed on the ground.

Amahle and Tara struggled though, trying and failing to protect the other Vangar woman as the skinwraiths grabbed her.

"We have to help them," Seth called to me.

A blur of screeches and black mist, rotten body parts, snarling teeth and the clash of steel overtook every thought as Seth and I fought our way back toward Tara and Amahle, trying to reach them before they were fully surrounded.

"Don't let them get between us," I yelled at Amahle and Tara, who fought back to back. Maybe a Vangar technique, but most definitely a Pendaran one. Brogan Ragnall had trained his daughter well.

Sweat dripped into my eyes as Seth and I closed the distance. Four of us, versus the remaining skinwraiths.

A sudden scream cut through the forest. Behind us, where we'd come from, a small group of Vangar emerged—but these weren't warriors. They were younger. Candidates.

The skinwraiths lifted their heads, their dead eyes locking on the weaker prey.

Not a chance they'd make it out alive.

We needed something more than our combined skills and strength.

Divine intervention. Magic. A protection spell.

If my gifts hadn't been Sealed, I might have done *something*. Even the damned vuk's powers from Seren's oath wouldn't be enough to help.

... but the vuk wasn't the only one to give me power.

A mad kernel of an idea formed in my mind.

Seren had gifts—latent ones that Lucia had hinted more than once hadn't been fully trained—and I had access to her through our bond. I knew how to open and close the pathway that allowed us to communicate now ... but what about one of those other paths I'd visualized in that space we shared?

If I could find the one that held some of her innate abilities, I might channel them. Lucia had suggested it was possible when she'd trained me the last few days. Hell, before realizing the vuk's blood had influenced the oath, she'd believed all my new gifts came from Seren.

But I needed to concentrate.

"Cover me," I yelled at Seth.

Then I dropped low, couching between his and Tara's legs.

Clammy, dead fingers reached for me, clawing at my face.

I ignored the scrapes of their broken, jagged fingernails raking against my cheek and forehead.

Concentrate.

My mind traveled to that shared space of our bond, the screams and hisses and stench fading away.

A twilit glade unfolds around me, the trees shadowed shapes, a liminal space devoid of color and light. Seren is here, the warmth of her, her every thought, humming through transparent leaves on grey branches.

I step forward. The ground beneath my feet shifts, sensing my intrusion, pushing me back. A crack forms in the earth.

I kneel, pressing my fingertips to the fissure. A pulse, below my fingertips.

"*Seren, they're going to die. I need your ice wielding, there's no time to explain. Show me where to find it.*"

"Rykr! We need you!" Tara's cry shattered the quiet.

Another crack spread, the fissure widening like a stream. Shim-

mering strands, white and blue light rather than water, filter through my fingertips. Strands of power. Threads of fate.

Will there be consequences if I take from her like this?

"Fuck!" Seth yelled.

Waiting, questioning the consequences will kill us. And my death will mean hers, too.

I dive into the stream.

CHAPTER 24
SEREN

A strangled gasp left me, the cold, lifeless eyes of a skinwraith flashing through my mind.

Above me, skeletal branches swayed in the dissipating storm, snow swirling through the air. I was on my back, on the ground, and I had no idea how I'd gotten here.

Darya leaned over me, Ciaran beside her.

I grasped my cheek, expecting to find blood there. Pain lanced through me, but my fingers came away clean.

Rykr.

I could feel him, sense him, as though he'd been right beside me. *"Rykr, are you there?"* I called out to him.

Nothing.

Both Ciaran and Darya were speaking, but I only heard a fierce ringing. My body was numb, strangely weak.

Ciaran lifted me and started forward. The rhythm of his hurried steps rocked me as I rested my head against his chest, shivering violently, unable to summon the energy to open my eyes again.

"Rykr."

Still nothing. He'd either shut me out or was ignoring me.

Time blurred. The last thing I remembered was being on a horse. *Was I thrown from it?*

That didn't explain why Ciaran was on foot.

Where had the horses gone?

Acrid smoke billowed in the air, stinging my nostrils, and I buried my face against Ciaran as he stopped abruptly.

Noise crashed back into me—wailing, tools clanging, voices shouting. Ciaran lowered me to the ground, and the familiar shape of my mother loomed over me as he bolted away.

I sat, still shaking, as Mother pressed a bottle to my lips—one of her bitter tonics that I knew better than to question. I swallowed, the medicine turning my stomach, but clarity rushed back to me. "What's happened?"

"Skinwraith attack," Mother whispered, her face pale.

Oh … no, no, no.

Anything but that.

She must have seen my panic. "Rykr encased the skin-wraiths in a wall of ice, then turned it to mist. They're gone, for now, but his powers didn't go unnoticed. Worse still, there's already a rumor snaking its way around the camp that Giulia Bernardi was killed by—and turned into—a skinwraith. That a blade of ice was found near her body."

Fuck.

The realization hit like a punch to my lungs. *Ciaran.*

He was the only one who knew besides my family.

Who else had he told?

I stumbled to my feet, searching for him. It didn't take long —his size and red hair made him easy to spot as he was hunched over on the field.

"Seren, wait."

I didn't listen. As I strode toward Ciaran, anger surged

through me, drowning out every other thought. I grabbed him by the collar, yanking him back. "You fucking son of a—"

His red-rimmed eyes, glassy with exhaustion, stopped me. His face was drawn, pale. Then I saw why.

Moira lay on a stretcher in front of him, deep gashes marring her arms and legs—one on her cheek. It would scar, but my mother could help her pain. I released him, fury momentarily checked.

"S-Seren," he sputtered.

I ignored him, dropping to my knees beside Moira. Pain twisted her face. I cradled her cheek, my fingers smearing in blood. "Moira, are you okay?"

"It h-hurts." Tears welled in her eyes. "But Rykr. He ... saved me."

My lips parted. *Rykr?* I'd been so busy focusing on my anger with Ciaran that I'd barely processed what my mother had said.

"Rykr encased the skinwraiths in a wall of ice, then turned it to mist. The skinwraiths are gone, for now, but his powers didn't go unnoticed."

He'd wielded ice?

A shiver rippled through me. What did that mean? He'd never mentioned having that power when I'd shown it to him.

Moira sniffled. "He saved all of us, really. There were so many. But he pulled one off me after he started wielding ice— it had me, Seren." Tears slipped down her cheeks.

Ciaran shuffled in beside me, taking Moira's hand. "All that matters is that you're safe now."

His voice reminded me of my anger and fears. "We need to talk. Alone." I stood, glaring down at him. "Now."

His face was incredulous. "Moira—"

Screw it. "There's a rumor about Giulia's death, that she was killed by a skinwraith."

Ciaran froze, paling further. "I-I had nothing to do with that, I swear."

Of course he'd deny it.

My throat constricted and I stepped away, feeling sick. How could he betray me like this?

Would he betray me like this?

He'd been so furious. So adamant that we needed to tell someone.

And he was the only one who knew outside of Tara and my mother. I couldn't believe either of them would let that information slip.

Raging at him here wouldn't get me the truth. Not with Moira bleeding on the ground.

I needed to find Rykr.

Without another word, I turned away. Despite his sister's injuries, Ciaran sprang up, following me. "Seren, you have to believe me—"

"I don't know if I do." I gave him a sharp look over my shoulder. "You hate him. You want to see him gone. And your love for the tribe—telling them what happened—"

"But I didn't!" Ciaran's face flushed red. "Godsdammit, Seren, I wish I *had* told them! Look at this forest! Look at the dead and injured, including my sister. I don't know who is dead, but those things got to the encampment first. They attacked the most defenseless in our tribe. If we'd said something, we could've been more prepared, but I didn't. And now I'm just as guilty as you are because I didn't say a fucking word."

Acid burned in my throat.

I swallowed hard and shook my head, unsure of what to think or believe. "I have to go. I have to find Rykr."

Ciaran reached for my hand, but I pulled it out of his grasp. "Seren, listen to me, I know you care about him but—"

"Not here. Not now." My voice was frosty. Turning on my heel, I dashed forward. *"Rykr!"* Silence had settled into the bond between us. I had to find Rykr. Something was wrong.

My arms and legs ached with each step, a reminder of the last few nights training with him and the sparring ring this morning. The strange weakness I felt—as though something had been taken from me—wasn't him, was it? That wasn't how the bond worked. He died, I died ... right?

The entire tone of the encampment had changed, and it was a whirlwind of movement as tents were broken down, wooden pikes sharpened and stacked, wounded cried in misery, survivors wailed in anguish. The stark remains of tents smoldered from destruction that must have happened in the chaos of the attack.

This no longer looked like a village, but a smoking ghost town.

A tribe on the move.

How long had I been unconscious, and what had caused that? It seemed several hours had passed. How was that possible? Ciaran had carried me straight here, hadn't he?

My mother appeared by my side once again, as though she'd been watching, waiting to talk to me. "Darling, listen to me," she said, hurrying to keep up with me. "The tribe is restless and looking for someone to blame. They fear what they don't know. Come with me. He needs you."

I gave my mother a worried look. "Rykr?"

She nodded.

"You know where he is?"

She took my hand. "This way. Seth and Darya are guarding him."

What in the gods' name?

I rushed behind her, dread filling me. "Has something happened to him?"

"I tried to tell you ... he used your powers, I think. But all the tribe saw was a powerful Lirien with magic that frightened them. The Vangar mobbed him in their fury. Seth fought them off, but Rykr was badly wounded. I think he did his best to keep you from the pain, but you were too lost to the intrusion on your soul to know."

Oh shit.

My knees nearly gave out on me.

My heart pounded with a fierceness I didn't understand as I ran behind my mother.

The Lirien who drove me crazy with his arrogance and charm. The man I'd fought to save, who'd saved me ...

The thought of him wounded, in pain—gods. It was like a dagger to my gut.

The Vangar must have known they couldn't take him one by one. The odds must have been stacked terribly against him if they'd gotten to him. "Did he hurt anyone?" That was all he needed to earn another sentence, especially with the rumor about Giulia.

"No. He surrendered. They struck him after."

We arrived in the center of the tribe, where the agitated crowd was gathered. At the sight of Seth, I shoved my way through toward him.

Seth wasn't alone. Darya knelt beside a crumpled, bloodied form on the ground—Rykr.

A choked breath left me, and I lunged forward. "What the fuck happened?"

One of the women in the crowd wailed, tears carving tracks down her cheeks. "My darling," she cried. "My darling girl. They must be punished. Both of them!" She lifted accusing, red-rimmed eyes at me.

The din from the crowd swelled. *"Punish them!"*

"Execute them!"

I fell to my knees beside Darya, who met my eyes with a worried look. She squeezed my hand gently. "He's still alive."

"Rykr," I murmured, touching his brow. His eyes were closed. He was unconscious, his body beaten, bloodied, and bruised.

"Burn them!"

"Enough!" Seth roared, sword in hand. "We are not a people who dispense justice in anger. Seren Ragnall and her husband may have flouted our laws before, but she's been tried and given a punishment. *This* is a new situation, and I don't have to speak as a member of the council or your waldren. What I say is truth. Rykr Westhaven saved our tribe today and you repaid him in blood—brought shame upon us all."

Darya flinched, her mouth pinching as she squeezed my hand.

Of all the people to help us, I never would have expected Seth. From the rage simmering in the crowd, it was clear Seth was all that stood between us and immediate execution.

But who in Nyxva had told them about Giulia?

My mother had pushed through the crowd by now, Tara and Amahle joining her. Tara's sword was already in her hands, and she approached Seth and stood at his side.

"Justice!"

Darya rose to stand beside Seth. I slipped my hand into Rykr's, noting the awkward bend of his fingers. *Dammit. They'd broken them.*

And his irons were gone. The lack of Bloodbinding mark was so clear to me now ... what if Darya saw it? I tugged his hand into my lap, shielding it.

Rykr didn't need any more suspicion on him.

"Seren Ragnall and Rykr Westhaven have already been sentenced to the Skorn," Darya said in a commanding voice. "If they are guilty of any other crimes, the gods will decide their fate."

The crowd didn't appear to waver, their clamoring growing louder.

Macklyn Bryce and his wife pushed their way through the throng. Macklyn stood beside Tara, throwing his arms out. "Rykr Westhaven saved my daughter and our tribe. He is no Lirien. He's proven his loyalty. If any one of you wants to harm him any further, you'll have to kill me first."

Morgana Bryce joined him, her face set with the same fierce determination that I'd often seen in Ciaran's.

A moment later, others followed. Members of the Vangar. Of the tribe. "He's one of us," Jabari Bankole shouted. "You will face us all to get to him."

Stunned, I watched as more warriors closed ranks, standing shoulder to shoulder with those who shielded us. The mob, so loud before, suddenly seemed small.

The Viori who had been rising against Rykr began to back away, their voices faltering.

"We'll leave tonight. All of us," Seth announced. "The tribe will seek refuge in Emberstone, and we'll transport both Seren and Westhaven under guard." He glanced down at me, lowering his voice. "You'll both be safer that way."

I nodded and tore my gaze away, my guilt bleeding through every beat of my pulse.

I wished Rykr could see this. The Viori, my people, standing here on his behalf.

Accepting him as one of their own.

Pride rose inside me—but also deep shame.

This time, I deserved the punishment that Rykr's attackers had wanted for me. My selfishness, my pride had destroyed so much.

My encampment was in ruins because I'd failed to protect

my people. Because, as Ciaran had said, my loyalty had been to Rykr, rather than my tribe—including my friends and family. People who now stood for me. For him.

I'd spent days training for the Skorn, believing if I found clever tricks in books or mastered bold fighting techniques, I could prove my innocence—not only before my people, but before the gods.

I've been so ... arrogant. Believing in my intellect and justified anger. But deep down, I knew the truth: guilt ruled me.

My baby sister is still missing.

What if I *was* to blame like the Viori believed?

Maybe I deserved punishment—and more.

PART TWO

EMBERSTONE

CHAPTER 25

RYKR

I woke to Seren hovering inches above me, wiping my face with a handkerchief, while a sharp, buzzing headache burned in my temples. A laughing groan left my lips, and I closed my eyes again, momentarily unconcerned about where we were or the lingering pain I felt. "We have to stop meeting like this, my lady."

"I don't know whether to slap you or kiss you." Then her soft lips pressed to mine in a quick, fleeting kiss—more relief than romance—a gesture filled with unspoken emotion.

Still, the feel of her lips tempted me more than she could have possibly imagined.

Any flirtation with her had long since crossed to a dangerous game with fire ... one that she ignited in me despite my better judgment.

She pulled away, wiping her damp lashes. Behind her, the iron bars of a prison wagon swam into view, a gorgeous sunrise beyond that ... and snowcapped mountains.

I tried to sit but she held me back. "They broke at least three of your ribs, your left wrist, and several fingers. I reset

267

them, though I suspect your own healing abilities will take care of the rest. Your face is still slightly bruised, but the cuts are gone. You'll probably wake tomorrow morning fully recovered. We've been traveling all night and most of the day, and the whole tribe is accompanying us to Emberstone—or what's left of us."

A shiver crawled through me at the idea of my body healing itself. What other, unknown abilities had the vuk given me?

"Why did you let them beat you?" Seren whispered, searching my eyes. "I saw you in that sparring ring. You could have easily defended yourself."

A low, humorless chuckle escaped me. "And risk killing someone? We both know that would have given your tribe more rope to hang me with."

"Ironically, Seth protected you. You must have impressed him when you fought the skinwraiths. I didn't think he had any honor left."

I swallowed, noticing bold streaks of blond in her hair—a marked change from when I'd last seen her. "Did you feel it? When I borrowed your powers?"

Her face was somber as she nodded. "I ... lost consciousness, I think." Then ruefully, she added, "I didn't know you knew how to do that."

"Neither did I. Truth is, I was born with fire wielding, but I haven't been able to use those powers since I was Sealed. So, this was ... a bit of change, for me."

Somehow my confession didn't shock her—and it felt strangely unthreatening to make. Her lips twitched. "Fire and ice. I knew we were opposites." Her hands squeezed mine. "You're Ederyn, aren't you? That's why you don't have a Blood-binding mark."

My breath went shallow.

"I've been thinking about it all night. You don't have a mark. At first, I thought that maybe it meant you could be Viori too, but that doesn't make sense. You're Sealed. Only the king of Lirien can do that. The only other Unbound are Ederyn. It's the only thing that makes sense."

She was too clever not to figure it out—what had I expected? I searched her eyes. "Who I was before I was Sealed ... it's not someone I want to remember right now." Someone I couldn't afford to think about. *Not when it reminds me so much of all the family I've lost.*

Despite her efforts, I sat and drew my legs up. The familiar bite of iron cinched my limbs again. I had a vague memory of being shackled when they threw me into the wagon. By then, I'd been in blinding pain, too far gone to care or focus on much. The image of boots stomping me remained at the fringe of my memory, each blow filled with utter hatred.

Unsteadily, I ran my hands through my unkempt hair, pushing it out of my eyes. "Did they hurt you?"

"No." Seren's eyes were wide and soulful. "But someone told the tribe about Giulia. That's part of what motivated them."

"Ciaran?" I asked sharply.

"I don't know. He swears he didn't, but I'm not sure if I can believe him." She swallowed hard, as though the memory was painful. The tug of grief that spilled through the bond was sharp with betrayal. "How did you keep me from feeling them beat you?"

Gods knew I'd used every ounce of concentration to block her from feeling the pain I'd felt. Maybe Lucia had known I'd need that skill the most. Blocking her out hadn't been easy, but I'd done it, just as I had so many times in the forest the last few days under Lucia's tutelage. "The same way I knew how to access your powers. I'll do my best to show you, if I can."

"You didn't have to do that—"

"They would have hurt you, Seren. And they're taking us to fight for our lives. But even if that wasn't the case, I'll always choose getting hurt if it spares you. I'd do it again. Every time."

"I know." Her eyes shimmered. "And I know you mean it. You've proven it. But ... why? You didn't even know me the first time you did it. Why keep putting yourself in harm's way? If I didn't know any better, I'd think you were punishing yourself."

My father's voice was a crescendo in my head. *"You're lazy and spoiled ..."*

I shook the memory away. Her words dug deep at something I didn't want to think about. "I don't have a death wish if that's what you're asking. But I'm starting to believe the king wasn't so crazy in forbidding Liriens from going into the Dreadwood. Hasn't worked out so well for me since I set foot inside."

She cracked a small smile, then sat back on her heels. "You can't make light of everything, you know."

"Can't I? I find that—and drinking—to be perfectly acceptable solutions to most problems."

"Well, you're lucky. In more ways than one. I'm still shocked that Seth, of all people, protected you back there. Especially after you insulted him earlier by forfeiting that fight." She gave me a curious look. "Speaking of which, why *did* you forfeit? You would have won."

I could lie. Make something convenient. But this didn't seem worth the effort. "He had my sword. And that sword would have killed me."

She frowned. "What?"

"The sword." I puffed out a short breath. "It's cursed with magic. Every time it's used, it kills. That rarely works out favorably for the person it's wielded against. I only use it if I have no other choice. I had another one I favored, but I lost it in the forest. But I wasn't about to fight Seth while he had my cursed blade."

She blinked at me, as though considering whether my admission was too ludicrous to be a lie. Then she murmured, "Thank you for telling me."

I looked down at my hands, wishing I could tell her more. But it wasn't possible.

The rudimentary splints she'd set came from twigs and strips of cloth—the missing shirt under her vest told me the source. It also called extra attention to the curves of her breasts against the leather.

"You're not cold?" I asked, my mouth curving. Any lingering on her breasts wouldn't help right now.

She followed my gaze and smirked. "I didn't have many options. We left in a rush and I climbed into the wagon with you. Mother and Tara are bringing my things and Amahle is following the wagon on horseback. She has my bag. Tara had to pack up all our belongings herself—Mother was too busy with the wounded. Hopefully my father and brother will know to find us in Emberstone."

Her worry pressed through the bond, deepening my own unease over Brogan and Madoc. Why do the Ragnall women speak of them so little? Their absence felt like a wound no one wanted to acknowledge.

I shifted over and peered out of the bars. A long line of wagons and carts stretched ahead, winding up toward the mountains.

Permanent villages, built of stone rather than tents, flanked the main road to the city in the mountain, dense with citizens.

Had my father been alive, he'd be foaming at the mouth for the intelligence I could provide. After what they'd done to

Dalric, I had no illusions what they'd do to me if they learned who I was. *And now that I've seen what I have.*

Yellow banners draped the streets and the massive bridge leading to the city's main gate. Here, as in Seren's encampment, the people reveled in the death of my family—only more brazenly. We passed drunken men and women sprawled in the alleys, and one brothel where revelry spilled onto the streets in a raucous, indecent display.

I had to guard my thoughts, careful not to react. The bond between Seren and me seemed to be deepening, her emotions slipping through when I wasn't prepared. A fierce protectiveness spread through me as drunken men called lewd remarks to her from the gates.

Damned Viori.

"What now? I take it we're being held as prisoners."

Seren sighed, removing my splints carefully. "I don't know. Some in the tribe demanded punishment for us, and Seth said he would transport us here under guard—supposedly for our safety—but I don't trust him. Either way, I'm sure the leadership here will have a say in our ability to go free in Emberstone before the Skorn, which isn't for a few more nights."

She cleared her throat and gestured behind the wagon. "The good news is that with the entire tribe seeking refuge at Emberstone, we'll have some friendly faces in the crowd— rather than an arena of people cheering for our deaths."

"You call that good news?" I chuckled dryly. "Solwyn, one of these days remind me to show you what an actual good time is. I have serious doubts if the Viori know anything about it."

"Do you take anything seriously?" She crossed her arms.

"Yes," I answered with a slow smile. "But your mother warned us we shouldn't do it so I can't show you. Unfortunately."

A blush heated her cheeks, her lips parting. "They must have kicked your head harder than I thought."

The outrage in her eyes was almost as appealing as the *desire*.

The wagon lurched to a stop and a guard in the courtyard strode toward the wagon. "Waldren Azad?" he said to Seth.

Seth jumped down from the seat. "Yes?"

"You and your wife are expected in the keep with your prisoners ... and *only* them."

Dammit. Word must have traveled before we'd arrived.

Seth circled to the back of the wagon, his somber gaze flicking toward Amahle. "Say your goodbyes now."

Amahle dismounted, handing her horse to a groom waiting in the courtyard.

"Will you be all right?" Amahle asked Seren, worry lining her features.

Despite the nervousness humming through the bond, Seren smiled bravely. "We'll be fine. I've uncovered something in the books I borrowed that might give us an edge." She leaned forward and hugged her friend through the bars. "Book us a room in the Bellwether—it's the only inn in Emberstone my father trusts. We'll meet you there to celebrate our win."

Amahle's shoulders flexed with defiance. "I should go with you—see for myself if they'll let me in. That's what I came for. You need an ally."

"I need an ally outside of the keep, too," Seren said gently. "If we don't get thrown in the dungeon, it would be good to have a room waiting. Tell my mother and Tara that I'll find them when I can."

Seren squeezed Amahle's forearm. "I'm not going down without a fight, Amahle. Remember that."

The wagon started again, an enormous iron portcullis

looming ahead as we moved deeper into the mountain. Armed guards stood at the entrance, clutching spears. Emberstone wasn't just fortified, it was a fortress.

"What's the intriguing information you found in the book?"

"I didn't find much." Her eyes were dark and troubled. "I barely had time to read under Darya's orders."

"But you did find something, right?"

She gave me a weary smile. "Some. I learned that the trial isn't *just* against the Skorn warriors. They usually prepare a surprise or two. Flesh-eating scarabs, poisonous vines—whatever they feel like throwing in."

"I'm beginning to regret I asked."

Her hand slid over mine. "Whatever we face, we'll face it together."

Somehow, the idea didn't seem as ludicrous as it had when I'd first woken in her encampment.

I'd expected Emberstone to be a dimly lit keep, with dusty, narrow passageways cut into the stone, maybe even a grand hall.

Instead, a sophisticated, colorful city sprawled before me, vast beyond anything I'd imagined.

The entrance had led us to a high vantage point in the road, flanked by guards in gleaming silver-plated armor. The wide, paved path cut a zigzagging switchback down into the city. From here, a labyrinth of streets twisted between alleys, the tiled rooftops of two- and three-story buildings glistening in the glow of streetlamps. A cacophony of sounds and smells wafted toward us as we descended.

In the distance, a majestic castle loomed, towering over the city, its white marble walls gleaming, ivy climbing the sides, as if sunlight streamed in during the day.

The Unbound Viori weren't as wild or savage as Liriens believed. The entire city brimmed with enchantment and ingenuity.

I tried not to gawk as the silver-clad guards escorted us down the switchback. At the bottom of the path, the cart creaked onto a cobblestone street. "*This* is the heart of your territory?" I asked.

A shy look crossed Seren's face. "I know it's nothing compared to what I've heard of Lirien but—"

"This is beautiful, Seren. A city to be proud of." Never in my wildest dreams had I expected this. Or thought I'd compliment the Viori on anything.

The cavernous ceiling arched high above the city, its finely hewn layers of stone smooth like a sky. Somehow the builders had found ways—through magic or sheer skill—to carve enormous shafts into the rock. The last rays of sunlight from the sunset filtered through.

I'd read about cities like this in old texts—tales of Murkhold, the dwarven realm of wealth and magic, carved into the mountains before Vornfall shattered the nine realms. But wasn't that all just myth? A long-dead world, lost to time?

Magic clearly existed, but everything else? Ancient texts, reading like fairy stories, hardly seemed like a reliable source of truth. Only Ibarrans truly put stock in the old gods and their legends.

Even they believed most of their gods had died ... which meant what exactly? If gods could die, who was to say the ones they still worshipped existed? Especially if their realms had been sealed off, forever out of reach.

The thought troubled me for other reasons now.

If I survived this and returned to Lirien as heir, my powers would be considered divinely granted. I would be the head of the faith.

The king's heretical youngest son. Troublesome. Inconvenient.

The king himself being a heretic?

Disaster.

"What is?" Seren's voice came through my head.

I stiffened, giving her a sidelong glance. *Dammit.* I needed to be more careful. *"I don't like not knowing what lies ahead."*

"I understand." Her eyes reflected that concern.

But what could we do? We were trapped, moving endlessly toward a fate neither of us could escape.

The wagon stopped abruptly.

"We're here," Seren said. Her dread only amplified my own.

More guards in silver armor were stationed here, standing before two massive, gated doors to the keep. The leader of the Viori clearly ruled like a king, even if he didn't call himself one —and this was his castle.

Green and black pennants hung beyond the gate, the crest emblazoned with the Everspire—the tree of life—its tangled roots curled into the shape of a dragon. I'd seen the symbol before—on Viori Vangar banners when they raided the border.

Seth and Darya, together with the silver-clad guards, helped us out of the wagon. The astonishment on Seth's face as I stood told me he hadn't expected to see me standing. Darya, however, narrowed her eyes in suspicion. I didn't blame her. I didn't trust her, either.

They led us inside, my chains dragging against the stone floor with a sinister scrape.

Deeper within, sentinels stood at attention, their armor gleaming in the torchlight. Rich tapestries lined the walls, depicting scenes from a history unfamiliar to me. From behind one, a boy darted out, clutching a ball, his wide eyes fixing on the irons around my wrists.

I pulled my gaze away, only to catch Seren watching him. A faint smile curled on those lips, sweetly.

She's Viori. These are her people.

It wasn't just Seth and Darya who were leading me here.

She was one of them.

I couldn't even trust her enough to tell her who I really was ... could I? Even Lucia had warned me not to.

Seth and Darya exchanged a glance, unreadable, their unease disquieting. Who waited for us beyond those doors?

Whatever confidence Seren had shown earlier was gone, too.

The doors swung open, revealing an opulent, breathtaking throne room packed with onlookers.

Nearly the opposite of the throne room in Suomelin in colors, but no less impressive, the room shimmered with dark, decadent splendor.

I'd expected to be deep in the mountain but, instead, the throne room was cut into the rock face, a row of floor-to-ceiling glass doors at the far side, open to the crisp mountain air. Golden sunset light streamed in, gleaming on the polished obsidian walls, where more green, silver, and black pendants hung. Silver thread embroidered the dragon sigil, its eyes sparkling with emeralds.

Massive black stone pillars veined with silver flanked the chamber, rising to a vaulted ceiling where chandeliers hung like constellations, each crystal shard gleaming like starlight. *And yet the Viori in the Dreadwood live so primitively.*

Most stunning of all, perhaps, was the majesty of the throne itself, carved from onyx inlaid with diamonds and perched atop a polished marble dais.

The man seated on the throne looked so much like my father that my breath caught, my pulse hammering in my ears.

"Kneel before Lord Haldron," a sentinel declared.

The name struck me like a blade.

Haldron.

The ground seemed to sink below my feet as Seth, Darya, and Seren knelt. A thick, oppressive silence settled over the chamber, all eyes turning toward me.

I hadn't seen Haldron since I was eight, but I remembered him well. Once, he'd been my favorite uncle, my father's youngest brother—until he'd became a traitor.

He had tried to kill my father. Had left his own wife in a coma. My father had barely survived the knife wounds my uncle had plunged into his torso.

The Regulation had hunted him down, chased him to Ibarra, where he was supposed to have died—trapped in a temple they'd burned to the ground.

But here he was, seated on a throne, alive and in power. Holding the fate of the Viori in his hands. *Seren's and my fate in his hands.* If I wasn't so shocked, anger would be flooding all my senses.

Like a lock sliding into place, the precision of the strike against my family suddenly made sense. Haldron hadn't just survived—he'd plotted, waited, and now seized power in a way none of us had seen coming.

He was behind their deaths.

With my nephew too young to be a legitimate heir, Haldron's claim to Lirien's throne was stronger than anyone's.

Except mine.

I tried to shield the surge of rage and dread, but it leaked through the bond, too strong to hide. Seren flinched, a ripple of unease echoing back at me. Her eyes shot to mine, concern flickering before she quickly looked away, as if sensing this was something I couldn't yet share.

It had been twenty years since the man on the throne had seen me, and given he thought I was dead, he wouldn't be looking too closely. But would he see the color of my eyes and see his brother? Would he see the shape of my nose and see my mother?

He'll kill me on sight if he recognizes me.

I had to survive this meeting.

I was the only one—*the only Warrick*—left to stop him.

And now my true purpose was clear.

CHAPTER 26
SEREN

A cold bead of sweat traced down the back of my neck, every sense hyperaware of the scene unfolding before me. The crowded throne room shifted and swayed with hushed, muffled whispers cocooning us. We were not welcome.

A chilly breeze swept in through the open windows, carrying with it the scent of snow, and the heavy curtains lining the stone walls rustled. It offered little comfort against the stifling weight of countless eyes fixed on us. Beneath it all lingered the cloying perfume of the gathered elite—an ever-present reminder of the luxury they enjoyed, a world far removed from the brutality of the Dreadwood.

My heartbeat pounded.

Rykr stood tall, defiant, in the middle of the room. *Refusing to bend the knee.*

"Kneel, Westhaven," Darya hissed.

"Rykr, please." What the hell was he thinking? This wasn't the time for stubborn pride.

Rykr's eyes narrowed. "I thought the Viori had no kings. I didn't leave one tyrant to bow to another."

"Lord Haldron was elected as our leader," Seth snapped beside me.

Haldron left the throne and crossed the room toward us. "Rise," he said, his voice as brisk as his pace.

He stopped before us, gaze fixed on Rykr. Thankfully, Rykr kept his eyes averted. "The rumors are true then. Waldren Seth Azad's tribe harbors a Sealed Lirien. Given the descriptions I've received, I expected someone more ... extraordinary. This is the man who caused such disorder? This savage, beaten, arrogant man?"

Seth stiffened, redness creeping into his face. "My lord, he may not be able to kneel because of injuries he sustained yesterday. If you could but allow us to explain—"

Haldron silenced Seth with nothing more than a pointed glance, the weight of his authority palpable. "Do you truly believe, Waldren Azad," he said, voice cold and cutting, "that I remain ignorant of the events in my own territory? That this ... aberration of our laws slipped into Emberstone unnoticed? No council hands down a Skorn sentence without my knowledge." His words carried quiet menace. "We've been waiting for you for days."

The cool fingers of fear wrapped themselves around my throat. Haldron *knew*? His reach and spies must be everywhere.

Haldron's attention turned toward me. "Seren Ragnall." Stepping closer, he took my chin into his hand, lifting my face, his gaze surprisingly intense. This wasn't just a frank, unforgiving appraisal—but something more. A display of dominance. His power to do with any of us as he pleased.

A hushed note of admiration curled through his voice. "Exquisite."

My gaze faltered. *What?*

Just like his inspection, it disarmed me. "Thank you, my lord." I bowed my head.

"You're nearly the spitting image of your mother at your age, though your eyes are something else entirely. They remind me ..." He didn't finish the thought, his face clouding, as though lost to a memory.

Then he blinked. "Brogan always had to fight Lucia's admirers away. And there were many—including me." He smiled.

I barely avoided gagging in disgust. My father had never spoken of any interaction with Haldron in their youth. Neither of my parents had.

Yet somewhere inside this intimidating man, there had to be someone reasonable—who'd freed my father to go after Esme.

Haldron clucked his tongue, his thumb and forefinger brushing against my chin with deliberate, unnerving gentleness. My skin crawled beneath his touch—not just fear but the suffocating awareness of powerlessness beneath his scrutiny. "I hear you've inherited Lucia's famed spellcraft prowess."

I fought to steady my breath. Every response felt like walking a razor's edge.

"The Oath of Bryndis. Clever. An ancient oath—one most of us have never even heard of—that is difficult to dispute. You must care a great deal for this Lirien, to place your life at risk in this manner."

If he'd heard so much already, then he must know I'd done it out of desperation, not love. Every word out of my mouth could be scrutinized and judged—used against me or to prove that I was a liar.

"I owed him a life debt, as he saved me from a vuk. Killing him would have brought a curse on me." The words felt like a tangle on my tongue. Even the illusion of confidence receded as I stared at the Viori leader.

I'd never met him before. Most in our tribe would have considered it an honor. But I hadn't been invited to court, I'd been dragged here for judgment.

"Another ancient curse—the Pendaran life debt." Haldron raised a thick, silver and blond eyebrow. "It seems your parents have taught you all they know. Still, tying your soul to a Lirien to save his life smacks of selfish desperation, I must admit. And it does beg the question of why he was in the forest ... or how your paths happened to collide."

More ominously, Haldron added in a low voice, "Then again, only one other Sealed man has ever left Lirien. And who would that be, Seren?"

His challenging tone made my resolve strengthen. Haldron meant to intimidate me before I even had a chance to speak a word. Paint us both as villains.

"My father," I said, lifting my chin toward Haldron. "And while that is an intriguing coincidence, that has nothing to do with the fact that I claimed this man with an ancient oath that makes him my spouse and soulmate. It cannot be broken. To reject the legitimacy of my claim would be to invite chaos into our ranks, undermining the very foundation of our people."

Haldron leaned forward, his blue-green eyes—so unnervingly *familiar*—fixed on mine. I tore my eyes away. "An oath made in desperation cannot bind us. You used it to save yourself, not for the good of the Viori. Tell me, Seren, why should we allow *you* the chance at the Skorn trial? Why shouldn't we strike you and this Lirien down right now?"

I didn't flinch. "Desperation doesn't invalidate the oath's power. The gods do not grant such oaths lightly, and they do not allow them to be invoked falsely. The Oath of Bryndis is ancient, yes, but ancient oaths cannot be ignored simply because they are inconvenient."

I couldn't afford to appear meek, nor could I come off as too bold. Every word mattered now. I glanced toward the gathered court, appealing to their fears and doubt.

"This isn't about my survival. The Liriens bind the gifts granted to us by the gods themselves. The Bloodbinding is a defiance of divine will. But the Oath of Bryndis was also given to us by a goddess. So was the Pendaran life debt."

Then my eyes narrowed at Haldron. "You claim to want to do the will of the gods. Any Ibarran scholar can tell you this oath makes this man mine to claim. Our lives—our very souls—are bound. I am his. And he is mine. If I am Viori, then so is he."

Haldron shook his head slowly. "And what's to stop other Viori from twisting ancient laws against us?"

A member of Haldron's council—a thick, corpulent man—spoke from the dais. "The Oath of Bryndis has not been invoked in living memory. The texts that she speaks of are locked away in restricted areas of our repository, my lord. The chances of it being repeated are slim. But that still does nothing to foster trust in *this* Lirien."

I seized the moment, my pulse thundering in my ears. "You don't have to trust him. Trust *me*." The words left my mouth faster than I could second-guess them. I forced myself to hold Haldron's gaze, fighting the tremor that threatened to creep into my voice. "Trust that I acted not out of fear, but faith in the divine will of our gods and the oaths—and curses—they gave us. If we discard those declarations from the gods, we are no better than the Liriens who support the Bloodbinding."

A cold silence followed, and for a heartbeat, I worried. Had I said too much?

Time stretched unbearably, every second like a death knell.

Haldron's expression remained unreadable, but I caught the faintest flicker of doubt in the faces around us.

Seth stepped forward, his voice steady. "Seren acted not for herself alone but for the sake of our people's laws. That is why our council chose to leave her fate to the gods through the Skorn trial. What's more, skinwraiths attacked our tribe yesterday. The Lirien single-handedly saved us all. I owe him my life. What remains of our tribe does as well. We've come to seek refuge."

Seth? The man who'd sworn he wouldn't help me? I struggled to keep my jaw from falling slack as the room gasped collectively.

Haldron's face colored. "Skinwraiths?" He stalked toward Rykr. "How did you defeat them?" His question was stated as a demand.

Rykr kept his gaze averted. "I froze them in a blast of ice, then crumbled it."

"Clever. A clever couple." Haldron studied Rykr for a moment longer, his eyes flicking toward his hair. "Though I can't say I've ever heard of a Pendaran with the ability to wield ice."

Worry hummed inside me, stemming from the bond. "The oath that bonded us transferred some of my abilities to him," I cut in sharply.

"I see." Haldron's lips formed a hard line.

He turned slowly, his eyes sweeping across the gathered councilors, as if weighing their reactions before speaking. "The Oath of Bryndis is not a matter to be taken lightly," he said at last. "Seren Ragnall has invoked it, and by our laws, we are bound to respect it.

"The Lirien will be allowed to remain among us, under the protection of Seren's oath. Both shall be admitted into the Skorn trial." He turned away.

"My lord—" I said sharply, my voice strong now. "When the Skorn trial was established, those sentenced were given the chance to cleanse and purify themselves before the gods. I request my husband be freed from his irons and granted this clemency—as was the tradition for centuries."

A hush came over the watching crowd.

Haldron paused mid-step. After a moment, he swiveled toward me. "As I said, you're a clever woman, Seren Ragnall."

"We are nothing without our traditions, my lord."

Please let this work. Both of us needed rest before the trial.

As the room held its breath, a gentle smile played at Haldron's lips. "Very well. If the Lirien has been as heroic as Waldren Azad claims, his irons can be removed as he heals and cleanses his soul before the gods. But understand this, Seren. If he betrays us, the consequences will be yours to bear. The gods will decide your fate at the trial in two days. You must present yourself at the gates of the keep at sunset."

Solric above. Had it worked? He was letting us walk out of here—*free*—until the Skorn?

Some of the tension in my shoulders eased. "Yes, my lord. Are we free to go anywhere in Emberstone we wish?"

An intrigued look crossed his features. "Of course."

"Aren't you concerned they'll try to escape, my lord?" one of his councilors said.

"They won't. No one escapes Emberstone without me knowing about it."

Something about this felt ... too easy. I didn't dare look back at Rykr.

"You are all dismissed from my presence," Haldron declared, but his sharp gaze lingered on me. "In the meantime, I'll send scouts to Waldren Azad's tribe to investigate this skin-wraith raid. If they have invaded the Dreadwood, it may be a sign of dark and forbidden magic that must be rooted out."

His tone made a prickle of unease stir in my chest. Though maybe it wasn't my suspicion and worry I was feeling. I caught Rykr's eye, and through our bond, his distrust shone clearly.

"Can our tribe claim refuge here, my lord?" Seth asked, wariness on his face. "Our homes were destroyed—over seventy of our people slain, with many more wounded. It will take some time for us to reassemble in a new encampment, and our people are scared and tired."

Haldron's face softened. "Of course, Waldren Azad. The gates of Emberstone are always open to our most destitute. We will give you lodging in the House of the Veil for the next month." Then he made his way back toward the dais, the conversation over.

With that, the room rustled to life once again. The onlookers resumed normal levels of conversation.

I stepped closer to Rykr as the guards unshackled his wrists. He rolled his shoulder, flexing his fingers. "Great," he murmured, his voice hard. "If you can trust anything that would-be king of yours says."

I swallowed hard. "We should go."

Rykr leaned closer toward me, his lips at my ear. "I'd advise you to get me a sword as soon as possible, Seren." Rykr's voice was low, edged with barely concealed hatred. "That man won't think twice about stabbing us in the back when the crowd isn't watching."

Through our bond, I felt the searing anger that burned within him, but beneath it lay something more—deep, consuming unease. Rykr didn't trust easily, and in this moment, neither did I. Haldron's kindness felt more like a trap waiting to be sprung.

I didn't know what or why I felt this way—maybe it was the intensity of Rykr's feelings clouding my own—but he was right: we needed to be careful.

CHAPTER 27
RYKR

The lack of irons did nothing to make me feel freer.

As Seren and I left the keep, Seth and Darya at our heels, I forced the faces of my brothers and father deep into the vault of my mind, forming a wall around them, as Lucia had taught me to do. The Unbound here had powers of many kinds. Some might be able to see into my thoughts, or even influence them. I wouldn't risk discovery.

Haldron's arrogance had likely saved me from immediate suspicion—he hadn't even deemed me worthy of interrogation—but I didn't and wouldn't trust him not to have some other plan at play.

Seth stepped in front of our path as we stepped onto the road. "Where do you think you're going?"

A weary look crossed Seren's face. "To get a room at an inn. Sleep. It's been a long day, and I have no desire to stay at the House of the Veil."

"You should stay with us," Seth said. "There's been enough trouble for our tribe."

"And that will keep us under their watch," I said wryly to Seren.

"I'm grateful to you both for your help, but let's be honest. We aren't safe with the tribe. I'd rather take my chances in Emberstone." Seren crossed her arms and smiled sweetly. "I've already made arrangements."

Seth opened his mouth to protest further, but Darya set her hand on his arm. "Let them be, Seth. There's enough division in the tribe as it is; Seren is right. Perhaps some space might do everyone some good."

"Thank you," Seren said, then grabbed my hand and yanked me down a bustling path lined with taverns. My stomach growled at the smell of food, but Seren pressed forward, as though she knew exactly where she was heading.

A sharp turn led us into a narrow alley. A black cat mewed and jumped out from behind a barrel, startling us both, then slunk into the darkened space, its tail held high. We stopped and Seren glanced behind us as if expecting Seth or Darya to follow.

"Care to fill me in on where we're going?"

Seren continued to inspect the alley. "I'm not staying with the tribe. Given the rumors about Giulia and the skinwraiths, there's clearly someone working against us. If Ciaran is telling the truth, then whoever started the rumor is no friend of ours."

At least we agreed on that. But what about Haldron?

Stepping closer to her, I cornered her against the stone facade of the nearest building. "Is there a reason you failed to mention before that the tyrant leading your people is Haldron?"

She bristled, tossing her braid over her shoulder. "Haldron isn't a tyrant. He—"

"Was elected?" I scoffed. "If that's what helps you sleep at night, Seren. All I saw back there was a tyrant—not that it surprises me. And it seems ruling the Viori isn't good enough."

Seren's eyes widened, her head reclining against the wall as she looked up at me. "What do you mean?"

I tilted my head, scanning her face for feigned innocence. "You have to know ... don't you?" My voice dropped to a whisper.

Confusion glittered in her beautiful, long-lashed eyes. No deception, only genuine curiosity, but that didn't ease the knot in my chest.

"Haldron is King Magnus's younger brother—a traitor who vanished after attempting to kill the king. With Magnus and his sons gone, Haldron can claim the throne of Lirien. He doesn't just mean to cut off the head of the snake, he wants to drape himself in its skin. He wants a kingdom."

Seren shook her head, though doubt raced through the bond. "That's ridiculous." But her voice wavered, and I could feel her mind racing. "H-how would you know?"

"Trust me. I recognize him. And why would I lie?"

Her face blanched. "Even if you're right, my people want freedom, not war ..." Fear crept into her voice before she shoved past me, unwilling to face the possibility.

I grabbed her wrist, forcing her to a stop. "Is it? Hasn't that always been the goal of the Viori? To break the chains *oppressing* Lirien? Reclaim the lands they left? Why else would your people have made war on us for centuries?"

Seren gave me an incredulous look. "No. The only thing my people want is to live in peace. The Viori help each other and people in need. You're the ones that have made war on *us*—not the other way around."

I palmed my face. "Oh gods, we're not back to this, are we? You might be in denial about who Haldron is and what his intentions are, but I'm telling the truth. And if you don't believe me, ask your mother. She was in Magnus's court. I'm sure she knows who Haldron really is. Mark my words, his next move will be to order your Vangar to advance on Lirien and attack. War is coming, Seren. There's no stopping it now."

Her gaze held mine, fear glistening in her eyes. "It's not true."

"Haldron always wanted my"—I barely caught myself, then managed—"my king dead. He wanted the throne for himself. And now it appears he's not only found a way but also has secured an army willing to fight his war for him."

"But Haldron has been our leader for over eight years. If what you say is true, why would he wait to strike?"

"Maybe it takes time to arrange the assassination of the king and his sons."

"Eight years?" Seren shook her head. "He could have picked them off one by one if all he needed was for them to be dead."

"Haldron isn't a fool, and neither was Magnus. If his sons had started dying, he would have put safeguards in place to secure the bloodline. Haldron waited until he could wipe them all out in one stroke. To make war on Lirien easier. There's probably chaos in Suomelin right now with leadership in question."

"You're blinded by hatred," she said softly and retreated a step.

"And you're blinded by naivety," I shot back, my voice with a hard edge.

Seren flinched, then yanked her wrist out of my grasp. "You might think I'm naive, Rykr, but I know what Lirien soldiers do. They've destroyed my family, turned my life upside down. So, don't call me naive. And honestly, I'm a little more preoccupied with the threats to *our* lives than a war that is probably justified in the first place."

"Dammit!" I caught her wrist, firm but not harsh, forcing

her to face me. "So, we should do nothing? Just sit back and let it happen?" My voice was tight, simmering with restrained anger.

She flinched, but I didn't let go. "How do I even know—"

"If I'm telling the truth? You have to trust me. *Believe me.* You might not care, Seren, or you're being shortsighted. I pray to the gods it's the second option."

I towered over her, my temper flaring.

"If you think I give a fuck about myself when millions of innocent Liriens could be caught in a war they didn't ask for, you've sorely misjudged me. I've seen crippled men, disfigured faces, and children's bodies pulled from the ashes. War will devastate the masses, Seren. And if you don't care about it, then I've misjudged *you*."

She stared up at me, eyes searching mine, shoulders falling with quick breaths. This proud, beautiful Viori woman.

Gods, be the honorable woman I believe you are, Seren.

A flash of pain crossed her features. She'd heard me.

Seren closed her eyes. "What would you have me do? Even if it's true, I'm nobody. And I'm scared."

"You're not nobody, you're my wife. And you have to be scared to be brave, Seren. You know this war won't just hurt my people. Countless Viori will die trying to satisfy Haldron's lust for a stolen crown."

Her shoulders sagged under the weight of uncertainty. "But what can you or I do to stop it? We have to fight in a deadly trial in two days and might not even live through that." The quiet defeat in her voice stirred something raw inside me —a need to prove she wasn't as powerless as she claimed.

I cupped her face, leaning in, searching her eyes. "You're stronger than you think. You've already risked your life for me once. Trust me, Seren. If anyone can stand up to Haldron, it's you."

I wished I could tell her everything, lay bare every dangerous secret I carried. But trust was a gamble and if I gambled wrong, we'd both pay the price.

"If we survive the Skorn, I have to go back to Lirien," I whispered. "Just get me back to the border and I can handle the rest—warn the Liriens about what's coming."

Her lashes fluttered, sorrow darkening her gaze. "And then what happens to me? If they find out I helped you escape, I really will be a traitor. And it won't be just me who's punished—my family will be too, Rykr."

I released her and stepped back, tension fizzling into the void between us. I'd asked too much—more than she could sacrifice.

Distant sounds filtered in—children's voices echoed as they ran through the streets, laughter from friends gathered for a meal. The hum of life.

"If you were to leave on your own, I wouldn't stop you," she whispered, her eyes avoiding mine. But through the bond, her emotions surged like a river after a storm—a torrent flooding me with doubts I couldn't ignore. Was she afraid for me ... or afraid of what might happen to herself if I left?

The bond didn't lie, but it didn't tell the whole truth either. Not this time.

"We should try to find anything we can about breaking the bond between us before you do," Seren went on. "And not just for that, but for the Skorn, too. The priests in the temple might know something. Or a Seidr."

"How is a mystic going to help?"

"I don't know, Rykr. I don't have a lot of ideas, but it's better than doing nothing. Unless you'd like to stay in this situation with me. Have every secret stored in that Lirien head of yours exposed to my perusal. Your life at risk if anything happens to me during the Skorn."

Right.

She stepped away one more time. "Let's go. Hopefully Amahle went to Bellwether. Maybe we can get a good meal and some sleep, then come up with a better plan in the morning when we're not both so exhausted. But we can't afford to wait too long, Rykr. If Haldron *is* planning something, we need to be ready. I'm not under any illusion that his decision to free us the next couple of days was out of sheer benevolence."

I followed her without protest, but the weight of her turmoil flowed to me through the bond. I didn't know how we shared emotions so easily, but I could feel her in my mind, always present, just beyond a closed door. What would happen if I opened it?

The temptation coiled, dark and dangerous.

The thought of looking into her mind made my heartbeat quicken, but something held me back. If I crossed that line, would she know? Destroy what little trust we had?

Power without control was dangerous. Lucia had said we could lose ourselves to the bond and I wasn't sure I was ready to pay that price. But I didn't know how to control any of the powers I'd noticed since I'd woken with this bond.

Maybe my other powers, long bound by the Seal, were closer to the surface than I realized. My father had restricted them with the Seal—a binding I'd never fully understood.

I'd focused so long on warcraft that I'd nearly forgotten their call. But before I'd been arrested and exiled, I'd set a building ablaze in Suomelin, the fire bursting from my hands like an extension of my will—wild, uncontrollable, as natural as breathing.

What was I capable of now? And could I control it, or would it control me?

We emerged from the narrow alley into a street lined with textiles strung between wooden posts, the bright colors at odds with the dim, uneasy mood clinging to me. Lanterns swung gently overhead, casting long shadows on the cobblestones, and laughter drifted from a nearby tavern.

I tore my gaze from the fluttering banners and focused on the woman in front of me. There was no cunning in Seren's delicate features, only a quiet determination that made me want to believe in her—to trust she'd see beyond the lines that divided us. Maybe, if she knew who I really was, she'd understand my cause.

I wasn't my father. I didn't want to rule, only to save what was left before it was too late.

If Seren could help me, perhaps there was still a chance. Her character, sense of duty, and fierce loyalty suggested she was the best of her people.

Even if she's Brogan Ragnall's daughter.

But the yellow banners flapping from magical breezes reminded me I was far from home.

With Haldron resurfacing, and the threat of war looming over my thoughts, trust was a luxury I couldn't afford. Not even with her.

CHAPTER 28

RYKR

We found the Bellwether Inn within minutes—a three-story building that reminded me of Volker's. Wooden beams traversed the plaster and stone facade. Window boxes with flowers decorated the large amber glass windows by the doorway.

Lamps smoldered in the windows, their candles burning steady and bright—yet the wax never melted. Enchanted light.

Ciaran stood abruptly as we entered and Amahle gave us a withered, weak smile, sagging into a bench in the dark foyer below the main stairway.

Seren gave Ciaran a deep frown. "Why are you here?"

"Because I didn't have anything to do with what you accused me of. Ask yourself if I'd be here right now if I were lying."

Seren crossed her arms then frowned at Amahle. "I had to watch," Amahle said, closing her eyes.

Seren scowled back at Ciaran. "Why did you let her—"

"I didn't," Ciaran snapped, running his hand through his red hair, the seam of his mouth making a flat line.

Let her what? Amahle wore her exhaustion like she'd been fighting in dueling pits.

"I only watched until you left the keep," Amahle argued, leaning her head back against a stained-glass window behind her.

"Watched?" I raised a brow.

"She can spirit glide into other places," Seren explained tersely. "But it drains her, and leaves her completely vulnerable to being attacked while she's in that state."

"Ciaran was here to protect me," Amahle said, trying and failing to sit straighter. "And I was worried. It's not every day my best friend gets dragged to Emberstone in a prison wagon."

I peered closer at the dark-skinned beauty. *Spirit glide?* That seemed like an incredibly useful craft. "So, you can glide your mind to any place, whenever you want?"

Amahle shook her head. "Not anywhere. I can only go where someone I know is."

Ciaran bent beside Amahle and helped her stand. "You need rest."

"Food will help. Besides, we should celebrate." Amahle mustered a half-hearted smile as we moved toward the tavern beside the inn. "Seren and Rykr are free to wander Emberstone. I was worried they'd end up in the dungeons."

"That's not really cause for celebration, though, is it?" Ciaran cast a look back at me as we went inside. "They still have to face the Skorn."

Seren dropped into a chair at a table, across from Amahle and Ciaran. "Yes, but Haldron gave us complete freedom for a couple of days. We need to use that time to our advantage."

Ciaran lifted his grey eyes to mine. "And if he's just trying to test whether Rykr's a Lirien lackey?"

Seren frowned. "Ciaran—"

But Ciaran continued looking at me. "We've never heard him deny it, or explain why he's here. Who's to say he's not?"

Fair enough. I'd irritated him before, and now he wanted to take his shot.

I sank into the chair beside Seren, stretching my arm out along the back of hers with deliberate ease. "Have you bothered to ask me yourself?" I gave Ciaran an unaffected smirk.

His nostrils flared, a few beats of silence between us. "Skinwraiths attacked our encampment. That's never happened before you came along. And you convinced Seren not to tell anyone that Giulia was turned into a skinwraith, too."

"Is that true?" Amahle's jaw dropped open.

"Neither Rykr nor I had anything to do with Giulia. She attacked me," Seren told Amahle. "And yes. Rykr *and* Tara thought it was better not to say anything. For good reason, apparently. Look what happened."

Ciaran still wasn't convinced. "If you had said something, then we might have stopped the attack."

Amahle bit her lip, uncertainty in her eyes.

"You knew, didn't you? Why didn't you say anything either?" I tilted my head. "We don't always make the right decisions when trying to protect those we love, do we, Ciaran?"

The shame in his face made it clear I'd won.

A barmaid approached with steins of ale, setting them between us. "Food?" she asked, barely glancing at any of us. Either she didn't notice the thickness of the tension at the table, or she didn't care.

I lifted my stein and took a slow sip of warm ale.

"Yes, for everyone," Amahle said. As the barmaid left, Amahle gave Ciaran and me a stern look. "Boys, this isn't the place for this conversation. If you want to have it out later, be my guest. But if you insist on spoiling one of the last meals I might get to enjoy in peace with Seren, I'll send you to bed and make certain neither of you gets any spankings for the evening."

Choking mid-sip, I cleared my throat, then set my stein down with a laugh. "No spankings? You really know how to ruin a night, Amahle."

I sat back in my chair, boots sliding over the sawdust-strewn floor. Everything in here felt sticky with ale, the scent permeating the dimly lit space. A roaring fire in a hearth along the back wall kept the tavern warm, though. Despite the relative, unexpected freedom here, my tension didn't dissipate—as though I expected Haldron to step from the shadows and attack.

Ciaran's face darkened angrily as he slung back a swallow of ale. "I have a right to be wary, Amahle. His life threatens someone we both care about." He shook his head bitterly. "Those skinwraiths mean something. Something abnormal is happening."

Seren, who had been unusually quiet, leaned forward, her eyes hard. "Did you know that Haldron is heir to the throne of Lirien?"

"W-what?" Ciaran gave her a baffled look.

Amahle's brows drew together. "What do you mean?"

Seren tilted her head toward me. "Tell them."

Dammit, this isn't the time or place.

But Seren trusted them. Given the shift in our circumstances, we might need all the help we could get. I wasn't even sure I'd be able to sleep tonight, knowing how close we were to Haldron.

With a slow sigh, I leaned forward, resting my forearms on the table. "Haldron is Magnus's younger brother. If King Magnus and all his sons are dead, Haldron is next in line. Magnus's grandsons are all too young to rule—none are above age fifteen."

My words settled between us like lead.

Amahle and Ciaran seemed to absorb the information differently than Seren had. Maybe they were older, more cynical. Or just more realistic.

Amahle exhaled through puffed cheeks. "Well, fuck."

Ciaran held my gaze, clearly assailed by multiple thoughts at once. "We can't be the only people in the territory that know this."

"I don't think so," Seren said, her mouth twisting. "But those who do are probably his allies. And even fewer know about the full line of succession in Lirien."

"You think he wants the throne," Ciaran to me.

"You think it's a coincidence that the king and all his sons —every legitimate heir—were murdered by your Vangar? Haldron commands your soldiers, doesn't he?"

Amahle bit her lip. "That is a good point."

Seren's face was still pale, as though the reality of what I'd suggested was still difficult for her to digest. "He's going to lead us all to war." Her voice was barely audible in the din of the tavern. A few beats passed, the heaviness of her words descending between us.

No one argued, because there was nothing to argue. War wasn't a possibility anymore—it was a certainty. One we were racing toward whether we liked it or not.

Ciaran shook his head with disgust. "People from Emberstone wouldn't care even if they did find out. They are not the Vangar. They won't be the ones out there fighting Lirien soldiers, either. They'll hide here in the mountain, letting the rest of us take the brunt of the fucking war."

Seren reached across the table, resting her hand on his. "It's how it's always been," she said softly. They exchanged a familiar look of sympathy and understanding, one that made my stomach clench.

The ferocity of my reaction caught me off guard. Much as I understood their closeness, the way I disliked it was unsettling.

Ciaran's tirade also surprised me.

"I take it Viori society is more stratified here?"

Seren nodded, withdrawing her hand from Ciaran's. "The tribes are the outermost rung of Viori society," she explained, her tone carefully neutral. "We're the bulk of the Vangar because we came here later—newer arrivals to the Dreadwood. The ones who first fled here centuries ago settled near Emberstone, tired of wandering. Over time, they built lives for themselves."

Wiping his mouth with the back of his hand, Ciaran said, "Now they leave us to fight their war with Lirien."

His bitterness was unexpected. "Didn't they offer your tribe refuge here?"

"Temporarily. They won't let us stay here forever."

Amahle set her arm around him. "We all need to keep our voices down. There are spies everywhere in Emberstone, and they'll drag us away and question us for treason."

Ciaran lifted his red face defiantly. "Let them try. They won't get within a foot of me."

"No, they won't," Seren said as the barmaid approached with plates of steaming food. "But if we get kicked out before I have time to eat, then I may fight with you myself."

A giant, torn hunk of crusty bread had been placed in the broth on the plate. It felt like months since I'd eaten food so rich and full. The last meal I'd shared with Thorne and Dalric had been like this. *Gods, I missed them both.*

I still couldn't get the images of Dalric's slaughter out of my mind. It only fueled my deep anger. Especially now that I knew my own flesh and blood had been behind the attack. Life had seemed simpler then ... *before the Dreadwood.*

Seren's friends intrigued me. Ciaran's family clearly had money and position within Seren's tribe—they owned horses, and Seren had mentioned his father was one of the council members I'd seen that first day. His irritation with the upper echelons of Viori society probably stemmed, in part, from that.

Amahle was more enigmatic. Friendly, but impersonal. She revealed little about herself, a guardedness in her interactions that reminded me of Thorne.

"Did your family come with the rest of the tribe?" I asked Amahle abruptly, testing my theory.

Seren's eyes widened. "Rykr—"

Amahle held out a hand, silencing her. "He's trying to get to know me, Seren. And it's better than a conversation that could get us all in trouble." She settled her shoulders back. "No, I'm an orphan. My parents died at the hands of Lirien soldiers in a skirmish when I was twelve. What gave it away? Do I wear my neglect on my brow?" She teased a smile, but her eyes remained a mask.

"No. You just remind me of someone I know. He lost his parents as a boy, too."

Seren gave me a curious look then, her body turning toward mine.

"Do you mean you?" Seren asked tenuously.

"A friend of mine. I was just disowned, remember?"

She must not have believed me, because she set her hand on my forearm. "Where are your parents now, Rykr?"

All three eyes at the table fixed on me.

I took a swallow of ale. "Dead, actually." The statement burned my gut.

Seren's expressive eyes softened with sorrow, and she bit that luscious lower lip of hers.

Godsdamn, I'd like to sink my teeth into it.

That thought came out of nowhere.

"I'm fine." I wasn't, but she didn't have to know that.

"Cheers to a fellow orphan," Amahle said, lifting her stein with a sardonic smile that didn't quite reach her eyes. "We've all lost people, but that doesn't make it easier. The Ragnalls took me in, though, so I can't complain." She paused, studying Seren with gentleness. "Which is why I see Seren like a sister. A pale, tiny, little sister."

Seren rolled her eyes, her posture relaxing more. Amahle wasn't exaggerating about that part—the two women were opposites in size and appearance. Where Seren was petite and lithe, Amahle was tall, lean, and graceful. Dark-skinned.

Both were beautiful, though.

Ciaran leaned forward on his elbows, unwilling to let go of his distrust of me. He watched me suspiciously. "So, you see, *Rykr*, we all have reasons to dislike your kind. Amahle's parents, my brother—who was burned alive, tied to a stake in a Lirien town—Seren's little sister, Esme, who was just fifteen when kidnapped by your—"

"Ciaran," Seren warned, her voice crackling with irritation.

Ciaran hesitated, glancing at her before continuing, "Look, I'm not trying to be cruel, but if you're trusting him with your life, shouldn't he know the whole truth?"

"You have another sister?" *What in Solric's name?*

Ciaran frowned at her. "You didn't tell him about Esme? You shared your blood and bed with him, but didn't tell him *that*?"

What the hell was he talking about?

Seren had a sister I'd never ever heard about? *Why?*

Amahle held Seren's gaze and then set her hand on Ciaran's bicep. "All right, Ciaran. I think my bed is calling me, after all."

Surprisingly, Ciaran didn't protest as he helped Amahle stand. Amahle slid a key across the table, a room number attached to it. "This is for the room, and your pack is already in there." She shot Seren an apologetic look, then led him away.

Hungry as I was, I ignored my food and turned my body toward Seren as they left.

"Esme?"

Seren kept her gaze down and picked up a fork. "My little sister. She's fifteen."

"You have a fifteen-year-old sister I've never heard of?"

Fuck it. I needed to eat. I tore off a piece of bread, sopping up the broth before stuffing it in my mouth.

Seren pushed a cube of meat around in her bowl. "Yes. Don't act so surprised. You don't know that much about me or my family. You didn't know about Madoc until a few days ago, either."

"True, but from Amahle's and your reaction to Ciaran telling me, it's obvious you didn't want me to know about Esme."

"That's not it." She took a bite, still not meeting my eyes. "She was kidnapped six weeks ago." Seren's voice quivered faintly. "Taken by Lirien soldiers led by an Ederyn spy. He took her to Ibarra, and is holding her for the bounty on my father's head."

She gripped the table, her knuckles turning white. "My father and brother have been trying to rescue her, but they've ..." She faltered, grief in each word. "They haven't returned." Her voice cracked on the last word, her burdens becoming clear —the guilt, the fear of losing more family. She didn't need me to tell her how dire things were. I already knew.

No wonder Brogan Ragnall hadn't been at the encampment.

The story certainly made sense—the bounty on Brogan Ragnall was sizable. He'd killed my mother, and my father had been desperate to see him brought to justice.

But the mention of an Ederyn spy gave me pause. Seren had spoken about Esme's kidnapping with a flat, practiced tone, but beneath it, the unease crept in. I didn't know Esme, but I knew how it felt to lose family to war. I had to tread carefully.

Seren's story didn't sit right with me—not because I didn't believe her, but because something felt off. Too neat. Too convenient. I had no doubt her sister had been taken, but by whom and why? That was what gnawed at me. And if someone had lied to her, she deserved to know.

"How do you know he was an Ederyn?" I asked, keeping my voice steady as I took another forkful of food.

"I—" Seren didn't meet my gaze. "Esme was with me when he took her. He attacked me and left a note for my father."

"And that note said he was Ederyn?" I took a sip of ale. That sounded unlikely. The barmaid returned to fill my nearly empty stein, her gaze flicking to Seren for a fraction of a second too long. I hadn't realized how much I'd had to drink, but that wasn't what set me on edge. The way the barmaid moved—careful and practiced—reminded me of a scout trying not to be noticed.

As she walked away, Seren lifted her eyes to me, confusion and anger sparking in her eyes. "Are you making fun of me?"

"I'm just saying, if he left a note with his name on it, he's not exactly the smartest spy."

"What difference does it make? He was Lirien, and he took her."

I chewed and swallowed, keeping my voice low as I sobered. "It makes a difference. The details matter. Ederyn doesn't have many spies of their own. There are some, but most of the warcraft belongs to Pendara. Truly gifted Ederyn spies aren't trained by the Sealed Masters in Pendara, so they don't rise up the ranks. And an Ederyn spy who could track your father to your encampment would have to be gifted, wouldn't you say?" I licked my thumb, then wiped it on a cloth napkin.

Seren stared at me, open-mouthed. As though she was just realizing I knew much more about Lirien than she understood. Or that I really *was* Lirien. *Which might not do me any favors.*

"You're missing the point."

"No, I'm not." I took another bite, chewing deliberately. "Because the only way that a spy would be leading a group of Lirien soldiers this far into Viori territory would be on the king's orders. So why take Esme to Ibarra, of all places, instead of to Ederyn? And if he was that close to capturing your father, why take Esme at all? Why not just take him?"

Seren bristled. "Are you saying I'm lying?"

"I'm saying someone is lying to *you.*"

She paled. "Who?" She hadn't touched her food.

"I don't know." I almost felt guilty for saying anything, but she had the right to know. No doubt the fact that Esme had been taken while with her weighed on her heavily. "You should eat."

Seren rubbed her forehead, her well-crafted poise unraveling. Grief commanded her face, her eyes mournful. "How the fuck am I supposed to just eat after that?" She scowled at me, then snatched her stein. Ale trickled from the corner of her mouth as she drained it.

I frowned as she set the empty stein down, then started in on her food.

"You didn't want to know the truth?"

"I *do* want to know the truth, you swiver. But you haven't put me any closer to it."

I didn't answer, unsure of what to say to her. Fury continued to mount in her posture.

She ate a few more bites, then slammed her fork down on

the scarred tabletop. "My father knows as much about Lirien as you do. He'd be smart enough to figure out everything you just said."

Had her father been the one to lie, then?

"I think we're being listened to," I murmured, keeping my eyes on the barmaid as she made another round through the tavern. She wasn't like the others—she was too poised, too aware of her surroundings. She wasn't just serving drinks. She watched *us*, waiting for something.

Seren stiffened. "Who?"

"The barmaid." I leaned closer to Seren. "If she's a spy, we've already said too much." I sipped my ale.

"Godsdammit." Seren took several more bites, then pushed her bowl away. "Let's just go." Seren threw some money on the table, glancing once toward the barmaid. Her movements were quick, controlled, but I could see the tension in the tight set of her jaw. She didn't trust this place, and frankly, neither did I.

I followed her across the street to the inn. "We should leave first thing in the morning. No sense in staying longer than we have to."

"Where the hell else are we supposed to go? There's nowhere safe for us right now." Seren strode up the stairwell just to the left of the entrance, as though she knew exactly where she was heading. The idea of the barmaid spying on us did little to warm me to the idea of staying here overnight. If she had been spying, all she'd needed to do was look out the window to see where we'd gone.

Seren unlocked a room at the end of the hall, her shoulders rigid as if she expected an attack at any moment. She didn't speak as we stepped inside.

The enchanted candles cast a soft, golden glow across the small room, but the warmth didn't reach her expression. She was retreating again, shutting herself off after that brief, vulnerable moment in the tavern. I didn't blame her—I wasn't exactly good at this sort of thing either.

A narrow bed, barely large enough for one person, stood against the long wall of the room.

That should be interesting. The bedroll had been cozy enough. This would be torture.

But what the space lacked in size, it more than made up for with a bathtub.

While I eyed the furnishings, Seren slid her pack from her shoulders, then unfastened her sword holsters and bandoliers. She set them down on a chair, her face flushed.

Her hands trembled as she unlaced her leather vest, as though all she wanted was to rip off the restrictive material, but her shirt was still missing below it.

I crossed my arms, leaning against the door. "What's wrong?" I asked, though I already knew.

Seren's head snapped up, eyes blazing. "What's wrong?" she repeated, her voice tight, trembling. "You can't be serious. Look at my life, Rykr!" Her breath hitched, and for a moment, I thought she might cry. But she didn't. She braced herself, holding it all inside like a dam ready to burst.

She unbraided her hair swiftly, shaking it loose over her shoulders.

I struggled to concentrate on her words after she'd untied her hair like that. Her dark, gold-streaked tresses cascaded over her shoulders in soft waves, reaching the middle of her back. In her normal braid, she looked fierce and untouchable, but this softened her, made her more human, more fragile.

Seeing her like this reminded me of why she'd risked everything to save me. She carried burdens too heavy for her slight frame. She wasn't weak but her strength came from a place I was still learning to understand.

My hands burned with the urge to run my fingers through

her hair, coil my fingers through it at the base of her neck and draw her head back. Kiss her until she forgot the weight of the world pressing down on her.

Fuck.

The ale, however minimal, was messing with my judgment.

I can't get involved with her.

She was fucking forbidden fruit in every way, and right now, the only thing I wanted was a taste.

I dragged my gaze from her, my fingers curling around my biceps as my arms tightened closer to my chest, as if that would keep me from reaching for her.

When I didn't respond, her expression shifted, and she looked away. "I get it. Your life is in shambles, too. I'm sorry."

Shambles was one word for it.

The exchange was enough to break the trance I'd fallen into, and I went to the edge of the bed and sat. "You're right. We have to start trusting each other more," I said, almost as much to myself as to her. "It's the only way either of us is going to survive what's happened to us, *and* what's coming." Even if I couldn't tell her the whole truth.

I removed the boots as she turned, her face drained of color.

"I never should have saved you," she whispered, her voice trembling. "I j-just couldn't ... I wasn't strong enough to l-let you die. And now it doesn't matter because we both know I won't survive the Skorn."

Her words hit me like a punch to the gut. She was blaming herself—for saving me, for not being ruthless enough to follow the Viori way.

Standing, I gently pulled her into my arms. She didn't resist. She sank against me instead, like she belonged there. "You are strong, Seren." I rested my chin atop her head.

"Stronger than anyone I've ever known. You didn't let me live out of weakness, you did it because you're better than they are."

Her arms slid around my neck and she stood on her tiptoes, her lips skimming my throat. I closed my eyes, tormented by the feel of her pressed up against me—the quiet, warm tremor of her breath.

She clung to me like I was the only solid thing in a world that kept shifting beneath her feet.

I tightened my grip, not knowing how else to steady her when everything else seemed to be falling apart.

As her lips crept up my neck, feather-soft, drawing closer to my jawline, the tension between us shifted into something else, more instinctive, more necessary.

It would be so fucking easy to slide my hands beneath her shirt, to palm the curves that had distracted me more than once over the last few days.

But she was vulnerable and had downed her ale as fast as I had.

Still, with her body pressed tight against mine, her mouth grazing my jaw, want took over rational thought. My cock hardened at the feel of her pushed up against my hips, my mouth aching to consume hers with the type of kiss that chaste peck in the wagon had stirred in my imagination.

My body was primed for something I shouldn't take.

Fuck. Me.

A taste wouldn't hurt. Just one small taste of those fucking full, luscious lips. One sip of her tongue ...

Fire consumed me as her lips inched closer to my mouth, heat flooding my body.

"We shouldn't," I managed, even as my fingers skimmed the lacing of her vest, sliding onto her bare waist.

She let out a throaty laugh, her breath hot against my skin. "Really, Rykr?"

Well, fuck, I sound like a prude.

"If you don't want it, we can stop," she whispered in my ear as her hand slipped down over the bulge in my pants. "But your cock is telling me otherwise." Her tongue darted against my ear. "And I like a man who takes what he wants."

A guttural groan tore from my throat. My mind was spinning.

"Want has nothing to do with it," I said in a low growl.

Want had everything to do with it. Wanting her was dangerous. Wanting her was also all I could focus on. Her softness, the velvet silkiness of her skin as my fingers glided up her spine.

Those legs I wanted to bury my face between.

"All that bragging, Rykr. Are you a tease, after all?"

"Fuck, solwyn." Pushing my hand up to the nape of her neck, I drew her head back and searched the deep pools of her eyes.

Our mouths were a whisper apart, all rational thought now gone.

Then she wet her lips with that tongue, waiting.

My mouth descended on hers as I forced myself to be slow. Gentle. Even as hunger roared inside me, demanding more. Demanding I shove her up against the wall, push her pants off her hips and take her hot and fast, right now. She tasted like salt and sweet ale—something forbidden. Something I would fucking die for.

But I can have control.

Her full lips melted against mine, a sizzling heat breaking through the surface of my skin, my want for her intensifying to an inferno.

Not want. Need.

I fucking need this woman.

I angled her head, holding myself steady as she leaned her weight farther into me. Her lips parted and my mouth slanted over hers, my tongue seeking hers in soft strokes. Her body yielded, fitting against me in a way that felt inevitable.

My mouth worked over hers, my hand slipping around her waist, and moving up until I palmed one perfect, full breast—

A knock rattled the door. "Seren?"

Amahle.

Seren tore away from me, her fingers brushing her lips as if she could erase what had just happened. She turned, moving past me without another glance.

"Wait." I grabbed one of her blades.

Seren gave me a baffled look as I sidled up to the doorframe, back against the wall.

"If the barmaid was spying, someone might be waiting to take us. We can't take chances."

Seren paled, then cracked the door open. "Hey," she said, her voice overly bright. Her posture relaxed. *"Just her."*

My gripped loosened, then I crossed toward the bed, removing the leather kilt above my trousers.

Amahle's voice was softer than usual. "You all right? I'm sorry about Ciaran bringing up Esme."

"It's fine." Seren gathered her hair over one shoulder. "It's just been a long day. I think I'm going to bathe and then go to bed."

Over my shoulder, I flicked a glance at Amahle, who studied me with that keen gaze of hers—like she saw too much but chose to say little.

"I'm right across the hall if you need anything. Ciaran's room in next to yours, but you might want to keep it down." Amahle met my eyes. "For his sake."

I smirked, thankful for Amahle's honesty.

"Noted. Only the necessary noises. I'll do my best to control myself but hopefully the bed doesn't squeak." I pulled off my leather vest, tossing it on the ground beside my boots.

Amahle rolled her eyes, then left again.

Seren shut the door, still facing it. "Swiver."

I chuckled. "I aim to please, solwyn."

She ignored me, climbing on the bed and pulling a book from her pack. "Why don't we take turns with that bath? There's warm water. It's one reason I like this inn." She nodded toward the tub. "You can go first." Curling her legs onto the bed, Seren opened the book.

"Is this your polite way of saying I stink? You didn't seem to mind so much a minute ago."

Her eyes flicked to me for half a second—just long enough to see me unbuckling my belt—before she stubbornly returned to her book.

I bit back a grin. "Don't worry. I won't use up all the hot water. Just most of it."

Seren rolled her eyes, but the faint curve of a smile betrayed her. "Go ahead, Rykr. You can wash off all that arrogance while you're at it."

That's it then.

We were back to pretending. Back to ignoring the kiss that had left us both breathless.

So be it.

That was safer. She'd run to the bed like a frightened rabbit who'd almost been ensnared.

But sleeping next to her—because there wasn't really space on the floor—was going to be its own kind of battle. And if I lost that battle, neither of us would come out unscathed.

Because I'd been wrong. One taste of Seren Ragnall would never be enough.

The weight of something large, heavy, and unfamiliar rested on my hip and I stirred, only dimly aware of my surroundings.

The Bellwether. The bed meant for one.

Rykr.

Drawing a shallow breath, I tried not to move. I couldn't blame him for curling his arm around my waist as we slept but he'd also unconsciously dragged us closer together. My ass was tucked neatly into his groin, his knees were pushed into the back of mine, and his foot was draped over mine.

Warm, intimate. Too close.

If we really were husband and wife, I would have rocked myself back against him. Through the thin fabric of my shirt over my backside, the hardness of his cock pressed against me. It was tempting. Waking up like this in a lover's arms would have been exhilarating, welcome.

But Rykr wasn't my lover.

He wasn't my real husband, either, no matter what Tara had implied.

Even if we survived the Skorn, he wouldn't stay.

And if I let him leave, I'd be a traitor. Especially if his plan was to return to Lirien and warn his people of the war Haldron was planning.

The consequences of his escape … I suppressed a shudder. I wouldn't think about that yet. If I did, I might lose my nerve.

What had I expected, really? That saving his life might mean something? That Rykr, of all people, would give up Lirien for me?

Fool. I was never seen as anything special. Needed. *Anything other than a pretend warrior.* The thought cut deep, but I shoved it aside. Feelings had no place here.

What mattered was breaking the bond, to give us each the best chance at survival. Imagining anything else was a dangerous fantasy. I would never force him to stay. *Which is exactly why I need to get out of this bed.*

Carefully, I reached for the small satchel of Ibarran spell powder on the nightstand. Dipping my fingertips inside, I took a small dusting and turned toward Rykr. I whispered a spell, then blew the dust from my fingertips toward his face. It settled there with a faint blue glow, then vanished.

The sleeping spell would deepen his rest, making it easier for me slip free.

With clever, slow-paced maneuvering, I got out of bed. Only when I was dressed and easing into the hallway, though, did I finally let myself breathe.

Crossing the hall, I tapped with a fingernail on Amahle's door.

A few moments later, she opened it, her dark eyes peering into the dim lighting. "You realize you're not in the forest, right? We can sleep past sunrise here."

I shrugged. "Speak for yourself. Next time get me a bed for two. Rykr practically spent the night on top of me."

Amahle lifted a brow. "That's easy. Next time, you get on top."

"Very funny. Care to take a stroll to the repository with me this morning? It'll be fun."

Amahle wrinkled her nose, considering. "Only if we stop by a bakery along the way. I'm not giving up the chance to eat all my favorite Emberstone foods for your side quests."

"Deal."

As I waited for her to dress, I leaned against the hallway wall, smiling to myself. Having her here grounded me. Even with the weight of everything pressing down, Amahle's presence was like a semblance of normalcy to the world I'd existed in before Esme had been taken.

Funny how I hadn't appreciated the simplicity of my life back then. My worries had been about small things—staying safe, finding food, enjoying time with Amahle and Ciaran when our duties permitted. Now, every decision felt like a step closer to failure, the weight of Esme's absence a permanent albatross on my shoulders.

A faint tingling spread through my fingers, the familiar aftereffect of spellcraft—but this time, it lingered, an odd numbness I couldn't shake. I flexed my fingers, unease curling in my stomach. My spells had always come easily, like second nature, so why did it feel like something was slipping?

Maybe I'd stop by the House of the Veil before heading to the repository. My mother might have answers.

We left the inn within minutes, heading into the quiet of Emberstone at dawn. Inside the mountain, the illusion of daylight and weather was cast by magic, the cavern ceiling shifting with the outside sky. The only advantage was that it never actually rained here, though lightning storms were interesting.

Amahle treated me to pastries from her favorite bakery, filled with cinnamon and fruit and drizzled with tangy, sweet icing, but the sweetness did little to ease the unease in my chest. My hands still felt strange, as though resistant to the spell I'd cast.

Now wasn't the time to doubt myself.

"To the repository, then?" Amahle asked as we headed back onto the streets.

"Actually, I want to stop by the House of the Veil, first." I hesitated, but this was Amahle, and she'd want to know. "I've been having some strange tingling in my hands. I want to ask my mother about it."

And if Haldron really was King Magnus's brother, she'd know.

But why didn't she ever tell me?

"Tingling?" Amahle raised a brow.

"I'm sure it's nothing. Just something I noticed after casting a spell."

"That doesn't sound good, Seren." Amahle's frown creased her forehead. "I say this with love, but you look ... tired. Rykr's not keeping you up all night, is he?"

I should have known she'd bring this up. I jabbed my elbow into her side. "Amahle, no."

"Don't pretend I didn't interrupt something last night. I felt bad enough about it. Hopefully, you were able to resume after I left."

"You didn't interrupt." At her skeptical gaze, I wrinkled my nose. "There may have been a kiss, but it was nothing. Just a momentary lapse in judgment."

"If a man like Rykr was in my room, I'd invite *all sorts* of lapses in judgment." Amahle grinned, rummaging in her bag for another pastry. "Don't pretend you don't like him, Seren.

The heat between you two sizzles. That performance in the sparring ring ... just *damn*."

Despite my protests, the memory of that kiss made me want to squirm—in a good way. His hands on my skin had been incredible, the taste of him better than I'd dreamed.

And I did like him.

More than that. *I care about him.* That's why the thought of him leaving was impossible to face.

Stop it, now.

This wasn't some ordinary Viori man that we could gossip and giggle about.

I tightened my resolve, jutting my chin. "It doesn't matter. He's Lirien, I'm Viori. That's never going to change."

We were nearing the House of the Veil on the city's eastern side when I saw it—a flash of a familiar light blue cloak in the distance, hurrying away. *Mother.*

I stilled.

Amahle followed my gaze. "Lucia?"

I nodded.

"Where's she going?"

"I don't know. But I think we should find out." I put my hand out to stop Amahle from stepping forward. "At a distance."

"You want to follow your mother and spy on her?" Amahle's dark eyes glittered with confusion.

Do I? But something in the urgency of my mother's movement worried me. She'd stayed with the tribe to heal the wounded—supposedly—so why was she leaving so early?

"Just for a little while. To see where she's going. We can catch up with her if needed, but she's acting strangely, don't you think?"

"Why do I get the feeling this morning is going to be less fun than you promised?"

"Feel free to go back if you want." I meant it, too. It wasn't fair to drag her into whatever this was.

Amahle rolled her eyes and started walking. "You know I'd follow you to the worst part of Lirien if you asked."

Amahle didn't just say things like that lightly. Her loyalty wasn't the blind kind—it was fierce, earned, and it made my throat thicken.

"Thank you," I whispered. "I don't know, I just get this *feeling* like I should let this play out."

"Oh yeah?" Amahle's eyes twinkled with amusement. "Well, Ciaran and I know better than to ignore those feelings of yours—and not just because you're brilliant and got us out of more than one tough scrape with your little spells and quirky bits of knowledge you tuck away for the right moment. Like when you saved Ciaran from the harpies."

A laughing groan escaped me.

Ciaran. The harpies. *Gods.*

In one of the encampments where we'd stayed, Ciaran had become obsessed with hunting the harpies—magical creatures with the bodies of eagles and heads of women who were all-knowing. He'd actually found one. And the damned thing had snatched him up in its claws, trying to carry him off.

Amahle had landed an arrow in its wing, forcing it to release him—right into a freefall to his death. Until I cast a spell, weaving the tree branches into a net that caught him.

He'd been bruised and bloody and broken an arm, but he'd lived.

"I didn't do it alone. We always were a good team," I said, but the words were bittersweet. I'd always thought the three of us—me, Amahle, and Ciaran—were unshakable. We had faced harpies, storms, and worse, always pulling each other through.

But this wasn't just about survival anymore. Rykr had changed everything, and no amount of clever spells or quick thinking could undo that. "Now Ciaran's upset with me because of Rykr."

We turned a corner, slowing as we searched the street for my mother.

There she was, far ahead, still moving at a brisk pace we could hardly keep up with. "Ciaran's just angry because you brought a Lirien home," Amahle said in a low voice.

"He'll come around," I said, but the words felt hollow. "Right?"

Amahle shrugged. "He's always carried a torch for you, Ser. Maybe it's not Rykr he hates. It's the idea of anyone who isn't him." Amahle frowned suddenly, squinting as she tried to trail my mother. "Where *is* she going?"

"You see? I'm not imagining things, am I? She's acting strange."

"If I can be honest, Ser, your mother has a level of strange that's also part of who she is. Not that I don't love her, but the Ibarran priestess in her scares the hell out of me, too."

I didn't answer—I was too focused on keeping up. My mother wove into a labyrinth of dark alleys with the ease of someone who knew exactly where she was going. *Curpiss.* If we didn't hurry up, we were going to lose her.

A sudden flood of confusion poured through my bond with Rykr, making my steps falter.

"Where the hell are you, Seren?" Rykr's voice was edged with irritation and grogginess.

"Good morning to you, too." The bond between us hummed faintly, a reminder of just how much he could feel. *"I slipped out with Amahle and went to talk to my mother."*

"Without telling me?"

My pulse quickened at the possessiveness in his tone. It shouldn't have mattered, but somehow, it did.

I closed my eyes briefly, savoring the familiar rasp of it before responding again. I wouldn't miss the attitude, but his voice? That was different. If this bond broke, would I still remember the way it wrapped around me like a spell?

Don't get sentimental. He wasn't mine to keep. He never had been. "*You were sleeping.*"

"*Yeah, well, next time maybe leave me a note or something,*" he snapped. "*Or, better yet, wake me up and tell me.*"

There was a pause before he added, softer this time, "*I would have come with you.*"

That stopped me in my tracks. I couldn't afford to let him come, but the offer—unexpected and earnest—tightened something in my chest.

"*Sounds like you slept as well as I did. Or is the jackass within just stronger before breakfast?*" I turned down another alley, no longer worried that my mother would see us. She was moving too fast to look over her shoulder for us.

His silence lingered for a beat too long. "*We were being watched last night.*"

The worry threading through his thoughts struck me silent for a moment. I forced myself to deflect. "*Maybe try trusting me. I've handled myself without your help until now.*"

I almost regretted the sharpness of my tone. "*Be careful,*" he said finally. "*For both our sakes. I don't take chances with your life.*" The intensity behind his words sent a shiver down my spine.

"Do you see her?" Amahle asked as we searched the alley.

"*Nope,*" I said to Rykr before I could stop myself, then cringed.

"*What?*" Rykr's suspicion was sharp enough to make me wince.

"*If you want something to do, ask Ciaran to take you to a*

swordsmith." Now I was the one starting to sound irritated. Figuring out how to control this free exchange of thoughts was crucial.

Yet another thing I needed my mother for.

But where had she gone?

As though she'd vanished, the alley ahead was empty.

Maybe she'd turned a corner or gone inside one of the buildings. I stomped my boot. "I should have just called her when I saw her."

We slowed as we approached the area where we'd last seen her—near an old, sputtering fountain by the city walls, the stone streaked with dark water stains.

This was a dead end. The city limits pressed against the mountain walls. If not for the buildings, we'd probably be able to see clear to the eastern gate.

The only way out was the way we'd come.

Or—

I stepped closer to a circular grate in the wall. Rusted iron bars spanned its opening, large enough for a grown man to fit through if he crouched. The entrance to the sewer.

Amahle stepped to my side, eyes flicking from me to the grate. "You don't think—"

"Mother?" I called softly, leaning toward the bars.

"That answers that question." Amahle scrunched her nose. "The sewer? Really?" She tested the lock. "It's locked."

A furtive glance around confirmed that we were alone. "You know my mother is better with locks than I am." I pulled the pin from my hair.

"Yeah, because she cheats." Amahle crossed her arms. "I don't know how Ibarra hasn't taken over all of Lirien. Spellcraft seems like the most useful divine gift when it comes to ruling."

I inserted the pin into the lock, peering closer. The lock was so large that my pin nearly vanished inside it, my fingers barely able to grasp the metal. "True, but the spellcraft that would be useful to the power-hungry is forbidden. Dark magic destroys the soul."

"Halt. What are you doing?" a deep voice snapped behind us.

I stiffened, my heart kicking. Glancing over my shoulder, I met the angry glare of a silver-clad guard striding toward us. I tucked my pin into my palm, straightening. "Are you attempting to enter the sewers?"

"Uh—no, I was just—"

"The sewers are strictly off limits." The guard jutted his chin at us. "Your name, rank, and tribe."

Curpiss.

Getting arrested for this wouldn't do me any favors.

Slipping my pin into my bracer, I pulled a pinch of spell powder from my satchel, extended my hand, palm up, whispered a sleeping spell. Blowing gently, I sent the powder toward the guard.

The air shimmered faintly, then dissipated, as if swallowed by an invisible force. My hands tingled again, stronger this time, a cold numbness crawling up my wrists.

Nothing.

Why wasn't it working?

What in Solric's name?

The guard's eyes narrowed and he sneered, towering over us both. "Did you just try to put a spell on me?"

My tongue seemed frozen by the sheer shock that my spell hadn't worked. What had gone wrong? *I just made this so much worse.*

Amahle jumped in. "Is this the sewer?" Amahle made a face. "Oh gods, thanks for letting us know. We were—"

"Name. Rank. Tribe. *Now.*"

The guard's voice dripped with hostility.

Before either of us could respond, footsteps echoed from the sewer. A violet glow flared from the dark and surrounded the guard. He swayed, then collapsed, his head hitting the ground with a sickening thump.

My mother stepped from the shadows, her hands on the bars.

Thank the gods.

She gave us a sharp look, then waved the gate open. "What are you doing here?" she asked, kneeling beside the unconscious guard. Violet light shimmered from her hands as she pressed her palm to his forehead.

"I—" My mother rarely displayed her powers at home, and never like this. "What am I doing here? What are *you* doing here? I was trying to find you and then—"

"We followed you," Amahle admitted, chagrin on her face.

Mother stood, her lips set to a line. After a moment, she waved us forward, drawing us away from the guard and the sewer.

"What about the guard?" I glanced back as we hurried down the alley.

"I erased his memories. He'll wake thinking he slipped near the fountain and hit his head." Mother didn't glance back at me, but irritation threaded her voice. "You never should have let her follow me, Amahle. I told you to watch over her. To keep her out of trouble."

My jaw dropped. She had Amahle spying on me?

Amahle cringed but shot me an apologetic look. "I didn't know there was any harm in following you," she told my mother.

Once we were deep into another alley, I grabbed my mother's elbow, forcing her to stop. "Wait. What's going on? Why were you in the sewer? Why were you—"

"One question at a time, Seren," she snapped. Then, her eyes softened, and she cupped my cheek. "I'm sorry. You don't need to put yourself in any more danger, my love." She gave an anxious glance back in the direction we'd come. "I thought I sensed ..."

I waited, but she didn't finish.

Amahle and I exchanged a look. Something was *wrong*.

My mother blinked again and frowned, as if shaking off whatever had distracted her. When she looked at me again, the vulnerability had vanished, replaced by cool disapproval. "No matter. What did you need me for?"

Amahle shifted with discomfort. "I'm going to give you two a moment."

She walked away before my mother or I could protest.

"Glad to know you're having my friends spy on me," I muttered, thoroughly confused by my mother's behavior.

My mother bristled, her face shadowed by grief and fear. "We're in grave danger here, Seren. More than you could possibly understand. You're facing the deadliest of trials *tomorrow*. Esme, Madoc, Tara ... I'm helpless to aid any of my children and I'm doing the best I can. To honor my oaths, to find out what's happened to your father ..." Her hands were shaking, now.

"I don't know what more I can *do*," Mother went on, more flustered than I'd ever seen her. "I have to do something. I have to *help*."

But why in the sewers? That didn't make sense.

I caught her by the arms, then pulled her into my embrace. She had always been so strong. So competent. I'd never been the one comforting her. Yet I understood her pain and her struggles. Her sorrow.

Maybe Tara, my mother, and I all carried the grief differently, but it had consumed us all the past six weeks. I'd been so wrapped up in my own pain, in the way I had made everything worse, that I hadn't seen how much she was cracking at the seams.

Over Esme. Over Madoc and my father. Over all of us.

I kissed her cheek, gently, then pulled away from her. "I love you," I said, my voice trembling.

"Oh, my darling." My mother sounded as broken as I felt. "I love you too. So much more than you will ever know. There is nothing I wouldn't do for any of my children—I hope you understand that."

My powers are failing me, I wanted to tell her.

Help me.

But she was burdened enough.

"What did you need?" my mother asked, sniffling and attempting to pull herself together.

"I—" I drew a breath, then chose the safest question. "I wanted to ask about Haldron. Rykr said he's King Magnus's brother. In the line of succession."

Her face darkened. "He's right," she said softly. "But you should be careful who you share that information with. *Rykr* should be careful, too."

I closed my eyes, absorbing the information. Despite not wanting to believe Rykr, I'd known he was telling the truth.

Which likely meant everything else was true, too.

War was coming.

Rykr had to leave.

But before that, I had to face the Skorn. And my powers were failing.

My hands still tingled, the numbness now crawling up to my elbows. Emberstone's wards couldn't explain this—my magic had never faltered, not even in the most hostile conditions. It wasn't just unsettling. It was terrifying.

My magic was more than a tool. It was part of who I was,

part of what made me valuable—to my tribe, to myself. My secret weapon to survive.

I couldn't rely on anyone else to save me now. Not my mother, not Rykr.

They had their own battles to fight.

Somehow, I was more alone than ever.

CHAPTER 30
RYKR

From the look on Ciaran's face as I tested the weight of the blade in my hand, he *hated* that Seren had insisted on arming me.

Not that I trusted him, either.

The swordsmith in front of me either hadn't noticed or didn't care about the Seal on my neck, though the Vangar leathers did a decent job of hiding it. The new clothing was comfortable and well fitted but I couldn't dislodge the contemptible feeling of being a traitor in the clothes of my enemy. *My brothers would be ashamed.*

Bracing his weight onto his hands, the swordsmith gave me a bored look. "Well?"

My fingers tightened around the grip. Truth was, I'd never purchased my own sword before. My father had always outfitted me with the best Volker steel—preselected from the finest craftsmen—in addition to my own heirloom blade, which Seth still held.

Would Seth give it back now that his hostility had cooled? He'd even shown me a semblance of trust since the skinwraith attack.

"Usually, I know if I like a blade once I'm using it." I avoided the swordsmith's gaze.

Ciaran's sigh was loud.

The swordsmith grunted. "If you don't know what you're looking for, you're wasting my time." He shoved his way through the side door of the forge, muttering about customers who didn't know steel from tin.

Ciaran pinched the bridge of his nose, then held out his hand. "Here. Let me take a look."

I raised a brow. He really thought he knew these weapons better than I did? But it was stifling in here and I doubted he wanted to waste any more time with me.

I handed him the sword, and he stepped back, studying the blade in the golden glow of the forge. Sweat beaded on his forehead and he slipped the guard onto his forearm, testing the blade against the palm of his hand. He frowned, then met my eyes. "The man's a crook."

Before I could ask what he meant, the door swung open again, and the swordsmith returned.

Ciaran didn't hesitate. "You called this Volker steel?"

"It is." The swordsmith sniffed, swiping a greasy hand across his face.

Ciaran didn't argue. He simply gripped the blade in both hands and bent it. The clean snap echoed in the forge.

Solric's name ... *how?*

The swordsmith's eyes narrowed with liquid fury. "Hey! You'll have to pay for that."

"We won't be paying for anything but Volker steel." Ciaran took a challenging step toward him. "I can't snap Volker steel once it's been forged, which means you were lying and trying to sell us a piece of junk. Now, if you don't want the whole city to hear about it, I suggest you fetch a real sword before I decide to test how many other blades in here are just as worthless."

Whether because of Ciaran's size or the fact that he'd been caught, the swordsmith blanched, then took a nervous step back.

Within minutes, we were on our way out of the shop, a new sword at my side.

"Thank you." I studied Ciaran's determined, serious profile as we waded through the crowded streets of the trade district. "But how in the fuck—"

"It's the power I was born with. And I didn't do it for you. I did it because Seren doesn't deserve to waste *her* money on a fake sword."

I rubbed the scruff of my jaw, his words having the intended, humiliating effect. A reminder of how much I owed Seren. How pathetic my existence here was.

Still, I stopped walking and turned to face him, meeting him head-on. A man like Ciaran wouldn't respond to anything less that blunt honesty.

"You might think this is about me, but I'm not thrilled about my wife's relationship with you, either. You couldn't keep your hands off her during that little chat in the forest."

Ciaran's lips curled. "Your wife?" He shook his head. "That's laughable and you know it. Seren is no more your wife than I'm a Lirien. But fine. You want honesty? Let's be honest. I don't trust you. I don't like you. And I don't believe a damn thing you say.

His voice dropped, rough with anger. "But more than that? I don't believe you deserve her. She's given up everything for you, and the only reason I tolerate you is because she says if anything happens to you, she'll be hurt—or worse. I'll protect her, even from her own bad decisions."

A muscle in my jaw twitched. He hadn't told me a single

thing I didn't already know. But I latched on to what he hadn't said, instead. "Sounds like you don't quite believe in her, either."

Ciaran's face reddened. "I believe in her."

"Enough to not want to risk her life, but not enough to accept that I'm her husband by law and by oath."

Ciaran's lips parted and a stupefied expression crossed the ox's eyes. "You're—"

"The better warrior?" I smirked. "Smarter than you? Sharing the bed of the woman you love?" I let the words land, watching as his hands clenched. "Or all of the above?"

Without giving him a chance to respond, I turned and walked away. I already knew the way back to the Bellwether.

The words I'd thrown at him had been reckless, and there was no satisfaction in them. Seren's warning to me rang in my head. *"... hurting my friends will never gain you my respect or trust."*

So why had I let Ciaran get to me?

I was leaving.

She *wasn't* my wife.

But somehow, she still felt like she was *mine*. The thought of Ciaran—or any other man—touching her, lusting after her made my blood churn, raw and possessive. Maybe I couldn't have her, but I sure as hell didn't want anyone *else* to, either.

Ciaran didn't share what I shared with her. She was a part of me, inextricable from my mind. My breathing. My every heartbeat.

What in the *fuck* was I going to do without her?

Apparently, Ciaran wasn't done fighting. He stormed up beside me, then grabbed a fistful of my shirt below my throat. As we squared off, my body readying for a spar, a strange, feral energy kicked through me, inviting the surge of adrenaline that twisted through my veins.

"Try it," I said in a hard voice. "Let's see how far you get, Ciaran. I haven't had a good challenge in a year."

The street around us slowed. People hesitated, watching.

A fight would put Haldron's eyes on us.

Against every desire curling through me, the more rational part of my brain took over. "Of course," I added, "Seren felt every blow as Seth flogged me. Lucia dulled the effects, but she's not here, is she? There's a chance if you punch me—she will feel it, too." He didn't need to know I could control that now.

Slowly, Ciaran's fingers uncurled, his chest rising and falling with struggled breaths. "You're a bastard." He lowered his hands and stepped closer. "I know you're not Bloodbound, Rykr. And the skinwraiths ... there's something you're hiding— who you are or what you're doing here. But I swear to the gods, if you betray Seren, I will find a way to hurt you. No, I'm not as smart as you. I'm not Sealed, but I'm loyal, and I was trained to kill my enemies."

Ah. Now I understood why Seren had questioned my missing Bloodbinding mark. Ciaran had planted that seed in her brain.

"You're looking too hard for a reason to hate me, Ciaran. Some of us just carry our secrets closer to the chest. You wear yours out in the open and she still picked me."

Ciaran's eyes flashed. "She's the only reason you're still alive. I know your type. You use people like stepping stones, then watch them drown from the other side of the river. Your honor? Skin-deep. But this time, you picked someone smarter than you. More capable than you give her credit for. She'll see you for who you really are—hopefully before you betray her and it's too late."

"I'm not going to betray Seren." Not that I could if I wanted to.

But I didn't want to.

Nyxva.

I cared about the woman.

Something cracked in Ciaran's fierce expression and regret panged through me. He loved her and she probably deserved a man like him—from her people, who could give her a life here. Be a real husband.

By taking that oath, she'd hadn't just isolated herself from her tribe, she'd cut off any chance for a future with them.

Even if we broke the bond ... what would happen to her if I went back to Lirien, like I needed to do? I wanted to delude myself into believing that she wouldn't be held responsible, but I'd seen enough of Viori justice—and I knew Haldron. If I claimed my throne, what would he do to Seren? To her family?

I didn't have long to dwell on it. Ciaran shifted, his face turning like stone. "Son of a bitch." He studied the cobble-stones beneath our feet as though they suddenly fascinated him.

Every muscle in my body tensed. "What is it?"

"We're being followed."

Not this again.

It didn't surprise me, though. I'd known from the second I'd stepped into that throne room that Haldron would be keeping a close eye on Seren and me—if we made it out of there alive.

"Male or female?" I asked.

"Male."

"If he's after me, we should split up. Any place around here we can lead him into a trap?"

Ciaran blinked at me, as if surprised I'd suggest working *with* him—and use myself as bait. He nodded after a moment. "Three streets down, make a right, then go straight toward the keep's wall. Wards at the top stop intruders, so he won't be able to climb. Before you get there, there's an alley to the left, then take a sharp right straight toward a dead end."

"Metal bending and a good sense of direction. You might be a better warrior than I gave you credit for."

I didn't wait for a reaction before starting off. Whoever was following me might not be alone, but I had the advantage. I was trained for this.

A thrill shot through me as I moved. I'd never been addicted to danger before, but something about this felt like a hunt—a restless, prowling need for prey rattling through me.

But it grated that Ciaran had noticed our tail before I had.

I didn't look back, trusting that Ciaran would be behind me. He might hate me, but his love for Seren made him a grudging yet unmistakable ally. Maybe the best I could hope for under the circumstances. If I had to give the Viori credit for anything, it was their loyalty—to their cause, their laws, and each other.

The crowd thickened, bodies jostling me from all sides. Each brush of a stranger's hand felt like a threat, a whisper of danger. At last, I found the alleyway. Ciaran's description had been apt—it ended at a tall stone wall, flanked by high buildings. Climbing the walls would require talent.

Footsteps sounded behind me, and I set a hand on my new sword, ready to draw.

A familiar scent reached me first.

"Thorne?" My voice was sharp, incredulous. "What the hell are you doing here?" Relief battled with dread. If Thorne had come, it could mean something in Lirien was terribly wrong.

He approached with a smirk, hands outstretched. "I thought I'd never catch you alone." The clothes he wore appeared to have been taken off the back of someone else—someone much smaller. A hooded cloak hung around mid-shin, but it looked like Viori clothing. Beneath it, the bulk of his ever-present bearskin confirmed he hadn't abandoned his old gear.

"I told you to—"

A soft step sounded. *Ciaran.*

Fuck.

Thorne caught the direction of my glance, then sprang into action. As the two men crashed into each other, each of them attacking, I hurtled toward them. "Stop!" I grabbed each of them by the shoulders, trying to push them apart, but it was like trying to move two boulders.

Ciaran gave me a wild-eyed look, a dagger still at Thorne's throat. "What are you doing?"

"You know this one?" Thorne growled at the same time, his own knife stopped perilously above Ciaran's gut.

Both men stared at me, distrust of the other clear on their faces.

I could try to make up a story, but it would do nothing to foster any trust in Ciaran. Telling him Thorne was a friend was a risk—but necessary. Maybe even help Ciaran feel as though we were on an equal footing.

"Yes," I said, releasing Thorne's shoulder. "He's my wife's friend. He's safe."

Ciaran paled as Thorne lowered the knife. A flash of betrayal twitched at his lips as he looked from me to Thorne, dagger still dangerously positioned. "He's a Lirien?"

"Well, I'm not a fucking Viori, if that's what you're asking," Thorne grunted. He scowled at me. "Excuse me if I heard you wrong—*your wife?*"

"I told you it was a long story," I hissed, crossing my arms.

Thorne knocked Ciaran's dagger away with a shove of his shoulder, then winked. "You're lucky we're in a mountain, *Vangar.* Might've caught a few flies by now with that mouth hanging open."

"His name is Ciaran," I said, inspecting my fingers as a faint tingling sensation pricked my right hand, out of nowhere. "Ciaran, this is Thorne Ursidor."

"H-how?" Ciaran's face flushed darker as he straightened, anger blazing in his demeanor. "How the hell did you sneak in here? The gates to Emberstone are warded to detect any spies."

"Aye, but apparently the sewers aren't." Thorne turned toward me. "We need to speak. Now."

I held his gaze for the barest moment. What could be so important that he'd risked crawling into Emberstone like this?

"No." Ciaran stepped back, shaking his head faintly. "No. I can't be party to this. How many of you are there?" He gave me a pleading look. "I have to report you. Both of you. Our laws—"

"Your laws will cause Seren's death, Ciaran." I flicked a bored look at Thorne, masking my urgency. "My Viori wife. I saved her life from a vuk. The Viori would've executed me on sight, so she took an ancient oath that bonded us as spouses. Unfortunately, if one of us dies, so does the other."

Ciaran's eyes bulged as I spoke, as though realizing how much I trusted Thorne. That was dangerous information and Ciaran knew it.

"Solric's balls." Thorne let out a low whistle. "I knew you stunk of vuk."

Rubbing his eyes, Ciaran grappled with the weight of what my trust had pulled him into. He wasn't just Seren's friend blindly following her schemes—he was a traitor in his own right. I tilted my head. "Not so easy to dispense with your swift, rigid justice, is it? Did you judge Seren too harshly, Ciaran?"

"You unredeemable son of a whore—"

Thorne raised a fist, nostrils flaring. "Who in Solric's name—"

"It's all right." I didn't think Thorne would give me away so easily, but I still needed to be careful. "Until me, Ciaran had probably never met anyone from outside the forest. Meeting two of us is probably overwhelming."

"We're not fucking unicorns," Thorne grumbled, lowering his hand. Then he gave me another impatient look. "But we really need to talk."

I gave Ciaran a hard stare. "What'll it be, Ciaran? I throw us both at your mercy. Can my friend speak to me, or do you need to summon more of your kind? Maybe some guards? They can't be far, this close to the keep."

"You never were going to join the Viori, were you? You're just a spy," Ciaran said bitterly. Maybe, despite his better judgment, he'd hoped he was wrong about me.

His loyalty to Seren made all the difference here. Somehow, I knew he hadn't been the one to tell the tribe about Giulia. His love for Seren was too deep.

I stepped closer, meeting his glare. "I didn't choose this, Ciaran. You think I want to be here? I was dragged into this forest, bound to a woman I didn't know, and thrown into your war. But yes, I need to go back. I have a kingdom to protect—a kingdom that will burn if I don't warn them about what's coming. Just like you would do anything for Seren, I'll do whatever it takes for my people. That doesn't make me a spy. It makes me a man with responsibilities—same as you."

Ciaran's shoulders squared. "And Seren?" he asked tersely. "What about her? What happens to her?"

"She's trying to find a way to break the bond. She knows I'm not staying. If you don't believe me, ask her."

He flinched and his throat bobbed. "I can't believe I'm doing this," he muttered, unable to meet my eyes. "You have five minutes. I'll be around the corner, keeping watch. If something goes wrong or someone comes over to investigate, I wash my hands of you both."

Then he looked at Thorne. "You can't stay in Emberstone. You may have gotten past the wards but they'll catch you eventually. Every Viori wears a rune on their wrist—the only exception to that is him"—he nodded toward me—"and he's been given special permission from Lord Haldron."

"How does one acquire this rune?" Thorne asked with a scowl.

"By being born Viori or claiming refuge here the first day of the Harvest Moon," Ciaran said angrily. "Don't even try forging it. It takes the incantation of a skilled priestess, and any attempt at a fake will be caught."

"Suppose I don't give a fuck about the rune? I doubt they go around checking that closely. And suppose you keep looking the other way?" Thorne growled to Ciaran.

"The first day of the Harvest Moon is tomorrow, Ciaran. Can't he claim refuge here then, even by your rules?"

Ciaran shifted his weight back. "This is madness." He jerked away and left us, desperate to flee.

"So, you're married now, huh?" Thorne asked, coming up beside me. He stank, and now that I knew what he'd crawled through, it made sense.

"It's complicated," I said with a smirk.

"Complicated? You're tied to the woman for life. Though, you skipped the messy part where she decides whether she likes you or not. Seems simple to me."

I barked a laugh, the familiarity of his wit welcome amid the dark shadows of the alley. "You're welcome to try it if you think it's so easy."

"Pass. I'd rather keep my freedom ... and my sanity."

I wrinkled my nose. "Considering the way you smell—and look—you'd be lucky if a woman got within twenty feet of you."

Thorne tossed back the hood of his ill-fitting cloak. "You know, I didn't crawl through sewers just to be insulted."

"No, you crawled through sewers because you're an idiot. I told you to stay away."

Thorne shrugged. "Fair point. But I expected a little gratitude. Maybe a drink. Definitely not the side-eye from your Viori 'friends.'"

"Ciaran is safe enough. He's in love with my wife—he won't risk her by turning either of us in." I turned back to Thorne. "But he's right. You can't stay in Emberstone. If you're found, it might put extra scrutiny on me. Now, what in the hell did you risk so much for and crawl through shit to tell me?"

Thorne's expression darkened. "They're calling for a coronation—within days. Maybe sooner. There's chaos in Suomelin, with the king's council arguing about the line of succession. If your nephew Ivar takes the crown, they'll use him as a puppet to cement their power. By the time you get back, it'll be too late to stop them."

The words drove the air from my lungs. I couldn't let that happen. Not after everything we'd lost.

I wanted—*needed*—to ask about my sisters-in-law, their children, Malin, but I couldn't. It hurt to breathe.

"You NEED to get back now, Rykr. As it is, it will take days just to reach Cairn Hold."

I closed my eyes, letting Thorne's words sink in.

"There's another claim," I said, my voice low. "And he's not just some petty usurper. He's here, in Emberstone. Magnus's younger brother—Haldron Warrick. Or just Haldron, as they call him now."

Thorne's thick brows furrowed.

"He orchestrated the massacre of my family," I continued. "And now he's planning something far worse. If he takes Lirien's throne, it won't just be our people who'll suffer. It'll be war."

"Godsdamn motherswiver."

I grimaced. "Exactly."

"Then you have to get the hell out of here. We'll find a way. I can shift into my bear form and drag you through the border if necessary—even the Viori aren't likely to get between a hungry bear and his dinner."

The thought of leaving Seren burned like a brand against my chest. If I left her now, I wouldn't just be betraying her. I'd be proving every doubt she had about me true. But if I stayed ... the throne would slip farther out of reach. And Lirien would fall to Haldron's schemes.

"I can't. I can't abandon Seren. Not yet. First, we have to go through a trial that might kill us both. If I leave beforehand, they won't hesitate to execute her."

He gave me a skeptical look. "Don't tell me a fine piece of ass is—"

"She's my wife," I said gruffly, a strange, protective feeling curling around me like a spell.

Stunned, Thorne bowed his head.

Where had that come from?

The bond wasn't just a chain, it was a mirror. Through it, I felt her strength, her doubts, her quiet pain. And she felt mine. Soon there was no hiding from her, no pretense. Maybe that's what terrified me most. She'd see the truth of me, stripped bare, and realize I wasn't the man she thought she'd saved.

Who knew what she'd do then? What her honor would demand of her?

Focusing on Thorne, I gritted out, "I already told you; our lives are tied together. I can't leave a liability like that behind.

If they kill her, I'll die too." Better to let him think that I was being strategic rather than sentimental.

"Yeah, that makes sense."

"While I'm here, I also need to gather some more information on Haldron and his plans—what we're facing. I'm certain he's planning to march on Lirien soon." Come to think about it, it made sense that Seren's tribe had suddenly been called to the training fields.

The tribe had been preparing for war.

Thorne straightened to attention. "What are my orders?"

A deep ache went through me. Dalric, Thorne, and I used to tease each other about who would end up commanding the others. Now Dalric was gone, and Thorne was ready to take orders without question.

"If you can get out again, send a raven to Warlord Ellison in Cairn Hold … if you can. Or go there yourself. He needs to know about Haldron and the threat he's posing."

"I'm not leaving this time, Rykr. What's this about a deadly trial?"

"The Skorn—a battle to the death with their best warriors. Tomorrow night."

Thorne's eyes gleamed with confidence. "A battle with Viori? You should be fine. And I'll be here to help you escape as soon as it's over."

"Maybe. Seren says there will be other obstacles. And it's not just me who has to fight. She does, too."

Thorne grunted. "You're right, that bond is a liability. A serious one." He nodded slowly. "Like I said, I'm staying. You may not think you need me here, but I think you do. But you should know, someone helped me find my way into Emberstone. A man I met in the forest."

What? A chill went through me. "And you trusted him? Who is he?"

"I didn't have much of a choice. But he's no friend of the Viori, that much is certain. And, like your woman, he didn't kill me either."

"A Lirien?" I searched Thorne's face. He wasn't gullible or easily trusting, but after the last few weeks, I had the right to be cautious.

"More of an outlaw. He thinks his daughter is here in Emberstone and he's come to rescue her. An ally, for now ... but you're not going to like it when I tell you his name—"

My breath hitched. Without a shadow of doubt, I knew who Thorne had met in the forest.

"—Brogan Ragnall."

CHAPTER 31

SEREN

A minute before the door to the room opened and Rykr strode through, Ciaran at his heels, I'd felt the bond between us hum, alerting me to his proximity.

I stared at him in his Vangar leathers, my heart lurching at the confirmation that it *had* been him I'd felt—and the fact that the sight of him was doing unacceptable things to my imagination.

"Nice of you to join us," Amahle said from her spot over on the bed. I tore my focus away from Rykr, my cheeks warming.

Amahle's gaze drifted to Ciaran. She sat straighter, more alert. "What's wrong?"

I frowned and peered at Ciaran as he closed the door. He was pale, but the blotchiness on his neck betrayed a recent surge of anger. "Did something happen?"

Rykr crossed his arms. "A solider, friend of mine, from the Regulation followed me here to Emberstone—long story short —and Ciaran isn't pleased to have been made an unwitting traitor."

I looked from Rykr to Ciaran, my mouth growing dry.

Another Lirien?

"Oh gods," Amahle muttered.

My own anger sparked as I stared at Rykr's unaffected gaze. "Don't just stand there with that smirk, Rykr. What the hell is one of your friends doing here? And how did he find you?" My glare intensified. "Have you been sending messages to Lirien? Spying on us?"

"Has it occurred to you, thistling, that if I were a spy and Ciaran had caught me, the easiest way to keep him silent—and myself safe—would have been to kill him?" He raised a brow. "So, either I'm a terrible spy, or just incredibly foolish to let him live."

Dammit, his logic made sense.

I crossed my arms. "Or?"

A smile curved at the corners of his mouth, a feline twinkle in his eyes. "Or you'll believe me when I tell the truth. Thorne is a shapeshifter who tracked me to the encampment and followed me here. That's how he's got past your Vangar. He's a loyal friend. Neither of us are spies."

My body went rigid. A shapeshifter?

I'd heard of people born with that gift—much like my ice powers—but never met one. I narrowed my eyes, my mind racing. "That's convenient. Almost too convenient. How exactly do you expect me to believe this, Rykr, when you've given me nothing but riddles and half-truths since the moment we met?"

"He comes from a long line of berserkers." Rykr crossed the room toward the sole chair and sat, stretching his legs out in front of him. With Rykr and Ciaran in here, the tight quarters felt suffocating.

Berserkers. Then he could turn into ... I startled, my eyes flying to Rykr's. *"He stole the prince's body, didn't he?"*

Rykr held my gaze, his expression unchanging, then dipped his chin in a subtle nod.

The blood drained from my face as I processed what the Lirien's presence meant for Rykr—both for his future here and for the real reason he'd been in the forest the day we'd met.

Ciaran cleared his throat, as though his own thoughts were equally muddled. The sharp sting of blame tore through me, and I slipped toward him, taking his hand. "You didn't do anything wrong, Ciaran."

He released a bitter laugh, his voice breaking. "Didn't I? I've broken my oath, Seren. Everything we stand for—the laws that keep us safe—I violated. How do I face the Vangar after this? How do I face myself?"

I stood on my tiptoes as I embraced him tightly. "I never should have put you in this position."

Amahle stepped toward us and set her hand on Ciaran's shoulder as I pulled back. "The Vangar may be rigid, but you're more than your oaths, Ciaran. Seren proved that when she saved Rykr, and you proved it today. Laws mean nothing if we lose ourselves trying to uphold them. Turning the Lirien or Rykr in would be disastrous, not only for Seren but for our tribe. The people in Emberstone protect themselves, and they don't have to face the same moral dilemmas that we do. Maybe it's illegal, but conscience matters."

Then Amahle turned toward Rykr, her face hardening. "That doesn't mean you've done *anything* to bolster our confidence in you. Seren could have been arrested today and meanwhile, you were out jeopardizing her life. Needlessly. What was so important that your friend risked coming into Emberstone for?"

The uneasy shift through the bond made my chest tighten as I turned to look at Rykr.

"To try to convince me to return to Pendara. The Regulation is charging me with abandonment of my post," Rykr said smoothly.

Too smoothly.

"You're lying," I hissed.

He crossed one ankle over his knee and held my gaze, unflinching, unwilling to admit anything. Then he tilted his head. "What was that about Seren being arrested today?"

I bit my lip, cringing. *Dammit, Amahle.* "It's nothing."

He raised a brow. "Clearly it's not."

"We ... just had a brush with a guard. A misunderstanding," Amahle cut in, exchanging a look with me.

"And what does that mean?" Rykr's voice was hard. *"Guess neither of us is innocent, right?"*

I flinched then glanced at my friends. Much as I appreciated their willingness to be here, I'd dragged them into something that could get them killed.

And right now, I needed to talk to Rykr without them. "Can you both leave us?"

Amahle's lips twitched. "Come on, Ciaran." She grabbed his hand. "We don't want to get caught in the middle of a marital spat." She tugged him out of the room, the door clicking shut behind her. I locked it, not looking at Rykr, my body tense.

"What happened?" Rykr's voice was clipped. Angry even.

I turned toward him, feeling his irritation through the bond. It fed my own anger. *"Smug bastard."*

"I heard that."

"I meant for you to."

"Good."

I set my jaw.

"Things didn't go to plan," I admitted. "When I saw my mother, she was already leaving the House of the Veil. I followed her to the sewer entrance—"

Rykr inhaled sharply.

I frowned at him but pressed on. "A guard caught us trying to go after her and demanded our names. I tried a sleeping spell, but it failed, and my mother had to intervene."

He stared at me, unblinking. My confidence faltered as I finished, "But I don't want to hear even a shred of condemnation, Rykr. You have no moral high ground to condemn me from this time."

"Thorne is harmless. And he's not going to get caught. *You*, on the other hand, have a way of drawing attention and putting both our necks at risk."

"Says the man who wouldn't kneel to Lord Haldron yesterday," I shot back.

"I don't bow to any man. Not anymore. And definitely not to the likes of Haldron."

I laughed without humor. "Another lie?"

"An inconvenient truth."

My mind spun with possibilities, each one darker than the last. Rykr had secrets—more than I could count. What if Thorne wasn't just a friend, but a scout? What if more Liriens lurked in Emberstone, watching, waiting for the right moment to strike?

And Rykr ... was he their leader, or just another pawn in a game I didn't understand? The bond hummed with his frustration, his tension, but it told me nothing of his true intentions.

Rykr chuckled.

"Something funny?" I glared at him.

"You seem to forget I can hear your thoughts. You're so self-righteous."

"I really don't have the patience for your lectures right now, Rykr. Yes, I almost got caught by a guard, but I was doing nothing wrong. If the damned sleeping spell I tried hadn't failed, it would have been *fine*."

His brows came together. "Sleeping spell?"

"I've done it dozens of times. It's always worked. I don't know what happened."

"Have you ever used it on me?"

I shifted, my eyes widening slightly.

What?

"I-I—I don't see how that's relevant."

Rykr advanced, shaking his head. "I knew something felt off when I woke up this morning. Like I'd been drugged. I was shocked enough that you slipped out of the room without you waking me but that's how you did it, isn't it? You used a spell."

Heat flushed my face. "So what? What difference does it make?"

He used his body like armor, approaching with an ease and power that forced me back until I was pinned against the wall behind me. "You know it makes a difference, Seren. If I'd done something like that to you, you'd be accusing me of gods-know-what. That's the pattern. Treat me like the enemy except when it's convenient. Everything I do is examined with suspicion of treachery and malice, even when I tell you the truth."

My breath hitched, anger warring with the thrill of his thigh grazing mine, the way he towered over me, the heat between us like a fuse waiting to be lit. "But you don't always tell the truth. Your friend didn't come to tell you about being accused of abandonment, did he?"

"As a matter of fact, he did tell me something, but I didn't want to risk sharing it in front of your friends—for your sake. Now I'm starting to wonder if I should even tell you."

"Yes, why would you tell me the truth? You're a Lirien. A godsdamned lying son-of-a-bitch *Lirien*. Ready to run back there as soon as you get a chance."

"The crown of Lirien summons me, Seren. *That's* the truth.

I've never pretended otherwise." He loomed over me. "You knew I was Lirien when you saved me."

"There is no crown of Lirien," I spat back, then shoved him away.

He blocked me as I tried to move past him. "We're already up to our necks with obligations to each other, Seren. You really want to know more? Every dark, dangerous secret that Haldron might torture out of you to use against me if he decides I'm a threat?" His eyes flashed with pain. "Is that what you really want?"

His words settled into my chest, thick and cording the tense muscles of my arms, still ready for a fight.

But the bond whispered something more.

He wanted to protect me.

Fiercely.

Struggling to breathe, I swallowed a lump in my throat, not believing the emotion flooding through me. "What do you care, Rykr? You're leaving. Whether or not we break this bond, right? Our debts to each other are paid. I'm nothing more than your greatest *weakness.* You said it yourself."

He flinched, then cupped my face. At last, his voice, strained and quiet, came. "I care about you, Seren Ragnall. More than I should. Not because you're not worthy but because my life is a threat to yours for reasons you can't possibly imagine. And still, I can't decide what worries me more—the thought of someone using us against each other, or the idea that if the bond is broken, I'll no longer feel you, hear you ... sense you."

His thumb traced my cheek, his voice barely above a whisper. "You've consumed me, Seren, and I fucking can't stand the thought of you not being a part of me."

My knees nearly buckled. He'd voiced my own fears and somehow that made them more real.

"What do you want from me, Rykr?" My breath shuddered. "Do you even know? Or am I a mistake you'll run from the moment you get the chance?"

His jaw tightened, his eyes dark and stormy as they held mine. "You're not a mistake, Seren. You never will be."

Before I could respond, his mouth crashed down on mine with a desperation that mirrored my own. The bond flared to life, an ache that turned to fire as his lips moved against mine. It wasn't just a kiss, it was an unraveling, every barrier between us falling away, leaving only the raw truth we couldn't ignore.

The feeling of his lips, his mouth moving as his breath clashed with my own, was enough to undo me.

I wanted him more than ever.

Needed him.

My soul felt incomplete without him.

I slid my hands behind the nape of his neck, tugging myself up onto my tiptoes so I could reach him better, my lips firm against his.

This.

My pulse beat faster, my eyes closing as I coaxed my lips against his.

His lips parted as he responded to the urging of my kiss. My tongue stroked his, drawing it more deeply into my mouth as one of his strong hands splayed at the small of my back. His other hand slid up to my neck, digging into my hair and holding the base of my head firmly against him. Anchoring me.

In that instant, my need for him grew, the kiss changing from a tender, hungry one to something I knew I couldn't control or come back from. My heart slammed into my ribs, an icy shiver traveling through my veins. The taste of his tongue, the soft caress of his lips, so full and delicious and just as sensual as I'd imagined they'd be, sent a molten ache through me.

I sucked on his lower lip, catching it between my teeth. A low growl rumbled from his chest as he shoved me back against the wall, hard, pinning me there with the iron strength of his hips. The cold metal hilt of his sword pressed into my side.

I fumbled with the sheath, unbuckling it, letting the sword clatter to the dusty wooden floorboards. My fingers found the waistband of his leather kilt as Rykr dragged his lips away from my mouth, trailing down my jaw as he undid the lacing of my vest. I tugged at every buckle and strap I found.

His breath was warm and ragged against my throat. "Solric above," he growled at last, eyes narrowed, his fingers tugging at the intricate lacing of my vest. "You Viori don't make this easy, do you?" His voice was rough, his fingers steady despite his frustration.

I teased a smile. "Need some help?"

Rykr's eyes, molten hot with lust, swept down the curve of my throat. His thumb traced the hollow at my collarbone, then lower still, between the swell of my aching breasts. I wanted his hands on me, teasing, tormenting, exploring. *Now.*

Without warning, he spun me, pressing me against the cool stone wall. "Impatient?"

The vest dropped at my feet. My shirt followed, then my undergarments. Rough, callused hands slid around my waist, grazing bare skin as his lips brushed against my neck, a whisper of a kiss beneath my earlobe.

"No. Starved." Hungry for his lips, I turned my face back toward his, catching his lips in a kiss and a tangle of tongues. One of his hands cupped one breast as he pressed me even harder against the wall.

His other hand unclasped the button at my waistband then

pushed into the tangle of soft, slick heat between my legs. I groaned, my body bucking in response to his touch. "Gods, Rykr," I managed, my voice breaking. "Please ..."

His fingertips teased me, finding my sensitive, swollen clit and it took all my power to stay upright. "*Is this what you want, solwyn?*"

"Yes," I moaned. "More."

"*More, Rykr. I need ...*"

I couldn't finish as his hand pushed deeper between my legs, two fingers sliding against the slickness there and pushing deep inside me. "Rykr—"

A strangled cry left my lips, pleasure crashing over me in waves. My knees nearly gave out as I ground back against his hard length, a promise of more to come. "*Fuck, yes.*"

"*You're so fucking tight.*" His fingers slid back, making slow circles that sent the room spinning, every nerve on fire, longing for not just this, but all of him.

A sudden chill seeped into my palms, sharp and biting. My breath caught as the stone beneath my hands shimmered, frost spreading like cracks in glass. I jerked back, my chest heaving, and stared in horror at the ice now encasing the wall.

Rykr lifted his head, the heat of his breath still on my skin.

I covered my breasts and whirled to face him, hoping I wouldn't find the horrified look on his face. But there it was, unmistakable.

"Seren." His voice was low, rough. "Does that happen often?" His gaze flicked to the ice, then back to me, the worry in his eyes sharp enough to cut.

"Freezing things accidentally or during sex?" I swallowed hard. "No, never."

"And if you had been touching me?"

I stared at the whorls of ice along the seams of the wall.

If my hands had been on him instead of the wall ...

The thought tore through me, leaving a hollow ache in its wake. The ice could have spread to his skin, to his heart. *I could have killed him without even realizing it.*

The tingle in my hands this morning.

I didn't answer his question, dread replacing every bit of lust that had been tearing through me. I snatched my clothes from the floorboards, my cheeks heating as I turned from him to pull them back on. "Something's wrong with my powers, Rykr," I whispered, a slight tremble to my voice.

"What do you mean?" Rykr came up beside me, his handsome face dark with worry.

"The spell failing earlier. My inability to control my ice. That's never happened to me before. My mother taught me how to control the ice when it manifested, and I've done it without a problem since I was a child."

Something flickered in his face, unreadable. "You think it has something to do with Emberstone?"

I trembled. "My powers have always worked fine here. The only thing that's changed ..."

The bond.

It had changed everything. I held his gaze, the bond thrumming between us, a pulse of warmth and unease. The soft press of the seam of his lips into a line told me he'd heard me.

"What can we do, Seren?" Rykr said gently, coming up beside me. He reached for my hand, but I snatched it away, afraid of what I might do. Of what I could have done.

"Let's go to the temple. We need answers. Now."

I was tired.

Exhausted.

And as Rykr stepped closer, his face shadowed with concern, I wasn't sure which frightened me more—losing control again or the fear I'd seen in his eyes.

Fear of me.

CHAPTER 32

SEREN

"**I**s the temple dedicated to Solric?" Rykr asked as we climbed the pillared steps to the enormous structure.

"Among others." I scanned the dark interior. The hour was getting late. Rykr had insisted that we get something to eat and drink before coming here, and much as I'd grumbled, the meal had made me feel slightly better.

Until I remembered that I'd almost killed us both by losing control.

Gloom gnawed at me, an ache that refused to let go. Every step toward the gleaming black marble arches of the temple felt heavier than the last, weighed down by the memory of what had happened.

Rykr didn't blame me—at least, not openly—but I couldn't shake the guilt. What if next time, I couldn't pull back? What if next time, I destroyed everything?

A statue of Bryndis loomed at the top of the stairs, arms outstretched, the feathered wings of her cloak unfurled behind her. Nude, powerful, mocking. Goddess of love—but also death. Magic. One of the few deities to survive the destruction of the Old World at Vornfall.

The statue's empty eyes pierced through me. I'd taken her oath, only to learn that it was more of a curse than a gift. Maybe that was the point. Maybe love was a curse and humans were too feeble-minded to comprehend that truth.

Love wasn't just pleasure and desire—it was loss. And the loss of it was the most painful wound of all.

Rykr's hand settled at the small of my back. "Do you really think we'll find answers here?" His analytical gaze searched the temple's vaulted shadows, where torches threw light into the spaces enchanted sunlight couldn't reach. Incense cloyed thickly, curling like unseen fingers, masking the movement of the many robed figures beyond.

"We'll be fine. There are laws about spilling blood in the temple." I sounded more confident than I felt. "And yes, the priests and priestesses could help. They know more about the old gods and Old World than most."

"Laws against spilling blood have never stopped anyone with malicious intentions," Rykr said flatly. His hand at my back sent a ripple of warmth through me, steadying, but unnatural in its intensity. The bond. Always there, amplifying every touch, every glance.

It was maddening how easily his presence steadied me, even when I wanted to be furious with him. Even when I wasn't sure if the feelings were mine, or the bond's. Was it me who wanted him near, or the magic threading us together?

I shivered and pushed forward. The longer we stayed here, the more the air around us felt threatening, the crowds too thick, the feeling we were being watched overwhelming.

A swish of robes up ahead caught my attention. A priest?

The cloaked figure turned, the silhouette of her profile

visible in the candlelight. A young and beautiful woman. She smiled at us, beckoning us forward.

The woman slipped behind a gauzy curtain, the fabric billowing in a breeze from an unknown source. Her hand extended from beyond it, one slender finger motioning us to follow her.

I exchanged a look with Rykr. His posture was rigid, alert.

"If they want answers about their bond, they must come beyond the curtain," a soft, melodic voice murmured.

Reluctantly, I pressed forward with Rykr close behind. "Are you sure we should ..."

I tightened my grip on Rykr's hand, stepping forward before he could object. "We came for answers," I said, my voice firm, though my stomach churned with unease. "We're not leaving without them."

The cloaked woman turned toward us, her face half shrouded in candlelight, a sly smile playing at her lips. "Brave words. But bravery and recklessness are often the same."

The area she'd entered was curtained on all sides, with pillows on the ground. Candles burned brightly on the floor and candelabras of various heights surrounded us. She came closer, then took my hand, leading me toward the pillows. "Be seated."

Rykr lowered himself beside me.

Slowly, the woman unclasped her cloak. It slid from her shoulders, pooling at her feet. Beneath it, she wore a nearly transparent dress that hugged her curves. Gold leaf barely covered her nipples, and the only other thing she wore was a delicate chain at her waist, dipping between her legs.

She was intoxicatingly beautiful, with thick golden hair that flowed down her back, unplaited, a circlet of gold around her forehead.

She wasn't a priestess.

She's a Seidr.

Known for their powers of seduction, they used trances and spells to travel into the spirit world and gain knowledge.

My mouth went dry, my gaze shooting to Rykr. Heat flared in my chest as I caught him watching her. She moved like a living flame, her every step a hypnotic sway, her amber eyes locked on Rykr with a predatory gleam.

My fingers curled into fists at my sides. I knew it was the bond amplifying my emotions, twisting my thoughts—but that didn't stop the sting. What did I expect? That he wouldn't notice her beauty? That he'd only ever look at me?

I forced my voice to steady. "If you're done gawking, maybe we can get to the part where she actually helps us."

The Seidr's amber eyes traveled to me. "She called upon Bryndis and yet the bond remains unconsummated. Unstable. Reckless."

She came closer, running her fingertips along my cheek. With a hint of a smile on her lips, she moved from me to Rykr, then gazed into his eyes. She knelt before him, those long slender fingers now tracing his jawline, his lips. "His blood is precious." She leaned forward, then kissed his mouth.

I shot up to my feet, the gauzy curtains swaying in response. "We shouldn't have come."

Rykr lifted a hand to her and gently pushed her back. Firmly. Each second his hand remained on her, though, my blood boiled.

With a slow smile spreading across her lips, the Seidr stood away from Rykr. Her hands dragged over her body, slowly, seductively, her hips swaying to some unknown music we couldn't hear. "They don't really want to break the bond. And why would they? It's delicious."

This woman was completely insane.

"Actually, I do. We both do. I need to know how to keep him out of my head."

She gave me a sharp look. "And yet she's desperate for him to be inside her. Her desire for him grows daily."

I swallowed hard, unable to look at Rykr as heat crept into my face. "We're leaving."

It didn't help that Rykr hadn't moved or said anything since we'd sat. Damned men. Always so easily distracted by the female form.

She turned in a slow circle. "Soul and mind connected. Now they need body. The bridge must be complete."

I shook Rykr's shoulder. "Rykr. Let's go."

His eyes shifted to mine, then beyond the curtain, narrowing slightly. "Can the bond be broken?" he asked the Seidr.

"That is beyond the power of this realm. Only divine power can extinguish a divine oath." The Seidr stopped, then her brow furrowed, deep with sorrow. Her eyes, once bright, grew dimmer, bluer, like a blind woman's.

"She will diminish. She's lost a piece of her soul and he is no ordinary mortal. A beast lives inside him, forged in the blood of the oath."

What was she saying?

Her breasts sagged before my gaze, her flat belly growing loose, the skin hanging. The golden hair turned white, and every inch of her face became lined with wrinkles.

I gasped and Rykr stood straight, his hand drawing me back toward him, curling me into his arm. "Diminish? You mean her powers won't work?"

"She cannot survive the bond."

My breath hitched. The words echoed in my mind, louder than the crackling of the candle flames or the muffled sounds of footsteps outside the curtain.

The Seidr's amber eyes glowed, her voice low and mournful. "It is unbalanced. He is too powerful, and her soul is incomplete."

Rykr shifted beside me, his hand tightening on my arm. "What does that mean?" he demanded, his tone sharp, almost angry.

"As the bond grows," the Seidr continued, her eyes growing distant, "her spirit will diminish. She will fade."

What in the name of the gods?

She cannot survive? It sounded as though she was saying ... the oath would kill me?

I gripped the edge of a pillow to steady myself. "When?" The word came out as a whisper. "How long do I have? Will we survive the Skorn?"

The woman's voice grew weaker, older, her shoulders rounding with age. "The bond will be complete, and with it, his power will awaken fully. But power such as his does not come without a cost."

I shivered, not only at her words, but at the chill in the air, the change in her face. "What cost?"

The Seidr's gaze turned toward me, heavy with sorrow. "It will rip her apart. Without balance, the power will consume one of you. And the war outside these walls will mean nothing if the beast inside him is unleashed."

The riddles made me want to scream, dig my hands into her and shake her for a straight and clear answer.

Rykr stiffened. "What beast?"

The Seidr gave him a faint, eerie smile. "You already know, don't you? She told you."

The spark vanished from her face. The Seidr blinked at us blindly, as though she could no longer see us there.

"Explain what you mean," I managed, despite my horror. "How can the bond be balanced?"

"He will take the bond." Some of the teeth that had once formed her gorgeous smile clattered to the stone floor. One by one.

I gagged. Was this Seidr going to drop dead before our eyes? "Rykr has to take the Oath of Bryndis so I don't die?"

She lifted mournful eyes at me, reaching a trembling hand toward my cheek again. Her words grew muffled, hard to hear. "Yes. But the consequences ..." She breathed out slowly, her ribs protruding with each breath. "He will release a great evil inside her. The threads of fate are fixed."

The Seidr reached for her cloak, then fled beyond the curtain.

CHAPTER 33
SEREN

Rykr kept his arm around me as we hurried from the temple. The Seidr's transformation had been appalling, but her words—those had been terrifying.

I wasn't even sure if I understood them correctly.

"Did she say I'm dying?" I managed at last.

Rykr didn't falter. "She was a deranged old woman. I wouldn't think twice about anything she said."

I pulled away from him as we reached the street.

Being under the mountain of Emberstone suddenly choked me. I wanted to run in a field, feel the wind on my face, see the stars. The noise, the streets, the dizzying amount of people overwhelmed me.

I need air.

Rykr searched my gaze, surprisingly calm. Then again, he hadn't just been told that a divine oath might kill him. "For all we know, that Seidr was a part of Haldron's games. She found us, rather than the other way around. She may have been ordered to say that."

"Then how did she know the things she knew?" I pointed back at the temple. "She clearly knew things—things no one could have told her. And if she's right, it means ..."

I'm really dying.

If the bond killed me, wouldn't Rykr die too? Wasn't that how it worked?

The Seidr hadn't said that.

Rykr scowled. "Seidrs are masters of manipulation. She could be lying ... or telling the truth in a way that only benefits her."

His words made sense, but my unease didn't fade. "What if she's right?"

Rykr frowned, but he set his hands on my shoulders. "Half the nonsense she spewed didn't make any sense. And why would my taking the Oath of Bryndis unleash evil within you? It didn't happen to me, did it?"

I hesitated. Seidr spoke in riddles, but their words weren't lies. Their magic was the same as Ibarran—and I trusted that.

"Seidrs pass along prophecy. Just because we don't like it doesn't mean we can change fate."

Rykr's mouth turned downward. "If you believe all fate is fixed. But we have choice, Seren. We can make our fates. If you didn't believe that you'd be more frightened of your twin brother and sister, wouldn't you?"

He was trying to make me feel better, but right now, I didn't want comfort.

"What now?" Rykr's calm tone grated against the storm in my chest.

"I don't know!" The words burst out before I could stop them. "We came here for answers, and all we got were riddles and death threats. How am I supposed to process that?"

He frowned, his jaw tightening. "I'm trying to protect you. Simple as that."

"Simple?" I snapped, my voice rising. "Nothing about this is simple."

His gaze softened, and I hated how it disarmed me. "I didn't mean it like that," he said, his hand brushing against mine. "I just don't want to lose you."

The words silenced me. *I don't want to lose you either.*

And I was suddenly exhausted. *Solric.* For all I knew, I had less than twenty-four hours. Either the Skorn trial would kill me, or the bond would. The desire in me to fight, to unravel the deeper meaning behind the Seidr's words was secondary to my need to simply *live.* The weight of everything on my heart might break me otherwise.

Moistening my lips, I nodded. "Okay."

"Okay." Rykr squeezed my shoulders then leaned forward, kissing my forehead, gently.

I think he meant to pull away right away, but he didn't. Instead, his arms wrapped around my back, holding me in a comforting embrace. The warmth of him seeped into my skin, steadying me as I closed my eyes, lost to the solid press of his body.

"She cannot survive the bond ... he will release a great evil inside her."

Either way, I was fucked.

Except in the literal sense of the word, and that's my fault, too.

Kissing Rykr had unleashed every desire I'd been denying the last few days. Even now, I could picture every hard ridge of muscle, the crimson and black tattoos lining his skin. When he'd stripped off his shirt and offered to take my flogging, he'd looked like something carved from legend.

The Seidr's words echoed in my mind. *"His blood is precious."* Precious. Why? Because he was Sealed? He'd been selected from millions by that—set apart. Or was there more?

He'd always been different—polished, disciplined, too

refined to be an ordinary soldier from Pendara. And the way he fought, the way he carried himself ... it didn't match the story he'd told me about being disowned by his father.

Who was he? And what wasn't he telling me?

I pulled away from him, wanting to stop the warring thoughts within my mind as we started back toward the Bellwether.

Truth was, despite the risk I'd taken, I couldn't regret saving Rykr's life at all. He challenged me in ways I didn't expect. Growing up with the Viori, whenever my parents had spoken positively of Liriens, I'd always just assumed they were reminiscing through nostalgic lenses.

The more time I spent with Rykr, the more I wondered if the Viori's stories were half-truths at best. The Viori taught us that Liriens were monsters, their Bloodbinding a symbol of their cruelty. But Rykr didn't seem cruel.

He'd bled for me, fought for me, stood by me when I didn't deserve it. How many Viori would do the same for a Lirien?

Maybe the Viori weren't so different from the Liriens. Both sacrificed their own for the illusion of safety, for power disguised as tradition. The thought left a bitter taste in my mouth.

The soft brush of Rykr's thumb against the back of my hand pulled me from my thoughts.

A sad smile crossed my lips.

I liked Rykr. *So much.*

Had he been anyone else, I would have fallen for him easily, and not just because he was so utterly attractive.

But our visit to the Seidr had affirmed what my mother had said—I needed to keep my distance from him. Guard my heart.

But it was too late for that.

I love him.

The bond hadn't done that. Even though he still kept

secrets, even though he mocked me at times, my feelings had taken root. There was so much to process, but what kept echoing in my mind were his words before we ... *before I nearly killed him.*

"I care about you, Seren Ragnall. More than I should. Not because you're not worthy but because my life is a threat to yours for reasons you can't possibly imagine. And still, I can't decide what worries me more—the thought of someone using us against each other, or the idea that if the bond is broken, I'll no longer feel you, hear you ... sense you. You've consumed me, Seren, and I fucking can't stand the thought of you not being a part of me."

That was why I loved him.

Because, like him, I couldn't fathom not hearing him, feeling him, sensing him.

"Tell me something true," I said, desperate to shake off the melancholy pressing in on me.

"It will rip her apart. Without balance, the power will consume one of you."

"Something true ..." He glanced at me, as though weighing my expectations. The movement on the streets was a steady thrum around us, somehow less threatening when he held my gaze.

He was silent for a long moment, then said, in a quiet voice, "I've been to every realm in Lirien, and I've never met anyone more fascinating than you, Seren."

Ugh. Was he trying to make me fall for him all over again?

When I didn't respond, he said, "Something the matter?"

"No," I choked out. "I just ... haven't ever met someone who's been to every realm of Lirien. Which realm did you like the best?"

"No, it's your turn. Didn't you ever want to visit anywhere outside of the forest? Make up your mind about Lirien for yourself?"

His question struck deep to the heart of me. Like he knew —somehow—the quiet war I'd fought within myself, torn between the love my parents had carried for their homelands and the identity I'd built as Viori.

"I *was* curious," I said, at last, voicing what I'd never admitted to anyone before. "But I knew it wasn't possible for me. So I read about them as much as I could."

"Of course you did." His voice was like a warm cloak inside me. "Which realm would you have visited if you could have?"

"Ibarra," I said without hesitation. "My mother used to tell me about the cities there, like Caral, where the streets shine with enchanted light. I used to dream of seeing them for myself."

Rykr's lips quirked in a faint smile. "Caral is as beautiful as they say. But Ibarra's magic doesn't hold a candle to Suomelin." His voice softened. "That's where I'd go if I could. One more day in the Golden City ..."

The wistfulness in his tone made my chest ache.

My parents had fallen in love there. "Is your family still in Ederyn?"

"I don't have much of a family anymore. Most of them are dead."

The tightness of his voice betrayed his sorrow, even if he'd said it flatly.

"I'm sorry." I stopped and brushed my fingers along his cheek, a gentle caress. "I didn't realize—"

"I know."

As we walked up the steps to the Bellwether, the depth of his grief carried through our bond, stealing my breath. Rykr had carried this pain alone, buried so tightly inside him it threatened to choke him. Compared to that, my complaints about my own life seemed like insignificant whining.

And he wouldn't have breathed a word of it to me. He

would have just carried it, his armor up, impenetrable shields around his heart well masked by sarcastic quips and charm and swagger. His life hadn't been as charmed as I'd thought, given the way he carried himself. He might be lonelier, sadder than I'd realized.

I couldn't imagine losing several members of my family—Esme's kidnapping had nearly destroyed us all.

"Rykr, I ..." Maybe it was stupid, but I wanted to soothe that wound inside him.

I didn't know what to say. We'd both had our secrets, didn't we? I hadn't told him about Esme, just like he hadn't told me about his family. Why hadn't I? Maybe because her kidnapping haunted me in a way I hadn't been ready to share with him.

And maybe he's not ready to share, either.

I unlocked the door and stepped inside. The enchanted lights flared on, flameless candles burning in their lamps.

I expected Rykr to follow me, but when I turned, he was still by the closed door, resting his back against it. Studying me.

"Do you want to remain Viori?" The question was blunt, his eyes narrowing in the corners, his gaze penetrating. *"If we survive the Skorn, would you go with me to Lirien?"*

He didn't have to explain why he spoke through the bond. Given everything we'd been through, this was safer.

He was offering his hand. Drawing a line in the sand and giving me a choice. My heart burned within my chest. *"Would you ever turn your back on Lirien?"*

"You don't know what you're asking." His voice was a sharp hiss inside me.

"Neither do you, Rykr. I love my people. This is my home. Yes, war may be coming, but I believe in the Viori cause. Don't you see how harmful the Bloodbinding is?"

'The war between Lirien and Viori is no longer just about the Bloodbinding." His voice was bitter. *"And going to Lirien may be the only way for you—us—to live."*

The conversation had veered far from where I'd intended. I closed the gap between us and slipped my hands into his. "Then let's not talk about it anymore," I said. "Let's go to sleep. Our next move can wait until tomorrow."

He nodded, his expression unreadable as his fingers curled against mine. "Speaking of our next move ... there's someone I need you to meet."

I stiffened. "Your friend?" Oh gods, had he remained in the city? If I was found in the company of a Lirien ... I took a deep, tired breath. "Not tonight. Tonight, I want to sleep. Forget that I'm dying because of the oath. That it doesn't matter whether I survive the Skorn—my fate is decided. That I betrayed my people, protecting you, enabling a skinwraith attack. That Moira was attacked, Giulia was killed, and Esme was kidnapped ... and I've dragged my friends into treason. I can't take anything more."

Something in his face hardened, became more distant. He released me and sat on the edge of the bed. "I ruined your life, didn't I?" He dragged his hands over his face, exhaling a breath heavy with sorrow.

When he looked up at me, his expression was raw. "All my life, Seren, I've only brought destruction whenever I tried to help. Those fire powers I told you about? I set more than one fire accidentally. I couldn't control it—the rage that came with anger. Justified or not. My father thought I was worthless and sent me away. The Seal changed that, but I lost everything I'd been up to that point. I'm not even sure I know who I am anymore, but somehow, I still keep destroying, even when I don't want to. Hurting those who don't deserve it."

I bent down and unlaced my boots, taking a moment to process his words.

That is his something true.

And he'd so bravely said something so raw and unpolished.

I'd wanted him to tell me who he was and, somehow, this cut deeper to the heart of him than anything else.

Sitting beside him, I tucked my legs up onto the bed and studied his profile. Neither of us was stronger than the other. We both had our fears, our wounds, our burdens.

And we both needed each other now. It was selfish of me to think that I was the only one in pain tonight.

"I know who you are."

He jerked his chin up, his frown deepening. "What?"

I offered a tentative smile. "I know who you are. You're Rykr Westhaven. The man who saved my life. You're honorable. Brave. And worthy of any role thrust upon him."

He shut his eyes, his throat bobbing as his jaw set. "But who's to say I won't ruin more, Seren? That my choices won't lead to more destruction? Make this world worse for the people around me?"

"You won't."

Incredulity shone in his blue-green eyes. "You don't know that."

"I do." I scooted closer and brushed my thumb against his lower lip, slow and deliberate. "Because only good men worry about things like that. And you don't believe in fate anyway, remember? Make your own fate, Rykr—if you dare. Defy them all."

"I'm going to kiss you, you know that?" His hands framed my face, fingers threading into the hair just behind my ears. "I'm going to kiss you, and I won't want to stop."

"You're not afraid of me?" I arched a brow. "After last time—"

He cut me off with a hard, possessive kiss. As his tongue swept into my mouth, colliding with mine, I had my answer.

I need him.

He pulled away, eyes smoldering as he stood, a slow smile curving his lips. "If we might die, this is a preferrable way, wouldn't you say?" He reached for the belt at his waist.

The Vangar leathers suited him—fierce, rugged, powerfully built. As he unlaced the leather bracers, I bit the inside of my lower lip. Forearms shouldn't be so sexy—or maybe I'd just never seen forearms like his.

Sinewed muscle, tightly corded to the elbow, a dusting of dark hair. The sculpted biceps, the broad shoulders—he moved with the ease of a warrior who knew his own strength. The feral instinct to glide my hands up those arms and be wrapped in his embrace took over rational thought.

He lifted his gaze to me then, as though noticing the heat of my stare, and the barest hint of a smirk tugged at his lips.

Gods, that chest.

He was so jaw-droppingly gorgeous that it made my thighs ache. I pressed my knees together. The tattoo from the rune oath on his neck and shoulder blended seamlessly with the Seal that wrapped around from the back.

Mine.

Possessiveness slunk through me. Plenty of women had watched him with admiration in their eyes during the sparring matches. But he was my husband.

And I want him. No matter who he is.

A shiver went through me as I stared at Rykr, the question burning deeply inside me. Though I could barely remember it now, Rykr's hair was golden when I'd met him. And he was Unbound ... *Ederyn.*

My breath went shallow as a possibility took shape.

He might *not* be Rykr Westhaven.

Or a spy, either.

"Rykr," I whispered. I didn't want him to *be* anyone else. The idea was terrifying, opening doors I didn't want to consider. "Are you ..." I couldn't force the words out.

Rykr's jaw tensed as though he knew and understood my thoughts. With a steady gaze, he came closer and pulled me to stand in front of him.

"I do need to tell you something." His voice was quiet, but sure. "I'm in love with you, Seren. And since we might die tomorrow, you deserve to know the truth. It's not the bond. Not magic. It's you. I love you with every beat of my heart."

I sucked in a shattered breath, the trembling in my body stilling. As I closed my eyes, he drew me closer, and I sagged against his chest. He'd become the air I needed to breathe, even when my mind couldn't fully accept or believe in his trustworthiness.

His lips dipped against my temple, kissing me with a tenderness I didn't expect. "I'm sorry," he whispered.

I didn't even know what he was apologizing for.

Then he pulled away. "I wish we weren't Lirien and Viori. There's no one I want to be enemies with less than you. I know you might not want to hear it, but I love you."

Despite my best efforts, despite the pain and the uncertainty and everything else between us, the tightness around my heart nearly suffocated me.

"Rykr ..." I lifted my eyes to his, my heart aching at the reality of what I refused to admit—of who he might be. "I love you, too," I managed in a whisper.

He cupped my face in his hands. "You're making it impossible for me to stay away from you, Seren." His thumb swept across my cheek, eliciting a shiver through me, then settled on the soft, fullest part of my lower lip. As he drew his thumb down slowly, my lips parting, I released a gentle, throaty moan, my eyes fluttering shut.

Then his lips were on mine, warm and insistent, one hand sliding around my waist and pulling me against him. He kissed that spot on my mouth where his thumb had been, as his hand cradled the nape of my neck, and his fingers tangled in my hair. With gentle pressure, his lips moved expertly against my own, urging them to part, his tongue teasing a gentle swipe against mine.

"Fuck, I missed the way you taste."

His voice in my head unraveled me. I clung to him, my arms twining around his neck, my weight melting into his. My mouth opened to his and the kiss deepened, his taste, his breath, his tongue consuming mine as my body burned with desire for him.

His hands glided down my sides, deftly unfastening my vest. The fabric slipped away, and before I could draw another breath, he tugged my shirt over my head, the heat of his gaze searing my skin.

His pants and shirt came off just as quickly.

His eyes darkened as they roamed over me, hunger sharpening every line of his face. "You have a fucking perfect body."

Oh gods. Only someone a lot stronger might have resisted the temptation he offered, but I didn't want to resist.

I wanted his hands on me. *Now.*

I pressed against him, our bodies fitting together in a way that felt devastatingly right. His tongue stroked mine. Claiming. Teasing. Taunting.

More.

More.

More.

My breasts were heavy with desire, my hardening nipples rubbing against the chiseled planes of his chest as his hand splayed across my back, pushing my waist against his rigid, impressively large cock.

I groaned, wanting to wrap my fingers around him—*no*—have all of him inside me, deep, relentless, until nothing else in the world existed but this.

Despite the difference in our sizes, I fit against him like I was made for him. Like we were inevitable. A perfect balance of fire and ice, strength and surrender. *Right.*

This was right.

How it should be.

Him and me. *Us.*

One.

I tore my lips from his, breathless, fingers tightening around his. His gaze was molten heat, his chest rising and falling in heavy, uneven breaths.

"Come with me."

His mouth quirked in a wicked smirk. "I'd like to."

I laughed and pulled him onto the bed.

Rykr wasted no time pulling me into his arms once again. "Fuck," he breathed, heavily. "I want you, Seren." Our mouths collided, and he pushed me back against the pillows, pinning my arms above my head with a strong hand. His other hand smoothed down to my breasts, and he dragged his lips away from my mouth, down my neck, then lower still.

His lips enclosed one nipple, his hand palming my breast. My back arched as he drew my nipple into his mouth, his tongue sweeping over the hardened peak. A low moan came from my throat, and my core ached for him.

I needed more. So much more.

I gasped, my senses swimming. "Aren't you afraid I might lose control again?"

"I'm willing to take my chances dying if it means doing this," Rykr growled, his mouth returning to my breast.

"Rykr, fuck, yes. I-I need—"

I gasped as he moved from one breast to the other. "What do you need, solwyn?" His breath was warm on my other nipple, then he took it into his mouth.

My body dissolved into an explosion of bliss.

Think clearly. Somewhere in the back of my mind, a quiet warning bell had begun ringing. I wanted to drown it before it was too late.

"Gods. *You. Please ...*"

Rykr's lips dropped to my jawline, the scruff of his face rough against my cheek, eliciting a shiver from me. "Are you sure?" he asked as his mouth caressed the side of my neck. "Remember what the Seidr said?"

Damn that fucking Seidr. Right now, prophecy and potential death seemed remote, ridiculous possibilities. What I needed and wanted was right here, in front of me. And I might never forgive myself if we stopped now.

"Fuck that. We might die tomorrow. I need you ..." I turned my face toward his, seeking his lips, which he gave me without hesitation. His mouth was like drinking from the most delicious, heady wine imaginable, and I wanted all of him. "Inside me. Now."

"I like it when you order me around." Rykr's arm wrapped around my waist, while the other dipped lower. His fingers brushed through the tangle of curls between my legs, then found my clit. A slow circle. I moaned, pushing myself against his hand while reaching for his cock.

As my fingers wrapped around the thickness of his length, his hand dipped lower still. I was soaked and slick for him and he pushed one finger deep inside me, my thighs clenching together reflexively. "Please ..." The pleasure of his finger inside me was driving me wild.

"I will, my love. I'll fill you deeply until every inch of me is inside you and fuck you until we can barely walk. But I like to take my time." His hand pulled back, then two fingers impaled me. "Fuck, you're so wet."

"Rykr, *please.*" Desperately, my hand glided against his length, hoping to tempt him into needing me as much as I needed him right now.

Maybe it was my body recognizing that part of my soul I'd given him, but this wasn't like anything else I'd ever experienced. My need for him tempted to tip over into something feral and uncontrollable.

I squeezed his cock.

"Fuck me, yes. Do that." He wet his lips, then slipped his other hand down, his fingertips finding my clit again. Slow circles gradually became faster, jolting me, my hips arching into his hands.

I could barely think straight, let alone concentrate on pumping his shaft the way he deserved, and I released a moan, my body trembling, pushing harder against him as he thrust with his fingers.

My head spun with molten desire. "So good ..."

Then Rykr knelt on the bed by my feet. His eyes were heated with desire as he pushed my knees apart, baring me completely to his view.

The way he looked at me.

Please. "I want your mouth on me if you won't give me your cock."

He smiled, then slid his hands up my calves, slowly, savoring every second. As his hands slipped onto the backs of my thighs, my body twitched with need. I was dripping wet all over the bed and he could see how slick I was, practically trembling for him.

He draped my legs over his shoulders, then trailed a slow kiss up the inside of my thigh, taunting me as he came tantalizingly close to my entrance. I sucked in a breath, waiting—*dammit, Rykr*—and he chuckled, then dragged those lips down the inside of my other thigh.

"You're a tease, Lirien," I growled impatiently, resting my hands back against the rough surface of the wooden headboard. Goosebumps had risen on my legs from the feeling of his lips, and I shuddered with delight.

"When you get to taste perfection for the first time, you don't swallow it down without appreciating it, my impatient little wife."

The words caused another moan, then his mouth dropped between my legs.

A soft, inelegant, *"Ohhhhhh ..."* left my lips.

His lips nuzzled my clit, a soft rub, then a flick of his tongue against it, sending my hands into his hair, dragging him closer. An enticing circle of his tongue made me ache.

Wife.

Was I his wife?

Did Rykr see me that way, or did he just enjoy teasing me?

This felt too sinfully delicious to be lawful.

And the rather inconvenient fact remained that, while I'd pledged him the protection of my body, given him a piece of my soul, and promised him my life—he'd pledged nothing to me in return.

But right now, I would trade every promise just to have Rykr fuck me with his mouth and make me come against his lips.

I barely felt as though I'd survive the feeling of Rykr's mouth against me, his tongue pushing inside me, his slow, generous kisses against my clit.

Giving me everything I needed. Taking nothing in return but the pleasure it gave him to be an unbelievably unselfish lover.

Wanton, demanding lust poured through me as my hips arched against his mouth, the strokes of his tongue against me bringing me closer to the edge. His fingers slipped inside me once again, thrusting as I panted. "Gods, Rykr, yes. More."

"I want you to come for me. Take what you need. Fuck, you're delicious."

My thighs clamped against him tightly, my entire body tensing like a coil, desperate for release. Then sweet relief cascaded down on me, every inch of me feeling warmth radiating like fire through my veins.

With shattered breaths, I moaned loudly and he held on, drawing every last second of my climax out of me, until I steadied myself against the bed, lying back in a crumpled heap.

As his hands stilled, I pressed my cheek against the pillow, a smile at my lips.

"This was not what I had in mind, Rykr Westhaven."

He chuckled, kneeling slowly, cock still rigid, unsatiated. Fucking gorgeous. He set a hand on either side of me, leaning over me. Then his lips dragged a kiss across my temple. "But was it good?"

I gave a throaty groan of approval, dropping my head back. "So good. Thank you," I said in a voice so low that I could hardly hear myself against the pounding of my heart.

He couldn't possibly know how much I needed that.

How much I needed him. For the first time in days, I felt whole.

Rykr pulled back, and he lifted my chin with his fingertips. Unbridled lust swam in his eyes.

But more than that.

Genuine warmth.

Love.

"Anything for you, my queen." He smiled, then dropped a kiss to my lips. "But we're not finished yet."

My heart nearly stopped at his words and my arms clamped around his neck, tears filling my eyes as I returned his kiss.

Sliding his hands to my ass, he pushed my knees apart with his hips. The head of his cock teased my entrance, which ached for him. "You're so fucking beautiful, Seren."

"*And mine.*"

His words made me arch against him.

I moaned loudly.

"*Say it, Seren.*"

"I'm yours," I ground out. My wrist was throbbing, the rune there stinging the muscle below it. And when my eyes found the rune on his neck, I found it black as ink, the pulse of his racing heartbeat below it. "Now and always."

"Now and always."

This felt like an ancient ritual ... the part we hadn't completed. Every inch of me burned for him, spiritually and physically. The thrumming of my heart, the rush of blood, the desperation I had for him.

He held the base of his shaft, a hint of a smile at his lips ... then had the nerve to fucking toy with me again, rubbing the dripping head against my swollen clit.

My gaze snapped to his. "If you continue to torment me, I'm going to tie you up, Rykr."

His piercing eyes were dark with passion. "Promise?"

Then pushed inside me in one hard thrust.

Fuck.

I hadn't had sex in so long, but I knew it hadn't ever been like this. As he thrust deeper, my legs locked around his waist, my hips arching to receive him until he filled me. I gasped at the union, panting as he stayed there, buried deep inside me, his eyes locked with mine.

My body trembled violently with the sensation, the void inside my soul filled by our union.

He retreated, then slammed himself hard inside me again.

Like he couldn't stand to break away from me.

Couldn't get deep enough.

Over and over.

"Fuck, you're perfect. Come for me, solwyn." His command was like smooth silk, equally gently and strong.

As I unleashed, coming apart against his thrusts, I screamed.

My climax had come hard and fast, the strength of my arousal tipping me over the edge immediately.

Nothing could be better than this.

No one would ever be able to touch me in a satisfying way again.

I was thoroughly wrecked. *Thoroughly his.*

He gave a fierce, guttural roar, then poured himself inside me, throbbing intensely as the muscles of my core clamped against him.

We both gasped for breath as he collapsed against me. His heart slammed into his ribs against my ear, and his arm curled protectively around my waist.

A slow smile spread on my face as I took in the tattoo of his Seal spreading over his neck and fused with the one from the oath rune. The ridges of his well-muscled back, the feeling of his cock, which was still buried deeply inside me.

Mine.

Every inch of him belonged to me.

"You were right," I murmured, closing my eyes again.

"About what?" His voice was a husky scratch.

"You're very good at fucking." My fingers spread out on the soft hair of his chest, and I watched them vibrate with his heartbeat.

His laugh rumbled in his chest.

"So are you."

I tried not to think about the consequences of this. It had been perfect. The restless exhaustion that had been stirring inside me was gone.

For the first time in weeks, I was whole.

Nothing else had happened, though.

All that fear and worry and denying ourselves ... and we were both fine. Somehow, I'd managed not to kill us—and neither had the bond.

I barely dared to ask the question. "What happens now, Rykr?"

"I'm not sure." His hand smoothed over my ass, then he gave me a sharp slap. "But we have a whole day to waste before we face death. So, I think maybe doing this would be a good way to spend it."

I laughed and kissed him.

That would be perfect.

CHAPTER 34
RYKR

Even though I'd shown her my underbelly, she still loved me.

Seren slept in my arms, her body warm as it pressed against me, the smooth skin of her ass tucked up so close that I'd woken hard all night. Fortunately, she'd been happy to wake up with me, and we had fucked on every possible surface of this room—not that there was much selection.

I wasn't spent, either. Even now, my hand rested on her hip and every irrational thought in my body urged me to wake her once more.

The oppressive silence of the early morning gave me too much time to think.

Lirien needed me—didn't it?

But how was I supposed to leave her here?

Her soul had been threaded with mine in a way I'd never known was possible. In a way that felt like obsession. I wanted her in every way—as a wife, a lover, a queen, a friend, a counselor. In ways I couldn't think of or verbalize.

She thought she loved me. That she knew me. Would she love the king of her enemies? The prince who'd once been labeled the scourge of her people? And if I turned my back on that divinely appointed path—would she love the man who'd chosen her over honor?

As the darkness of my thoughts sprouted long claws that dug into my chest, my lips dropped to her jaw, my hand smoothing forward across the flat plane of her stomach.

She groaned softly, a light laugh leaving her lips as she woke. Her lips found mine immediately and she kissed me softly, then smiled. "You don't intend on letting me sleep at all this morning, do you?"

"Sleep is a waste of time," I growled possessively in her ear, my hand sliding down to stroke her swollen, slick clit. "Especially when you're facing death."

Gods, she's so wet already.

"And if we survive tonight?" She moaned as I pushed her thighs apart with my knee, teasing her entrance with my cock.

"Then we'll fuck in celebration all day tomorrow." I flipped her onto her stomach. "Get on your hands and knees."

She complied readily and I set my hands on her ass, admiring the view of her, splayed before me. The sight of that quivering, slick pussy made me somehow harden even more. I'd coated it with my cum so many times already tonight, claimed her, made her thoroughly mine and it wasn't enough.

It would never be enough.

I thrust myself fully inside her, taking her so fast that she cried out in pain and pleasure, a groan ripping from her throat. "Did I hurt you?" I asked.

"Yes." She reached between my legs and squeezed my balls. "But I liked it."

This woman was going to drive me insane.

How could I satiate myself with fucking her? Nothing was enough.

This bond made sure of that.

Nothing would ever be enough—*would it?*

Or was it that lack of balance that had me this feral? I wanted to give her everything I had—but what if what I needed to give her was a literal piece of my soul, as she had given me?

A knock on the door made us both look back and I moved to pull away from her, but she clamped her hand harder against me. "Finish first," she demanded.

I smiled and leaned down, my hand sliding around her waist to find her clit as I continued to thrust. "My pleasure, darling wife."

Her moans began to grow louder and she reached for the pillow to bury her face against it.

I tugged it away from her with my free hand, thrusting harder.

As cries of ecstasy left her lips, I felt her tighten against my cock, her body shuddering and shaking against me. That undid me. I groaned and gave one final thrust as I released inside her, pulsing deep.

Gods almighty.

My fingers traced the curve of Seren's spine. She was warm against me, soft despite the strength I knew lurked beneath. I'd spent a lifetime fighting battles, yet this was the first time I feared losing. Not a war, but her. Not the kingdom, but this.

A sharp knock shattered the thought. Seren tensed against me, and I cursed under my breath.

Heart hammering in my chest, I pulled away and lay back on the mattress. "I'm not sure I can walk."

"Swiver. You're going to make me answer the door?" Her

cheeks were pink, her face flushed with pleasure. Combing her long hair over her shoulder, she shook her head at me, then stole the sheet off the bed and stood, wrapping it around her. "I'm dripping, you know," she hissed.

The thought made me grin. "You're the one who wanted to finish."

She walked toward the door and cracked it open a slit.

"You need to get dressed," Ciaran's voice said stiffly from the other side of the door. "Rykr's friend is back, and this time he has company. We're in Amahle's room. It's bigger. And … quieter."

Thorne?

Shit.

I hadn't allowed myself to think about that whole situation all night. After the experience with the Seidr, my mind had been plenty occupied.

Seren closed the door but didn't turn around. "I guess that means he heard us last night," I said, getting up from the bed. I went over to the tub. Drops of water were still on the bottom of it, from when we'd used it during the night. Turning the water on, I soaked a cloth in the warm stream, then carried it to her.

Turning Seren to face me, I knelt in front of her, then cleaned the mess I'd made on her. She set her hand on my shoulder. "Company?"

I stood and held her gaze. Would she be angry that I hadn't told her? "It's not what you think. Or who you think."

Seren crossed her arms, pressing the sheet against her perfect breasts. "Who do I think it is?"

"More Regulation soldiers. But it's not." I went back to the tub, wiped myself clean, and shut the water off.

The truth was, I hadn't been ready for this meeting last night. I wasn't sure if it would have changed things between Seren and me.

And after everything … I hadn't wanted to risk it.

The night we'd had, despite how it had started, had been incredible. Selfishly, I hadn't been willing to let anything take that from us.

We dressed in silence, a heaviness creeping in. Her thoughts, a hum in my head that I'd learned to block out, were unusually quiet, as though she was afraid to think too much.

I tensed as I finished strapping my sword at my hip. Seren gave me an odd look. "It doesn't quite feel real, does it?"

"What?"

"Last night. It was like a dream."

A smile played at my lips. "A dream? Or a recurring nightmare?"

She chuckled. "Hilarious." Then she came over toward me and kissed me. "Ready?"

"Does it make a difference?" I arched a brow. I wasn't sure that I was.

We crossed the hallway and Seren knocked. Amahle opened the door immediately, ushering us in.

The room was only slightly larger than ours, but it had the benefit of a window to the street. Thorne occupied a large space over by the window and at his side—Brogan Ragnall.

Seren's knees nearly buckled. A strangled cry tore from her throat and she was gone from my side, flying toward her father.

I'd tried to prepare for this meeting since the moment Thorne had told me the man was here and helping him, but the sight of him stirred fury in my blood, my hand dropping instinctively to the hilt of my sword.

Brogan caught his daughter in a tight embrace, and I tore my gaze away. The man who murdered my mother should be a savage, heartless monster, not a loving father with a family. I *wanted* him to be the former—needed him to be.

Ciaran sat awkwardly on a chair, looking absolutely miserable. Amahle sidled up to me. "Nice work," she whispered with a wry smile. "Ciaran spent the night on my floor just to get away from you two."

Seren pulled away from Brogan, wiping tears from her cheeks and then whirled back to look at me. "Did you know my father was here?" Then she stiffened slightly, as though remembering the hatred I'd relayed before—and the fact that I'd never met her father. "Father ..." She pushed back a strand of hair, nervously. "It's a long story, but this is—"

"I know who he is—what's happened." Brogan lifted his chin and held my gaze.

The simplicity of his words was clear enough: he knew me as Prince Calix Warrick.

Odd how, in many ways, I no longer knew myself by that name.

"I spoke with your mother," Brogan said in a gruff voice to Seren, still watching me. "You were wise to stay here. The House of the Veil is filled with spies."

"That's where Mother was going, isn't it? The sewer ..." Seren's eyes widened and she glanced at Thorne.

Thorne shifted beside Brogan, watching us both with caution. I'd given Thorne an earful about trusting Brogan. No matter what the man had done or claimed, I couldn't and wouldn't trust him. Anything else would mean sheer stupidity.

But Thorne had insisted. Brogan had found him in the forest. Helped him, rather than killed him. Led him to Emberstone. "Did you claim refuge with the Viori?" I asked Thorne.

Thorne lifted his right wrist with a scowl. "I got a shiny new brand and everything." The Viori rune gleamed on his skin. "I still have to present myself for a loyalty test and pledge tonight. Before your trial."

"Thorne, this is my wife, Seren," I said, directing Seren's attention to him.

"My lady," Thorne said with a bow. "Thorne Ursidor, at your service." He gave me a knowing look. "Now I know why you don't want to leave."

Seren looked him over carefully. "Thank you," she said, but the anxious set of her features remained. Her gaze snapped back to her father. "Did you bring him here, Father? What are you doing here? Where's Madoc ... and Esme?"

Brogan's grim expression shifted.

After a tense moment, he said, "Haldron has Esme."

Seren gasped, her shock seeping through the bond, the strength of her pain like a gut punch.

Wait. *That* daughter? *That* was the daughter Ragnall had come to rescue?

I felt the way Seren's mind shifted. The way her thoughts raced, boiling with rage and questions as her eyes turned toward me, lips parted, shaken to her core.

The leader of her people was the villain she'd been looking for all this time. The one who'd taken her beloved sister.

Both Ciaran and Amahle looked equally stunned. "What the hell?" Amahle breathed.

"Why?" Seren gripped her father's arm. "Why did he take her?"

Brogan rubbed his bearded jaw. His shoulder-length brown hair was in disarray, as though he'd been living in the wilds for some time. "To manipulate me. To force my hand into something he knew I'd never have agreed to otherwise. He ordered me to plan and execute the assassination of King Magnus and his sons."

Thorne reacted faster than I could. The cold clang of metal rang as Thorne's sword left the holster at his back, the edge of his blade stopping inches away from Brogan. "You son of a bitch," Thorne growled, betrayal and rage on his dark, golden face.

But my own rage was silent, deeper. A slow, festering thing. It clawed up my throat, threatening to consume the logic I barely clung to.

My ears rang with a sharp sense-dulling scream, my heart numb and cold. My pulse beat harder, and I blinked at Brogan, as the meaning of his declaration sank slowly through my skin. I'd been blocking the connection between Seren and me since I'd come into the room, but I threw further effort into it now.

The truth would endanger everyone here.

My breath left me in a slow, shaking exhale, and my vision blurred at the edges. I wanted to drive my sword straight through Brogan's throat. Not just for my mother.

But for my father. For my brothers.

My hand was already on my hilt, the leather warm beneath my grip.

Brogan met my stare with something unreadable.

"You don't deserve to speak their names," I said finally, voice tight with control.

Seren threw herself in front of her father. "No!" She breathed hard, her eyes meeting mine. "Wait, please. *Please*, Rykr, tell your friend to stand down."

"Your blade is perilously close to my wife, Thorne," I managed, noting the tension in both Amahle and Ciaran. Their worry and confusion ... and hands inching closer to their own weapons. I took slow, deliberate steps toward Ragnall then set my hand on Thorne's shoulder. "If anyone executes Brogan Ragnall, it's me."

Seren's eyes widened. "Rykr, you don't understand—"

"No, he understands." Brogan's voice had an edge of exhaustion to it. "And I deserve it. What I did is unforgivable.

Haldron threatened unspeakable consequences for Esme ... *he knew exactly how to manipulate me.*" His gaze met mine over Seren's head. "But I made a vow to Queen Eldis to protect one of the princes and I wanted to honor that—spare him. Instead, I replaced him with an impostor, not knowing that Haldron had a means of detecting my failure. Now he's hunting for me and Madoc. And the prince that escaped."

Had Brogan come ... *to warn me?*

Seren flinched.

I can barely breathe. He killed my family.

He.

Killed.

My.

Family.

At last, I forced out, "Does he know which prince escaped?"

"No." Brogan's eyes glittered. "If he did, the prince would already be dead."

"Aye." Heat radiated from Thorne's furious form. "Then you'd better be willing to keep your oath to protect the prince at all costs, before we kill you for slaying the king."

"You won't be killing anyone," Seren snapped, protective, and ready to fight. "Why are you here, Father? Isn't it dangerous for you to have come to the Bellwether?"

"Why do you think, Seren? I went back to the encampment to try to hide the rest of my family away and found ... you'd been pulled into all of this. I don't know what Haldron has planned for you in the Skorn—if he puts you through the trial at all—but I have no doubt he's using you to bait me. And, considering that I'm here, it worked. But the Bellwether is safe. The innkeeper is a friend."

"What would Haldron bait you here for though? To learn which prince escaped?" Seren turned toward her father, her body tense.

"Yes, to use you and Esme to force me to track him down. Finish what I started. I don't know how he knows I failed, but he needs the prince dead for whatever he's planned."

"War. He has war planned. He's next in line for the throne, and you knew that before you did this." I bored my eyes into his. "The question is, do you plan on killing the surviving prince to save your family?"

Brogan watched me closely, as though measuring how quickly and easily I could end him. His confession was the only thing staying my hand.

"I can't," he said lifting his chin.

If Lucia had told him about the bond, then Brogan knew Seren would die if he killed me.

Once again, the bond might be the only thing keeping me alive.

"And Madoc?" Seren's hands trembled. "Where is he?"

Brogan's eyes grew sadder. "I helped him escape to Lirien through the northern mountains. He'll never be safe in the territory now. Then I came back for the rest of you."

Seren lifted trembling fingertips to her mouth. "No—"

Brogan pulled Seren into a fierce hug, and I didn't interfere, shooting Thorne a look to stay where he was. If Madoc had gone to Lirien, then he wasn't coming back. *Ever.*

"Why?" Seren's voice broke, muffled. "I don't believe he would just leave so easily."

"You're right, he didn't want to. I forced him to. It was only by Madoc's help that I was able to save the prince who escaped. He shot him with a whistler quill then protected him until the effects wore off. But the cost was knowing his name. If Haldron catches Madoc, he'll torture him for it."

His words sickened me. Madoc had been there—when the Viori came after us. Thorne knew it too. His expression was dark, his thirst for vengeance unmistakable. Madoc had been involved with Dalric's murder. Had he lifted a hand against him?

I couldn't bring myself to be grateful for Madoc's help in saving my life.

Stepping away, Seren pushed her braid back, her face drained of all color. "What can I do? Is Esme here in Emberstone?"

Brogan nodded. "I believe so."

"Then find her. We'll take care of Haldron—he'll be at the Skorn trial. Between Rykr and me, we can find a way to kill him, right?" Seren shot me a look, waiting for my support. She glanced back at her father. "You find Esme and we'll kill Haldron. End this once and for all."

Kill Haldron?

Her determination, her honor sent warmth through me.

Even Thorne looked impressed. "You'd kill the leader of your people?" He raised a skeptical brow.

"He kidnapped my sister, manipulated my father, is hunting my family, and wants to lead my people to war. I owe him nothing. He's not worthy of my deference, and I won't submit to such a leader."

"Your people won't see it the same way, though. They'll kill you before you set foot out of Emberstone. Your family will be exiled from the Viori, and your father is already an exile from Lirien. There will be nowhere for your family to go." Thorne sheathed his sword, and some of my tension fizzled with the motion.

Amahle, who had been silently listening to every word, moved beside me. "Seren, it's not just your family, either. Our entire tribe is in the House of the Veil—your mother and Tara. If something goes wrong, who do you think will suffer first?"

My gaze shifted to Ciaran. He may have concealed what

had happened to the skinwraith, but his sister had suffered the consequences. I doubted he would take that risk again.

"Ciaran is a liability," I told Seren.

He shifted under my hard stare, as though reading my thoughts. "I'm here, aren't I?" he snarled. "Not in the House of the Veil."

Seren's eyes softened as she looked at him. "Your family—"

"You're my family too, Ser." Ciaran's voice was thick with emotion.

The room was suddenly too crowded, the air rife with distrust.

Brogan drew out a slow sigh and looked at his daughter. "Thorne is right. You can't kill Haldron without risking your life and the safety of the tribe." He took Seren by the shoulders. "But you and your husband can escape. Right now. Give Haldron one less hold on our family. Go with Thorne through the mountains and don't stop until you reach Pendara. It'll be dangerous and risky, but it's the best choice. Haldron may be furious, but the tribe may have time to leave Emberstone. I'll keep trying to save Esme."

"If I die, I die, but I'm not leaving here without doing my part, Father. You can't ask me to run now," Seren gritted out fiercely. "You didn't raise me to run."

Brogan dropped his hands from Seren's shoulders. He met my gaze. "I'd like to speak to you alone."

"No," Seren and Thorne answered in unison.

Thorne crossed his arms and glared at Brogan. "Given what you just admitted, you can understand why I don't trust you."

Ragnall's request intrigued me.

"I can handle myself." I gestured back toward the door. "We can go to the other room."

Thorne opened his mouth to protest, but I cut him down with a look. "Ragnall won't kill me. He knows the consequences." I pushed past them all, my footsteps hard against the floorboards.

A few moments later, Brogan followed. I opened the door, scanning the room that, minutes ago, felt like a private refuge. I hadn't cared that Ciaran or Amahle knew Seren and I had spent the night together—but Ragnall? He might loathe me even more for it. He stank of sweat and unwashed clothing, and the sound of his breath filled the quiet.

The man who had murdered my mother was in my grasp.

And even if he was as innocent as Seren claimed—he had orchestrated my father's and brothers' deaths. Maybe even killed some of them himself.

Hatred wasn't enough to describe what I felt toward him. And still. He hadn't murdered me. He'd honored his oath to my mother and kept me alive.

"Do you regret not killing me when you had the chance?" My voice was low, flat as I turned to face him. I should be more wary of this man, yet I didn't fear him in the slightest.

"Yes." The word echoed in the room. Brogan's eyes narrowed. "I should have. My family wouldn't be in danger right now if I had."

His certainty left no room for doubt. "You've always picked your family over honor, it seems."

"The love of family is a powerful magic and motivator. I won't lie to you. If I could have picked any Ederyn prince to save, it wouldn't have been the 'Scourge of the Viori.' But I vowed to protect you. Now my family is suffering for it."

Guilt blazed through me. The depth of his knowledge was startling.

He changed the subject abruptly. "Do you know why Haldron tried to kill Magnus years ago?"

"Because he wanted to be king. That's clear enough."

"No." A soft chuckle left his lips. "Not at all. Haldron was a good man. Sympathetic to the Viori. Beloved by the people. And most especially, by his wife, Thyra."

I jeered. "Thyra, who languishes in Suomelin, still trapped in a half-life after his abuse?"

"Your father only gave you the version of events he wanted you to know. Thyra bore the cursed Hrafn mark, and your father destroyed her life—Haldron's life—for it."

"Hrafn?" I repeated, dragging the *H* and *R* together like he had. The word meant *raven* in Old Ederyn but I'd never heard of the mark.

"The divine mark—a sign of the old gods that Ragnor Ederyn rejected out of fear."

A slow, sickly feeling curled in my stomach. "Fear of what?"

"That the old gods would return through their chosen." Brogan's expression darkened. "It was how Magnus justified taking Thyra from Haldron."

"Taking her?" My brows furrowed. "You're saying my father *stole* Haldron's wife?"

"That's exactly what I'm saying." Brogan rubbed his jaw. "She bore the Hrafn mark—though no one knew until an accident forced her to shave her hair. The mark was hidden beneath it, waiting."

I crossed my arms. "And you expect me to believe my father kidnapped her *just* because of a mark?"

"No," Brogan said grimly. "Because he believed she was a vessel for something far worse."

He spoke with such openness it nearly made his story sound true. But in all my years living in Suomelin, I'd never heard a word about Thyra bearing this mark—or my father interfering in Haldron's marriage. "Why would he take her?"

"It's Ederyn tradition. Anyone born with the Hrafn mark is taken—locked away in a dungeon beneath the keep, where they can never be a threat. Most are imprisoned as children and go mad before they reach adulthood."

Ederyn children seized and thrown in the dungeons?

The idea sounded preposterous.

But was it? Twins were murdered at birth. The Bound realms were subjected to the Bloodbinding. Lirien's traditions were built on fear and superstition. "Why?" I demanded.

Brogan drew a sharp breath. "Because the gods might have died at Vornfall, Your Grace, but their spirits endure. They want to return. They should return. But which ones? Valtheron, the all-knowing? Gaelric, god of storms? Or Sly, the traitor who sided with the enemy at the end of the Third Age?"

His brow furrowed as he went on. "A child born with the Hrafn mark has been touched by the divine. Given the right circumstances, one of the gods could resurrect through them. Ragnor Ederyn had everything in his power to eliminate that possibility through the Bloodbinding.

"The only threat left, Ederyn children born with the Hrafn mark, are taken when they're found. Every infant is searched at their naming ceremony."

I stared at him, dumbfounded and chilled.

Is it possible?

Could Brogan Ragnall be telling the truth?

I shouldn't listen to another word of his poisoned lies. I knew who he was. What he'd done.

"But if Thyra was an adult, what difference did it make if she bore a divine mark? Why would my father care?"

His lips pursed. "Haldron asked the same thing. Begged Magnus to see reason—that she was no threat. But Magnus took her all the same. Insisted she had to be locked away."

He held my gaze, unflinching. "After years of trying to get her back, Haldron lost control. He stabbed your father in his rage. Stole Thyra and took her to Ibarra, where a priest promised to remove the Hrafn from her with an ancient spell. But it failed and she was left clinging to life, her mind shattered. The Regulation caught up with Haldron and he fled, unable to take her with him. After that, he came to the territory."

"How do you know? You would have already been here when Haldron left Lirien."

"He found me in my encampment. Begged me to help him plot his revenge. I refused." Bitterness twisted his scowl. "Turns out he found a way to force my hand."

I averted my eyes, staring at the floor.

It made too much sense.

And worse, it didn't contradict what my father had told me. The lies had been in what he *hadn't* said. I'd filled in the blanks myself.

Brogan's voice softened, an insidious mist blanketing all my certainty. "You were born with the mark. Your mother begged Lucia to conceal it after your birth and made us swear to protect you and keep your secret. When the time came to call in her debt, she helped us escape Lirien."

Lucia had spoken of my birthmark, of concealing it with a rune. But a divine mark? Was that why I'd always had stronger powers than my brothers?

More sickening was the way he spoke about my mother. *With admiration.* "And yet, you killed her. Even though she helped you."

"I did not kill your mother. I swear it," Brogan said, his eyes like flint. "And I don't know who did or why. But whoever it was found it convenient to blame me and remains beyond suspicion."

I held his stare, my heartbeat dull. He had every reason to lie. But something in his words *felt* true and I loathed the inconvenience of my instincts. "That doesn't change that you murdered my father and brothers. *My* family. I should run you through right now."

"You see, Your Grace, we're more alike than you know. Willing to sacrifice for the women—the people—we love. I can't kill you without hurting Seren, but I'd give everything to go back a few weeks, when the only consequence of your death would have been destroying what remains of my honor. Now, I've risked my entire family. I have no love for you or for Lirien. Not anymore. No loyalty to the Viori. My only loyalty is to my family."

My jaw clenched at the brutality—and honesty—with which he spoke. "What do you want from me?" I asked at last.

"Tell Seren who you are. Convince her your life is necessary and to flee with you into the mountains. Take her away from this. She won't go otherwise. She's too good—too loyal. She will never leave her friends and family. I will do what it takes to save the rest of my family, but she's in your hands now. Please. Save my daughter."

Of course.

The coward wanted, once again, the easy way out from all this.

Seren had spoken of her father with such admiration ... would she still idolize him if she knew what he really was?

His pleading eyes may have convinced someone else. Maybe I should have considered it, but he was Brogan Ragnall. His pleas meant nothing to me.

I shook my head, gently. "When have you known your daughter to do what anyone else wants her to do? I've only known her for a short time and even I can tell you that. It will make no difference. She still won't leave and the knowledge of who I am will only endanger her further."

"You have to try," Brogan growled.

"I *have* to do nothing." I gave him a hard look. "You forget yourself, Ragnall."

"She might die and then where will you be? Where will Lirien be? Going through the Skorn is lunacy."

The corners of my lips turned up as I felt her at the edge of my consciousness, trying to push through the walls I'd put up while I spoke to her father.

Beautiful, loyal, fierce Seren.

Temptation filled me. When I'd arrived in the territory, thoughts of escape had consumed me. Return to Lirien. Now I knew it was my duty to go back. But without her?

That was torture.

Practicality aside—yes, she was a huge vulnerability. But I couldn't stomach the idea of her staying behind while I went to Lirien.

Brogan's plan was interesting. *Force her to come with me.* Take back my kingdom now, before Ivar could be crowned, and prepare for the coming war with Haldron. But she might hate me for it. She didn't want to go and would be separated from her family and people forever.

The options before me were grim, my head aching as I considered them. I'd spent the night with Seren in my arms and, for that one moment, the outside world had slipped away.

I wouldn't leave without her. But I would never make her leave, either. Not if there might be another way.

I rubbed my eyes.

And what if the war could be stopped?

Seren's idea had merit.

"We do it Seren's way. We kill Haldron during the trial. End this war before it ever starts. You'll get your family back, I'll give them a place to live in Suomelin, and you'll turn yourself over to me to face the consequences of murdering my family. It's a much neater ending for everyone, wouldn't you say?"

Anguish lit his features. "You can't guarantee—"

"And neither can you. But we can try."

Brogan pinched the bridge of his nose. "Seren will never survive that trial. Haldron will make certain of it. And he may not know who you are yet, but it's only a matter of time before he does."

"How *did* you learn? Only two people knew my name in exile and I'm sure both would be willing to die for that secret."

Brogan nodded. "One of your father's guards—Ulf—confessed under torture that you'd been Sealed to Pendara. After that, it was a matter of finding the right Sealed man. Only Madoc and I a knew your name after that ... but if I was able to find you, others can too. Haldron has many spies."

Ulf?

The disgust I had in Ragnall had no bounds. He was a mercenary, but damn if a man with Brogan's knowledge and skill wouldn't be an asset in the future. Yet a man without loyalty was more trouble than he was worth.

"It doesn't matter. Seren's plan is sound. I'm staying. And rather than argue with her, I'd suggest you learn not to underestimate your daughter. If you're here to help, then *help her.* Otherwise, you're a waste of breath."

A few beats of silence passed, then Brogan nodded. "I won't sacrifice any of my family, Your Grace. We have to get them out of the House of the Veil. And my tribe deserves better than to suffer for our actions. They've suffered enough, wouldn't you say? They're innocent."

Innocent was an exaggeration, but I focused on those moments after the skinwraith attack—when I'd seen children and women, elderly people, crying or dead. Injured. Men who'd tried to help their families and failed.

And then turned their wrathful savagery on me.

"There are innocents among them, yes," I admitted at last.

"And they may not acknowledge me, but I will protect all the people of Lirien as best I can. I'm not my father, Ragnall. I never will be. This wasn't a role I wanted or prepared for, but I won't hide from it or from Haldron, either. I'm no coward."

Shame burned openly in his eyes. "All I wanted was to be left in peace."

I stepped closer. "Then you shouldn't have started a war. But this may be your chance to redeem yourself. Once and for all."

CHAPTER 35
SEREN

Amahle and Ciaran were silent as we made our way from the Bellwether toward the House of the Veil.

Under any other circumstances, there would have been chatter between us. Light banter, maybe even reminiscing over old times. But now, each of us wore our worries like a shroud.

Rykr and Thorne had stayed with my father at the Bellwether to plan. The book Giulia had given me on Emberstone had come in handy, but my father also knew more about the city's layout than I'd realized.

But there were two more people whose help we needed—unlikely allies who cared about the tribe and who might have a role to play today: Seth and Darya.

With her expert knowledge of Emberstone from years of living here, Darya might be able to help us figure out where Haldron might be keeping Esme. And Seth ... Amahle and Ciaran were convinced he truly loved our tribe, pointing to the way he'd protected Rykr after the skinwraith attack.

Trusting Seth could be a huge misstep. We couldn't afford

to tell them all we knew, just enough to help us and our tribe. But what if they didn't believe us about the danger?

And then there was what my father had revealed about his role in the murder of King Magnus and his sons.

... except one.

I swallowed hard, my heart falling all over again.

One prince, replaced by an impostor.

One golden-haired Ederyn, chased into the Dreadwood unwittingly.

Could it be possible?

But my heart already knew the truth. When the news of the king's death had reached our encampment, I'd felt the depth of Rykr's pain—*gods, that's not even his name.*

He'd lied to me.

I'd lain in his arms, made love to him all night. Fallen in love with him, without even knowing his name.

Tension crept into my shoulders.

The signs had been there, hadn't they? The way he hesitated when talking of his past. The way he deflected, dodged questions with wit and charm.

I should have seen it. I should have *known.*

What a stupid little fool I was. Everything made so much more sense now. Everything he'd said—a half-truth meant to make me hear what I wanted to hear and see what I wanted to see.

His queen.

Bile tore at my throat.

And the worst of it was ... no matter how much I loved him ... no matter how much he said he loved me ... we could never be together. The heir to the throne of Lirien couldn't marry a Viori Vangar woman, could he? And even if he could, I didn't want to be a queen. And *never* the queen of Lirien.

It was almost déjà vu. Would I survive the Skorn only to

watch the man I loved marry his true queen while I was cast aside once again? What I'd felt for Seth was nothing compared to what I felt for Rykr.

How would I withstand that?

Amahle squeezed my hand. "You look like you're going to fall apart or murder someone."

"I might do both," I admitted, meeting her warm gaze.

"Do you think they'll be able to get out in time?" Ciaran murmured. He looked so tired that my heart broke a little. His whole family was in the House of the Veil.

"We have to hope." I looked from Ciaran back to Amahle. "I'm so sorry—"

"What are you apologizing for?" Amahle's brow furrowed. "You need to stop blaming yourself for everything. You know that, right? Haldron started all this."

"True," I admitted, bitterly. "But Haldron didn't make the skinwraiths attack our camp and that's what forced our tribe to come to Emberstone. I could have—"

"I've been thinking about that," Ciaran said, his gaze low. "Even if we had warned everyone, you were right. Tara was right. They would have thought Rykr was involved and still wouldn't have been prepared. The outcome would have been the same. You're not to blame for that. No one is."

Sweet Ciaran. I paused mid-step, turned, and threw my arms around him, his words a balm I hadn't known I'd needed. Ciaran caught me in his embrace, everything about him so comforting and familiar. I'd hurt him so many times over the last few weeks, even questioning his loyalty, yet he'd remained by my side. Steadfast.

My eyes misted and I stepped back. "I'm sorry," I managed. "I'm so sorry for everything I've put you through. I've tested our friendship and you're still here. I love you, Ciaran. I never should have questioned you."

Ciaran's expression flickered. A heartbeat passed before he cupped my face, his grey eyes warm and gentle. "Nothing will ever change how I feel about you, Seren. I'm proud to be your friend. Always."

Amahle grinned. "Oh, thank the gods. I was worried we might die with you two never figuring out how to talk." She stepped between us as we started forward again. "Do you have any idea how much I've wanted to shake you both?"

"We're not going to die," I said firmly. "I'm not going to let that happen. Once we warn the tribe, I want you all to stay with them and leave Emberstone. That's your part in all this. Get them to safety. Between Rykr, Thorne, and my father, we'll figure out the rest."

"No way," Amahle said, her lips vibrating as she expelled a huff. "We're not leaving you, Seren."

"You have to." I gave them both pleading looks. "I don't have a choice. If I don't show up for the Skorn tonight, I'll be hunted. But it will be a lot easier for me to do what I need to do if I know you're safe."

"What about what we want?" Ciaran asked skeptically. "Doesn't that matter?"

"Of course it matters." My heart throbbed as I looked at my brave friends. They were my family. Closer, really. And they were also Vangar—brave and fearless, no matter the challenge. "But I'll need all my wits to get through tonight. I'm already worried to death about Esme. I can't afford to be worrying about you, too. Please."

They exchanged a look, their faces troubled. "It's not your responsibility to protect us," Amahle said firmly. "But we'll do our best to make it easier for you, all right?"

We were getting closer to the House of the Veil and, somehow, it didn't seem like enough time to say everything I wanted to say to them. This could be the last time I saw them. "I just—"

Amahle squeezed my hand. "We know, Seren." She stopped and drew me into a hug. "But sometimes, when you're going through a trial, it's better to know that you're not alone. That matters too."

I inhaled shakily, wanting to draw from her strength.

There would never be enough time with the people I loved.

Tucked behind the market corridors, the House of the Veil blended seamlessly into the city's jagged architecture. The unassuming facade—a broad, arched doorway framed by weathered stone columns—gave little clue about what lay beyond the threshold. Even from here, though, faint, eerie chanting drifted from the numerous stone windows cut into the stone, the voices of the Veiled brothers and sisters who served the poor and destitute of the Viori.

Goosebumps rose on my arms as I followed Ciaran and Amahle inside. My reaction had to be more about my wariness than the sanctuary itself. Just because Haldron was evil didn't mean the rest of Emberstone was.

Beyond the threshold, the cavernous interior stretched before us, dimly lit by the ever-burning lanterns lining the walls. Smooth stone floors echoed beneath our footsteps, and low-hanging beams narrowed the corridors. In the central chamber, clusters of tables and chairs were gathered before a broad hearth, the flickering firelight casting shifting shadows on the high walls.

I recognized men and women from my tribe, their low murmurs echoing against the white walls and high vaulted ceilings that rose in places to reveal skylights chiseled into the mountain's surface. Thin shafts of daylight pierced the gloom, illuminating the smoky air.

"Seren." Tara's voice reached me before I saw her, then my sister stood from one of the tables.

I hadn't realized how worried I was about her until she strode toward me, a laughing scowl on her face. "I take it they didn't throw you in the dungeon, after all." She crossed her arms as she stopped in front of me. "But Mother and I had to hear about it from Seth. Guess you forgot we were here, did you?"

"I saw Mother yesterday. Didn't she tell you?"

"She's been busy with the wounded. I think she went out to stock up on her supplies, though. I haven't seen her all day." Tara scanned my face. "Is everything all right?"

"Not exactly. Anywhere around here safe? Free from listening ears?"

Tara frowned then nodded. "Follow me."

Ciaran gave me a worried glance. "I'm going to find my family. I'll meet you back here in an hour."

Amahle and I accompanied Tara down another corridor, a winding passage cut deep into the rock. Closed doors lined either side, offering sanctuary to the weary souls who found refuge here. We didn't stop until we reached the one where Tara was staying.

There was no bed inside, just a bedroll on top of clean straw, and the space was small and windowless, crates stacked high against one wall, filled with what little my family still owned. Nowhere to sit.

Tara closed the door behind us. "What's going on?"

"Father's here." I surveyed the space, my pulse beating faster. "Haldron has Esme. He's the one who kidnapped her."

Quickly, I explained everything my father had told me.

Tara's expression darkened with every word. By the time I finished, her entire body had gone rigid.

"No." The word escaped her like a breath before her jaw

clenched. Her hands curled into fists, shaking at her sides. "No, no, no."

Faster than I could react, she grabbed the nearest crate and flung it against the wall. The wood splintered, trinkets spilling onto the ground.

"He took *Esme*?" Her voice cracked, her chest rising and falling with shallow breaths.

I nodded, throat tight.

"I'll kill him," Tara hissed. "I *swear* it. I'll carve his heart out myself."

She turned toward the door as if she might storm out right then and there.

I grabbed her arm. "We need a plan first." Considering her state, I stumbled over my next words. "And there's something else I need to tell you." The news of Madoc would devastate her. Maybe Mother or Father should be the ones to tell her, but I couldn't do that to Tara. She deserved to know.

Tara's wild gaze snapped to mine, filled with fury and pain. "What is it?"

"It's ..." I struggled for the right words. Madoc and Tara were more than just twins—they were best friends. They could sit in perfect silence and still understand each other, reading every shift in body language. "Madoc had to flee to Lirien. Haldron's forces were hunting him and Father helped him escape. He's not coming back, Tara."

She didn't meet my eyes. Didn't blink, her gaze growing distant.

"I just—"

"Don't." She set a hand on my forearm, her voice raw, rough. "Don't say anything."

We all knew the consequences for going to Lirien without permission—and this time we had no one to turn to for mercy. Madoc would never be coming back. If I knew

Tara, the news wasn't just painful—it was like a death to mourn.

I could barely think of Madoc without feeling sick. I wanted to be proud of him for what he'd done ... my brother was the most honorable of men and I understood, now, why Father hadn't let me be a part of Esme's rescue mission.

But none of it changed the fact Haldron had orchestrated a plan that had destroyed my family. Nearly destroyed *me*. I'd spent weeks drowning in guilt ... only to learn that I'd been played like a puppet.

"We don't know what the future holds, Tara," I offered as optimistically as I could. "If we succeed in getting rid of Haldron, maybe we can get him back."

"Fine." Determination showed in her face—a fierce, protective light in her eyes. But she was done talking. "Then tell me what the hell we're going to do, Seren, because if you're expecting me to sit here and do nothing while Esme suffers, you can go straight to Nyxva."

"Get our people out of Emberstone. Get Mother out. If I fail to kill Haldron, who knows what the retribution will be."

"That's a job for Seth and Darya. Not a job for someone who stands to lose just as much as you do," Tara snapped.

"Thank you," Amahle said.

Of course they would be on the same side of this. "Do you really think we can trust Seth?"

"Seth was weeping after the skinwraith attack," Tara said. "He may be foul in other ways, but he loves our people as much as we do. And don't forget ... he stood for you and Rykr in the encampment. He's not a complete villain."

Thoughts crowded my head.

Could they be right?

Despite Amahle, Ciaran, and Tara's assurances, I wasn't so sure. And I'd sensed Rykr's hesitation, too. He'd left the decision up to me, but I couldn't help but worry. My prejudices made it hard to see clearly.

And then there was Tara's resistance to leaving. Gods knew that she could hold her own among the Vangar and her bravery surpassed mine. But my mother ...

"Mother needs your help, Tara. You're the only one of us that can help her right now. Father and Madoc are being hunted and I'm walking into the Skorn. One of us has to protect her."

"You're underestimating our mother, Seren. She's an Ibarran priestess—your spells and tricks are children's games compared to what she can do. And she's not leaving here without Esme, either."

I drew a slow, deep breath. "If I can't convince my own family and friends to listen to me—"

Amahle leveled a determined look my way. "We are listening. And we're all telling you the same thing. We're not going anywhere. Now, why don't we do what we can do and get Seth to help?"

Maybe I should have expected this, but frustration bloomed inside me at their stubbornness. But I was out of time and options and every moment I spent here arguing with them was a moment lost.

"Fine," I said, at last. "Let's go."

SETH PACED IN THE ROOM, Darya watching him closely. Worry was written on her face, though neither of them had spoken yet.

"And why is it that you think we need to leave Emberstone again?" Seth asked, his emotions guarded. The old Seth—the one I'd known—never revealed too much. He'd risen to his position by being cautious and smart. Of course, I couldn't say he'd followed that pattern the last few weeks.

"Haldron has Esme, Seth." I chose my words carefully. "My father managed to get a message to me through secure channels, but Haldron is using her to manipulate him. What Haldron did to coerce my father is evil. It violates all our principles as Viori."

"If your father did as Haldron wished and killed the king and his sons, why hasn't Esme been released?" Seth asked.

"I don't know. Only that Haldron won't release her. Maybe he wants to conceal what he's done. Esme may know that it wasn't Liriens who took her." The lie was necessary. At least, that's what I told myself. We couldn't risk telling Seth and Darya about the prince my father had allowed to live.

"And you think he'll retaliate against the tribe if you attempt to rescue Esme." Darya bit her lip, then nodded slowly. "That makes sense. He won't want a whole tribe that knows of his treachery this close to Emberstone. He'd see us as a threat. He's not a king, after all, and he can be deposed if the public turns against him."

"How are we supposed to move our people out of Emberstone without him noticing?" Seth shook his head. "We can't just declare that we no longer need refuge. The skinwraiths may still be out there and most of our tribe needs time to resupply. We have wounded."

"Tonight, during the Skorn. The trial is held outside the city in the Havamal, right? The amphitheater holds thousands, so take one large group there while another group of Vangar remains and leads the wounded and the weaker members of the tribe out of Emberstone. Then, when the trial is over, the group that went to the Havamal can join them, rather than return here."

Seth exhaled sharply, pacing again. "That's assuming

Haldron doesn't have men watching the exits. You're talking about moving *hundreds* of people without arousing suspicion."

"That's exactly why we have to do it in stages," I countered. "The Skorn will be a distraction."

Seth stopped pacing. His frown deepened, but he nodded once. "It's risky." Seth glanced at Tara and Amahle. "And you'll help Seren find Esme after the trial?"

"Probably during the trial." Tara studied the backs of her fingernails with a disaffected air that I'd come to admire in Rykr as well. I envied their poise.

Hopefully, between them, Thorne, and Father, they'd be able to locate Esme and rescue her, but Rykr and I would still need to kill Haldron. Another thing we couldn't afford to reveal to Seth and Darya. They might be furious with us later for keeping it from them, but that would be a problem for later.

Darya stood and moved to a trunk by the wall in their room. Kneeling, she retrieved a wooden scroll case. "This holds a map of all the known secret passageways of Emberstone," Darya said, holding the scroll out to Tara. "It won't help you find Esme, but it may give you a way out of the city without being seen."

I fought to keep my jaw from dropping. She was just giving it to us?

"Thank you," Tara said, grasping her by the forearm. "I won't forget this. You have my gratitude and my debt."

Darya's eyes were wide and solemn. "I know that's not a small thing. The Ragnalls keep their oaths."

"Will you lead the tribe out of Emberstone?" I asked Seth. He'd been watching quietly, his handsome face more relaxed now. Darya's influence seemed to be softening his resistance.

"I'm not certain if this is the best decision for the tribe." Seth's brow creased with worry. "But if Haldron has over-reached in this manner, something needs to be done about it.

I'll try to summon the council—see if there's a precedent for this. I worry about leading us out at night with nowhere to go."

Darya nodded then set her hand on his arm. "There may be a way to get some of the people out of Emberstone before the Skorn—the frailest and most wounded—but we'll need Lucia Ragnall. She's one of the best healers we have. We might find shelter in nearby villages for the night, then begin searching for a new encampment."

Amahle stepped toward Seth. "You know how the tribes work. They respect strength. The strongest tribes get the best encampments, the best outfitted Vangar, more power in trade deals. We chose you as our waldren because you can lead us to greatness. Haldron's actions didn't just endanger and threaten the Ragnalls, it was an attack on our whole tribe. He violated our borders in a way that could have been deadly for any of us."

Maybe it should have been me pleading and trying to get Seth to see reason, but I couldn't bring myself to do it. Yet, as I saw the doubt flicker on Seth's face, I remembered the man I'd once loved. The way he'd dreamed of what he might accomplish for our tribe. I'd been young and naive but listening to him had made me hopeful.

He'd told me not so long ago that he'd even sacrificed *us* for the love our tribe.

"Please, Seth," I said at last, cutting through the tense silence. "I know you love our tribe fiercely. Don't let the sacrifices you've made for it be in vain."

He flinched and met my gaze.

I'd never forgiven him, and he hadn't asked for it.

But maybe it was what we needed to move forward. Maybe not as friends—that would never be possible—but as allies for the same cause.

"I don't fault you for your choices," I added in a soft voice.

Maybe Darya would think I meant the flogging and sentencing to the Skorn, but it didn't matter.

If Seth hadn't chosen Darya, I wouldn't have fallen in love with Rykr—my soulmate.

Even if he might not be mine forever.

I knew now that I had loved. Truly. Deeply. Everything I'd had with Seth had paled in comparison.

Seth exhaled slowly, rubbing the back of his neck. "I don't like this."

He met my gaze, his expression unreadable. For a long moment, I thought he would refuse. That he'd walk away, leaving us to handle this alone.

Then, finally, he sighed. "All right. We'll do what we can."

"You have our word," Darya added with a taut smile. "Solric protect you during your trial, Seren."

I thanked her. "Where will you be taking the sick and wounded before the trial? I'd like to say goodbye to my mother before I present myself."

"Go past the west gate and look for a tavern called the Ruby Rose. I'll have her wait in the alley behind it for you," Darya said. "About an hour before sunset. That should leave you time to get to the keep and present yourself for the Skorn."

I nodded, then left with Tara and Amahle, exiting back into the corridors. As we reached the main chamber again, I caught sight of my destitute tribe and desperation gripped my chest. Despite Seth and Darya's assurances, I couldn't help worrying that my actions tonight might cost them even more than I already had.

Please gods, just let this work.

But as I looked at their weary faces, a terrible thought clawed its way into my mind.

What if it doesn't?

CHAPTER 36
RYKR

Amahle's bedroom resembled a war room more than sleeping quarters, with maps sprawled across every flat surface, the air thick with sweat and the heat of too many bodies crammed into a tight space, and the scent of half-eaten food and ale rising from the stacked plates and cups beside the door.

Seren had returned with her friends and Tara in tow, which had even surprised Brogan Ragnall. While I respected their desire to help rescue Esme and fight rather than flee, the logistics of involving so many people were fraught with room for error. If any one of them was caught, we could all suffer for it.

It was also problematic that I wanted nothing more than to take Seren back to our room and relieve the unbridled lust I couldn't seem to control when I looked at her. She sat across the bed from me now, her legs crossed, the tight fabric of her leather trousers hugging her hips. Despite my best efforts to find a less alluring place to fix my gaze, there wasn't any place on her body that didn't lead my thoughts back into temptation.

I'd enjoyed sinking my lips against the curve right below her hipbone. Trailing kisses to her inner thigh and tasting the sweetness of her—

"Pay attention," she hissed, a faint blush on her cheeks. She leaned forward then, setting down the book on the Skorn.

I held her gaze, a feline smile twisting on my lips. "I was."

"Really." She arched a brow. "What did I just say?"

I sighed and leaned back on my hands, stretching my shoulders back. "You said that the Skorn trial's first challenge is the Hall of Echoes—a tunnel leading into the base of the amphitheater. Most of the sentenced don't know it exists and it eliminates two thirds of them."

She smirked, an impressed look in her eyes. "And do you remember *why* it's the first challenge?"

"Because it's filled with Nyxwraiths—shadow creatures that make you face your deepest fears. They feed off doubt. The more you give in, the stronger they become."

"And you Viori just so happen to keep these creatures on hand for your trials?" Thorne shook his head with a scoff. "Tell me there's not something deeply twisted about that."

"You're right," Tara shot back from her place beside her father. They were both poring over the map Darya had given her. "It's much more barbaric than stealing infants out of their mother's arms and cutting them with blood magic."

Thorne narrowed his eyes. "Why do the pretty ones always have to have loud-mouthed, bossy older sisters? Better you than me, my friend," he said to me with a chuckle. He crossed his arms and looked back at Tara. "Just how many violent criminals are there among the Viori that this trial needs to exist in the first place?"

Brogan's face darkened and he silenced any retort from Tara with a look. "The Skorn *is* barbaric. Losing the ability to admit that is a loss of our own integrity." He locked eyes with

Thorne. "The Viori leadership uses it to sow fear of their authority into the hearts of the people. There are far more people in that arena every year than deserve to be there, though I would argue that no one deserves such a cruel punishment. But Haldron needs his spectacle, so there is never a lack of souls condemned to the trials."

Amahle frowned, then sat beside Seren. "You mean there's more than one trial before you face the Skorn warriors?"

"Apparently there are two other challenges." Seren lifted the book and held it out to her. "The Hall of Echoes, the Surfacing, and the Arena of Skorn. To be honest, the second challenge worries me the most. There's barely any information on it. All it says is that once the sentenced make it through the Hall of Echoes, they have to face the Surfacing before reaching the main arena of the Havamal. But I'm not sure what that involves."

"Do you think the name has a clue?" Ciaran asked. He sat on the floor beside Thorne, preparing bandoliers of weapons they'd collected in the city, both looking too large and too squished to be comfortable sitting there.

"Probably." Seren sighed and took the book back from Amahle. "I feel like I must be missing something." She bit her lower lip and flipped through the pages again.

My gaze fixed on her mouth, my willpower slipping fast. I stood abruptly. "A word?" I asked holding a hand out to her.

She gave me a puzzled look, then a knowing look came into her eyes. Taking my hand, she let me lead her out of Amahle's room and across the hall. Maybe everyone knew what I was doing, including her father, but right now I didn't care.

I closed the door behind us, and she crossed her arms. "A word?"

"All right, three. I want you. Right now." I pushed her back against the door and crushed my mouth against hers.

"You're ridiculous," she breathed against my lips, but sank into my arms just as readily, a soft, contented moan in her throat as she returned my kiss. "We need to be preparing for the Skorn."

"We have two or three hours before we face certain death, and I can't think of a better way to prepare." My hands slid down to her waist, quickly working the buckle of her trousers.

I pushed her trousers down over her hips and turned her to face the door.

"My father's right across the hall ..." she warned as my lips dropped to the curve of her neck.

I undid my own trousers, releasing my hard length from the restraint of the fabric. "So what? He was there this morning too."

"Yeah, but I didn't *know* about it then."

"If you think I'm worried even slightly about Brogan Ragnall's discomfort, you're in love with the wrong man," I hissed, more irritated about the turn of the conversation than I wanted to admit.

She froze and threw a contemptuous look over her shoulder. "So, you've just been politely pretending all day that you're fine being in the same room with him?"

Dammit.

This wasn't going the way I had hoped at all.

"I haven't been pretending anything. We have a deal. Once Esme is safe, he'll turn himself over to me to face the consequences for his role in murdering my king. And queen, for that matter."

She went utterly still.

Then she shoved me away. Hard.

She squirmed out of my arms, pulling her trousers up hastily.

I dipped my forehead against the cool surface of the door. *Fantastic.*

"Are you serious?" Her voice shook with accusation. "When were you planning on telling me this?"

"Right now ... apparently. I have great timing. Or angering you is my favorite form of foreplay."

"Sometimes I really hate you," she spat.

I readjusted myself, then buckled my trousers again. "I love it when you lie to me." Turning toward her, I rested my weight against the door and crossed my arms. "What do you want me to say? I love you, Seren. But that doesn't change the fact that your father murdered my—"

"Your what?" Her eyes narrowed, gleaming with fury. "Who, exactly, was the king of Lirien to you, Rykr? Why do you care so much?"

Maybe I should have anticipated this.

Or prepared for this conversation better.

But I hadn't and here we were.

I searched her gaze. My secret would be safe with her, that wasn't what worried me now. But telling her the truth would change everything in ways I wasn't ready to face. And it put her in danger. The truth was dangerous.

But this might be the last moment we had alone together.

"I think you know," I said at last.

She flinched and tore her gaze away, as though she hadn't wanted to hear that. She hugged her arms to her chest, unable to look at me.

My throat tightened. *Gods, don't look away from me, Seren.*

"What's your name?"

I swallowed, but the lump in my throat wouldn't go down.

I should lie. I should stall. I should say anything but the truth.

But I couldn't.

"Calix," I said at last, my voice quieter than I meant it to be. "Or it was. I've gone by Rykr Westhaven for two years now."

When she looked back at me, her eyes were red-rimmed. "Why were you in the forest?"

"My friend was attacked, dragged away by Viori. They used whistler quills on Thorne and me ... I woke up hours later, alone." I lifted my chin, the words difficult to push out. "The crucified man they brought into your encampment ... that was my friend. Dalric."

When she was silent, I stepped closer to her. "I couldn't tell you because I—"

"I get it." Her eyes were glassy. "But I don't understand. Why are you Sealed to Pendara?"

"It was my father's punishment. I burned down some buildings in Suomelin and he was tired of my lack of discipline, as he put it. So, he Sealed me to Pendara, Bound my other powers, and exiled me for two years." That was about as succinct as I could put it.

She drew a sharp breath, then her eyes filled with tears. "What I don't understand ... you know we can't be together, Ry —um."

"Rykr." I took her hands in my own. "I'm Rykr. To you, always. And maybe just in general. The man I was? He died, in many ways, after I was Sealed. And there are things about who I was before that I'm not proud of, Seren. Things I'm sure you'll hear of in time. But that's not who I am now."

"Name aside, you're the heir to the throne of Lirien. We can't be together. We may be bonded by the oath, but your duties and loyalties lie elsewhere. My life is here. And that's if I even live past tonight. Who knows how long I have. The Seidr said I was dying, Rykr."

I had no answers.

Nothing to say that would make any of this better. The thought that she'd choose to stay here, rather than go with me, made a knot form in my stomach. I couldn't think about it too much, but I was sure the reverse must be true, too. Would she doubt my love if I didn't stay here—give up my kingdom for her?

After a few beats, I said, "Whatever is waiting for us after tonight ... we can face it together—figure it out then. But I think we have enough to worry about for now, wouldn't you say?"

I moved around behind her, unable to face her right now. The pain of losing her ... I couldn't consider that.

Gathering her braid, I moved it gently, then set my hands on her shoulders and dug my thumbs into the muscles below her shoulder blades. "I don't forgive you," she murmured. "You're the man who wants to kill my father."

"Good." I kneaded my hands down the length of her spine, continuing past her lower back. She quivered, her body betraying her in an instant, but my hands moved back up to the safety of her back and I kissed her neck.

My voice was soft like silk, my fingers stroking her gently. "The angrier you are, the more likely you are to claw at me like that wild thing I first met in the forest. I wake up hard thinking about that."

She turned her profile toward me, eyes flaring. "You think you're so charming."

"If it's working, then I *am* that charming." I set my hands on her hips then turned her to face me. Lifting her chin with my thumb and forefinger, I brushed my lips against hers.

"Prick. You can't just expect me to forget everything."

I ran the backs of my knuckles against her cheekbone with a featherlight touch.

"Yes, but also *your* prick. Willing, ready, and able to be used exactly how you like, my love." I smiled before I kissed her once again. "And I know just how you like it." My lips crushed against hers, devouring, consuming her with a fire that singed us both.

She sank against me as I tugged her against my hard cock. "You don't fight fair," she managed between kisses. She pushed her hand past my waistband and grabbed my length as I groaned.

"Feel free to punish me however ..." I trailed off as she glided her hand up and down, then managed a strangled, "What was I saying?"

"However?" she prodded, then bit my lip, our tongues lashing against each other's. Maybe this conversation could wait.

"No, I think you were describing how you were going to punish me." I stepped back, a wicked grin tugging at my lips. "I highly encourage your roughest, angriest punishment."

Her eyes stormed, dark with lust. "Fuck it," she groaned, then tumbled back into my arms.

The quiet of the room was soon replaced by our moans.

"I'm going to miss you," she managed in a choked voice as I leaned over on the bed.

Don't say that, I wanted to tell her. *Don't talk like we've already lost.*

But I couldn't bring myself to lie.

My precious warrior. She just showed me in her tears how much she loved me. It was the only time I'd seen Seren cry. *And I felt so helpless to take those tears away.*

The foreboding worries of the coming night seemed to push in from all sides, her tears flowing down her cheeks with each kiss as she whispered, "I wish we could just stay here. In this room. Together."

"I'm still here." I kissed her, moving inside her, our bodies and souls joined in a way that I knew I'd only ever find in her. "One moment at a time. Tonight has enough troubles for us both."

SEREN

The Ruby Rose stood in one of the less savory parts of Emberstone, the west side of the city that I'd rarely stepped foot in. Somehow, the city seemed darker here, the air filled with smoke, the surface of the buildings grimier.

With Ciaran and Rykr flanking me, I didn't fear the lewd looks cast my way as I might have if I'd just been with Tara and Amahle, who trailed us. Then again, Tara and Amahle would have been just as willing to kick the asses of anyone who dared cross us.

But we looked out of place. Here, the people didn't bother to conceal their stares as we passed them.

My father had parted ways with us at the Bellwether to begin exploring the most promising passageways into the keep. Esme might be there; Haldron might want a close watch. But she could also be in the dungeons, which were well guarded and difficult to break into.

Thorne, in the meantime, had gone to the refugee receiving

ceremony held before the Skorn trial. He planned to find my father directly afterward.

The Ruby Rose was tucked on the corner of a darkened square, the whole building leaning, as though it were trying to escape the street it had been planted on. The sign above the door hung at an awkward angle, one chain rusted clean through. The paint had long since peeled away, but enough of the deep red lingered to hint at what it once was—a rose, or something meant to look like one, though now it resembled more of a bloodstain dripping down splintered wood.

The windows were worse. Grimy, warped glass distorted the faint light flickering inside, casting strange, jagged shapes onto the cracked cobblestones. Someone had boarded up one of the panes, but the boards were loose, creaking like the place breathed. The door itself sagged on its hinges, its surface gouged with deep scratches—as if something had tried to claw its way out, not in.

As we drew nearer to the building, Rykr's hand grazed mine. I longed to reach out, intertwine our fingers, cling to him just a moment longer. Even though I hadn't expected him to pull me back into the room for one last time together, I'd realized afterward how much I'd needed it. Not only to say all the things that we'd said.

But because I was terrified.

Surviving the Skorn had become secondary to everything else. Haldron had Esme and this had all started that night when he'd come for her.

Had he been one of the people there?

The man in the cloak, who'd taken her from my grasp ... somehow, I was now certain it had been Haldron.

"I don't like the look of this place," Rykr gritted.

"I don't either," Tara agreed. "There aren't enough exit points."

"A place known for crime is also a good place to sneak our tribe out of the city. The sentinels at the gate are probably easier to bribe here." I tried to sound more confident than I felt. I glanced at Ciaran and Amahle. "You'll go with my mother for now, right? Until the start of the Skorn?"

Amahle gave me a reassuring nod. "We will. And then we'll go to the arena."

"Moira should be coming with the group of injured, too," Ciaran said with a grim expression. "I want to help get her settled if I can."

We continued past the building, then turned into the alley, as Darya had instructed. Farther ahead stood a small group of Vangar, including Seth. Their silhouettes were barely visible in the dim torchlight. I recognized my mother's familiar light blue cloak, the hood over her head.

A footstep behind us made me stiffen.

A quick glance back revealed a group of Vangar, armed with swords, who closed off the exit from the alley.

My heart fell. "Fuck," I breathed, locking eyes with Rykr.

He whirled around to see them, just as the woman in the blue cloak turned. Not my mother, but another Vangar warrior —this one dressed in the silver armor of Haldron's guard.

Oh gods, no.

A sharp pain ripped through me, knocking the breath from my lungs. My head snapped up.

Seth held a crossbow in his hands.

And a bolt protruded from my chest.

I gasped, but it came out wrong—wet, strangled. Something was burning and bubbling inside me. The pain spiraling through me was icy, but the fire in my lungs screamed hotter.

"No!" Rykr's voice split through the ringing in my ears and the sound of metal clanged as my friends drew their swords.

A strangled breath gargled in my throat, my consciousness

swimming as a swirl of torches drew closer, my body convulsing as Rykr held my shoulders, keeping me upright.

"Seren!" Panic was on that handsome face. He snapped the shaft of the bolt. "Seren, look at me. Gods! *Fuck.* I'm going to slit his fucking throat."

His eyes scanned mine desperately, but I blinked slowly, my brain unable to form words.

Fine. I'm fine, I wanted to tell him. But my tongue was thick, pushing against the roof of my mouth like some swollen, useless thing.

Two sets of firm hands grabbed me roughly under my arms and by my legs, wrenching me from Rykr.

A grating shriek sounded as a gate lifted at the end of the alley. *What is happening? Are they fighting ...*

Dizziness washed over me, my eyes closing. I must be in shock.

But it didn't explain the way my thoughts felt so sluggish.

Or the numbness traveling through my nerves.

A disconnect seared through me, one I couldn't understand, almost as though I was drunk. Aware, but barely able to comprehend. Sounds became muted, the passage of time disturbed.

I couldn't open my eyelids now, darkness consuming me. Somewhere in the deepest recesses of my mind, I saw myself plunging, falling deeper and deeper into a pit of darkness. Wisps of gold, whirling and twisting like lightning, reached for me.

Rykr.

Every instinct told me to hold on to him. But I kept falling, faster, and harder, out of his reach.

Darkness swallowed me whole. The cold of the alley, the sting in my chest—gone, but not gone enough.

My body rests on the cracked ground of a wooded glade of greys and black.

The scent of blood still lingers. The faintest echo of Rykr's voice drifts on the wind. Seren—

Golden embers swirl from barren tree branches in the woods around me, dancing, drifting through the inky black.

A flash of blue tears through the darkness.

Someone shook my shoulders.

"Seren!" Rykr's voice was in my ears. "Seren, please!"

I pushed my heavy eyelids open. My tongue drew over my lower lip, where the taste of blood seeped into my mouth.

Rykr touched my brow, his eyes searching mine. "Your skin is ice cold."

"I can't," I rasped. "Pain ..."

Gods, the pain was excruciating. My body felt as though it was being ripped apart from within.

Rykr's fingertips drifted to my lips. "Don't speak. Save your energy." I could see nothing but his face. His lips dipped against mine. *"Stay here with me, Seren. In this space we share. I don't care about the pain. Give it all to me."*

I'm back in the glade.

The tendrils of golden magic swirl closer. Rykr's trying to get in, to break past my thoughts. I shudder and nod, despite the excruciating pain that flares through me.

"Steady now." His voice fills me. Shimmering transparent leaves appear on the trees. "Don't look at anything or anyone. Just give the pain to me."

A flash of agony radiates from me, and I see it in wisps of blue flames that curl into the golden waves pushing forward, through cracks in the earth, from the spaces behind trees. A dance of fire and ice that seems to burn us both.

"Don't hold me back. Don't fight me." His voice is stronger now, a deluge of fire in my veins.

"I can't!" I wail as fire bursts from the cracks in the earth, singeing me with its strength.

A wave of gold crests hard against the dying blue light surrounding me, extinguishing it with such force that the pain vanishes.

I see myself, dragged by my arms and legs, the shaft of a crossbow bolt sticking out of my chest, where a wound seeps crimson blood onto my vest. We're in a stone tunnel, being dragged and prodded by silver-armored guards.

Tara, Amahle, and Ciaran are behind us, their swords … gone.

Everything through Rykr's eyes.

From my own eyes, I see nothing. No light. No movement.

I am Rykr.

Seren is no more than a distant memory.

A name slipping through my fingers.

Her body, still bleeding, is dumped on the dusty rock as I'm dragged away from her.

CHAPTER 38
SEREN

I barely noticed the approach of booted feet as I rested on the ground, tears seeping from the corners of my eyes into the dust below me.

A hand grasped my throat, and the bolt was yanked from me, ripping my flesh further.

My eyes flew open, startled. I gasped for air, unable to draw it into my lungs as the damage on my chest blistered to life.

Seth loomed over me, every inch of his face filled with hatred. "You and Westhaven are finally going to die, Seren. Dragon's blood has no antidote and that bolt was drenched in it."

My brow furrowed together, my body quivered uncontrollably.

But then I saw it.

Deep inside his pupils, a glowing yellow light.

What the hell?

Before I could answer, Seth stalked away, leaving me in the dark space. The barest flicker of torchlight glowed in the distance.

Where was I?

A dungeon of Emberstone?

My thoughts were clearer now, despite the excruciating pain. I had no idea how long had passed or where Rykr, Tara, or my friends were. Whatever magic Rykr had used in the alley must have kept me alive, for now—maybe he'd even found a way to pass some of his ability to heal to me through the bond. I should be dead, shouldn't I?

But that wouldn't save me from dragon's blood.

Seth had betrayed us. He'd gone to Haldron. Who knew what he'd told him, but it might mean that my father and Thorne would be walking into a trap. That Esme might never be found.

Tears slipped down my cheeks, and I wiped them away with trembling hands, sitting. Each breath was agony, the metallic tang of blood in the back of my throat. I had no spell powder to heal myself with.

Maybe if I froze the wound from the bolt, to keep it from bleeding ...

I set my fingertips against the hole in my vest, gasping and swallowing a scream. Closing my eyes, I tried to conjure the magic that had been a part of me since birth.

The tingle in my hands, that sign that my powers were failing, rushed into my palms instead.

Dammit.

"Rykr," I croaked out into the bond. The doorway to his mind was firmly shut, though. He couldn't hear me, or he wasn't letting me in. Gods knew why.

I was alone here—wherever the hell I was—and I was dying.

I struggled to my feet, the pain nearly unbearable. I needed to get my bearings, figure out what options I had, if any.

Heading toward the distant glow of light, I hunched over,

keeping one arm tight against my wound. The only hope I had lay in the fact that they hadn't killed me yet ... at least not outright. But Seth had bragged about hitting me with a dragon's blood bolt, which meant that death would be imminent.

Not yet, though.

Maybe Haldron wanted to torment me for a while longer.

But what had that glow in Seth's eyes meant?

Seth wasn't a skinwraith. And the vuk hadn't been either—even though I had jumped to that conclusion after Giulia.

Which meant this had to be something else. Something I hadn't considered.

My head ached so severely that it felt as though a spike had gone through my skull.

I appeared to be in some sort of narrow corridor chiseled out of stone. Each step toward the light made me wonder if this wasn't all just part of Haldron's plan—to lure me into something else. But what choice did I have? Curl up and die?

Another step took me past a doorway, and I trembled as I went past. The stone door groaned shut behind me, and the sound echoed through the narrow corridor like the final toll of a death knell. I flinched, not at the sound itself, but at the silence that followed—a stifling, unnatural stillness that pressed against my ears, my skin, my very bones.

I was alone.

The quivering torchlight ahead of me died with the closing of the doors, leaving only a dim, shifting glow from some unseen source—I could barely see.

I reached out toward the wall, using it to guide myself forward. It was slick with moisture, the rough surface veined with roots that pulsed faintly beneath the stone, like veins in a corpse. The air was thick, heavy with the scent of damp earth, moss ... and blood.

My heartbeat thundered in my ears, loud enough to drown

out my thoughts. I forced a breath through clenched teeth, willing myself forward. *I know what this is.* The first of the Skorn trials. The Hall of Echoes. A place designed to strip you bare, to drag your deepest fears into the light and watch you bleed beneath their weight.

"You should have let him die."

The voice slithered through the darkness, soft and cold, like frost creeping over glass. I froze mid-step, my pulse leaping into my throat. I turned, scanning the shadows behind me.

Nothing. Just the oppressive dark, the flicker of distant, failing light.

"You should have let him die."

Closer this time, almost brushing against my ear. I spun again, my heart pounding so hard it hurt.

"Who's there?" The sound was brittle in the vast, empty space.

Silence answered.

I forced my feet to move. The corridor narrowed as I pressed forward, the walls closing in until my shoulders nearly brushed the slick, pulsing stone. My fingers itched to reach for a weapon, but mine had been taken away. And this wasn't a battle of blades. It was a battle of the soul.

"You can't save them."

I clenched my jaw, pushing the voice aside. It wasn't real. None of this was real.

Up ahead, a faint glow became brighter, as though moonlight spilled through a window cut into the tunnel. Silvery, cold, and eerie.

Illuminating *her*.

Esme.

She stood at the edge of the dim light, her small figure fragile and still. Her clothes—the Vangar leathers that had been too big for her the first night of her training—were torn, the fabric stained dark with dirt and … blood. Her hair hung in tangled clumps around her face, and her eyes—gods, her *eyes* —were too wide, too empty.

My breath hitched. My legs moved without permission, carrying me forward as my heart clawed against my ribs.

"Esme?" I whispered, the word tasting like ash in my mouth.

She didn't move. Didn't blink. Just stood there, staring at me with that hollow, soulless gaze.

"Why didn't you save me?"

Her voice filled the air around me, seeped into my skin like poison.

"I—I tried," I gasped, my voice shaking. "I tried, Esme."

"But you failed."

The corridor trembled with the words. The shadows stretched, lengthened, and bled into the space around her. I stumbled forward, reaching like I could pull her from this nightmare, from my failure. My heart screamed at me to move faster, to *do something*, but my legs felt like stone.

"No, listen to me, Esme. I wanted to save you. I wanted to go with Father."

"I've been in Emberstone this whole time, Seren. I was in the keep, watching when you came in with your lover. But you were too distracted to see me. Too worried about him. Too busy fucking to look for me."

I was only inches from her now and the impact of her words seared me. Was it true? Had she been there? I swallowed back thick saliva. Is that what she really believed? That I'd been thinking of Rykr—of myself—more than her?

With a struggled breath, I set my hands on her frail shoulders as tears left her eyes. "No, Esme. No. I just didn't know—I-I had no idea that Haldron had taken you."

I lifted my hand to her cheek and swiped the tear from her skin.

Ice-cold skin. *Scaly.*

A smile on her face spread, too wide, too horrifying to be human.

My heart froze with terror. This wasn't Esme.

The Nyxwraiths.

The hands wrapped around my wrists, sharp, long claws biting into my skin. I'd made the creature more real by believing its poisoned lies and now it had grabbed hold of me.

"Let me go," I screamed, trying desperately to pull my hands away.

The grip tightened. *"I am you. I am a part of you. You share your soul with mine."*

In the blink of an eye, Esme's small form morphed, her body elongating, her skin rippling as if something inside her struggled to break free. My breath came in ragged gasps as her human teeth sharpened to jagged points.

No, no, no.

My feet sank into the floor like it had turned to tar.

"You could have saved her," she whispered, her voice warping, splitting into two voices—one Esme's, one Rykr's.

The walls pulled away, stretching infinitely in all directions —no ceiling, no floor, just endless dark. Rykr stood where she had been. His face was carved in cold stone, his blue-green eyes void of the warmth I'd come to rely on.

"You chose wrong," he said. "You should have let me die."

The veins of my arms had turned a horrifying blue, from where the Nyxwraith clung to me, as though feeding off my body as it became more corporeal.

"You're nothing to me. I'll choose my kingdom over you."

I staggered back, the breath ripped from my lungs. "No," I

whispered, but the word felt thin, fragile, like it could shatter under his gaze.

"You could have saved *her*," he continued, stepping closer, his expression hardening into something cruel, unfamiliar. "But you chose me. You bound yourself to me." His lips curled into a bitter smile. "And I will betray you. I will never choose you in the end, Seren. I have a duty to something bigger, *more important*, than you. You're frail. My weakest link. Not strong enough to be my queen. If I survive tonight, it won't be because of you."

The words hit deeper than I wanted to admit. Because, beneath the surface, a part of me—the part I tried to bury, to smother—believed him.

He *was* going to leave me. I knew that. He'd told me he had to leave.

But I didn't want that. I wanted him to choose me, however impossible that was. However selfish that was.

"You're weak."

"You can't save anyone."

"Why would I ever choose you?"

The whispers merged with his voice, rising in a chorus that drowned out reason, smothered me under the weight of my own guilt. The shadows thickened, and from within them, more shapes began to emerge.

More Nyxwraiths.

They slithered from the darkness like liquid shadows, their forms barely solid, their eyes empty voids of endless black. Their limbs were too long, too thin, and their fingers ended in curved claws that dripped with inky darkness. They moved without sound, but their hunger screamed in my mind.

They fed on fear.

And I was drowning in it.

I sent a kick toward the Nyxwraith holding me, straight

toward its core. It released me, dropping back enough for me to wrench my wrists away.

The Nyxwraith lunged, its claws slicing through the air with a hiss that sent terror surging through my veins. I stumbled back, barely dodging the swipe, but another was already there, its shadowy form flickering like smoke as it reached for me.

I couldn't fight them. Not like this. Not when my mind was unraveling, my heart gripped in icy claws of doubt.

I dropped to my knees, my breath ragged, my vision blurring with tears I couldn't hold back. The Nyxwraiths closed in, their whispers merging with my own.

I squeezed my eyes shut and through the darkness, I felt a tether.

The bond between Rykr and me. Always there. Always shimmering beneath the surface of my mind, entangled in the very fibers of my soul. He had a solid wall up, blocking me from him ... to protect me.

Because he *loved* me.

Because even amid all this ugliness, we'd found love. Real love. Love that didn't make sense and *shouldn't* be but love all the same. A love that had brought me hope during my fears, during the worst betrayals I'd ever known.

The Nyxwraiths' claws dug into my skin, their voices louder in my ears.

"*I won't stay.*"

"*You're pathetic.*"

And yet the bond, the feel of *him*, there, in my heart. In my soul. He had brought me calm. Fear could destroy everything, yes, but not where love and hope existed.

But it couldn't be that simple, could it?

Or maybe it was. Maybe fear had sufficient force that it could swallow some people whole.

"He doesn't have to choose me over his kingdom. That's not what matters," I whispered in a trembling voice. "I don't have long left to live anyway. Those fears don't matter. I love him. Our love is enough to survive this trial."

The shadows thickened, twisting around my throat, squeezing.

"You're weak."

The words wrapped around me like a noose.

"You could have saved her."

A clawed hand plunged into my chest, gripping my heart. My vision blurred, black spots spreading across my gaze. The Nyxwraith was pulling something from me—my very soul.

It's not real. But the pain was. The terror was real.

I squeezed my eyes shut. What if I stopped fighting? What if I let them take me, so Esme could live?

The whispers shuddered, faltering.

That was it. They didn't fear love—they feared self-sacrifice.

"I will give my life to save Esme," I screamed in a shaking voice. "I will save Rykr, Ciaran, Amahle, Tara—everyone I love—even if it kills me."

The Nyxwraiths screamed.

Then, the entire space shattered.

The illusions burned away, leaving only a long, empty corridor.

I was alone.

A sob wrenched free from my chest, shaking uncontrollably from the horror of what I'd just experienced.

Was Rykr going through this? *Gods, this is terrifying.*

I wiped my face. If they'd brought him here, maybe I could find him. Help him.

I struggled onto my feet once again, feeling drained of life.

The sound of footsteps drew closer and Ciaran stood before me, his face wary, hard, untrusting.

Shit. It wasn't over after all.

"You're fake," he said, his eyes narrowing at me.

Tears slipped down my cheeks, and I wiped them away, waiting for him to taunt me with my failures. If I answered, the Nyxwraiths would only grow stronger.

"Seren is dead," he shouted. "Leave me alone!"

I lifted my head sharply, my eyes widening. He felt real. So real. Not like the other illusions I'd encountered here. Esme had looked different.

And Rykr would never condemn me the way the Nyxwraiths had.

But Ciaran ...

Was it possible?

Could he *be* real? Or would the Nyxwraiths only grow more convincing the more I believed in them?

"Do you remember the harpies, Ciaran?"

His brow drew together in grief. "No." He wiped his eyes. "No, you don't get to talk to me about her like this. I loved her. *I loved her!* And she loved him instead. She picked him, instead of me."

Gods.

I swallowed hard.

A fake Ciaran might say this, if I was honest. Torment me with the guilt of what I'd done to him by choosing Rykr.

But Ciaran *felt* real.

The sharp bite of my nails into my palms grounded me in the present and I forced myself to my feet. "I said I would always catch you when you were falling, Ciaran. And I always will. Because I do love you. You're my best friend. And that's just as valuable as a lover."

Ciaran stared at me, eyes wide with shock, then took a hesitant step forward. "Ser?"

I released a cry, then tumbled against him, my arms wrapping around him.

Rather than the cold, scaly grasp of a Nyxwraith, Ciaran's arms were warm, his embrace tight as he wept against my neck. "Gods, Seren, it is you. Fuck. I thought you were dead. I thought Seth killed you." His body shook, his chest racked with sobs.

All around us, a sharp hiss filled the air, more Nyxwraiths dissipating into the shadows, until the corridor brightened, the oppressive weight lifting from my chest like a vise torn away.

"What are you doing here?" I asked, pulling away. I gasped with pain again, clutching my chest.

"You're bleeding." Ciaran gaped.

"I'll be fine," I lied. He didn't need to know how much pain I was in—or that I'd been poisoned.

"Seth dragged us all here. Left us in different cells. I guess we're all in the Skorn trial together." Ciaran mopped his brow with the back of his hand. "I wouldn't have even known what the hell was going on if I hadn't heard you and Rykr talking today. Those things ... they're fucking terrifying."

"We have to find the others. If we were able to find each other, chances are these corridors are connected. And who knows how many other people are in the Skorn this year." I took Ciaran by the hand, unwilling to let him go.

"You were right," Ciaran said as we hurried through the space. "We shouldn't have trusted Seth."

"It doesn't matter now." My teeth chattered, and my legs were weaker. I'd lost blood, and maybe too much of it.

A familiar hiss made my feet stumble, then the space in front of us lightened.

Rykr stood at the end of the corridor, his chest heaving, his eyes wide with something between relief and disbelief. Sweat clung to his brow, his shirt was torn, but his eyes—those fierce, blue-green eyes—were *alive*.

Our gazes locked, and for a moment, the world stilled.

"Are you another test?" Rykr asked suspiciously, staring at my grasp on Ciaran's hand.

My chest ached. "No, it's me."

"That's what she said," he muttered.

My stomach twisted. "What?"

He exhaled sharply. "They made me see you, Seren. Over and over. Each time, you stabbed me. Betrayed me. And each time, I had to kill you."

My breath hitched.

"I don't trust what's real anymore," he admitted, his voice hoarse.

My heart clenched. I had to break through to him.

"Then let me prove it," I whispered. "Touch my wound. I'm still bleeding. If I were a Nyxwraith, I'd be whole."

Slowly, he reached out. The moment his fingers brushed my skin, the bond flared—familiar, undeniable. His breath left him in a choked sound, a haunted look in his eyes.

"Seren." His arms crushed me against him. "Gods, it really is you. You don't move like them, you know—the Nyxwraiths."

His words reminded me of the first time we'd met in that forest. "And you know how Nyxwraiths move?"

His eyes held a tired smile. "I've seen enough." Then he added, "You talk too much for someone who's bleeding out."

I inhaled his familiar scent, felt the heartbeat of the man I loved. "And you're too kind for someone who doesn't run."

CHAPTER 39
RYKR

Maybe I had been arrogant, but nothing could have prepared me for the terrors I'd faced in the Hall of Echoes. Besides visions of Seren betraying me, I'd had to face illusions of my father and Dalric, each of them whispering of my failure, their voices speaking to my deepest fears.

Whatever Seren had faced must have been just as difficult and she'd done it badly wounded. *My brave, amazing warrior.*

Even though we'd survived the Nxywraiths, they'd left their mark. A deep feeling of helplessness filled me as we dragged ourselves through the endless, dripping tunnels, each corridor filled with the stench of death.

I might not be able to save her. Seren clung to me, but she was weak.

One by one, we found those sentenced to the Skorn with us tonight, including Tara and Amahle, who were both dirty and ragged, but alive.

Some of the people we'd encountered had screamed for help before vanishing into the dark, lost to the Nyxwraiths.

441

Others had been left behind, too far gone to continue. We had to keep moving. Had to push through the slick, narrow passages, ducking beneath crumbling archways and climbing over the twisted, shriveled bodies of those who hadn't made it. The walls seemed to close in on us with every turn, the weight of the mountain above pressing down like a tomb.

We stumbled over a fresh corpse—one of the trial's sentenced, his body twisted in agony, his face frozen in a silent scream. The Nyxwraiths had drained him completely—his flesh was withered, his eyes nothing more than hollow pits of darkness. I checked every body we passed, fear gnawing at my ribs. *Thorne. Where the fuck was Thorne?* Each time I lifted a lifeless face, my stomach coiled tighter, waiting for the worst.

I tried to stop looking—tell myself it wouldn't change anything. But my hands betrayed me. Every corpse I passed, my fingers curled against cold flesh, my breath held, waiting for the impossible. Waiting for Thorne to be among them.

I didn't find him. Or Brogan Ragnall.

For now.

Seren's hand in mine was the only thing grounding me. I hadn't let go of her since I'd found her, except to freeze the bleeding wound on her chest, and the moment our fingers touched again, my pulse steadied. But the fact that she couldn't use her powers terrified me more than anything. She needed help that I couldn't fucking give her.

A group of about twenty people now remained in what we believed was the exit from the Hall of Echoes—a large, circular space chiseled out of stone. Cold, dark, lifeless.

The ceiling above us was an enormous, wooden, trapdoor. Drips of water seeped between the seams in some spots but gave little clue as to what may be ahead of us.

Seren sat on a low, flat boulder in the middle of the space— large enough for only a couple of people to sit—and I knelt at her side. She leaned against Tara, who'd put an arm around her in a display of affection unusual for the elder Ragnall sister. She was clearly worried about Seren.

"We have to get you out of here." I lifted her hand to my lips and kissed the back of it. "You need medicine."

"She needs my mother." Tara gave me a pained look. "But I'm not convinced she's safe, either. Dammit, we never should have gone to Seth and Darya."

"We should have listened to you," Amahle said with a shake of her head. "You knew what Seth was this whole time. I'm so sorry, Seren."

Seren shivered violently. "I'm not happy to be right." Her eyes scanned mine. "What happened after he shot me? I ... *felt* ..."

I knew what she'd felt. I'd *felt* what she'd felt—the all-consuming pain from the crossbow bolt. It was my intrusion into her mind once again, like I'd done with the skinwraith attack, but this time as I'd searched for a way to give her my ability to heal and to take the pain away.

I didn't have to say any of it, though, because from the way the bond thrummed between us, she *knew*. And while I'd helped her in the short term, I had the feeling that these intrusions into her soul were causing the loss of her own powers. "I can't do it again," I said in a soft voice. "The bond is getting too unbalanced, Seren. I feel it now."

"I know." She tore her eyes away from mine.

"How did you survive that shot?" Ciaran asked from his place beside Amahle.

"Lucia gave me some training back at the encampment." I glanced at Tara, whose expression remained like flint. Truth was, if Tara hadn't arranged for Lucia's training we might not have gotten this far. *The Rúna be damned.* Maybe Madoc was the evil twin, but he'd saved my life. I just knew that *Tara* wasn't. Which meant that my father had been wrong to enforce that cruel practice in Lirien.

My father—and I—had been wrong about many things.

"Well, Seth did us a favor, even if he didn't intend to." Seren closed her eyes for a moment. "He put us in this trial with the people we know the best—who we'll die fighting to save. That probably helped all of us in the Hall of Echoes. And it will help us with whatever we face next."

Gods, she looks so weak. The thought gutted me. "Any clue what comes next?" I asked. The night already felt too long, and the trial wasn't over yet. How on earth would Seren survive the best warriors in the Vangar like this?

Seren shook her head wearily, but she seemed to understand what I was thinking. "Hopefully now that I've got my closest friends and sister with me, my odds just went up. But none of us have weapons, do we?"

We didn't. Seth and Haldron's guards had taken them all.

Ciaran leaned down toward us. "The other people here have weapons," he said in a low voice. "Not great ones. But better than nothing."

I held his gaze, understanding his meaning. We might have to take them from the other survivors if we were going to survive the last part of the trial. Or maybe even the next one. Thankfully, the Nyxwraiths hadn't required weapons to defeat them.

The sound of grinding stone echoed above us. A monstrous, mechanical groan.

The doors were opening.

I looked up just as water began to spill through the seams of the wooden doors above, dripping in steady, rhythmic beats.

Then the drips became rivulets as the doors inched open.

Then a steady stream.

Tara stood, helping Seren. "How much water do you think is up there?"

I surveyed the room. "Probably enough to flood this area. And more."

"Surfacing," Seren breathed, closing her eyes as she rested against Tara. "Of course. They're going to try to drown us out. They probably filled the Havamal with water and it's going to inundate us as soon as those doors open fully."

Amahle frowned. "I know better than to argue, but how in the hell are we supposed to get into the Havamal if we don't know how to swim?"

Ciaran removed his belt. "Latch yourself on to me, Amahle. I can swim us both to the surface."

That wasn't a half-bad idea. "Mind if I take my wife off you?" I asked Tara, reaching for Seren.

"I wouldn't dare try to get between you." Tara gripped my elbow, tugging me closer. "But she might have a hard time holding her breath, Rykr. That bolt went into her lung."

Dammit, she's right.

A low groan, then a crack. The water gushed in like waterfalls.

A woman near the far wall whimpered, then the first real scream tore through the chamber.

"We're going to drown!" A man shoved past another, nearly knocking him to the ground. He bolted for the far end of the room, hands scrabbling at the slick, crumbling walls like there was some hidden door he could force open.

The ground rumbled again, but this time, it wasn't from the doors.

A thick, gnarled tendril shot out, twisting around a man's ankle. His scream was cut short as the vines yanked him under, the thorns slicing through his flesh like razors. His body spasmed, jerking once—twice—before he was pulled deeper into the water, his mouth opening in a silent cry. Then he was gone, leaving only a crimson stain that spread through the water.

"It's vodavine," Seren gasped. "They're carnivorous water plants that grow rapidly in fresh water."

A woman near the far wall let out a panicked scream. "I can't—I can't—" Her hands clawed at the walls, slipping on the wet stone. Another man shoved past her, scrambling for a foothold, his wild eyes darting between the dripping ceiling and the vines creeping along the ground.

The boulder was the only temporary reprieve, and the others knew it. The remaining survivors rushed us, clawing at the rock, their desperation turning feral. This wasn't about honor. It wasn't about trials.

This was about survival.

No wonder no one survived this damned trial. It was a feat just to make it into the damned amphitheater.

I grabbed Seren and hoisted her onto the boulder as the flood of water crashed around us, a deafening roar filling the chamber. "Get on the damned boulder," I shouted to Seren's friends. "Before you can't."

As Amahle and Ciaran scrambled onto it, a cascade of water burst through the widening cracks above, slamming into the ground like a beast breaking free of its cage. The rush of it swept two people clean off their feet, sending them crashing against the jagged stone wall.

Then the room exploded into chaos.

A man near the center turned on us, wild-eyed, brandishing a blade.

"Give us the boulder!" His voice was shrill with desperation.

"No. Fuck you!" someone else screamed.

Fists flew. A knife slashed across someone's thigh, blood

mixing with the rising water. Another woman tried to climb the boulder, slipping, screaming as she was yanked back down into the flood.

The vines spread at an alarming pace, wrapping around the ankle of a nearby man. He jumped, trying to slash them away with a knife. The vines weren't just attacking. They were watching. The moment someone slowed down, or a foot faltered or a breath hitched—they struck. A man to my left screamed as a tendril wrapped around his throat instead of his leg this time, yanking him up like a slaughtered animal.

"Solric's balls," Ciaran breathed, kicking a vine away as it lashed toward him.

I set Seren down between us. I hadn't taken off my belt yet like Ciaran had and it might be the closest thing I had to a weapon right now. "Stay here," I ordered Seren, yanking the belt from my waist.

I can help, Rykr.

I stood once again.

"Not right now you can't." I snapped my belt in the face of a woman who came at me with a knife. She fell back, swallowed immediately by twisting vines that pinned her to the ground.

"I'm not helpless." Seren's voice sounded tired through the bond. Seth must have known what she'd be facing. I was going to cut that man's heart out if it was the last thing I did.

"Just stay there." I whipped my belt at a large man with a sword, aiming for his wrist, rather than his sword. He paused, surprised. But the belt had done nothing, either.

I let him come.

The moment he swung, I ducked low, slammed my elbow into his ribs, and drove my fist into his throat. He gasped, staggered, and I kicked him backward into the rising water, snatching his sword out of his grasp.

A vine lashed out and impaled him instantly.

I had no time to register the horror of it as another vine shot out and coiled around my leg. *Fuck.* I wrenched my leg forward, cutting the vine before it could drag me down, but more were coming, lashing out like striking vipers, hunting, wrapping around anything they could take.

The doors above our heads opened fully now, and a giant torrent of water headed straight toward us. I cut down the remaining survivors in front of me, then dove toward Seren as I released the sword.

As I caught her in my arms, I gasped for a breath, then let myself be swept under the surface of the water. Water closed over us, and the world became cold and dark.

I had Seren. That was all that mattered. I expelled a few bubbles from my nose, trying to hold tight to my breath. *"Hold on to me. Whatever you do, don't let go."*

My words were nothing more than thought, carried through the bond, but I felt her answer—a faint squeeze of her fingers.

The current was brutal, yanking at us like a beast trying to rip us apart, to tear us from each other. My lungs ached, burning. Seren struggled—I felt the spasms in her body, her instincts fighting to gasp for air that wasn't there.

I kicked us forward, doing my best to fight against the current. Without the use of my arms, though, swimming was impossible.

"Rykr, I don't know how long I can hold my breath." She was clearly trying to stay calmer than she felt.

I tugged her face into mine. *"Seal your lips to mine. Tight. As tight as you can. We can exchange breath."*

As I set my lips against hers, she followed my instructions, her lips pliant. Our mouths molded together, and I dug my hands into the hair at the nape of her neck, giving her the breath she so desperately needed.

The exchange of breath had to end, or we'd both end up lightheaded and deprived. *"Pull back now."*

A burning feeling rose in my chest.

Somehow, I could see the outline of shadows around us in the dark water, my superior vision at night both helping and terrifying me. But I couldn't see anyone else. I just hoped Tara and Seren's friends had gotten away from the vines.

"We can't swim holding on to each other like this. Hold on to my shirt and we'll swim together, to the surface."

We started forward then I stopped, a sharp tug at my leg.

Not a tug.

A vine. A fucking vine. Wrapped around my ankle, tightening, twisting, dragging me back into the abyss.

"What is it?" Her voice was faint. Alarmed.

I didn't answer.

"Go. Now." I shoved her toward the surface. I didn't have a knife. I didn't have a sword. I clawed at the vine, but the thorns bit deep, sinking into my flesh, cutting through muscle, the water turning black with my blood.

My gaze traveled up to the surface. I closed my eyes, trying to keep myself going. Breath wouldn't materialize by hoping, but panic would speed my drowning.

Noises muffled as water filled my ears, my pulse the loudest sound of all. I bore through the pain, reaching down and tugging at the vine. My fingers tore into the thorns, razor-sharp against my skin, and a swell of panic rose with the crushing desperation for air.

I ripped with everything I had. But it kept pulling.

I didn't have time.

I couldn't fucking breathe.

The pressure in my lungs reached a breaking point, and the edges of my vision darkened.

"Seren." I reached for her through the bond, but my mind was fogging, slipping, spiraling into the void.

I need air.

I need—

I couldn't fail her.

But the only powers I had right now were from her and everything I took from her made her weaker. Less likely to survive.

Dammit, I need to breathe!

My lungs screamed, a hollow ache that turned to fire. My limbs felt heavier, slower. The vine coiled tighter, like it could feel me weakening, feel me giving in. The pressure built, a vise around my ribs, crushing, strangling. The darkness in my vision stretched wider.

My grip on the vine slackened, my head spinning.

"Seren…"

CHAPTER 40
SEREN

Rykr's soft call filled my head as I dove back into the water.

"Rykr?"

Nothing.

Dammit! A wave of fear surged through me and I swam faster, trying to return to him. What if I couldn't find him?

"Rykr!"

Still no response.

Oh gods.

My heart pounded so hard that my chest felt as though it would burst. *Dammit, dammit.*

He only had precious seconds or he'd drown.

Bryndis help me.

Panic surged through me, raw and primal. I kicked harder, clawing through the freezing abyss, but I couldn't see a damn thing. The water churned, rippling echoes of something moving beneath the surface—a presence shifting through the gloom.

Solric, please. Bring me some light.

As if in answer, a flash illuminated the shadows of the bottom.

If I hadn't been freezing from the water already, goose-bumps covering my skin, they would have risen now. Maybe Solric had heard me after all.

Then I saw him.

Limp. Motionless. Several feet below me, his body drifted, his arms weightless, his face slack—too still. My stomach clenched so violently I nearly choked on what little air I had left.

No. No, no, no.

I dove for him. A thick, gnarled vine had coiled around his ankle, its barbed thorns buried deep in his flesh. The sight of it jolted me into action.

I yanked the pin from my braid and stabbed the vine—hard.

Nothing. It was too thick. Desperation roared inside me. I hacked at it again and again, my hands shaking, my lungs screaming for air. *Don't black out. Don't black out.*

The flash came again, and the vine shifted, jerking away slightly from Rykr's leg as though wounded.

Then—a shimmer in the dark. Another flash of light.

It wasn't Solric.

It was a sea serpent.

A monstrous form, long as a full-sized ship, its glowing body pulsing with energy as it coiled through the water, its gaping maw parting to reveal rows of gleaming, jagged teeth.

Coming straight for us.

I raked the pin through the vine one last time, felt the sharp snap of it breaking beneath my fingers. Rykr's body loosened instantly, free. I snatched him into my arms, kicking for the surface.

But the serpent moved faster.

The water around us shifted, a crushing current pulling me backward as the creature surged, its glowing eyes locked on us. I tightened my grip on Rykr, waiting for the exact moment—waiting for it to lunge.

The second its mouth snapped open, I struck.

I jammed the pin straight into the slit of its eye, twisting hard, a gush of blood clouding the water in front of me.

A horrific, high-pitched screech rattled through the water, vibrating through my bones. The serpent thrashed violently, its tail whipping around in a frenzy. Bubbles and current exploded around us, throwing us forward, straight toward the surface.

I kicked harder, my body screaming, Rykr heavy in my arms.

Air.

Behind us, the lifeless body of the serpent rose to the surface of the water, sending a monstrous ripple toward us.

That last cry of the serpent had shaken me in a way I didn't fully understand. Like Haldron not only wanted to strip me of my life, but my humanity in the process—and I'd played into his hands.

But what choice did I have?

As soon as the water became shallower, I dug my feet into the mud, dragging him onto the bank. Ciaran and Amahle were already there, and they ran into the water, Tara following them, and together, we dragged Rykr's heavy form out.

His head lolled to the side, and I laid him down, beating my fist against his chest. Desperate, I opened his mouth and set my lips against his. Under the water, he'd given me the very air from his body to keep me alive.

"Please, Rykr." The bond between us was silent, distant.

I held his nose and breathed into his mouth, my cheeks puffing slightly. Once, twice ... five times.

"Come on, Rykr. Please. Please come back." I slammed my hand against his chest.

That I wasn't dead yet was my only reason for hope.

Tears stung my eyes, and I lowered my mouth to his once more.

"Please."

Then he coughed, choking and spitting up water, his lungs expelling what he'd taken in under the surface. He drew a rough breath, and a cry left my lips as I dropped back, giving him space as his eyes opened.

"I'd ask if I died and went to Evermere, but you're here," he rasped.

Swiver. Despite everything, I laughed, relief filling my every pore. I bent toward him again and kissed his mouth, gently. "The cruel Rúna have sent you back. Even the weavers of fates don't want you."

His lips tipped in a smile. "Every time I'm staring death in the face, you decide to snatch me from it." Rykr raised a hand, stroking my cheek softly with the backs of his knuckles.

I shivered, and not just because I was freezing after the plunge into the water and the frosty night air we'd come out to.

But because Rykr's touch set my skin on fire, even when it was innocent. A lump rose in my throat as I remembered how his hands had brought me more bliss and satisfaction than I'd ever felt in my life. I sat up straighter, looking around me.

"Don't thank me yet. I've dragged us out to the Havamal." Cold, slick fear went through me as the stands of the arena swam into my view. Spectators watched, waiting to see us battle for our lives against the Skorn.

The crowd wasn't just watching. They were feeding off this. Their laughter filtered down from the stands, together with drunken shouts, the clinking of goblets as if they were watching a troupe of dancers in a festival square, not people fighting to the death.

A celebration of suffering.

The Havamal, built on the side of the mountain at the base of Emberstone, held thousands of spectators. An enormous parapet protruded from the side of the arena carved into the mountain. Haldron and the other leaders of the Viori were seated there.

That would be where Rykr and I would have to find a way to strike, if we were going to be successful. Even if we'd ruined our attempt to rescue Esme, if we could still kill Haldron, we might be able to free her. Seth didn't know it, but he'd given me more motivation than ever to strike—if I was going to die from poison anyway tonight, I had nothing to lose.

"How many other people made it out of the water?" Rykr asked, looking toward the dark, murky surface that now looked like a placid lake in the center of the Havamal. The ground we stood on was muddy—no doubt it had been flooded before this.

"I've seen three," Ciaran said, panting. Water dripped from his face. "I'm not sure if any others will make it out at this point."

"Where are they?" Rykr stood, alert and wary. "They're as much of a threat to us as anything that's coming next."

"I'll guard your backs for now. I think I'm the only one that kept a sword after swimming," Tara said, her damp hair clinging to the sides of her neck. As much as I wanted my sister to be safe, having her here had proven to be a comfort, too. Her competence reassured me.

I scanned the arena of the Havamal, familiarizing myself with it. Besides the lake, the basin of the arena was barren, the only significant features consisting of enormous boulders that the amphitheater had either been built around or had fallen from the cliffs and mountains around us.

The pale light of the full Harvest Moon shone down on us. My shivering had gotten worse, my strength thoroughly sapped. I gripped Rykr's forearm, hating how weak I felt. Any training he'd given me might be in vain after all.

Torches flared to life in the stands of the Havamal. The amphitheater erupted into cheers, the spectators reveling in our success—so far. All my life, I'd heard of the Skorn but never attended it … and yet it had never occurred to me how cruel— how vicious it was.

Even though he was some distance away, I felt Haldron's eyes on me, knew he looked directly at me. Any reverence or respect I'd had for him had vanished, replaced by loathing. Every single ounce of pain and suffering that my family had endured over the last six weeks was owed to him.

To his hatred for Lirien.

His malice.

Maybe once I would have wanted to see our enemies defeated at any cost, but he'd involved my family in such a way that my eyes had been opened to the truth—we were the villains just as much as they were.

Peace would be the only thing that would heal our people, but that wasn't what Haldron wanted. He wanted war and power.

I didn't have much time left, but if my life counted for anything, then I would do whatever it took to stop him from leading my people to death and destruction in a war with Lirien.

Haldron raised his hands, settling the noise of the Hava-mal. The crowd leaned forward, their smiles and jeers sickening me to my core. This was meant to be a trial where the gods determined our fate. He'd turned it into a vicious game and allowed the crowd to think they were here for a show.

"Praise Solric on this sacred Harvest Moon!" Haldron's voice boomed through the Havamal, clearly assisted by some form of magic.

Another cheer erupted and I inched closer to Rykr.

"Whatever happens, stay by my side." Rykr's voice filled my head. *"Haldron will have tricks to play."*

Once the cheers ended, Haldron said, "We have a unique Skorn this year. With not just the normal sentenced, but traitors to the seat of Emberstone and a Lirien—a Sealed Pendaran who represents the best of their warriors. Let us see how he does against the mighty Skorn!"

All around us, gates opened on the walls below the risers where the spectators watched.

Cold gnawed at my bones as Skorn emerged from the tunnels, their faces painted with ash, dark kohl around their eyes.

They looked just as soulless as the Nyxwraiths had been. A quick, inexact count put them at over thirty in number. Haldron wasn't taking any chances.

I backed closer to Rykr, each breath a ragged plume of mist in the night air. My clothes clung to me like a second skin, heavy with water. The moon's pale light spilled across the Havamal's vast, unforgiving basin, turning the jagged rocks and dirt into a silver graveyard.

"Stay together, in formation," Rykr commanded with authority. My friends and Tara wouldn't question him here. He was our best shot at survival.

The roar of the crowd slithered down the stone walls of the amphitheater, seeping into my skin until the sound filled my head like a war drum. They wanted blood. Our blood.

Pain was a fire licking through my ribs, spreading with

every heartbeat. I pressed a hand to the wound Seth had given me, but the effort was in vain. I'd already lost too much blood and the poison spreading through me couldn't be stopped. But I couldn't afford to be weak now. Not here. Not when every moment of my life had led to this.

"Stay close, Seren." Rykr's voice, rough and urgent, echoed through the bond, grounding me. I felt his worry like a pulse, steady and insistent. I wanted to answer, to tell him I was fine, but the lie stuck in my throat. So I nodded, forcing myself into a fighting stance, feeling his presence like a shield at my back.

The Skorn encircled us, their blades gleaming in the light.

How in the hell were we going to defeat them when we didn't even have swords?

"Ice," I managed to Rykr. *"Use my powers."*

"I can't do that. It weakens you more." Rykr's back was flat to mine. *"And you're fading. I can feel it."*

"Do it, Rykr. At least until we get a sword or two to balance the scales."

A sudden flurry of activity interrupted the Skorn warriors' steady progress toward us—one of the other sentenced jumped out from behind a rock, seeking to use the element of surprise.

One Skorn warrior turned in an instant, his blade slicing through the air with precision ... and cutting straight through the attacker's neck. The man's head fell back, a bright stain of crimson jetting from his body as it fell forward, onto the mud of the basin.

"Do it now, Rykr!" I cried out, then lunged away, hurtling toward the Skorn. We'd never survive if we didn't get weapons.

"Fuck!" Rykr yelled. Ice then shot out from his hands, shooting like daggers and impaling three of the Skorn closest to me. My knees collapsed as my power left me. I hit the rock and dirt, my consciousness teetering.

The stunned crowd cheered at the display of ice, the bodies of the dead Skorn thudded against the ground, and my friends bolted forward.

Scraping myself up, I blinked numbly as a Skorn lunged for me.

Tara met him with a roar, her blade flashing as it collided with his in a shower of sparks. The metallic scream of steel against steel rattled through my skull. Rykr was a shadow beside her, fast and lethal, his fist connecting with a warrior's jaw with a sickening crack that echoed through the arena.

Amahle dove for a fallen sword, her movements swift and precise, and drove it into an enemy's side with a grunt.

I tried to move, to fight, but my legs wouldn't budge. The pain in my chest spread through me fully, gnawing at my strength. Through the blur of battle another Skorn warrior approached, his spear aimed straight for my heart, his eyes cold and unfeeling.

Before I could even raise my arms in defense, Rykr was there. He moved like a storm, his growl tearing through the chaos as he tackled the man to the ground. They struggled, bodies twisting in the dirt, until Rykr wrenched the spear from the warrior's grip and drove it through his chest with a brutal, final thrust. He pulled the spear out, then pressed it into my hands.

"You're not dying on me, Seren." His voice was a raw, desperate whisper. *"Get up. Get moving."* He lifted a fallen sword and stood at my side, his handsome face splattered with blood, his eyes fierce cand unrelenting.

I barely had the strength to stand. My vision swayed, dark spots creeping in at the edges, my limbs felt sluggish and unresponsive. But I couldn't fall again. If I fell, I would never get back up.

A Skorn warrior lunged toward me—fast, brutal. I barely

managed to lift my spear before he slammed into me with the force of a charging beast.

Pain exploded through my ribs, my breath strangled from my lungs. I hit the ground hard, my fingers going numb around the spear. The impact sent a fresh wave of agony through my already failing body.

The Skorn grinned down at me, his black-painted eyes filled with bloodlust. He lifted his sword, ready to bring it down—

Rykr was a blur of motion, raw power unleashed.

He was on the warrior before he could react, catching the blade mid-swing with his bare hand.

His bare fucking hand.

Ice crackled over Rykr's palm, rapidly spreading up the blade. The Skorn's face twisted in shock just as Rykr wrenched the sword from his grip—then slammed his fist into his throat with bone-breaking force.

The warrior collapsed instantly, choking.

Rykr didn't hesitate. Didn't stop. He turned, a predator among prey, his movements blurring with unnatural speed as he tore through the Skorn like a god of war.

Another warrior leaped at him from behind—

But Ciaran was already there.

I saw his movement first—fast, brutal—as he slammed a dagger straight into the warrior's kidney. No hesitation. No wasted movement.

Blood spurted from the Skorn's lips as Ciaran ripped the dagger free, then slammed his boot into the man's chest, sending him sprawling.

Amahle was a blur of golden light and flashing steel, her stolen sword singing as it clashed against a Skorn's blade. The Skorn warrior snarled, swinging hard.

Amahle didn't block. She sidestepped the attack, ducking

low, sliding past him with eerie grace. Her sword whipped through the air and the next moment, the Skorn staggered, blinking, before his throat split open, blood pouring down his chest.

She was already moving on before his body hit the ground.

Tara fought with sharp, controlled precision, her blade a viper's fang, striking fast and true. She parried an attack with deadly ease, twisting the blade in a flourish before carving a brutal arc across the enemy's chest.

Another Skorn came for her, swinging a massive axe.

Tara dodged just in time, spinning out of the way. A knife in her hand flashed, burying itself deep into the warrior's thigh.

The Skorn roared in pain, staggering, and Tara took off his head.

One clean, effortless stroke.

Blood sprayed across her face, but her expression was as cold as ice.

Gods, they were all incredible. Fierce. Unstoppable. Fighting for their lives and for each other. *For me.*

And I ... I was on the ground. *Fucking useless.*

No.

I shoved against the pain, forcing myself upright, using the spear to steady myself.

My legs were weak. Too weak.

The world tilted around me, but I forced myself to move.

Around us, the battle spiraled into madness. Ciaran took a brutal blow to the shoulder, his cry of pain sharp before he gritted his teeth and pushed forward, blood streaming down his arm. Tara was a whirlwind but even she couldn't be everywhere at once. Amahle's quick reflexes saved her from a fatal strike, but not before a sword sliced across her thigh, bright blood staining the dirt beneath her feet.

Seth—and Haldron—had underestimated the lengths we would go to for each other. One of us alone may not have survived this. But together? *Together* we had everything to live for. Everything to fight for.

Pushing myself forward, I summoned my strength, every movement a scream of agony. My vision swam, but I locked eyes with a Skorn within reach of my spear. Gritting my teeth, I dove toward him, my fingers closing around the shaft of the spear as I stabbed him through the neck, the head of the spear connecting with a nauseating crunch of bone and sinew. The shock of impact rattled up my arm, but it was enough.

I yanked the spear out then struck again.

Again.

Again.

Each twirl of my spear, each stab through a living body made my friends—my love—safer. The harder I fought, the more I felt the stickiness of blood flow against my skin, but my exhaustion had faded, my will to protect them dominating all else as I dodged, struck, slashed.

One large Skorn man loomed over the others, fighting his way toward Rykr, who was already surrounded. I raced toward the warrior, blood pumping through my veins like fire.

"Seren, don't!" Rykr's mind called out toward me.

I pressed forward, then pushed the blunt end of the spear into the ground, catapulting myself onto one of the boulders nearest to the Skorn man. I landed lightly on my feet, dancing across the stone as I gathered speed, then hurtled toward the Skorn warrior.

The warrior was fast—too fast. My foot barely grazed his shoulder before he twisted, his blade slicing toward my side. I spun in mid-air, narrowly avoiding the tip, then used the momentum to drive my spear forward—

Straight through his eye.

The impact jarred my bones as I landed, rolling through the mud. Blood spattered my hands.

My breath came in ragged gasps.

Then I lifted my head slowly.

The Skorn were dead. So were the rest of the sentenced.

All of them.

Only Tara, my friends, me, and Rykr remained standing, each of us wounded and covered in dirt and grime. There was no relief in the victory. Our blood mingled with theirs in the dirt, the scent of iron thick in the air.

Haldron stood above us, untouched. Unbothered.

The crowd laughed and cheered as if we weren't standing in pools of blood, as if we hadn't just fought for our lives.

But it wasn't the crowd I cared about.

It was him.

Haldron.

The man who had destroyed everything. The man who had sentenced me to death. Who had stolen my father, my sister, my people's hope. Who had made us nothing but pawns in his war.

The taste of blood coated my tongue, and my fingers itched to rip his heart straight from his chest.

I couldn't reach him. But I could do something.

The spear was solid and strong in my grip, every fiber of my being burning with fury.

End this. *Here. Now.*

My muscles coiled as I reared back ... and hurled it with everything I had.

The spear cut through the air like lightning, a streak of silver in the moonlight.

For a heartbeat, I thought it would hit.

For a heartbeat, I thought I had him.

But metal clanged against stone. Sharply. Emptily. The

spear missed by mere inches, splintering against the rock beneath the parapet, like a child's toy thrown in a tantrum, now broken and meaningless.

Silence.

A breathless silence formed from the stunned crowd.

Haldron's silhouette loomed over the arena, his expression cold and distant, as if he were a god gazing down upon his broken creations.

Then he laughed.

It slithered through the air, smooth and mocking, sinking into my skin like poison. He tilted his head, watching me with amusement.

"You think this is over? All you've done is proven that you are not worthy of a pardon." Haldron purred. "It will never be over for you, Seren Ragnall."

With a snap of his fingers, a cage appeared, creaking and swaying over the water of the lake. My heart stopped.

Esme.

Her terrified face pressed against the bars, her wide eyes searching the arena until they found me.

Her hands curled around the iron, her eyes locking onto mine.

"Seren!" she sobbed, her voice barely carrying over the roaring crowd.

A raw, broken sound tore from my throat. I stumbled forward, my limbs moving before I could think, before I could process anything but the sight of my sister. Alive. *Alive.*

I could save her.

Haldron's smile was cruel. "Let's see how well you swim, little one."

With a flick of his wrist, he released the cage.

"No," I whispered, my voice breaking. "No, no, no—"

The cage plummeted into the dark water, the splash swallowed by the roar that tore from my throat. I screamed until my voice gave out, until my knees hit the ground, until the world narrowed to the sight of that cage sinking beneath the moonlit surface.

Rykr's arms wrapped around me, his grip ironclad as I thrashed against him, my screams muffled against his chest.

"We'll get her," he promised through the bond, his voice like steel, but all I could hear was Esme's fading cries as the lake swallowed her whole.

CHAPTER 41
RYKR

Tara and Ciaran streaked toward the lake as Amahle reached Seren and me. "Let me go," Seren gasped, pushing against me. "Let me go to her."

"You're not in any condition to get into the water," I said as gently as possible, holding her by the shoulders. "Tara and Ciaran will get her out."

Before she could protest further, the gates to the tunnels opened once again.

Two glowing eyes came from the darkness, the fiery white eyeshine of some animal. A vuk emerged, slowly stalking forward.

"Rykr Westhaven, you claim to have killed one of these mighty beasts," Haldron taunted. "Or was it yet another lie? I suppose we'll find out."

Smite me.

My shoulders tensed at the memory of the last vuk I'd encountered. I wouldn't have been able to kill the damned vuk if it wasn't for my sword, and Seth still had it. I couldn't help but wonder where the treacherous couple had gone, or if they were enjoying the spectacle of the Skorn from the luxury of the seats.

The gate swung closed and the vuk bared his teeth, growling.

Maybe I couldn't kill the damned beast, but I could wound it.

As though he'd read my thoughts, Haldron leaned forward on the parapet. "We wouldn't want to have a repeat of Seren's display of anger toward me, though, would we?" With a wave of his hand, all the Skorn weapons vanished from sight.

"Curpiss," Amahle breathed, her eyes going wide.

I had to get Seren to safety. Without waiting for the vuk to come closer, I hoisted her over my shoulder, hooking my arm around her legs as I searched for any place that I could set her down while I fought the vuk. "Help me," I called to Amahle.

Grabbing the biggest rock I could find with my other hand, I backed up slowly, only to hear another gate screech open. Another hungry, snarling vuk emerged.

Haldron intended to let us be ripped to shreds and eaten alive here.

The second vuk was closest to me, but the first seemed to sense the threat to his meal. He pounced, charging toward us at full speed.

We were going to die here tonight if I didn't get moving. I ran for the tallest place in the Havamal—a large boulder near the center. Scaling it as quickly as I could, I flung Seren onto the top, setting her down just as teeth dug into my calf, excoriating my skin.

I cried out, then kicked the vuk that had bitten me with my undamaged leg. Amahle clambered up beside me as the vuk fell, but it jumped back to its feet immediately. "Stay here. Together," I instructed them.

I didn't have time to wonder whether they would listen.

Seren hadn't done the best job of that already, but I'd never seen her so unleashed, either. If I hadn't been busy fighting for my own life, I would have wanted to watch her, marvel in the fluid, graceful way she'd taken on the Skorn, despite being wounded so terribly.

No time to think about that now, though.

I hopped down from the boulder away from the vuk. I had to draw it away from Seren.

A blur of teeth and scales approached, and I readied myself. Just when the vuk drew near, I rolled to the side of it, then reached out, hooking my fingers into the scales of its back. I swung my body onto its back, then mounted it.

The beast was more unwieldy than any horse I'd ever ridden, yet the scales provided a natural hold. The vuk bellowed and snapped below me, furious at the intrusion. The second vuk came closer, thick spittle dripping from its mouth as it assessed both me and his rival.

What the fuck am I supposed to do now?

The beasts could be killed, but without my sword I couldn't hope to stab them. As the second vuk pounced, I yanked back on the scales, as though the vuk under me *was* a horse and the scales were its reins. It howled and reared backward and the two vuks clashed on their back legs, a tangle of teeth and paws.

I dropped off the back of the vuk and landed on my feet, then ran for another boulder. With any luck, the two beasts would at least injure each other.

Scaling the boulder with a speed born of desperation, I dragged one foot, then the other to the top and stood straight. The vuks, realizing their meal had run out on them, turned toward me. Those glowing eyes caught the light of the full moon above us, casting a pale silvery glow amid the torches.

The torches.

My body went stiff. They weren't much, but they were the closest thing to a weapon here.

The fire itself might keep the animals at bay momentarily, but the torches themselves could help.

But I'd need to get to the outer edges of the basin to grab a torch, and I doubted I could outrun two vuks.

I might have to take a ride on one of them again.

My hands grew slick as they neared, encircling the boulder as they tried to get to me. One of them leaped and I braced myself, then caught the damn thing with a strength I hadn't expected.

I threw the beast toward the ground, and it landed with a heavy thud that shook the earth and then it rolled, yelping as it got back up again.

I didn't have time to think about how I'd managed that— the other vuk charged me. I jumped, then landed on its back.

Maybe it was the same one I'd mounted before, but this vuk didn't react and kept running instead. The torches glowed in the distance. I dropped onto my knees and dug my hand between the scales again, holding on as I tried to direct the vuk toward the gate.

If I hadn't been riding the vuk, the torches would have been out of reach—twice my height off the ground. But I got my feet under me, crouching as we drew closer. When we'd nearly reached it, I sprang from the vuk's back, my hands grasping the torch. I wrenched it free from its metal bracket, then lowered myself to the ground.

The heat from the flames singed my face, the smell of burning hair greeting me as I turned it in my hands.

The vuk I'd ridden over here doubled back. The other still thrashed on the ground, yelping. Maybe I'd hurt it after all.

I needed more torches, but that wasn't an option. This one would have to count.

With only a few feet left between the vuk and me, I swept the torch in wide arcs and the animal paused, keeping a wary distance.

To make this work, I'd have to let the beast get closer.

I drew my hand back toward me, my heart pounding as the vuk approached. This would hurt me—there was no way around that.

I lowered the torch, my chest heaving as the vuk sized me up, ready to make a meal of me. Then it lunged, mouth open. The first vuk that had attacked me in the forest had shown me the way they handled their kill. As this one snapped at my neck, I turned, thrusting the torch into the vuk's open mouth as deeply as it would go. Its claws shredded my shirt front, leaving me practically bare-chested, scratches bright and red with blood down my torso.

Fangs dug into my arm, sending shooting pain through me, then I yanked my arm back. A few jagged gashes marked my skin, but the stunned vuk fell back, a hiss of steam and smoke coming from its mouth. A foul, nauseating smell of flesh burning filled the air, and then it stumbled onto its haunches, legs wobbling.

Then the vuk pitched onto its side, dead.

My arm throbbed, the torn skin there feeling as though it had its own pulse. The vuk I'd thrown from the boulder continued to thrash and cry.

I might have broken its back.

This time, a large rock might do the trick. Even if I didn't kill it, I could incapacitate it.

Despite everything, my heart squeezed with guilt as I approached the yelping beast. My fingers curled around the rock I'd grabbed. Better to put the damned creature out of its misery than to let it die slowly like this.

I crouched beside it and lifted the rock. Some of my blood dripped down from my elbow, splashing on the ground near the vuk. The white glow of its eyes lessened and it stilled, eyes meeting mine.

Soft. *Sad.*

It bowed its head, struggling onto its front paws as it knelt before me.

The tongue flicked, its great chest heaving. Grey fur poked out from between those scales and, for the first time, I saw the tame animal that Seren had said these vuks normally were.

The vuk held my gaze, a plea in its eyes.

Something shifted inside me. That they'd attacked me might be instinctual, but no worse than any other creature trying to survive might do.

"You deserve a better death than to be bashed in the head with a rock."

I stood, tossing the rock to the side.

Blood oozed down my arm. A hush had gone over the crowd again. "Good enough for you?" I called to Haldron.

I glanced back toward where I'd left Seren and Amahle.

They were gone.

Godsdammit. I found Amahle in an instant—by the edge of the lake, leaning over the water.

A crack of lightning cut across the sky, then struck in the center of the amphitheater. Clouds billowed in, a sudden gale stirring the wind, the very ground trembling.

Searing pain ripped through me as lightning struck once again, nearer to me, then flowing through me, the sky seeming to rip in two as I fell to my knees, my head falling back.

A whisper filled the wind, a chorus of voices. Not Old Ederyn or any other language I knew, but something eerie and beautiful.

A scorching feeling came from my chest and I dropped my chin, my eyes widening as a rune sizzled against the surface of my skin, the remains of my shirt and vest burning away from my body, as though the rune had been drawn by the finger of the god of light himself.

Not just any rune—but one I'd seen many times before, the black and crimson tattoo of my father's sigil, the Everspire— the tree of life, encircled by rune marks of the gods and goddesses of old.

My throat constricted, my body robbed of breath as the whisper continued, a vision filling my mind. A crown placed on the head of a boy, too young for the weight. Too young for the role. My nephew, Ivar.

The words of consecration, spoken by the High Magister filled my mind.

Ivar had been crowned.

But the gods had chosen me.

As though shackles had been around my wrists, a great weight fell away from my body, the powers my father had restricted in me with the Seal now loose. A torrent of heat blazed at my fingertips—the fire I'd never known how to wield as a youth.

The dark clouds parted just as suddenly as they'd come, the silver hue of moonlight draping me in a cloak. The whisper that had filled my ears fell away, and the wind stilled.

The entire assembly was motionless.

I inhaled slowly, the air that filled my lungs somehow sweeter. As though I was a newborn taking its first breath.

I lifted my head. Haldron's face was pale, his lips parted in stunned silence. His knuckles had gone white where they gripped the parapet, his mouth slightly open—not in scorn or amusement.

In fear.

He knew.

"Who are you?" he whispered.

A slow, dangerous smile curved my lips. "Don't you recognize me, Uncle?" I said, fire swirling in my hands.

"I'm Calix Warrick, King of Lirien."

And I let the flames rise.

CHAPTER 42
SEREN

Screams reached me as I broke through the surface of the water. Rykr's connection to me had somehow broken and I lifted my head, horrified as I watched the stands burst into flame.

My alarm only deepened as I saw the source of the fire.

Rykr.

The fire roared toward the parapet like a living thing, tendrils of flame licking at the stone, curling hungrily toward the wooden beams. Screams echoed—high, sharp, and endless. The scent of burning flesh thickened the air, and through the haze of smoke, I saw people falling, their bodies still alight as they tumbled from the stands.

Haldron and his council scrambled back, their robes catching fire as they slapped at the flames, their shouts lost beneath the howl of Rykr's fury.

I rasped a breath.

All these people—the Viori screaming and fleeing for their lives—were going to die if I didn't stop Rykr. Some power inside him had been unleashed. But Esme was still in the water, along with Ciaran and Tara—my gods, were any of them even alive still? What if there were more serpents?

This time, I was going after Esme.

I dove back under.

My eyes stung in the water as I searched, though the fire burning in the Havamal made it easier to see in the murky water.

They'd been under for so long. Was it even possible for them to hold their breath this long?

Please. Don't let them die.

My lungs were already burning.

Then I saw them: Tara, Ciaran, *and* Esme.

My gods.

They were alive ... and swimming toward me.

I surfaced, my breath shallow, sending ripples across the water. then their heads popped through. "What happened?" I managed, swimming toward them. "How did you get the cage open?"

Tara kept an arm under Esme's frail torso, swimming with her toward the edge of the lake. "Ciaran. He bent the metal bars back." Tara cast a worried look as he lagged behind us. "He's losing blood in that arm though. We need to get him help and soon."

Thank the gods for Ciaran. If he hadn't been here ...

I shuddered at the thought.

Amahle helped us out of the water, then I caught Esme in my arms, embracing her with a sob. "I'm so sorry, Esme," I managed, dipping my forehead against hers. "I'm so sorry it took us this long to save you."

"I'm okay," she whispered, teeth chattering. "I'm all right, Seren." Her voice was small. Too small. And she wouldn't quite meet my eyes.

I swallowed hard, pretending to believe her, and grasped her shoulders. "Did he hurt you?"

"No, I'm okay," Esme repeated, her face drawn and tired.

I nodded mutely, too overcome with emotion to speak, then Tara and I helped her stand.

"We have to get out of here," Amahle said, her voice urgent, her eyes dark with worry. "Your husband lit the whole place on fire."

I had to stop him. Handing Esme over to Tara, I bolted, flying past the bodies and mud between Rykr and me. The roar of fire and screams melted into a low, distant hum. My body felt distant, sluggish. The poison. Solric's light, how much time did I even have left? As I reached Rykr, I grabbed his elbow.

But something inside me hesitated.

What if I didn't stop him?

What if I let him burn Emberstone to the ground?

No. Gods, no. This isn't who we are. This isn't who I love. "Rykr. Stop. It's finished now."

A wet trail moved from the corner of my mouth, and I wiped it away, seeing the blood on the back of my hand before I tasted it.

Rykr turned sharply, his eyes glowing red, sending fear spiraling through me.

The man I loved was in there.

He had to be.

But standing in the center of this inferno, flames curling around his shoulders like a mantle of destruction, he looked more like a god of destruction than the man I loved.

I rose to the tips of my toes and kissed him. "Stop," I begged. "Please stop."

The redness faded from his eyes, then Rykr's arm tightened around my waist. He blinked down at me. "Seren." Sweeping me into his arms, he strode across the Havamal through pockets of smoke and flame.

He stopped in front of my friends. "Get her out of here," Rykr ordered Ciaran, handing me over to my friend. "Out of the Havamal and out of Emberstone. Don't stop and for gods' sake, don't wait for me. I'm going after Haldron—ending this once and for all."

"No!" I gasped, reaching for Rykr. Ciaran held me close, though, his grip as strong as iron. "No, please."

"Let me help you," Amahle's voice was low, her dark eyes appealing to Rykr. "You can't do it alone." But she was wounded too, blood continuing to seep from the gash on her leg.

"No, I have to do this alone. Go, now." Rykr set a hand on Ciaran's shoulder. "Please. Guard her with your life."

Rykr turned to go.

"No, Rykr, no." I pushed away from Ciaran feebly. "No, don't do this. I love you."

He bent near me and kissed my forehead. "And I love you. Now get out of here."

I attempted to lunge for him, but my efforts were futile. Ciaran was far too strong.

"I don't want you to go," I begged Rykr, my tears flowing more freely as I reached for him.

"I have to. For my father, and my brothers." He kissed my hands then strode away, disappearing into the thick smoke.

I whirled to look for Tara, Esme, and Amahle, who flanked Ciaran as he hurried through the Havamal. I rubbed my bleary eyes, coughing against Ciaran's chest. Spatters of blood accompanied each cough.

Tara touched my forehead, concern written on her face. "That bastard, Seth. Gods, Seren, you look terrible. We need to find Mother. She might be the only one who can heal you."

Amahle stroked my back. "We have to keep moving, Seren. We'll fight our way through the Vangar to get you out of here if necessary, but the more time we take, the more people we'll have to face."

Get me out of here?

"What do you mean?" I managed, my body shaking more violently.

"Your husband just announced to the entire Viori—and Haldron—that he's the king of Lirien, Ser."

Ciaran and Tara stumbled, then exchanged a look. Even Esme's eyes went wide, though she couldn't understand what had happened in her absence. "Wait a second—what?" Ciaran asked.

"There's no time to explain right now." Amahle panted as we ran. "But it turns out Seren didn't just bond herself with a Lirien—she bonded herself with the prince. And if we don't get her the hell out of the Dreadwood right now, she's going to have every Vangar warrior in the territory hunting her."

Tara still held Esme close, but there was a tension in her shoulders now, something *different*. Amahle, usually so quick to reassure me, didn't say anything.

I looked at them—really *looked* at them—and saw what I hadn't wanted to see.

I wasn't one of them anymore.

They knew it. *I* knew it. And yet, some stubborn part of me refused to believe it.

I wasn't just running for my life. *I was running because I'd been cast out.* I couldn't remain here anymore.

I'd made myself an enemy of the Viori. Proven Ciaran right.

I *was* a traitor. *My husband is the king of Lirien. Gods!*

"And my family?" I managed. "Where will you go?"

Tara ran her fingers through her short hair. "The hell if I know. One problem at a time right now."

I shook my head. "No. I refuse to be dragged away like this. Seth poisoned me with dragon's blood, and I don't know if I have much time left. Don't you see? You're the ones who have to escape. You're the ones they're going to punish."

The fire from the stands singed us, the heat intensifying as we drew closer to the tunnels. Would there even be a place to escape from? The gates into the arena were all closed.

I didn't want this.

Didn't want them to die for me.

But Ciaran kept barreling forward, his speed increasing as we drew closer.

"This way!" a familiar voice called. Ciaran nearly skidded to a stop.

Darya stood near one of the tunnels on the inside, turning the crank to open it. Her face was filled with worry, fear, and defiance. After Seth's betrayal, I didn't trust her, but we had no other options.

We ran toward her as smoke and ash rained down on top of us, a shower of sparks and embers landing on our hair and skin. A massive wooden structure—the roof attached to the parapet—began to collapse.

If it fell, it would block our path into the tunnel.

My friends ran faster, Tara hauling Esme so quickly that my younger sister's feet stumbled. Amahle left a trail of blood, the movement speeding the loss of blood.

At last, we tumbled into the open gate, just as a deluge of flame and smoke landed behind us.

Falling to his knees, Ciaran still held me close, but I pushed away, onto the ground.

"Thank you," I rasped, the only one of us not gasping for air.

Darya's hands were still on the crank. *She wasn't shaking.*

My stomach twisted.

Too calm. Too steady.

"No," Darya murmured, and I barely heard the shift in her voice before she moved. "Thank *you*."

The blade flashed.

My breath caught—too late, *too late*. I saw the blade coming, but I couldn't move fast enough.

But Ciaran could. *Did*.

His hands slammed into my shoulders—a hard, desperate shove that sent me crashing against the tunnel wall. My head snapped back, pain ricocheting through my skull. My fingers brushed his sleeve before Darya's blade found him instead.

The sound it made was sickening. Soft, almost.

Ciaran gasped, his fingers jerking around the blade buried in his chest. Darya wrenched the sword free. Blood sprayed, a warm mist against my skin.

And Ciaran staggered. His mouth opened, lips forming my name ...

Then he crumpled.

CHAPTER 43

RYKR

"*Rykr, help us!*"

Seren's voice, which had gone quiet for a while now, came into my mind unexpectedly clear.

But weak.

Fading.

A rip went through the fabric of my soul.

Seren was dying.

Concentrate. I couldn't let myself slip into her thoughts now. Leaving Seren had been foolish, but I had abandoned my duties to my people too many times over the last month not to take this opportunity.

I jerked my chin up, grabbing on to a handhold on the cliff I'd scaled as I followed Haldron and his council taking a mountain path back into Emberstone. If they reached the protection of the city, I might lose the chance to strike.

Conveniently, my ability to climb seemed to have improved, along with every other skill I'd once possessed.

The possibility existed that my uncle was unaware of the

fact that I'd followed him—which I doubted—but there was an equal chance that he lay in wait for me.

I was willing to take my chances, but I prepared myself for the second option.

With the added protection from my powers, a sense of indestructibility had settled into my bones. Reckless, maybe, but what did it matter? Going after my uncle was the best way to strike a blow for my kingdom.

My kingdom.

Did the High Magister know what had happened? Surely, he had to know something hadn't gone right with Iver's coronation.

But now that the divine gifts had been given to me, I had a fighting chance. I had no sword, but I had newfound powers and strength at my disposal.

My feet dug into the toeholds of the rough rock, and I hoisted myself up, then stopped short.

My uncle waited on the path, on a horse.

What I hadn't expected? Lucia Ragnall, bound by heavy chains and gagged, held at knifepoint by one of his guards. Vangar soldiers flanked them—about ten in all. But I'd be a fool to assume that the only strength these soldiers possessed were their swords. I'd been in the Viori territory long enough to know these Unbound people had imperceptible skills.

"I don't have a weapon," I said, taking slow steps toward them, my hands in front of me.

"You *are* a weapon, Calix. I saw that well enough in the Havamal." My uncle narrowed his gaze at me. "Not another step or my man will slit the throat of your darling wife's mother."

Fear pulsed through me, but I couldn't allow it to show. I shrugged, still inching closer. "And why should I care? Do you really think I love a Viori gutter rat? I have many far more beautiful women waiting for me in Suomelin."

Lucia's eyes widened, pleading with me as the guard pressed the knife closer.

"You're lying." Haldron's mouth turned up in a cruel smile. "You think I haven't had you watched this entire time in Emberstone? You're in love, Calix. Maybe it's the effect of the Oath of Bryndis or maybe you're just a simpering fool, but you care about Seren Ragnall. How long do you think Seren would continue to love you if she knew you didn't even try to save her mother?"

I ground my teeth. *Fuck.* Despite my temptation to ignore him, he was also right. But I wouldn't give that away, either.

Seren loved her family deeply.

She might never forgive me if I didn't help Lucia.

I stopped my approach, weighing my options. Fire would be expected—and a sure way to make certain Lucia was killed. My fire wasn't as precise as Seren's ice was. Not yet.

"I must admit, I didn't anticipate you, Calix. I'd heard of your powers, but you impressed me. You were magnificent in the Havamal, and that was before the gods chose to bless you with their divine gifts." Haldron's eyes glittered. "It will be a pity to kill you."

I had to get Haldron away from Vangar protection. No doubt they'd interfere if I tried something from here.

"Then I suggest you do it yourself, Haldron. You wouldn't want to leave the task to someone else and have them fail you again, would you?"

Haldron held my gaze. "I didn't get where I am by being a fool. You shouldn't underestimate me, dear nephew. Or what I'm capable of."

"This from the man that murdered my entire family?" I

threw him a hard glare. "I'm already well aware of what you're capable of." I shifted my weight forward with one foot.

"Clearly you don't. That was yet another step ..."

Before Haldron's words had fully sunk in, the guard plunged the knife into Lucia's gut, without the slightest hint of emotion on his face. She cried out, her voice muted by the gag, but a red stain appeared on the front of her dress as he pulled the knife back.

"No!" The word escaped me as the guard lifted Lucia and tossed her, face forward. She tumbled off the path, barely catching herself as she hung from the edge.

If I went after her, they'd kill me.

But I couldn't stand here.

Fire burst from my hands once again as I plunged toward her. One Vangar member lifted her hands as a shield and the fire bounced against a transparent wall harmlessly—a protection charm.

I was going to die saving Lucia Ragnall.

Several of the other Vangar soldiers released ironstones from slings—small, sharp, flat, triangular weapons with sides as sharp as razor blades and points that pierced flesh easily when thrown with speed. Each sling released several ironstones, and they sliced through the air toward me.

With an unpracticed gesture spell, I sent a gust of wind, knocking the ironstones off their trajectory. I dove onto the path heading straight for Lucia.

As I reached her, more ironstones pierced my skin. *Gods.* They'd fired another volley. Pain lanced through me as I yanked Lucia by the chain at her back, dragging her up and over the side of the cliff.

She heaved for breath, the gag impeding her, and I tugged it out of her mouth as I heard another volley of ironstones fired. As I shielded her with my arms around her, the iron-stones embedded in my back and the back of my neck. *Nyxva.*

Somehow, despite the agonizing pain that flared through me, I remained standing.

Bleeding.

But standing.

How?

I plucked the ironstones I could reach from the backs of my arms, then turned slowly to face Haldron.

"You should be dead," Haldron whispered, awe and fear in his eyes.

I *should* be.

I had no idea in Solric's name how I was still standing.

"And yet, I'm not. You keep failing to kill me, Uncle."

I started for him and Haldron kicked his heels into the sides of the horse, taking off at a gallop, leaving the Vangar to close the path behind him.

Grabbing Lucia, I hauled her behind me as one soldier rushed toward me. I sidestepped him, grabbing his shirtfront. A savage twist to his arm yielded his sword, which I caught with my left hand as I lifted him and sent him hurtling over the cliff. Dropping closer to the face of the mountain, I turned to face the Vangar.

The other soldiers fell into formation around me. Then they attacked.

The rawness of my powers had been the source of my ability to defeat anyone who'd challenged me in the sparring rings during the harvest festival, but I'd sensed that power growing. And now, despite my pain, despite the ironstones still embedded in my flesh, every obstacle in front of me felt nonexistent—no more difficult than snapping a twig.

Above our heads, dark clouds stirred to life once again, as

though the sky seethed with my anger, reflecting the violence in my heart.

I caught my breath, each exhale dissipating like mist in a fierce wind that battered us. My eyes locked with the commander of the Vangar as I deflected his soldiers' inferior attacks.

The commander stood with relaxed poise, ready to strike.

My muscles twitched with the hum of energy that poured through me, barely contained. I lunged forward again, leaning into the power that filled my fingertips with surging heat. The commander met the blow with a deft parry, but the strength of my blow knocked him back several feet.

Surprise showed in his eyes. He spun, aiming a precise thrust at me that forced me to move with superhuman speed to block.

As our swords clashed, the sound echoed off the mountains around us. But he had time to recover that I didn't have. I needed to thin the herd. *Now.*

I plunged my sword into the gut of the next soldier who attacked, not bothering with anything less than a killing blow. This wasn't the time for a spar.

The scorching heat that now seemed to live within me roared to life and I adjusted my fingers over the hilt of my sword as it grew hotter.

Concentrate.

I risked letting go of the sword with one hand, then thundered my hand against the face of the slippery ridge—just to knock them off balance. The mountain gave a mighty crack and rumble, then stones fell as the cliff split open instead.

What the fuck did I do?

The Vangar commander stared at me, horror in his face as he caught his balance, the ridge splitting in two. A gap, about five feet wide, appeared between us. Two of the soldiers who had been standing near it tumbled into the chasm that had been created.

"Rykr!" Lucia screamed.

I turned to see Seren's mother backing up. The path had split in two, and one of the remaining soldiers closed on her.

I charged, slicing through him before he could swing, but not before she slipped.

As the man fell dead, Lucia's scream carried in the wind. I lunged for her, catching her by the chains that bound her.

"Hold on," I yelled, flattening myself into the blood that poured from the man I'd just killed. It dripped onto my forearm and face, splashing down on her.

I darted a glance back. The remaining soldier jumped across the gap, charging at me.

He'd almost reached me when another man jumped from the ridges of the cliffs above us.

Brogan Ragnall.

He attacked the soldier who had crossed over, and I turned my attention back to Lucia.

The chains are suffocating her.

"Don't let go." I'd have to crawl dangerously close to the edge to get a better grip on her.

"I can't breathe," Lucia cried, tears streaming down her cheeks. "I can't!"

A body went flying from the cliff—the last soldier.

Where in the hell had the Vangar commander gone, though? I hadn't seen him go down.

Then Brogan was at my side. He lunged for the front of the chains, grasping it farther down. Together, the two of us pulled, hauling her up the cliff and over the ridge.

Brogan pulled his wife into his arms. "Oh, my love," he murmured as she wept.

My shoulders heaved, my muscles aching. A sound

rumbled above us—something shifting in the shadows of the cliffs. I barely had time to process it as I turned to stand and find the Vangar commander when Brogan tackled me. "Get down!"

A dagger whizzed past the tops of our heads as my forehead connected with the rock.

"Brogan," Lucia's voice whispered behind us.

The dagger had speared deeply into her chest.

Horror spread through me as Brogan gave a cry, releasing me to catch his wife before she fell backward again.

I whirled to see the Vangar commander standing on the other side of the gap, ready to throw yet another dagger, a wicked smile on his face.

An unexpected growl came from above me. From seemingly out of nowhere, a black flash leaped from the top of the cliff above us, landing on the commander and pinning him down.

A vuk.

The dagger tumbled uselessly from the commander's hands as the vuk's enormous, sharp teeth dug into his neck and ripped out his throat.

The guard went limp as the vuk raised its head, still growling, flesh in its teeth. Blood dripped from his snarling spittle onto the rock below it. The vuk's eyes met mine, holding them, something familiar in its gaze.

Could it be?

I took a step toward the vuk, holding out my hand. It swallowed back the flesh in its jowls and then came toward me, leaping across the gap easily, its tail *fucking wagging.*

I palmed the top of its head, leaving a trace of blood from my fingertips on its black scales.

My uncle was long gone—no doubt hidden safely within Emberstone, but I wasn't here alone.

Turning slowly, I faced Brogan and Lucia Ragnall. Tears streaked his face as he cradled her in his arms.

Brogan Ragnall, who had participated in the murder of my entire family.

"Brogan," Lucia whispered, her lips a deathly shade of blue. The color had drained from her face and a bright spot of blood pooled in the corner of her mouth. "Brogan, you came back."

"Don't speak, Lucia. Don't speak. Save your energy."

"King Calix ..." Lucia held a hand out toward me, her movement still restricted by the chains.

Brogan lifted his face, a dazed look in his eyes, as though he was surprised to see me standing there. He said nothing, staring at me without wonder or interest, lost to his own sorrow.

Forgiveness was a small mercy that I did not want to grant him, but Lucia Ragnall had been kind to me. Helped me. Bitterly, I crouched beside her. "Why am I not dead, Lucia?"

Her watery gaze met mine. "The blood of the vuk." She wet her mouth, but only blood stained her lips. "Vuks are immortal creatures ..."

The Seidr's cryptic words rang in my head.

"... he is no ordinary mortal. A beast lives inside him, forged in the blood of the oath."

Lucia reached for my hand, tracing her thumb against my palm as she searched it. "It is one the gifts the bond has given you. I saw your lifeline was unbroken."

Immortal?

My head swam with her words. What in the hell did that mean?

I swallowed hard. "And Seren? Is she immortal too?"

"No." She shook her head, softly. "And she's dying. The bond's killing her. You must take the oath. Use ... this. Search the memory I showed you. Y-you'll find you'll ... remember."

She pulled out her amulet, streaked with blood, then pressed it into my palm. "You must."

The Seidr had said something about that, too. That I had to take the oath for Seren to survive. Her words crept back with eerie precision. *"He will release a great evil inside her. The threads of fate are fixed."*

"Am I a beast?"

Lucia's face was solemn. "A-an immortal *man*. Immortals can be killed … b-but you won't die on your own."

My head had stopped processing her words.

Immortal man.

The depth and breadth of *forever* was incomprehensible.

Every single person I would ever know, every love, ever hate, would die … while I continued living.

Including Seren.

No wonder the bond between us was diminishing her but not me.

I had to get to her. Had to save her.

Releasing Lucia's hand, I stood to give Brogan and his wife a moment alone. "Rest, Lucia. I'll pray to the gods for you."

"No, I-I have to—" Lucia reached for me once again, but more blood came from her mouth, her words drowning with a gargled gasp.

"No!" Brogan's shoulders shook with broken sobs. "My darling. Lucia, my love. Lucia!"

Lucia held his gaze for a moment longer, then the life faded from her, her body going limp.

Thunder cracked through the sky, as my hands clenched into fists. Already, the pain in my body had started to fade, though I was certain I'd need the gifted hands of a healer to remove the ironstones.

What in the hell have I become?

Lucia had died too quickly. I needed more answers from her. Answers that I might never have.

Would Seren ever forgive me for this? No matter how little part I'd had in the death of her mother—my presence here had cost the Ragnalls everything.

And I still had this murderous traitor in front of me.

I would never forgive him. *Ever.*

"Brogan Ragnall," I said in a low growl.

Brogan's head snapped up, grief written in his face. "Your Highness. *Please.* Spare my children. The fault in what I've done is mine and mine alone."

"And Madoc? Didn't he slaughter my family too?

Brogan bowed his head. "No. He came to help me save you. I instructed him not to kill you. It was the only way we could convince the world that you were dead. But I never expected —" He gritted his teeth, his eyes red with tears.

I blinked at him, his words like soft blows against my numb heart.

It would be so easy for me to kill him now. To make him suffer as my family had suffered.

He deserves it.

"*Rykr* ..." Seren's voice floated through my head.

I couldn't delay. She needed me now.

"Bury your wife, Ragnall. But you won't die an old man. When I come for you, you'll wish you had." I turned to go.

"Your Highness—"

I glanced back at him.

He shook his head, as though deciding whatever he'd wanted to say no longer mattered. "Thank you."

I ignored him.

I have to find Seren.

CHAPTER 44
SEREN

The Vangar that surrounded us in the tunnel beneath Emberstone were entirely from my tribe. Every last one of them. Including Seth.

Turned against me.

I cradled Ciaran's head in my arms, my hands shaking as he struggled to breathe, blood flowing freely from the wound from Darya's blade. My hands were pressed against it tightly, but blood seeped between my fingers, not slowing despite my pressure.

The only thing keeping me alive right now were Tara and Amahle's bodies, standing shoulder to shoulder in front of Ciaran, Esme, and me. They didn't have swords—they'd lost them when Haldron had waved them away—so they didn't have a way of defending us. But I knew they'd give their lives trying.

"S-S-Seren," Ciaran breathed, blood trailing from his lips.

"Shhhh," I whispered, leaning down and pressing my lips against his. As if I could just breathe the air he needed back

492

into his mouth. My tears fell onto his cheeks, leaving a trail on the dust there. "You're not allowed to leave me, Ciaran."

"Just surrender now, Seren. No one else you care about has to die," Darya taunted with a smirk. "You're trapped."

She was right—the gate behind us held us in ... and beyond that, fire and smoke consumed the Havamal. Smoke that was creeping slowly into the tunnel, making it harder to breathe.

And the only way farther into the tunnel was through Seth and the Vangar who had swords at the ready.

"I-I lov-ve you, Ser," Ciaran whispered.

"I love you, too." I kissed his mouth again, my voice breaking. "Don't go. Please!"

But Ciaran's breathing was shallower, his body growing limp. Ciaran tried to lift his hand to my face, but it fell back to his chest, as a wet, rattling breath wheezed from his lips. His mouth moved, forming words I couldn't hear. His fingers curled slightly, as if reaching for me.

Then his face went slack, his eyes growing still.

"No!" I screamed. "No, Ciaran."

"You didn't care about him. You mocked him. Shamed him. Took advantage of his love," Darya hissed. "You think you're special, Seren? You're just a little girl playing games you're not strong enough for, and everyone you love will die for it."

My shoulders squared as I glared at her. "Shut up, you stupid bitch."

"Stupid, am I? Somehow I managed to get to you, didn't I? Got you to trust me, to come to me in your hour of need." Darya's eyes glittered with triumph. "Poor, unloved Seren. Unwilling to fight for what she wanted and so easy to predict. All the Ragnalls are. So that's exactly what I did, just as my lord Haldron had commanded. Go to your tribe. Watch. Wait. Learn. And strike."

Her words collided into my gut with ferocity. Beside me Esme trembled in her cold, wet clothes.

My Esme, who Haldron and his men snatched, who'd known exactly where to find us.

Because he'd had help from inside our tribe. A spy reporting to him. Telling him how to manipulate the Ragnalls.

"You're nothing but Haldron's puppet."

She arched her brow. "I'm the puppet? That's naive, even for you. Not a single person in your tribe was free from my influence. Do you really think the council would have condemned you to the Skorn if not for my suggestion? They all did whatever I wanted."

"Are you hearing this, Seth?" I called out, my voice echoing down the tunnel. "You're just a pawn in Darya's—and Haldron's—game."

Seth didn't move though, his face like flint. Lethal.

The side of Seth I'd come to know after Darya.

"It wasn't hard to get him to cast you aside for me. An alliance with the daughter of the Vangar's vice command ... and a woman who knew how to actually take care of him in bed?" Darya tilted her head, her eyes cruel. "He fell easily."

The way Darya spoke now, though, it was as though Seth wasn't even here. Like she could say anything she wanted, and he was just a brainless, soulless skinwraith who would ...

I inhaled sharply, and pain flared in my chest.

The skinwraith.

The yellow glowing eyes.

The vuk.

"He's bewitched, isn't he?" I set Ciaran's limp body down carefully, then struggled to my feet. "You bewitched him today, just like you did Giulia, after you turned her into a skinwraith. And the vuk that attacked me in the forest. Seth was going to help us today and you bewitched him. You probably even had all those skinwraiths attack us in the encampment to turn everyone against us, and it didn't work. People still stood up for me."

Darya's lips pursed. "Even Ciaran. Who you'd betrayed." Her face was cruel. "Yes, Seren, that's true. But you're only as strong as your friends. You wouldn't have survived the Skorn without them. And you're about to lose them all."

Seth didn't stir ... and neither did the men and women at his side. They stood eerily still, their swords raised, their breathing in perfect rhythm.

The hairs on the back of my neck rose.

"They're all bewitched," I whispered.

Darya flinched, then gritted through her teeth. "Step aside, Tara. Amahle."

They only stood straighter.

With a smirk, Darya flicked her hand out in a gesture spell and yellow magic flowed from her fingertips.

"Tara, duck!" I called out.

But it was too late. The glow descended on them both, then sank into their skin.

"Seren!" Esme cried out behind me, terror in her voice.

My heart hammered, my vision growing blearier. I sank beside Esme once again, hugging her into my arms.

"Step aside," Darya commanded again.

This time, Tara and Amahle moved out of the way without hesitating.

"You see? It's that easy. Now let go of Esme or she'll get hurt next."

"No, Seren. Don't," Esme begged. "Don't let them take me again."

"Why not just bewitch me like everyone else?" My eyes narrowed at her. "Why make this more difficult on yourself?"

Her face hardened. "Gods, you pretend to be Ibarran and

know something of spellcraft. You're such a disgrace in every way. *You* can't be bewitched, Seren. Or I would have done it long before now."

Her goads could do nothing to me now.

Tears streamed down my cheeks as I looked over at Ciaran's dead body. He'd died for me without hesitation. I was already dying, but I wouldn't leave Esme in her power.

If I could kill Darya, her spell on the bewitched would break. They would all be free.

The sounds of running footsteps provided a momentary distraction, then Thorne roared into the tunnel, a torch in one hand, a sword in the other. "Stay the hell away from my queen," he growled, running straight toward the Vangar.

The poison in my body had overpowered me, and my arms and legs trembled uncontrollably.

Without blinking, Darya turned toward the Vangar, then pulled a sword from the sheath at her side. Rykr's sword.

A sword that would kill when used.

I had no doubt Thorne was a superior fighter—stronger and better—but he was going to die, too.

"*Rykr.*" I reached out to him through our bond, almost as an instinct. *Is he still alive?*

I squeezed my eyes shut as the pain grew, my shivering so intense now that I couldn't prevent my body from twitching.

"*Rykr.*"

AMID MY PAIN, I revisited that moment after I'd met Rykr when he'd been dying and I'd stared at that handsome face, trying to decide whether my damnation was worth the trouble of dragging him back to the territory.

Fate had brought him to me.

And now I would be damned if I didn't do everything to save him once again.

I drew a deep breath, seeking the wisps of gold in my mind that were Rykr's spirit. My mother hadn't taught me how to block or access my power—or his—but he'd been in my mind enough that I recognized where I ended and he began.

Sucking in a shallow breath, I noticed the frost on the floor below me.

As though it had come from my fingertips. Like I'd seen fire shoot from Rykr's hands, except this was my power with his strength.

I sat straighter, my shaking gone, my heartbeat strangely slow. The clash of swords sounded as Thorne fought his way through the Vangar, not knowing that even if he reached me, he would die.

Esme trembled in my arms.

I had to save us.

Spreading my palm in front of my lips, I blew a cold, icy chill from my fingertips toward Seth. Not the type that would freeze a form, but something that would go deeper inside him. If the ice could wrap around his heart, maybe it would be enough to sever the connection Darya had placed on him.

It might also kill him.

Much as I didn't want that to happen, it was a risk I wasn't willing to take on anyone else.

Desperation filled me as Seth stood straighter, a cry of pain leaving his lips. "Seth, please. Darya bewitched you. Everyone here. Please. I need your help, Seth."

His face clouded with disbelief as he braced himself on the wall of the tunnel beside him. "Why would Darya bewitch me?"

"Because she doesn't love you. She never has. Her one and only goal here has been to serve Haldron."

"Stop this!" Darya whirled to face me. "What did you do?"

I held my breath, my gut churning.

Darya turned back toward Seth, sending another bewitching spell over him. "Tie her up, Seth. We'll take her to Haldron and see what he does to her."

If she hadn't turned her back to Seth, she might not have seen it, but I did.

The flicker in Seth's face. The lack of the yellow glow in his pupils.

Her spell hadn't worked.

Seth rolled his shoulders, straightening, his eyes clearing. He flexed his grip around his sword. He turned to Darya, voice cold. "You've been using me this whole time, haven't you?"

Seth took two steps toward us, then spun, swinging his fist against Darya's face. A bright spurt of blood erupted from her nose as she screamed, drawing back.

"Seren, run!" Seth cried out as Darya plunged the sword into his shoulder.

She was going to kill him.

He rasped a breath and stood as Darya approached. She held Rykr's sword in her hands, her face burning with fury, blood streaked from her nostrils to her ear where she'd wiped it back.

Seth unsheathed his own sword.

"Seth, no!" I screamed as he lunged toward Darya.

Their swords clashed with a sharp, metallic crash. Seth was a stronger fighter. A better one.

One of the best in the Vangar.

But Darya had Rykr's sword.

That's why Rykr had refused to fight Seth.

No matter how quickly Seth lunged, Darya seemed to move with a speed and ability that I'd never witnessed in her before. Seth feinted left, swinging with brutal force, only for Darya to pivot, impossibly fast. She wasn't just dodging, she was moving like something more than human, her body unnaturally fluid, her strikes too perfect.

"No, Seth!" I released Esme, then ran straight toward them.

Seth's eyes locked with mine. "Seren ..." he whispered.

A sob left me, an inexplicable pain enclosing around my heart.

I had to end this.

For Rykr.

For my family.

For my terrified people. Even if they'd never accept me again.

I steeled myself to calm, this time reaching for what remained of my own power. As the iciness drifted through my fingertips, I thought of how Rykr had started that fire with his hands.

He was fire.

I am ice.

So I let the iciness flow through my palms. I drew to my full height as I stalked closer to Darya. "You will not harm another person in this territory while I draw breath."

Darya whirled toward me. "Then I'll just kill you."

"But you can't," I lied, coming closer, still. If she swung that sword at me, it might kill me before I could get any nearer. "You couldn't kill me with dragon's blood because I'm blood bound to the King of Lirien. And the gods have favored him. It's his power that I wield. And his sword answers to him and him alone."

Fear sparked in her eyes.

I extended my palms and let the full force of the icy power flow through my hands, like a conduit from my mind to my fingertips.

A blast of blue spiraled forward, cascading over Darya.

My power flowed through me—not just my fingertips, but my arms, my torso, spiraling, searing, cutting like a knife at the very fabric of my soul. A flood of images tore across my mind ... of Esme, curled against me as a toddler, Ciaran, splashing in a brook with me, Amahle, laughing.

I saw Tara teaching me to throw a dagger, over and over, patience in her brow. Madoc, hoisting me onto his shoulders when I was a girl and carrying me across a wobbly tree branch, while my mother waved below us. My father, his kind, patient smile, as he taught me to hunt.

And *Rykr*. My love. Holding me in his arms. Kissing me.

Loving me for who I am.

The world around me blurred, the moment holding as I saw frost creeping into Darya's cheeks, spreading with a crackle into the whites of her eyes, turning her dark irises blue.

Darya gasped, her lips trembling, the ice creeping up her throat. She raised a shaking hand, fingers sparking with golden magic. "No," she rasped. "No, I—"

But the words never finished. Her magic fizzled out, and the ice swallowed her whole, a scream freezing in her throat, a wisp of cold mist hanging from her lips.

The power that flowed through me was relentless, unstoppable, out of my control.

When it ended, Darya stood frozen solid, like ice, the sword still firmly in her hand.

I took a step to wrest the sword away, but a sharp sting filled my mind, splitting through my ears. *I've spent too much of my power.* Used the last of my reserve.

Dizziness overtook me, and I collapsed, my face smacking against the ground.

A gentle set of hands tugged at my shoulders. Seth turned me onto my back, and I blinked into his face, riddled with grief. "Seren! Oh gods, Seren!"

In the background, distant now, I heard the clang of a sword. Thorne continued fighting toward us.

"Help my sisters and tell the Vangar to stand down. Please," I rasped.

"Rykr," I called out again in my mind. A tear slipped from the corner of my eye and slipped down my cheek. *"Rykr, I love you."*

Then the world slowly slipped into a deep shadow.

CHAPTER 45
RYKR

As I extinguished the fire in the Havamal, walking between plumes of billowing smoke, Thorne emerged from a tunnel.

Tara and Amahle were behind him ... followed by Seth and a group of Vangar.

"Thorne?"

Seren was in Thorne's arms. Limp.

I raced toward him. The vuk who had followed me down from the mountain quickly caught up, running at my side, like a hound.

Thorne saw me and knelt, then held her out toward me. Tears flowed freely from Tara's and Amahle's faces ... and Esme's. I didn't have to ask to know who she was. She looked like Seren.

My beautiful, sweet Seren.

I bent beside her and took her into my arms.

Her face was pale, her lips nearly tinted blue.

And her heartbeat was a faint, barely-there echo.

She was dying. The closer she got to death, the deeper the rip went through me.

She was being torn away.

I took her hand in mine, but her skin was like ice.

I pressed her fingertips against my lips. "I love you, Seren."

I would love her forever.

My throat constricted.

If I had to live an immortal life, if I had to watch everyone I loved die, then why couldn't I have more time with her?

"I don't want to live without you," I whispered, leaning forward and pressing a kiss to her cold lips.

I had to take the oath. Now, or I'd lose her forever.

Agony ripped through me at the thought.

I had a kingdom to take back. A war to stop.

A duty to my people.

But none of it would mean anything ... *without her.* She had given me what no one else could—a love so deep and real that it had become a living, breathing thing between us. In spite of our prejudices. In spite of logic.

Tears—*gods, how long has it been since I last shed tears?*—cut down my cheeks as I cupped her face in my hands.

The bond wasn't magic, love was. Love had made the bond real. Without it, without *her*, my reason for existing would fade away.

The Seidr's warning had held me back but there was no time left to wonder what might happen. To ask questions.

"You must take the oath," Lucia had said. *"Use this. Search the memory I showed you. You'll find you remember."*

The memory Lucia had shown me floated through my mind as I took out the amulet and placed it around us both. Tears filled my eyes.

"This world isn't worth being in without you, Seren. I want

you." I leaned my forehead against her temple. "Please come back to me."

I closed my eyes, letting my mind wander to Lucia's altar, when she'd shown me the moment when Seren had taken the oath.

She'd shown me the oath and ...

... I remember it clearly.

My hands trembled as I unsheathed the dagger. The Seidr's warning clawed at my mind.

This would unleash something inside her, but if I did nothing ...

Her breath was a ghost of sound.

Damn the Seidr. Damn fate. I would not let her go.

I gritted my teeth and pressed the dagger to my skin, then cut the rune into my wrist, as Seren had once done for me, ignoring the pain. Cutting the rune into her wrist, I pressed my wound to hers.

The moment our wounds touched, a jolt of white-hot pain shot through me, a pulse of energy rippling outward like a stone dropped into a lake. The air crackled, the fabric of the world shifted.

I barely registered the figures around me—Thorne, Tara, Amahle, Seth. Even the vuk at my side had gone still, but none of them mattered. Not now.

Only Seren.

Only her fading heartbeat, her cold skin against mine.

CHAPTER 46
SEREN

T he sweet scent of Paionia flowers hung in the air and I wrinkled my nose, stretching. I'd been dreaming I was flying, and I hated to tear myself from the sensation. My wings were getting stronger each day and I could fly higher each time I tried jumping from the mountainside.

With a jolt, I opened my eyes, the dream abruptly leaving me.

The unfamiliarity of the room, the luxury of my bedding, startled a cry from my lips.

I drew a deep breath and sat, squinting at the streams of light that greeted me, unhindered by a tree canopy or tent panels. Instead, the light cascaded through floor-to-ceiling glass windows. The ceiling itself shimmered like crystals in a dark cave, vaulted high above me. The sunlight reflected on the dark stone walls with an iridescent glow.

Maybe I died and went to Evermere?

My fingertips drifted over velvety fabric as my eyes adjusted. Thick green velvet draped from the four posts of the bed I occupied. A strange energy hummed beneath my skin, thrumming like a second heartbeat. My limbs felt foreign, lighter and heavier at the same time.

A creak from a few feet away alerted me to the fact that I wasn't alone, and I turned as a woman stood from a chair. "You're awake."

"Where am I?" I managed.

"Be still," the woman said with the hint of a smile, one that didn't meet her eyes. "You've only just awoken. One question at a time."

She came over to the side of the bed and sat beside me. "We're in Cairn Hold. In Pendara."

Pendara? I was in Lirien?

"But ..." I searched my memory for those last moments before Thorne had carried me. "I died. Why am I here?"

The woman crossed her arms. "You didn't die—obviously. The king took the Oath of Bryndis. He saved you."

My eyes widened.

Rykr had taken the oath?

Fear snaked through me. "What about—"

"You're alive, my lady." The woman took my hand in her slender fingers. She scanned my gaze. "That's all that matters."

I tossed the sheets to the side and stood. A desperate feeling filled me. *What happened to my family? My friends?* We couldn't all have crossed the border so easily. "I'm fine. But I don't understand what happened. Where's my family? What—"

The words died on my lips as I caught sight of myself in the mirror. I stepped closer to the mirror, my heart rate slowing. A dark tattoo showed on my right arm, the same shape as the one I'd cut onto my wrist when I'd taken the oath.

But my entire right arm also appeared to be covered with a unique pattern of iridescent tattoos on my skin. Beautiful and *... shaped like dragon scales.*

"What the hell?" I gasped.

"The dragon's blood," the woman said. "The poison never left your body. It was inside you when the king took the oath."

"What does that mean?"

The woman lifted her chin, watching me warily. *With fear.* "It's better for the king to explain everything. I'll summon a servant to help you bathe."

My heart throbbed with sorrow as she turned to go. "What about my family? Please tell me."

The woman didn't look back, but she paused for a step. "The king will be here soon. I promise."

A foreboding feeling rose in me. *What isn't she telling me?*

"What is it? Please!"

But she'd already gone out the door.

Within moments, female servants arrived. They bowed toward me, saying little as they took me to the adjoining bathroom, pulling and poking and prodding in a blur of activity that was overwhelming.

Just as they'd finished pulling me from the bath and slipping me into a robe, the door to the bathroom flew open.

The tug in my heart pulled tight, Rykr's presence flooding my body with warmth before I saw him.

Then he was there, striding into the room, and my heart stumbled at the sight of him.

Every trace of the Pendaran warrior had nearly disappeared. His hair was still dark, but his clothes spoke of the Ederyn prince I'd never really known. His striking features were even more beautiful, the chiseled jawline and strong cheekbones set in an unreadable mask.

His piercing blue-green eyes met mine, the rawness in his intense gaze nearly making my knees buckle.

He wore a thick tunic over woolen trousers, which were tucked into sturdy fur-lined leather boots. On his broad chest was a leather vest, adorned with metal studs, leather bracers carved with dragons and wolves encasing his arms. The thick, fur-lined cloak fastened with a silver Valknut brooch swished as he strode toward me, then stopped a few feet away.

Rykr gave the servants a hard look as they curtsied. "You're dismissed."

They rose quickly, scrambling toward the door.

"Should we expect you for your midday meal?" one servant, an older woman, asked as she stopped at the doorway.

"Not likely," Rykr snapped, not taking his eyes off me.

She bowed her head, then left.

The door closed behind them.

I rubbed my arms, mystified at my sudden desire for them to return. "Rykr," I managed in a soft voice, feeling oddly exposed.

His dark brows drew together, the hint of a line between them, then his gaze softened. A smile curved at his lips. "Gods, I've missed the sound of that name. Everyone has taken to calling me Calix once again."

"Missed?" I asked, searching his gaze. "It can't have been that long since we left the Havamal."

"You've been asleep for a month, Seren."

Tears pricked my eyes at his words. "What?" My legs felt suddenly weak, and I searched for something to sturdy myself on. My fingertips gripped the edge of a chaise in the bathroom.

A chaise. In the bathroom. Absurd.

"How is that possible?" I whispered, beginning to understand the woman's hesitation at answering my questions. So much must have happened between now and then. *Where is my family?* I wanted to scream. But I held back, fear pressing in on me from all sides.

"The High Magister thinks it may have to do with the dragon's blood that was inside you when I took the oath."

He rested his hand on the hilt of the sword at his waist and stared at me, as though afraid to come any closer.

Touch me. I'm right here. I've come back to you, I wanted to scream.

But a chasm seemed to exist between us, where once there had been nothing but all-consuming passion, there was hesitation and *distance*.

A month had passed and I'd been asleep. What had he gone through during that time? "Rykr ..." I managed, then stopped. "Am I allowed to call you that?"

A smile curved at the corners of his mouth. "Yes, Seren."

I lifted my chin. "You'll always be Rykr Westhaven to me, I suppose."

"I can live with that."

Still, he made no move to come any closer. His eyes raked over me, like he was afraid I might vanish if he blinked ... as if he was staring at a ghost.

What if he no longer loved me?

But he'd come rushing back to my side when he'd heard I'd awoken. That wasn't nothing.

Drawing a deep breath, I closed the gap between us and touched his cheek. "I'm real, you know. This isn't a dream."

A light laugh left his lips, and he lifted his hand, his fingers enclosing mine. He closed his eyes for a moment, his breath shallow. He kissed my knuckles softly. "I'm sorry. I did dream of this moment, often, and now that it's here, there's so much to say, and I don't know how to tell you." He opened his eyes, holding my gaze. "Not having you in my life the last month has been the hardest part of my existence, Seren."

His voice was deep and tender as he cupped my face in his rough, callused palms. "I never want to wake from this if it is a dream."

My eyes filled with tears. I couldn't imagine what he'd

been through, or what I would have felt if the situation had been reversed. Even though my mind burned with questions, the peace, the *completeness* of his presence calmed me. "I love you, Rykr." I rose to my tiptoes, sliding my arms around his neck.

His arms tightened around my waist, encasing me in a gentle embrace, then his lips met mine. "I love you, Seren."

I laughed as he swept me off my feet, then he set me down, his eyes bright with emotion.

I pressed my cheek into his chest, a strange mixture of uncertainty and happiness going through me.

Then something fierce and uncontrollable wrapped around my heart, squeezing it.

The slick feeling of *utter darkness*.

The feeling twisted, as though something inside me had shifted. My heartbeat faltered. Heat curled through my veins— wrong, unnatural heat.

Fire, burning my soul.

I stepped back and looked hard into his eyes. "What the hell did you do to me, Rykr?"

EPILOGUE

The burned grounds of the Havamal glistened in the moonlight. The fire that King Calix had created had burned for days.

The king had destroyed much more than the amphitheater, though. My entire family had been torn apart. Haldron's retribution on my tribe had been swift and merciless—only a few of us had escaped.

Every chance I'd had to escape back to here, though, I had taken, with one goal in mind.

The spade in my hand turned the soil, dust and rock spilling from it onto the careful line I'd dug across the floor of the amphitheater.

Night after night.

The arduous task seemingly unending.

I pushed the spade into the soil once again and this time, I heard the soft *chink* of metal grating against metal.

Dropping to my knees, I sifted through the dirt and ash in the spade.

My fingers brushed against the chain first, my breath catching in my throat.

For a moment, I thought I'd imagined it. Just another piece of scorched metal, another fragment of ruin. But then, as I brushed away the soot, something gleamed—dim, but unmistakable.

I found it.

For so long, I'd questioned myself, wondering if I'd really seen it drop from the king's grip as he strode out of the Havamal, holding Seren in his arms, wreathed in smoke and flame.

But here it was.

The amulet.

I'd found it at last.

NEWSLETTER AND
NEXT BOOK

Want to keep up with me and hear what's going on in my world? Join my newsletter on my website! I have freebies and giveaways, exclusive content and, of course, you get to hear all about upcoming book news, my life, and my small army of children.

I hope you enjoyed Seren and Rykr's story. Thank you so much for reading; my readers really are what make this possible and I am so grateful for you! If you enjoyed this book, I'd love it if you took the time to leave a rating or review at your favorite book retailer. It truly goes a long way.

The next Heirs of Lirien story continues with *Blood of the Bound,* coming in 2026.

ACKNOWLEDGMENTS

The journey to this book started when, as a lonely girl of 12, I first cracked open a journal and started my first full length novel—an epic fantasy.

It was the first book I'd written, and the first time I truly fell in love with the written word.

Coming back to this, after years working in other genres, was a full circle moment where I had more fun writing than I had in years.

This was a massive project and I couldn't have done it without the support of an incredible team of publishing professionals and artists. That said, many thanks to:

Christi Bushar, my darling sister, for the first, second, third, and fourth draft reads. You put up with all the multiverse iterations of this and give me valuable advice the whole time—plus let me rant about imaginary characters far more than anyone else should.

Melissa Frain, for seeing the potential for a real story in that first version and giving me the map to make it shine. You are amazing.

Marion Archer—you know I love you. I couldn't do a book without you. Thank you for always being such an incredible editor.

Robin Seavill, the most incredibly detail-oriented and thorough copyeditor a girl could be lucky enough to hire. I always love our conversations and am so thankful for you.

Caitlin Lengerich ... your notes in my edit absolutely made my day. Love ya, girl.

Huge thanks to Maria Spada, the most kind and incredible cover designer who was able to take the seed of my idea and really make something with that wow factor I was looking for.

Claire Bushar, Mary Begletsova, Pandora Young for the incredible artwork that has brought my characters to life. You are all wonderful and so massively talented.

Kayla Burchfield at Ink and Lore Maps for the most amazing map of Lirien. I adore it.

Anna-Lena Spies at Atra Luna Design for the stunning chapter headers, edge artworks, and heading backgrounds, and for being so wonderfully kind.

Crowns and Chaos PR and my fantastic street team: YOU ALL are the BEST and the energy I need to keep going when the business side of this business gets difficult to navigate.

Ellie at LoveNotes PR, you've been so lovely to work with and I'm incredibly grateful to you for your help with this project.

...and last but not least, my beta readers, with a special note of thanks to Cayce Hoffman and Shawna Sherell, who really were so wonderfully helpful in providing me with feedback.

Okay ... man, it takes a village, doesn't it?! And in that spirit, I just want to say thank you to my wonderful husband Patrick and my darling children, who are my village, my inspiration, and my home. I love you more than words can say.

ALSO BY ANNABELLE MCCORMACK

The Windswept Historical Fiction Saga

A Zephyr Rising: A Windswept Prequel Novella

Windswept: The Windswept Saga Book 1

Sands of Sirocco: The Windswept Saga Book 2

Whisper in the Tempest: The Windswept Saga Book 3

A Spark in Ashes: The Windswept Saga Book 4

The Brandywood Small Town Romance Series

All This Time

I'll Carry You

Once We Met

Until Forever Ends

Ever With Me

Wanderlust Contemporary Romances

See You Next Fall

He Loves Me Knot

One Time in Paris

The Route to You (August 11, 2026)

Heirs of Lirien Fantasy Romance

Carved in Crimson

Blood of the Bound (November 3, 2026)

To find out the latest about my new releases, please sign up for my newsletter or Facebook Reader's group! I love hearing from readers and have some great offers lined up for my subscribers.

ABOUT THE AUTHOR

Annabelle McCormack writes historical romantic fiction and contemporary romance packed with sprawling adventures, epic love, and soulmates who just can't stay away from each other (even when the world is falling apart). If there's a sweeping love story with high stakes and deep emotions, she's probably writing it—or at least dreaming about it while chasing down her next cup of coffee.

When she's not wrangling words, she's wrangling five home-schooled kids, a couple of dogs, and an unreasonable amount of books in Maryland. If life had more hours (and less laundry), she'd be traveling, painting, or becoming a professional pastry chef. For now, she's content with baking, reading, lifting heavy things at the gym, and plotting her next great escape—er, novel.

Visit her at www.annabellemccormack.com or http://instagram.com/annabellemccormack to follow her daily adventures.